Other Books by: Christie Palmer

Shadow Play (A Tracker Novel)

Lost In Time (A Fallen Novel)

Reaper Mine (A Reaper Novel) – Oct. 2014

Dedication:

This book is dedicated to Debbie and Connie, women who have shown me what it means to be strong and courageous. I can only hope it shows in my life and the female characters I write. I love you two, I couldn't ask for better best bitches.

And their husbands who put up with them. And as always to my husband, whom I love and who does everything in his power to make all my dreams come true.

Beautiful, majestic and powerful. She wanted to leap down and grasp him in her arms hold him close, feel his power and strength, pretend he loved her as much as she loved him. She wanted him to know all the times she had cared for him while in the Infernos. She sighed and looked back over the city. They were fairy tales.

"Can't we have just a little fairy tale, with a happy ending? Is that too much to ask?" she said it knowing how wistful her voice sounded. It was something she would never dare say to her brothers or her father. They dealt in death; they didn't do happily ever after. But her mother had told her they existed, and she hoped that her daughter found hers one day.

"Yes," Marcus sighed heavily.

That pretty much summed it up for her, and she pursued her lips together. She had fantasized about this man for two centuries, and the reality was a disappointment, but really, what did she expect? To spend five minutes in his presence, and he would drop to his knees and promise his life and love to her for all of eternity?

A tear slipped from her eye, and she whipped it away. She needed to grow up. Marcus was right. There was no place in their life for a fairy tale ending.

She turned to face the city, blocking out the blinking lights and the beauty for something other than the red, orange and dusty light of the Infernos where time passed in the blink of a mortal eye.

Jinx Fantasy Fiction LLC
Salt Lake City, UT

Cover Design by: Jaycee De Lorenzo of Sweet N' Spicy Designs

Ebook formatting by www.ebooklaunch.com

ISBN: eBook: 978-0-9885557-3-0

Paperback: 978-0-9885557-4-7

Manufactured in the United States of America

First Edition February 2013

Second Edition September 2014

Table of Contents

Prologue

Ash billowed into the heavens on the wings of the screams and cries of the mortals. Their bodies were cloaked in boiling lava from the erupting volcano. Marcus believed he could smell the stench of the burning flesh, hear the tortured screams of the poor souls. He knew the sounds of the burning and the dying would stay with him for a long time if not forever.

He doubled over in pain. "Make it stop," he gritted out between his teeth, trying to keep from screaming out in pain.

"They are deserving of their fates," an unearthly voice boomed over him the voice pounded d into his head like an anvil.

Marcus looked down into the ash and smoke covering the once beautiful and serene countryside. The screams dying along with every living creature in the valley.

Once, it was a prospering metropolis. Filled with people who hoped and dreamed. Now they were nothing.

"This is unnecessary," he ground out, still feeling the pain of the dying souls. The souls would not be recycled. They would not go into Limbo, they were lost forever. The pain of the loss making Marcus wretch. So many lost souls, it was incomprehensible.

"Really?" a female Angel flew over to him where he lay. Her wings stirring the air around them. "And what makes you think that? What right do you have to question the Judgment?"

Marcus pushed himself to his feet. "We murdered children and innocence today? Are we really any better than the Damned?"

Several Angels gasped in outrage. "Blasphemy," one Angel cried.

"You would be wise to watch your tongue," a voice echoed from the crowd of gathering Angels.

Marcus could still feel the lingering pain of the dying mortals. "I will not stand by while light and innocence is murdered without regard."

"It is not your choice." The voice shook the heavens again driving several other Angels to their knees in pain. "You do not have the gift of free will," the voice bellowed in rage.

Marcus pummeled his fists against the granite he knelt on. "This is wrong. The God I love would not have chosen this fate for his children."

"It is ordered the mortals pay the price for their sins. False Gods, greed, treachery, lust," the voice boomed with disgust.

Marcus felt the weight of those lost souls descend on him. He knew what he had to and do and that it would change his very existence. That his decision would drive him from the love and peace of his creation. And the only existence he had ever known. He pushed himself to his feet and expanded his wings, thrilling in the power he sensed flow through his body. A collective gasp at his actions echoed through the gathering of Angels at his show of pride.

"Think carefully before you speak, Marcus," the voice whispered over him.

He looked out through the assembled crowd of Angels, their beauty and love all he all he had ever known. Marcus looked up at one of the most beautiful Angels. He would miss that beauty, the love grew in his heart for every member of the congregation. He may not approve of the decision, but it didn't change the fact he loved them all.

"Even we sometimes lose our way, and the actions today prove that," he said cementing his fate. Several Angels took flight disappearing into the heavens not wanting any part of Marcus. "His love would have extended to those that had wandered from the path. He would not have wiped them from the face of the mortal plane."

"Marcus, stop." Sariel ran toward him on bare feet, her wings flowing behind her. She was the closest thing he could call a friend in the unconditional love of the congregation.

"No, Sariel." Marcus held up his hand to stop his friend from coming any closer. He had felt disconnected for many years now. Now would be the time to take a stand.

He looked up into the clear blue sky, the ash and smoke having cleared from the visage of heaven and the fields where the Angels lived. "We are to be the compassionate ones. We are to show mercy and love when none other exists. Guide and care for the mortals. Be the light He gave us for them. Today we had none of this to give. And I would rather live among the ones with free will, then abide with the now corrupted power of the Angels."

"So be it," the voice boomed from the heavens shaking the ground Marcus stood on.

Marcus felt the voice from deep in his head, spiking pain throughout his entire body. The sound of his screams alien to his own ears. He clamped his mouth shut biting his lip as he did so. The unfamiliar taste of blood filled his mouth, and he spat it out gagging.

Lightning lit the darkening sky as his body writhed in pain.

"You have chosen, FALLEN." The voice had turned into a screeching sound.

"FALLEN!" It repeated over and over again, making his ears pop. Something trickled from them, and he knew he was spilling his own blood; blood that had never been split until this day. He was proud to spill it on behalf of the poor souls that had been condemned.

Unfamiliar pain spread through him as his wings were ripped from his back. Marcus arched into the pain and heard his own voice begging for mercy he knew would never come.

If the collective could wipe out all the people of the valley, then the screams of one fallen brother wouldn't sway them. He screamed anyway begging for the pain to stop. Finally, blackness swallowed him, and he sank into its arms gratefully.

Chapter 1

Celeste motioned for the other women to leave as she leaning over Marcus. His lash marks raised and bleeding freely. He had been there countless times, received countless punishments. She cared for him each time, tending the wounds of his body, ensuring his recovery. Thoughtless of his immortality, the very idea of him suffering could bring her to her knees.

Soaking a cloth in the special herbs that would aid in the healing processes, she pressed it gently against the flesh that lay open. She drew comfort from the small stone room, shelves carved into the walls held everything from ancient medical tools to state of the art medical equipment found in any emergency room. The bitter smell of the plants and antiseptic competed against each other. The old and the new, the room was meant for the woman of the Fortress, not for the Reapers or visitors.

Marcus was the one exception to the rule, he was tried held accountable and treated. Celeste could only imagine that he knew of the great honor Dante gifted him by treating him after his punishment instead of sending him back to wherever he belonged and to whatever Fate awaited. No, Marcus was treated and left under his own power, a testament to his fortitude and willpower.

Celeste gentle washed away the blood covering Marcus's back she flinched when he flinched. She added a painkiller to the bowl. It bubbled and smoked, she dipped the cloth back in wanting to comfort him. But this wasn't the first time he had lain here, and she didn't think it would be the last time either.

Haunting emerald green eyes stared up at her, glassy with pain. "And here you are again, my own personal Angel of mercy." She didn't smile, the first time he had said it, it had brought a smile to her lips, but now— she understood those words to be the mutterings of a man driven out of his own mind from pain.

He often called her Jessica. It tore at Celeste's heart. And although she had no idea who the woman was she wanted nothing more than to find her and tear her limb from limb and she would do it with a smile.

"Why spend the time cleaning them? They won't kill me. There is no death for a Fallen," he muttered more to himself then to her.

"Is that what you seek, Fallen? Death? Oblivion from your immortality?" Celeste wondered if death was his ultimate goal. Why else cavort with Reapers, and everything else an Angel would find repulsive? Breaking rules like he did. Taking the punishments as required, seemingly seeking nothing in return. Celeste had never been able to put a finger on exactly what the "something" could be.

"If you seek oblivion then why not ask, Dante? As the ruler of the Infernos and the Keeper of the Gate to Hell, he alone answers to none other than Lucifer himself. He is capable of providing it. Instead of the torture and punishment you continually endure." Celeste commented as she continued to clean his back.

She was surprised when a smile played at the corner of his full lips. "I seek the feelings of being alive. And your gentle touch. You are what I seek." The words were like a caress, she soaked it up knowing she would pay for it later. The Sex Demon in her stirred, deep in the pit of her stomach, causing spikes of sensation to tingle down to the base of her spine.

Celeste finished cleaning his back, staying with him until he drifted off to sleep. Luckily he said nothing further, and she gently brushed a stray curl of his short brown hair off his forehead. It was not possible to stay with him the entire time he convalesced, although it was what she truly wanted. She stifled the urge to stay with him and comfort him when he woke. If her father knew she looked after the Fallen he would be very displeased. A person did not displease Dante, doing so often led to a different kind of punishment altogether.

Victor found her lingering in the hall outside the Infirmary fighting with herself. She toyed with her long braid of red hair hidden under her long cloak, the feel of the tightly braided strands a tactile anchor to her world.

He shook his head at her. "Stay away from the Fallen," he ordered.

Celeste dropped her heavy braid and pulled herself to her full height, unfortunately she still stood more than a foot under her brothers over six foot frame. But that didn't stop her as she pushed past him. "I don't answer to you, Victor.

"So you would have me go to Father?" he threatened following her.

Celeste rounded on him. "And just why would you do that? Marcus is unconscious and delirious with pain. He doesn't know anything much less who cares for him. Each time he has come and been punished, I have treated his wounds. Not once in all those times has he recognized me as the one that treats him each time. He will be healed and gone soon, no harm, no foul."

Victor snorted. "Don't go and bat your pretty violet eyes at me. I'm immune, just stay away from him. His recovery is not your concern."

She crossed her arms over her ample chest and watched her brother stalk away. No way would she tell her brother she had actually fallen in love with Marcus. It had happened so long ago she couldn't remember a time when she hadn't loved him. How did she explain to her brothers, or even her father for that matter, her general curiosity had turned into an obsession? An obsession that had driven her to taste his blood, to cement his essence in her very soul. She could Trace him on any plane. She could feel his presence when he entered the Infernos. Feel it when he left. There was no place he could hide from her, and it was a gift as much as it was her own personal torture device. One she had given to herself, in the vain hope that one taste would satisfy the lust and want she had for him. More her the fool.

Celeste shook her head, it was wrong, this obsession with Marcus. After all, why in the world would a beautiful Fallen Angel ever even look twice at a half Demon, half Reaper abomination? She was small with wild red hair thc hung to the back of her legs when braided. She had the full hourglass figure of all Sex Demons, they were breed to attract males, and it was totally out of her control. As a fighter she hated she couldn't control that part of herself. She had trained her entire life to control every action she made. Maybe it had something to do with the response her brothers and father had to her physical appearance. They would see her and shake their heads saying she needed to stay hidden.

Just thinking about all that pissed her off, so Celeste made her way to the training area, needing to burn off her frustration before it consumed her. Several of her brothers were training. Perfect. Stripping off her robe, she wore dark blood red pants and a cropped tank top that hugged her upper body. The tight leather may show her off, but it also held her in, leaving her free to move as a fighter should, move the way she had been taught and trained. Her long red hair pulled back in its normal braid at the top of her head hanging down to just below the back of her knees. The mental spikes she wound into the ends of her hair tinkled as she rolled her shoulders and walked onto the mat.

A couple of her brothers took one look at her and stepped off the mat. "She isn't in a good mood today," one of them mumbled.

"When the hell is she ever in a good mood?" another asked. They all laughed. She rolled her eyes. They always thought they were so funny. But they were also the ones walking away from a woman, and they were Reapers. What the hell did that say about them?

One brother remained— Christian, and he smiled at his sister beckoning her forward. With a come and get it motion of his hands. "No holding back?" he asked with a lecherous smile on his face. He had won the last sparing match, but she wouldn't hold back this time. Celeste learned from every encounter she had, and she knew exactly what had gone wrong last time and wouldn't make the same mistake twice.

"When do you ever hold back?" she asked before stepping into the fight.

He caught her off guard with a round house that connected solidly to her face. She tucked and rolled out of his reach, moving into a crouched position. Celeste spat out blood, and shook her head. Endorphins rushed through her blood stream awakening the Demon in her. Her fingernails elongated, turning a burnished shade of purple. She racked her fingers down the mat leaving cleanly sliced holes in their wake.

"Well now, you've just gone and pissed me off." She laughed bitterly. She needed this, the fight. The endorphins and rush of power, the feel of a good fight.

When they were done, she had a split lip, two broken fingers and aches and bruises on most of her body. Christian, however, lay unconscious in the center of the mat.

She looked around. All her brothers had stayed to watch. Shaking her head she accepted a towel from Victor and wiped at the blood on her face and hands. Victor took her and wrapped her in his arms, she felt his flinch of pain as he felt what she had gone through. Victor had the ability to heal his brothers and sister, it was his curse. For he did it without regard, unfortunately he went through the same pain his siblings experienced.

"Didn't like hearing the truth earlier?" he asked once he released her. "Feeling a little hostile?"

"When aren't I feeling hostile?" Her brothers were right, as much as she hated to admit it. And it continued to get worse. She had to visit the mortal plan and find a man to relieve the tension that built inside of her as a Sex Demon. It made her brothers and father nuts when she did it. But they knew if she didn't get the sexual release her body needed, she could become a menace to them all. Damn her mother for being a Sex Demon and her father for falling for her tricks. She didn't know who she hated more. Especially since she couldn't have sex with the one individual she most wanted. No, she had to settle for second rate, one night stands.

"Are all our visitors finally gone?" If anyone remained in the Fortress other than family she remained fully cloaked, and she hated it. It kept her safe, but after a few hundred years, it had officially run its course.

"Yes, except for Marcus, however, he should be leaving soon." She nodded and grabbed her cloak. She swung it over her shoulders and headed for her room. She needed to get out of the

Infernos for a while. But to take any extended time away, she first had to get her father's permission.

Celeste showered and put on a clean linen gray Grecian style dress that bared one shoulder and hung on her lithe form. She wound red beads around her waist showing how slim she was and went barefoot to find her father. A half-skeletal house servant stopped her, which could only mean her father entertained someone. Swearing to herself, she grabbed a cloak from a peg and wrapped it around her shoulders, pulling up the hood.

Celeste opened the door quietly and stepped through, letting it close behind her.

Marcus stood at the foot of her father's dais. At first she wanted to demand that the Fallen return to his sick bed. He couldn't be healed all the way. She tamped down her reaction and stood quietly by while they spoke.

His hair caught the light of the candles that lit the room, turning it golden brown. Celeste took the opportunity to just stare at Marcus. Green eyes sparkled with the pain she knew he tried to hide. His hair was just long enough to run her fingers through. She knew from doing it while he had been unconscious. She also knew it felt like silk through her fingers. He had a strong brow, and even though she rarely saw him she knew he was quick to smile which emphasized his strong cheek bones and jaw making his green eyes sparkle. Slight stubble covered his jaw, which she found sexy. Her fingers itched to run along the planes of his face. The face of an Angel. She started to shift uneasily from foot to foot. That Sex Demon in her was fully awake now with the combination of the fight she had earlier with Christian it was taking everything she had to hold herself back from doing something stupid.

"Thank you for, you're..." Marcus's words faltered. "Hospitality?" He finished with a sly smile on his lips. Celeste smiled herself. Marcus played a fine line with the Reapers and Dante.

Dante laughed. "How many times will you come to us Marcus? Ask favors that force my hand?"

Marcus shrugged, and Celeste could see the pain that passed through his beautiful green eyes even from across the room. "There is very little I would not give in order for light and good to triumph." She could be wrong, but she thought she sensed a slight bite of sarcasm in his voice.

"Bullshit," Dante barked. "Your quest to feel alive is going to leave you a broken and beaten man and nothing but a shadow."

Dante's words didn't seem to faze him. Marcus took a step up the dais and extended his hand, shocking Celeste. "We will, of course, meet again, Dante." One should never offer a hand to Dante. Not in all of her existence had she known someone to willing be Touched by Dante. Celeste's mouth sagged open in shock for a moment. To be Touched meant you owed your soul to Dante, and you didn't want to owe your soul to the ruler of the Infernos.

Her father stared hard at the Fallen's offered hand. "You offer more than you have to give."

Marcus shrugged again, this time hiding the pain. "I offer only what I am willing to."

"And you grow weary?" Dante asked. Marcus said nothing, leaving Celeste to wonder about his motives. Dante reached forward and took the Fallen's hand. Marcus shuttered, but otherwise showed no other emotion of being touched by Dante. "When it is time, I shall claim your soul myself," Dante promised before releasing Marcus's hand.

Marcus stepped back and nodded. "I would be honored, Dante."

Again her father laughed. "We shall see, my friend. We shall see."

He turned to leave, but stopped when his eyes fell on Celeste. She very much wanted to step back when piercing green eyes seemed to focus too deeply into the shadows of the cowl she wore. But she held her ground. He didn't know she existed, but his green eyes burned into her for a moment. His deep stare created a shiver that worked its way down her spine and into her lower back, making her ache with such need. After what seemed like an eternity, he looked away and continued out of the hall.

Dante didn't turn from the dais and his seat. "And what brings you to see me, Celeste?" He asked once the door closed behind Marcus.

She shrugged out of the cloak, letting it fall to the floor. She strode up to stand next to her father. He smiled when he turned to her.

"You must want something. You're wearing a dress, and your hair is down." He knew her too well. She sank to her knees and laid her head on her father's lap.

"I need to visit the mortal plane." Her body burned for touch, she hated and loved it at the same time.

"Yes, I had assumed so. But the mortal plane is fast becoming a very undesirable place to be," he said looking down on her.

"You know of another plane where I can get what I need?" she asked, knowing she pushed her luck with her sarcasm. As Dante's only daughter, she had leeway where her brothers did not. But even she knew how far she could push him. And they both knew she could go to Lust, the fourth degree of the Infernos, where the female Sex Demons had been banned thousands of years ago. But in doing so it could backfire on them all, driving her insane instead of easing the pain. Too much lust and sex could sometimes kill or drive a person crazy. Not something either of them would chance.

Dante's hand fisted in her hair, where he had been stroking just moments before. But just as quickly released her. "You go too far, Celeste."

"I apologize, Father."

"You may go. However, if something happens, and you are called home, you will come immediately." She had been known to dance around the requests of her return, for days and even weeks at a time. "I will not allow you to go until you agree to that one point." He had never demanded this of her before.

She turned and looked up at her father. "And if I refuse?"

"If you refuse, then I will deny you the right to go to the mortal plane. And if you accept yet fail to heed my call, you shall be punished." She shivered knowing he would punish her, regardless of her being his only daughter.

Dante shook his head. "You sometimes are far too similar to your mother."

She smiled. Her mother had lived in the Fortress for the first hundred years of Celeste's life. And even though in the end, her mother had gone mad needing and craving the touch of a man, she still remained her mother, and Celeste loved her. Celeste had visited her mother several times in Lust. But when her mother's ravings had become too much, Celeste had deemed it unwise to continue the visits. Besides, her mother came in and out of sanity, and Celeste never knew exactly what she could expect when she visited.

"I promise to come when you call, Father," Celeste promised standing, she kissed his cold cheek.

He squeezed her hand a strange look in his eyes. "Be safe, daughter."

She laughed. "Even you have to admit that of all your children, I have the ability to defend myself with the most success."

Dante nodded. "Yes, you are a warrior at heart, with the abilities of a Demon, and a Reaper combined. However," he said, touching her chest where her heart beat strong, "someday I believe that you will need to let someone in. And I wonder if after everything I have done to keep you safe, you will be unable to do so. I fear that in doing so it will crush the spirit I love so much."

"I will never allow anyone that close. There is no mortal, or immortal with the ability to crack me." Her mind immediately pulled up a picture of Marcus, but she disregarded it just as quickly. Having agreed to her father's conditions, she left the great hall and went toward her room. She had no intention of ever letting anyone in. She was nothing but an abomination. No one would be able to understand who or what she was.

Celeste entered her room and threw some clothes into a bag and braided her hair, pulling it up so that the spiked ends were tucked into the base of her neck. Mortals didn't understand the spikes that she had weaved into the ends of her hair. She changed into leather pants and a t-shirt before she opened a portal and appeared in a back alley in the back streets of Chicago. She waited for several moments. She sensed nothing that could track her entrance into the mortal plane. However, with her ability to Trace Marcus, she knew he was close, which could mean he could be in the same state, or on the next street. She couldn't help but feel some comfort at the knowledge that he could be so close.

She pushed him out of her head and headed downtown to the club-district. She needed a man, and that should be the only thing she should be concerned with.

****

Three days later she lay in a bed with a man she had spent the last two days with. He had satisfied her need for sex, but she remained empty inside. An existence she now realized she couldn't keep up much longer. It was looking as if she would end up with her mother in Lust, craving for the touch of man she could never have. The thought sent a shiver of dread through her. She would rather die, have her soul dispersed never to be recycled again, rather than spend eternity wanting something she could never have. Pay for her sin of coveting Marcus, in the Infernos. After all she had grown up there and knew for herself that ultimately there was no other fate for her, it was why she trained so hard, fought so diligently to gain control of herself. But after this visit, she understood her current existence was going to drive her insane if not kill her.

Celeste glared at the dingy ceiling and swore, causing the man next to her to murmur in his sleep. She should leave, go back to the Infernos at least there she had more control of her Demon side. The mortal planes decadence offered a near sensory overload that was harder and harder to control.

She was about to climb from the bed when out of the corner of the Motel room, Victor appeared. "Argghh." Celeste scrambled for a sheet to cover her nakedness.

Victor grunted and looked away. "Heard of a door?" Celeste snapped.

"It's time."

"And why is that?" she asked sarcastically.

Victor growled, which meant she shouldn't have asked. Celeste swore under her breath and wanted to kick something.

He must have sensed her hesitation, because he swung around to her. "Do you really want to fight with me?" His eyes black as death he looked from her to the sleeping male.

She flipped him off and grabbed her clothes. Throwing them on, she snatched up her bag and gave her brother a sweeping gesture. "After you."

Victor snorted and opened a portal. Celeste leaned over the bed and whispered a few words of power into the mortal man's ear, making him forget everything that had happened in the last two days, and then followed her brother back into the Infernos and complete and utter chaos.

Something that looked eerily like an arm disconnected at the elbow, flew at her. She ducked out of the way just in time. Screams of pain, terror and rage ripped through the air. More than just the screams of the damned where the sounds of fighting and panic rendered through the Infernos like a wildfire. Terror seized her for a moment.

Victor looked at her. "Keep it together." He handed her two deadly short Swords she sheathed in her boots. "Calliope broke in," he said over the noise. "Mason is dead." His voice was flat and emotionless, he turned to fight off a damned soul that came at him.

Unexpected tears stung Celeste's eyes. "What are you talking about?" she screamed kicking off an attacker. "What level are we on?"

"Heresy. When Calliope came through, he killed Mason, and the inhabitants felt the loss of power and broke through." Another soul attacked, and for a moment Victor and Celeste fought back to back as they moved to where their other brothers were making a stand.

"He has moved to Dante's Peak," Christian bellowed. "We were just waiting for you two."

With a flash of fire they all transported to Dante's peak. They stood in the shadows of Dante's garden. They could hear the fighting and as a group ran toward one of the bases, hidden by rock and shadows, stood the opening to Pandora's Cave. Dante stood there with a long Sword in his hand. He fought to protect another brother. Celeste wanted to crumble to the ground at what she saw. Victor shoved her behind him as a huge black winged figure flew from the mouth of the cave.

Calliope laughed, his head thrown back as he taunted Dante. "Do you honestly think now that I am free you will be able to put me back into one of those boxes? That I would submit to you and your pitiful offspring?" Calliope looked at each Reaper that stood with Dante.

Dante laughed. "I'm not going to put you into one of those boxes, Calliope." Calliope hovered just out of reach. His eyes narrowed, but Celeste could see the hope there. "I'm going to cut you into a million pieces and send you straight to Hell."

This time Calliope raged. "I will rule the Infernos like they were meant to be ruled. And when I do, you shall beg for forgiveness on your knees, *Father.*" He slurred the last word. Dipping down he attacked.

"Get into the Cave, Celeste." Victor pushed her toward the opening.

"I can fight," she growled.

"No. Go get the Black Sword," Victor said.

Celeste wanted to slap herself in the forehead. She scrambled past her brothers and into the Cave, sliding her short Swords into the sheaths in her boots.

Calliope had ransacked the place. Boxes and treasures littered the floor. She wondered briefly what he had been looking for and prayed to the gods he hadn't found it. She started throwing things aside, climbing over precious objects, and avoiding dark objects that would suck her very soul out of her body. Tripping and falling several times, the bellows of pain and rage and her brothers drove her forward.

Dante had brought her down to Pandora's Cave when she was old enough to know what she was, he showed her the treasures he had collected through the ages. Showed her the Sword and explained that being half Demon and half Reaper it made her the only creature in this world or the next that would be able to hold it and not be consumed by its darkness. Celeste had conflicting sides in her soul that would keep her safe.

"Then how did it get here?" She had asked.

Dante had looked so sad when she asked that question. And it frightened her; she had never seen human emotion on her father's face before. "An Angel gave herself to the dark in order to in-tomb it here." That was all he had said, and she was too frightened to ask him anything else. Something that upset Dante, would terrify her.

The Black Sword remained where she had seen it with Dante, buried deep in the red bedrock, and Celeste hoped it didn't kill her as she wrapped her hands around the hilt and tugged. A tingle spread up her arm and into the base of her skull, she could feel it probe her. Trying to decide if she was evil or not. For a moment her brain was flooded with images she couldn't explain, and then it was filled with light. As quickly as it had started, it ended, and she was left staring at her hand wrapped around the hilt of the Sword she tugged.

It didn't budge.

More screams from her brothers at the mouth of the cave. "Please," she begged the Sword. Pulling with everything she had, it still didn't move. She felt tears fall down her face, and she wiped them on her shoulder. Then she tugged at the Sword again, again it didn't budge.

"You bitch," Celeste screamed at the Sword in frustration. She put her leg next to the hilt and heaved and pushed with her foot at the same time. It came loose with a grinding noise. Her momentum sent her across the cave to land in a collection of boxes in a heap. Ribs cracked and Celeste saw stars for a moment.

Shaking it off, she scrambled to her feet and out of the mouth of the cave, just as Calliope disappeared through a portal. Several of her brothers lay in the dirt, but she knew they were still alive by the subtle rise and fall of their chest.

She stepped forward gasping for air. Victor took her by the arm, stopping her. "There is nothing more that can be done here."

"It wouldn't come loose," she offered lamely looking at the Sword in her hand.

Victor nodded. "It wouldn't have made a difference. He is testing the waters, seeing what our strengths and weaknesses are."

"And?" Celeste asked.

Dante stepped forward vibrating with rage. "He knows as a collective he cannot take us. Individually, we are weak. That's why we are two down. However, what he doesn't know is that we have a secret weapon."

There was quietness at his pronouncement, Celeste could feel the air being stolen from her as she looked at her father. His eyes shown with rage, and she knew there was no getting out of this now. Calliope had broken into the Infernos. He was going to cause havoc and destruction, and someone had to destroy him. Unfortunately she was the only one that could hold the Sword, and they all knew it.

Victor pushed past Celeste, tucking her behind him protectively. "You cannot use her that way."

Dante slammed a fist into Victor's chest. He sent Victor flying backwards, Celeste barely moved out of the before he flew past into hard red stone. He fell unconscious into the dirt.

Celeste had never seen her father so upset, and she pursued her lips together to keep from saying anything. She knew her place, knew that rushing to Victor would be showing weakness. Not something you did in front of Dante, Victor had been wrong to try to protect her.

"You shall fight him on the mortal plane, and bring his pieces back to me." He took Celeste by the shoulders and shook her. "Promise me you will bring him back to me for retribution. For your home? For your brothers? For your very existence," Dante growled. Celeste nodded, and Dante threw his head back and howled to the heavens and hell with pain and rage.

Chapter 2

"They want to speak with all the Trackers?" Marcus looked at Victor as if the Reaper had suddenly sprouted horns. Marcus couldn't remember a time when anyone had ever asked to speak with the Trackers and Fallen at the same time. In fact until recently the Trackers, an ancient race of hunters with the ability to find any creature be it human or Other with three sense's; taste, touch, smell, had believed to have been extinct.

"Did I say something that would allude otherwise?"

Victor's dry humor not cracking even a little. "You have forty-eight of your hours to pull it together."

He was gone in a spectacular ball of fire causing Marcus to stumble back in surprise. When had they started doing that? It was very unlike the Reapers to call attention to themselves in such a showy manner. He couldn't imagine what could be bad enough to warrant a meeting with both he and the Trackers. He did know it didn't bode well for anyone.

Swearing, Marcus grabbed his phone. He wasn't looking forward to calling the Trackers, they didn't take direction or demands well. And this definitely fell under the demand category.

Falcon picked up on the first ring. "What?" he barked into the phone.

"Good morning, Falcon," Marcus said with mock pleasantry. "It's good to hear your voice."

"Marcus, if you have something you need to say, say it or I am going to hang up this bloody phone." He had to give it to Falcon the Tracker never beat around the bush. It was something to respect in the man.

"I just had an interesting visitor. Victor is demanding all the Trackers and the myself be at Staten and prepared for a visit within forty-eight hours." Marcus couldn't wait to hear what Falcon had to say to that.

Falcon didn't respond immediately and the pause was enough to make Marcus just a little nervous. Would he flat out refuse? Finally he spoke. "Excuse me? A visit from whom?"

"I would assume the Reapers."

"All of them?" The slight inflection in Falcon's voice meant the news had shaken the unflappable Tracker as much as it had Marcus. "Where are you?"

Marcus looked around the drear church he had been searching. "I can be at Staten by nightfall."

"It will take about thirty-six hours to get everyone here," Falcon said.

"Just make it happen, Victor didn't act as if we really have a choice in the matter."

"Did he threaten you?" Falcon asked.

Marcus snorted. "Your sense of humor is hysterical."

"I'll see you by nightfall." Marcus looked down at his phone and shook his head. Since spring, when he had met up with Ryder and his brothers, his life had changed drastically. The Trackers considered him a brother, which meant being treated like a brother, and entailed pulling asses out of fires. And being talked to like an idiot, this was apparently a trait brothers had. Marcus had nothing to compare it too, his brethren in the Congregation of Angels would never dream of talking to each other the way Trackers did. Moreover, he didn't know if any of his fellow Angels or Fallen would have his back the way the Trackers did either. With Fallen disappearing like they were, Marcus never complained about having a backup plan of the Trackers either.

He walked out into the fresh air of the fall morning, leaving the musty smell of the old church behind him. He searched his memory for any time in history he knew of when the Reapers had requested an audience with anyone much less Trackers and Fallen. He came up blank. Yeah, his week was about to get a whole lot more interesting.

****

"Marcus." Kyra smiled and stepped into the circle of the Fallen's arms as he came through the door. Ryder stood behind his bonded mate growling, to irritate the Tracker he pulled Kyra in closer.

"It's good to see you," he whispered into her ear.

"Let her go, or I'll break you in half," Ryder snarled.

Marcus laughed and let her go, then extended his hand to Ryder. "It's good to see you as well, Ryder. I see your territorialism regarding Kyra hasn't lessoned since the summer." Ryder took his hand and pulled him in for a bone-breaking pat on the back. "It is good to see you, Fallen. And no, it hasn't, so keep your hands to yourself. How has the hunt gone?" Marcus snorted. "Not good. Calliope might as well have never existed for the amount of evidence I have found on him."

Kyra laughed and it brought joy to Marcus's heart it sounded like the tinkling of bells. "Did you expect him to just swoop down from whatever perch he has claimed and say, 'Here I am, would you please lock me up in a Pandora's Box again?'"

Kyra leaned into her bonded-mate who wrapped an arm around her waist. Ryder looked down at Kyra and smiled. Marcus had to acknowledge the stab of jealousy that flickered through him. As a Fallen Angel he knew ultimate love, but the love of mortals, and specifically the love Ryder and Kyra shared, shook all the beliefs he had built regarding love. Something deep inside of him craved it so profoundly it physically hurt. He thought he had it once. But what Kyra and Ryder shared eclipsed anything he had ever seen or felt before. It spoke volumes of the love he thought he had found so many years ago.

"How many are here?" he asked to cover his envy and jealousy.

"Everyone but Bowen, and Cameron. By the way, what happened between the two of you? Cameron came back pissed as hell three months ago and said you were impossible." Ryder laughed.

The information didn't surprise Marcus. Being young and stupid, Cameron didn't listen to a damn thing anyone said. He thought he knew everything. He continually did stupid and reckless things just for the adrenal rush. Marcus had worked with him for four months before sending him packing.

"He is hot-headed and should be locked up until he grows up a little," Marcus mumbled, not really wanting to speak ill of the Tracker.

Ryder threw his head back and laughed. "He doesn't work well with others, Marcus. We had hoped by sending him with you he might learn some patience. But he came back so angry at you and the world, Falcon ended up sending him to South America to ask the Amazons if they knew anything."

"What the hell kind of punishment is that?" Marcus asked.

"He came back with a broken arm and four festering arrow wounds," Ryder said, leading Marcus down the hall. "He's been pretty calm since then."

Marcus laughed. Leave it to Cameron to mess up an opportunity to stay among some of the most beautiful and powerful woman in the world.

"Bowen is in Germany, but he will make it. Cameron is in Chicago. He said he would show up at the appointed hour and not a minute before."

Marcus raised an eyebrow. "And that is calm?"

"He is staying out of trouble, that's all I care about, brother," Falcon said stepping into the hall he exchanged a hand shake with Marcus.

"So any ideas yet?" Marcus asked.

The Trackers had contacts everywhere, and he wouldn't be surprised if they knew exactly what was going one and why.

Falcon gave Marcus a black look. "All I know is the Infernos, and all the portals into it have been locked. The last intel we received was something had attacked."

Marcus released a pent up breath. "Calliope." It was a statement not a question, which meant bad news for all of them.

"It was our assumption as well."

Marcus had a sinking feeling things were going to get a hell of a lot worse before they got any better. Why was it when the Trackers were involved a well laid plan always went up in smoke?

****

All eight Trackers sat at the large dining room table with Kyra next to Ryder. Marcus standing behind Falcon. They had all been informed of what this was possible about. The tension in the room was palatable. And, he wondered, who would crack first? The Trackers or the Reapers when they showed up. Either was possible.

Expecting a portal to open, they were all shocked when, in a flash of fire, seven cloaked figures appeared. Marcus, being the only one standing, took an involuntary step back. The heat from the flash of the fire scolding him.

One slight figure stepped forward and lowered his cowl. Dante stood at the other end of the table. He heard Kyra suck in a shocked breath. Marcus had never heard of the man leaving the Infernos for any reason, and Marcus was left utterly speechless.

"Thank you for taking the time to meet with us." He nodded toward the cloaked figures behind him. "We call upon you because the Infernos have been attacked. Portals are compromised, and Reapers are dead."

Removing his cowl, Victor stepped forward. "Calliope has taken the last months to assimilate to this time period and now understands the comings and goings of the Reapers. He was able to get in via a portal that has not been used for centuries. It went directly to the seventh level. He fought his way forward. Samuel was beheaded and hung from the gates of Limbo, disemboweled. The inhabitants mutilated him, leaving almost nothing." Each word was tinged with steel, Marcus felt for the Reapers. They had never had to deal with the death of a brother.

Another brother stepped forward removing his hood. "Mason was slain defending Pandora's cave. His fate was similar to that of Samuel's."

"The balance of the planes of existence as we know them is now in jeopardy," Dante said, taking back the conversation. "I will not lose another son to this monstrosity. You have been given the task to find and destroy him, Fallen. And the Element..." Dante looked pointedly at Kyra. "...will bear the weight of the innocence lost on her shoulders when her time of redemption comes."

Ryder growled and made to stand, but Kyra placed a hand on his arm holding him back. "He is not telling us anything we didn't already know, Ryder."

"Your soul belongs to know one," Ryder snapped.

"What exactly are you looking for from us?" Falcon asked. Marcus cringed eyeing Dante warily, he knew the leader of the Infernos sanity often balanced on a thin thread. And the Trackers often took and individuals last shred of sanity and wore it thin, but one did not play with Dante.

"I want you to find Calliope and bring him to me for retribution." The words came out in a growl and bounced off the walls of the room as if trying to escape the small space. "He is a liability that should never have been given the opportunity to escape."

"You said Samuel fell defending Pandora's cave," Marcus said, not sure he wanted the answer to the question he was about to ask. "What was he doing trying to get into the cave?"

"There are many things you do not know nor understand, Fallen. There are things in that cave that are there for a reason. Hidden from the world. Hidden from everything including time. Releasing them would wreak havoc on every plane of existence." Dante looked at him his dark eyes cold, holding secrets Marcus couldn't even begin to fathom. His stare caused shivers to spread over his arms and Marcus had to fist his hands at this side to keep them from rubbing his arms. Dante finally looked away releasing Marcus, and he felt warmth return to his extremities.

"Then why don't you explain them to us before we put our own lives on the line?" Marcus asked losing sight of the fact he shouldn't piss Dante off at the moment.

"You—" Dante stammered, and slammed his hand on the table cracking the wood down the center. Marcus was surprised the table didn't crumble to dust beneath the blow. "You were charged with finding Calliope, and the blood of my sons is on your hands as well Fallen. Do you have any idea the chaos running wild in the Infernos?"

A small figure, still cloaked, stepped forward and placed a gloved hand on Dante's shoulder. He seemed to calm slightly, but his cold stare racked the room. Marcus wouldn't be surprised if he breathed out, and was able to see his breath the room had grown so cold. "I don't think you fully understand the ramifications of what this means. The portals are compromised. Anyone using them could be killed entering or leaving the Infernos. Beside the fact that the open and closing of portals can be tracked by Calliope. Souls will be lost to the in-between. Trapped. The Angels will forsake those they deem unworthy, and no redemption will be found in the hands of Reapers with the portals compromised. We will have to move one soul at a time or risk letting Calliope back into the Infernos. Do you have any idea what will happen if we leave tainted souls to roam this plane?" Dante's words echoed through the room making several people shudder. Evil souls, left to linger will haunt and terrorize the innocent. It would cause wide spread panic, terror and insanity among mortals.

"How exactly did you get him out of the Infernos?" Ryder asked in the silence that followed. "Once he obtained what he wanted he left," Victor explained.

"What exactly does Calliope want?" Falcon demanded.

"To rule the Infernos," Victor provided. "And in order to do that, he will need to destroy all of the Reapers and Dante."

"So why leave the Infernos if he was able to get there? It doesn't make any sense," Skylar asked.

"He wanted to know what our defenses were, what weaknesses we have. He was able to make it from the seventh level to my Fortress in Limbo before we were able to open a portal and force him through it. However, I believe he left of his own accord. He could have stayed and fought but chose to let us drive him out. He is up to something, and the end result is him ruling the Infernos," Dante spat.

"Again, I'm not sure how this pertains to us?" Falcon said.

"There are several ways to get into the Infernos portals, Flashing, and by way of souls that belong there. But even those souls aren't a guarantee that a Reaper will come for you," Dante said slanting a look at Marcus as he spoke, making Marcus's stomach pitch and roll. Marcus was almost afraid to ask his next question. "Exactly what type of soul would guarantee entry into the Infernos?"

"Only one of my Touched would guarantee a portal to the Infernos. Now that the portals have been locked, once he has a way to kill us Calliope will go after anyone that has access to the Infernos by other means. Enter the Infernos and kill us to obtain the right to rule over the Underworld." Dante looked at Marcus and then at Kyra. "You are both Touched by me. Killing either of you would be a gateway to the Infernos."

"Son of a bitch," Ryder bellowed slapping his hands down on the table. "How many others have you personally Touched?"

"Hundreds, but there are a select few that are not only Touched but guarded, those souls would be his one true way into the Infernos. Besides, the Fallen and the Element, there are six souls that are Touched by myself and guarded by the Angels," Dante explained. "I need you to find them and either kill them yourself or keep Calliope from killing them."

"And exactly what are you going to be doing?" Marcus couldn't help but ask.

"I will be attempting to restore order back to the Infernos." Marcus was surprised when he saw genuine sadness in Dante's face. "And, of course, replacements for my fallen sons."

"Wait." Kyra held up a hand stopping the conversation. "You said he was going to find a way to kill you. How is that possible? What types of things will kill you?"

Victor shook his head. "The majority of items deadly to immortals have been collected either by the Angels or Dante."

That comment shook Marcus to the core, Dante held items that could kill immortals? It was staggering. "You have been collecting these items? Why?"

Dante slapped the table again in agitation. "Because items such as those should not be left on any plane for mortals or others to trifle with." He pinned Marcus with a glare. "And your dear Angels have been helping me."

"So what then?" Kyra said breaking the standoff between them.

Several items that Marcus knew of had been destroyed by Angels, or Reapers. But then he questioned even that. Maybe he didn't understand the workings of the Other's as well as he believed.

"The only item that remains on this plane besides the Book Of Deaths, which has been missing for over two thousand years. Is the Blood Rite Dagger," Dante explained.

"And does Calliope know of either of these items?" Falcon asked.

Dante snorted. "Of course he does, he helped in the creation of the Dagger."

"Well that's just great." Ryder swore. "So he probably has some type of connection with the damn thing."

Dante nodded. "You should not bother yourself with finding the Dagger. Calliope will find it if he hasn't already, and then he will do everything possible to get back into the Infernos."

"What can he do with the Dagger?" Marcus asked wanting to fully understand what they were going to be facing."

"The Blood Rite Dagger was imbued with the blood of the first Reapers giving the carrier the ability to reap the soul of an immortal," Victor explained, his words made Marcus light headed with worry, and his legs shook slightly.

"Something like that should never have been created," Kyra said to the silent group. "What was the purpose of it?"

Victor shook his head sadly. "Many wars have been fought between immortals, gods and demi-gods. Weapons were created and destroyed for the purpose of winning those wars. Then lost to the world and time."

"So unlike other weapons created by the Others, this Dagger can be held by anyone?" Marcus really didn't want to hear the answer. He only hoped whoever had the Dagger now didn't know what it was used for.

"Yes." Dante's word fell like an anvil on the table between them. "You must find him and bring him to me."

"And exactly what are you going to be doing?" Marcus asked again.

"We cannot be in two places at once," Dante explained. "If anarchy continues to rain in the Infernos, it will eventually bleed over into the mortal realm."

"It sounds like it already is," Falcon snarled slapping his own hand on the table. "The souls bound for the Infernos will be trapped on this plane."

"Answer me one more question, Dante," Marcus said interrupting Falcon. Dante leveled him with a black cold stare. "How do we kill Calliope?"

The slight figure at Dante's side stepped forward throwing off its cloak. A beautiful red haired woman in blood red leathers unsheathed a Sword as long as her arm and as black a pitch. "With this." She stabbed into the oak table.

Everyone scrambled away from the table. Chaos reigned for several minutes as chairs were tipped over and the inhabitants of the room, excluding the Reapers, moved as far as the four walls containing them would allow.

"That was to have been destroyed," Falcon bellowed glaring at the Sword.

"Yes, well, something's should never be destroyed," Dante said calmly.

"And what exactly is holding the Sword?" Kyra asked nearly hissing the words. Then she directed her next statement at the woman. "What are you?"

Dante placed a hand on the woman's shoulder. "This is to never leave this room."

Marcus and several of the Trackers snorted in disbelief, after everything Dante had said to them he was now asking them for their confidence?

"You're asking for favors now?" Lykar barked. "I know you're the ruler of the Infernos, but you must have the largest set of balls on any plane."

Nobody spoke for a long moment. "She is my daughter, Celeste."

Kyra snorted. "Heaven sent? Are you kidding me? Her name means heaven sent?" she turned to Ryder, as if he would understand the irony of that. "Can you smell it? She's a Demon."

"Just Reaper enough to hold the Sword, and just Demon enough to not let it take her soul." Skylar shook his head, and glared at Celeste "Bitch, you're trouble, that's what you are."

Dante held up his hands. "Celeste will be partnered with Marcus in order to find the Guarded Touched. Calliope will go after them after finding the Dagger. Kill the Touched yourselves if you have to, but do not allow Calliope to get ahold of them."

"I will not kill innocent mortals," Marcus demanded. "There has to be another way. And how can that be all you are worried about, he is out there right now trying to find a dagger that could very well kill you and your telling us to kill innocent mortals to keep the Infernos safe?"

Dante shrugged casually making Marcus itch to shake him. "I care little for how the situation is handled when it comes to the Touched. Those souls belong to me regardless. Calliope cannot have them," Dante said with no feeling at all. "Celeste will ensure that

Calliope pays for his deeds." He exchanged a look with Celeste, and she nodded slightly.

"I don't want her," Marcus balked. The last thing he needed was to have to deal with a female Demon/Reaper mix.

Dante sneered at Marcus. "That Sword is the only thing that will kill Calliope, unless you have another blessed Sword?"

"We shouldn't have this one," Marcus snarled. There was something about the small Demon/Reaper that just had his hackles up. Some recognition flickered in the back of his mind that he couldn't place.

"And just what happens to the rest of us if we happen to come up against Calliope?" Falcon asked. "If that Sword is the only thing that will kill it, then the rest of us will be sitting ducks. Especially if he as the Dagger."

"You must find and protect the Touched," Dante explained.

"You said yourself there are hundreds of Touched," Falcon shouted. "How do you expect us to find and protect hundreds of Touched?"

Dante glared at the Tracker. "Hundreds of Touched, but only six that I have Touched and that the Arch has guarded. Find them that is who Calliope will be going after. Besides, you are Trackers. You are able to sniff out the Touched. Then the Elements will be able to hide them."

"And then what?" Marcus asked. "No one can touch that Sword but her." He glared at the small woman. He would have bet money a strong wind would blow her over, she was so tiny. He wasn't even sure how she was holding the large broad Sword up by herself.

"Celeste will hold her own. And no, I would not recommend anyone hold the Sword for any length of time. Any more than a few minutes will blacken your soul, and the Sword will feed on your light. But it cannot be helped," he said. "It is going to take us all to correct this problem."

"How in the world am I supposed to get the Elements to agree to hide these Touched?" Kyra asked.

Dante slapped the hard oak table again and pointed a finger at Kyra. "You opened the box." Kyra stumbled back hugging her arms she screamed in pain.

Ryder caught her as she collapsed. "Hurt her again, and you won't have to worry about anything but me." Ryder's voice was low and deadly. He carried his mate from the room, not turning back.

"Marcus you were charged with finding Calliope, and you are failing miserably," Dante taunted. "Celeste is the only one I can spare. The only one Calliope is unaware of. The only one that can carry the Sword. If there was any other way, I would take it. She is the perfect weapon against him."

He swept the rest of the group with a disgusted look. "The rest of you know what is at stake. Either find the Touched and keep them safe, or allow Calliope the means to destroy the Reapers and myself and open the doors and portals around the world to the Infernos. Not to mention the terror and insanity that the left evil souls will cause on the mortal plane."

Dante made eye contact with each person in the room. "Is this something you are willing to take on?"

The Trackers turned to Falcon. "Our brother's bonded mate is Touched, and one of our own brothers carriers your mark," Falcon said to the Trackers then turned to Dante. "We will do this for a price." Falcon held up his hand as Dante attempted to interrupt. "You must remove the marks on Kyra and Marcus."

"And if you fail?"

Falcon was forever the calculator. "What would you consider a failure?"

Dante laughed. "All the Touched could die, but if one of their deaths results in Calliope gaining access back into the Infernos, you fail."

"You care so little for the souls you have marked?" Falcon's voice dripped with acid.

"Either way, they belong to me," Dante quipped. "I will remove the mark on Kyra, but Marcus," Dante's eyes went to Marcus. "His is nonnegotiable. It was given freely, not taken. Therefore, I have nothing to release, he has the right to, of course ask me to remove it, otherwise it will not be removed."

Marcus hadn't said a thing about his mark to the Tracker brothers. And they hadn't asked, but now he was going to have to give them answers he wasn't willing to provide.

"You have nothing to bargain with if we fail, Dante," Marcus said stepping forward.

"If you fail the only answer is hell on earth. Because if you think for one second Calliope won't throw the gates of hell open, then you are all deluding yourselves. He was a vengeful and cruel Reaper." Dante stepped back, joining the Reapers that stood at his back. "And his vengeance and anger has only grown in the several millennia he has been trapped in that box."

Chapter 3

Marcus knocked softly on the door. He wasn't sure if he was going to be allowed in, but he had to try.

"Go fuck yourself," Ryder bellowed from behind the door.

Marcus couldn't help it. He smiled. "I don't do that anymore. But I would dearly love to make sure Kyra is no longer suffering before leaving." The Element in Kyra had revolted, and she had gotten sick right after the Reapers had left. Marcus was concerned for her health.

Arguing ensued at his statement. Then, "Thank you for checking on me, Marcus. I truly appreciate it," Kyra said appearing in front of Marcus.

More swearing from the room as Marcus stepped aside the door was thrown open, and Ryder stormed out. Coming nose to nose with Kyra, "I said no."

Kyra rolled her eyes and looked over her mates shoulder to Marcus. "He thinks that's going to stop me," Ryder growled.

Marcus directed his next question to Ryder. "What are you going to do to protect her?"

Ryder threw his hands in the air and turned to Marcus. "At this moment I have no idea. She is just as much a part of this as you are. But I will not put her in harm's way."

Kyra wrapped her arms around Ryder from behind. He was so broad her hands didn't touch, but her hug seemed to calm him. "I opened that box, Ryder. I can't run from it."

"Where are you headed first?" Ryder asked.

"Victor gave us a couple of leads," Marcus explained. "There is a Guarded Touched in Australia and another in New Orleans. Those are the only two we currently know about. After that we will have to have more information.

Marcus felt helpless. They couldn't have said no even if they had wanted to, and Dante knew it. It made Marcus want to strangle the deity's neck.

Marcus pulled a piece of paper from his pocket he and Falcon had made. "There is a family in Wyoming. The women have passed the touch down from generation to generation. Dante is waiting for something to come of it. He also wants to send someone out to look for the Dagger."

"We can do that," Kyra said, still behind Ryder. Her excitement obvious as she bounced like a child in a candy store from foot to foot.

"No," Ryder muttered. But he had a resigned look on his face. "We should set the Enforcers up to find the Dagger, they would have more luck finding an object then we would."

Kyra huffed a deep breath and threw her hands in the air. "You take all the fun away," she muttered to her mate who only rolled his eyes.

"Dante is a sick bastard," Ryder snarled. "His Touched are in danger, and all he wants is his revenge on Calliope."

"Sick doesn't begin to encompass who and what he is, although he is correct. If we do nothing, then Calliope will tear the walls down between the mortal realm and the Infernos and ultimately between hell proper and our world." Marcus shook his head. "Humanity will be destroyed."

"You need to stay here and coordinate. Get the Druids to bless the house and everything between here and the Haven," Marcus said to Kyra.

She stomped her foot and both Ryder and Marcus knew that wasn't a good sign. "I am a fighter, just because I don't have a—" Ryder covered her mouth with his hand.

"Do you really want to finish that sentence, Blue?"

Her eyes narrowed, but when Ryder moved his hand her mouth was closed. "And what about you?" she asked Marcus.

"I am going to find those Touched with Guardians. They are the ones in the most danger. Guardians are like beacons. If Calliope knows what to look for, then there is no way we will be able to keep the souls from him. He will take them and with the aid of the Dagger he will storm the Infernos."

"Do you honestly think bringing them all to one place is a good idea?" Ryder asked.

Marcus didn't have a single idea at the moment which sounded like a good idea or not one was as good and because he honestly thought he was throwing knives in the dark at this point.

"I don't have any other ideas. Why don't you come up with something while I'm on my way to Australia?" Marcus said.

"Please tell me you didn't agree to work with that She Demon?" Kyra asked incredulous.

Marcus sighed. "I wasn't really given a choice Kyra."

"Marcus, she is a DEMON. A female Demon and you are a Fallen Angel."

Ryder snorted. "I think he is aware of all of that, sweetheart."

Kyra hit Ryder in the chest with the back of her hand. Marcus smiled. "I promise I will not let her drag me to hell."

"I don't want you anywhere near her," Kyra argued.

Both men gave her the same dubious look. Ryder recovered first. "You're kidding, right?"

Kyra put both hands on her hips. "What the hell is that supposed to mean?"

"It means you're not his mother." Ryder grabbed her by the arm and pulled her back into the bedroom. "You will keep in contact?"

Marcus nodded. "Yes and you?"

"I agree we need to make Staten and the Haven safe, which is what Kyra and I will work on as the rest of you go in search of Dante's little prizes. The Enforcers will be in charge of finding the

Dagger." Marcus could hear Kyra starting to argue as Ryder shut the door.

Marcus shook his head. They were meant for each other, but it didn't stop them from fighting like cats and dogs. He envied their love. It was beautiful.

****

Celeste looked around the rooms on the first floor. Once her father left, she had been left alone. None of the Trackers had even looked at her. She understood why. She was an abomination and they wanted nothing to do with her. But none of that mattered. All that was important to her was that they find the Touched or kill Calliope. She wasn't going to lose another brother. She stuffed her pain down deep inside of her knowing she would be able to pull from it when she needed to.

As she looked around, she found a beautifully decorated living room. She was amazed at the old world furniture and style. It made her feel as if she had stepped into an English drawing room in the early eighteen hundreds.

She was so engrossed, she didn't see or hear the attack. One moment she was running her fingers over a wonderfully cross-stitched pillow, and the next she was flying through the air. She hit the wall with a force that would have broken another person in half. Celeste allowed her body to crumple to the floor.

Her attacker came at her like a rabid wolf in female clothing and stilettos. As she closed in, Celeste rolled forward cutting the other woman off at the knees.

Her attacker let out an ear-splitting screech as she somersaulted into the air. The crazed woman landed on her feet and crouched down into an attack position just as Celeste swung the Black Sword stopping as it rested against the crazed woman's carotid artery.

Celeste narrowed her eyes. "I don't believe we have been introduced."

"Demon," was all the Lycan snarled her eyes feral. She scratched at the antique rug with her long fingernails. Rending the coiled fabric down to the wood floor beneath.

"Lycan," Celeste returned with just as much fury and rage.

"Get your knife off my throat."

"You attacked me. Bitch," Celeste said pressing the point of the Sword into the woman's throat until a small drop of blood beaded on the edge of the Sword. "So you'll pardon me if I keep my Sword exactly where it is."

"You have no idea what bitch is," the Lycan snarled. She backed away, rolling from the tip of the blade. Celeste matched her speed, but not her cunning and her Sword was knocked out of her hand, and she was tackled with the force of a raging bull.

Celeste threw her palm into the woman's beautiful face smashing her perfect nose and sending blood spraying across both of them.

The Lycan screeched again bringing up a knee she drove it into Celeste's midsection. All the air was pressed from her lungs and Celeste stumbled back a step. The Lycan must have sensed she was vulnerable and advanced. However, Celeste was anything but vulnerable and the Lycan stepped right into a round house to the temple and hit the floor like a ton of rocks.

The doors flew open and Marcus was the first one in followed by the Element and several Trackers she didn't know.

She stood up refusing to show them any weakness. "Someone should keep that bitch on a leash."

"If I've said it once, I've said it a thousand times," the Element said, shaking her head. Celeste couldn't believe the Element was taking her side on this and to hide her surprise, she moved and picked up the Sword, swinging it into the scabbard she wore.

"What happened?" Marcus asked.

"She attacked me." She wasn't about to admit it had come as a surprise attack.

A man she didn't recognize stepped forward. "I am Lykar, and I apologize. Marlee often acts first."

Celeste raised an eyebrow. "Really?" she whipped blood from her face. "I hadn't noticed."

"Are you hurt?" Marcus asked. Celeste looked up into green eyes she had seen a hundred times, generally filled with pain and unrecognizing. Something in her screamed for him to remember all the time's she had been there to clean his wounds wipe his brow.

She saw nothing there, not even real concern. Pushing past those feeling, feelings she should never have allowed herself to feel, she shook her head.

"It's going to take more than that feral bitch to hurt me."

"I'll be happy to try again," the woman said, being helped to her feet by Lykar.

"Marlee, Celeste is a guest in our home," Lykar said with false calm.

"The fuck you say?" Marlee said. "When did we start allowing Demons in the house? Cause I didn't get that memo? What next, Satan's pygmies?"

Celeste took a step back in utter shock. She had never known a louder or annoying creature in all her life. The Lycan's voice had taken on the sound of a screeching banshee on helium.

"That's a misnomer, by the way," Celeste said more to herself then to anyone else. But Marlee whirled on her.

"Did you have something to say, Demon?" she snarled. At least she wasn't screeching.

"Satan doesn't keep pygmies. They run wild in hell, but they aren't his, they aren't anyone's. They are like—" she thought for a moment. "What you would consider a rodent on this plane?"

Marlee threw her hands in the air. "I need a god damn drink."

She stormed from the room, Celeste cataloged everything the woman did. How she had moved, the sound and smell of her. She wouldn't be caught off guard by the Lycan again.

"What are you doing?" Marcus asked accusation lacing his words.

Celeste looked up at him. "Excuse me?"

"Your eyes turned a little red and you blinked very quickly, what were you doing?" Celeste was left speechless, and had to remind herself she wasn't around people that new or understood her. She was something none of them had ever come across before, nor ever would.

Her defenses immediately went up. Her father's words pounded through her head. "They will not understand you. They will use you to help them find and kill Calliope. They have no other choice, but don't for one second let your guard down. They will use that against you, possibly kill you the moment they have the chance and the moment you are no longer necessary."

"I don't have to explain anything to you," Celeste said pulling her cloak around her shoulders, imitating a stance she had seen her brothers and father use a million times.

The only reaction from Marcus was the flare of his nostrils. Then he leaned down so only she could hear his next words. "We are to work together, are you sure you want to start this out by keeping secrets from me?"

It wasn't the words so much as they way he uttered them that jarred her. It was as if he were asking how the weather was.

She let the blood of her Demon side bleed into the iris of her eyes. Marcus's nostrils flared again and she knew her next statement would be drawing a line in the sand. That was okay with her. The things she felt for this Fallen were forbidden. And the more they could maintain a distance between themselves the better.

She spoke slowly as if he hadn't understood her the first time. "I have nothing to explain to you."

****

Marcus had never wanted to strike a woman more than he did at that very moment. The Demon was pushing her luck and she needed to learn her role on this team.

He grabbed her by her arm, she tried to pull away, but he only tightened his hold on her.

"If you'll excuse us, we have something we need to discuss," he said to Ryder and Kyra.

She stopped fighting him when they were out of sight of the others. He picked a side room and, throwing the door in, he shoved her into the room. Following her, he slammed the door behind them.

He leaned back against the door, crossing his arms over his chest. He took several breaths to maintain his calm. There was something about her. Something he recognized, but couldn't seem to put his finger on it. He must have come across her in the Infernos at some point. He spent a great deal of time there. There was just something about her that pulled at him and tightened his gut, made his blood run a little hotter. He realized suddenly he was aroused. The fury that caused boiled through his body astounded him. In less than two hours this tiny thing had wound her way through five hundred years of sexual defenses.

He couldn't control the growl that erupted from deep in his chest. He glared at the woman. Her forehead would barely touch his chin.

Marcus had to admit she was beautiful, but also dangerous has hell. Shaking it off, he stared at her. Waiting for her to blink. Because he wasn't about to back down, she had some explaining to do and she would do it. He was a very patient man.

****

Celeste looked around the room, it was lined with books.

She watched Marcus out of the corner of her eye. He leaned against the door, arms crossed over his chest. He looked like he was waiting for something. She had no idea what, so until he explained she would have to wait. But she could smell his fury. Of course she would know that from tasting his blood. She could tell things about him that not everyone else would be able to. Celeste was about as in tune with him as he was with himself. It was something she didn't think he would appreciate knowing. However, she was amused because at the moment he was sexually frustrated and totally pissed. Two totally opposite emotions. She wanted to shake her head. He was a mess.

She finally turned to him, forgetting she had want to wait for him to speak. After all, she had been raised with Reapers and Dante. They spoke what they felt and be damned if your feelings were hurt in the process. Her change and puberty had driven them all close to murder.

"What?" she demanded from Marcus.

"Are we partners?" he asked his voice calm and quiet almost to quiet.

So, he was going to be reasonable was he? She wondered if he ever lost his composure. "I think partners would be a very broad classification of what we are."

"Then why don't you narrow the definition down for me?" he demanded without even raising his voice.

"We are being forced to work together, Fallen. It's not something you or I obviously want. So let's just make the most of it. Would you like to go to New Orleans or Australia?" she moved over to the book shelf. Unable to stop herself, she turned and started reading the titles. Acting like she wasn't completely aware of the the man at her back or the fact he was going from mad to furious. She wondered if he struck woman, but a sideways glance at him reassured her he wasn't really the type. His arms had come uncrossed and he fisted his hands at his sides. His green eyes sparkling, she was glad to see something in them other than pain and delusion.

After several minutes of silence she turned to him. "Australia then?" she crossed her own arms over her chest staring him in the eyes.

"Be ready in two hours," he ground out between clenched teeth.

Celeste gave him a bland look. "I'm ready now."

He growled.

Celeste took several breaths through her nose so he didn't see the distress she was suddenly in. Because the sound he had just made, was causing the Sex Demon in her to scream out with desire. She turned from him so she could look out the window, knowing her eyes had gone red. If she didn't control her reaction, her skin would take on the same red hue. She would attack him against the door. She was sure she had no way of explaining that type of action to him. Gods, she wouldn't be able to explain it to herself. "Wait here," was all he said. She heard the door slam behind her. Celeste lowered herself into a chair and put her face in her hands. This was going to be harder than she thought. Everything in her wanted to run screaming back into the Infernos. Fighting dead, evil souls was preferable than being stuck with a man she desired. She shook her head. She thought briefly of going back and trying to convince Dante that they should formulate anther plan. But her father had been clear, he wanted her out of the Infernos and he trusted no one, he said that the Fallen and the Trackers would protect her or pay his price. That way, he and her brothers could regain control of the lost levels of the Infernos. Plus, she was the only one who could wield the Black Sword and everyone knew it.

Unfortunately, that meant she was the only one who could kill Calliope, and that price could very well be her soul. It was something only she, Dante and her brothers knew. She could wield the Sword, could hold it without it taking anything from her. But when she used it to kill Calliope, the backlash of his evil could and probable would kill her. Or worse, stain her soul with his darkness, which would result with her in Lust for eternity, with the rest of the Sex Demons tortured by empty desire and longing. What her brothers and father didn't know was, she was prepared to die. Her existence had come down to this mission and her life taking on some meaning before she left the world.

Celeste closed her eyes and concentrated on her breathing. She could do this. She could fight this evil. This was her destiny and if it meant giving her life for those she cared about she would do it. She rolled her shoulders, feeling the black steel at her back. Directing herself on her surrounding she stroked the buttery soft leather of the chair she sat in, and saw the light that surrounded this house. It brought a smile to her face. This was a safe haven. A place where love and light flourished. It warmed her to know Marcus had a place like this. Calm again, she waited.

Ten minutes later, the door was thrown open and one of the Trackers she hadn't been introduced to poked his head in. "Let's hit it."

She stood, assuming that meant they were ready to go. She was going to have to pay close attention to the way everyone spoke and their movements or she was going to make herself look the fool.

Celeste didn't see Marcus again until she climbed on the personal jet. He tossed her a blanket, his anger radiating through him.

"There's a bed in back, and it's a long flight. You might want to get some rest."

Celeste shrugged. He obviously didn't want her anywhere near him. Well that was fine with her because the Sex Demon inside of her wanted nothing more than to climb on him and show him how fast this flight could go by with the right type of entertainment.

Instead, she took the blanket and went to a seat. She pulled the Sword off and laid it in the seat next to her. Celeste watched out the window as the plane taxied and then took off. It was an amazing sight and feeling. Her stomach gave an excited jolt as the wheels left the ground. She had never traveled by plane. She always Flashed or used a Portal to get everywhere she went.

The rumble and hum of the giant engine vibrated through her, making her smile. It was a strange and exhilarating experience to fly, she decided. As they flew up into the clouds, she wondered what it would feel like to be able to take flight, to have wings of her own, just lift up into the wispy clouds. She knew these were whimsical thoughts she didn't have time for.

"So, why Australia?" Marcus asked after an hour or so.

Celeste turned to him. They were alone on the jet. Celeste had contemplated what she should and could tell him about fighting Calliope.

"Like Dante explained, he has assimilated himself to our time. This was not something we had expected. He believed Calliope would go to ground and stay, unable to understand modern ways. Or outright attack either the Angels or the Infernos. Taking the time to assimilate, he now understands who are allies are, who the Reapers spend time with. That means he knows about you and the Trackers. He knows you are stationed in the United States. For that reason he will strike as far from there as humanly possible. I doubt he thinks we have the means to fight him in a global sense."

Marcus seemed to relax slightly and his smell changed just a little. "That would make sense. How assimilated is he?"

Celeste shrugged. "To be honest, I have no idea." That was about all she was willing to admit. She hadn't actually fought him after all.

"So he could just be waiting for us when we get off the plane? Or attack us in the air?" Marcus snarled.

"You should work on controlling your temper," Celeste offered.

"Excuse me?"

She looked him dead in the eyes. "You should work on controlling your temper." She emphasized each world. "I can fill the hostilely rolling off of you. Plus, I smell your irritation. It's something you should work on. If I can smell and sense those things, then Calliope will be able to as well. It will be a weapon he will use against you."

His mouth opened and closed so many times it reminded her of a fish out of water. Celeste actually thought for a moment his head might explode. As the vein at his temple started to throb.

She leaned back in her chair, easing closer to the Sword. Celeste had her two short swords tucked into each boot, but she wasn't giving up any weapon. Especially with how pissed the Fallen looked at the moment.

"And just how the hell do you know those are weapons he will use against me?" Marcus ground between his teeth.

She really wanted to ask him how he was able to talk with his teeth clenched together so tight. But she changed her mind and gave him what she hoped looked like a casual shrug.

"Because I would and with that information you wouldn't stand a chance. I would cut you down before you even knew I was there, what with all your senses focused inwardly like they are." She ignored his reaction to those words by flipping out the blanket and curling into a ball, one hand on the hilt of the Black Sword. She pretended to sleep, as he huffed and puffed for several minutes before stalking off. She couldn't help but smile, he was easily irritated, something he would have to get over very quickly. Like her brothers loved to tell her, she worked a man's last nerve with her outwardly calm attitude.

****

She didn't know how long she slept before Marcus roughly shook her awake.

"Why did I never meet you in the infernos?" He demanded.

Celeste was shocked at the question, and tried to pull herself together so she didn't say something stupid like: *You have you dumb ass.* But she kept that to herself.

"I'm not generally introduced," she said pushing hair that escaped her braid off her face. "Why do you care?"

"Because, I feel like I should know you. But for the last six hours I've been racking my brain trying to figure out how I could have met you." He lowered himself into the chair across from her. He looked tired. "And all I come up with is a blank. Care to explain that to me."

She shook her head. "No."

Marcus raised an eyebrow at her quick response. "Because I spend time, a lot of time, in the Infernos. Have for centuries. And never in that time have I been introduced to you."

She noticed he didn't say 'see' her, and she wondered if he was remembering the time she had spent tending his wounds.

"Like I said I'm generally not introduced. Why do you spend so much time in the Infernos?" she asked changing the subject with a question she had always wanted to know the answer to.

"You are a Fallen Angel," she prodded when he didn't answer right away. "I mean, I would think you wouldn't want anything to do with Reapers."

Marcus leaned back and crossed his arms over his chest. She didn't sense anything from him and couldn't help but smile at him. He had taken her advice pleasure flooded her.

"And why would you think that?"

"Because Reapers would be the last thing a Fallen should be associating with."

"And why is that?"

Celeste huffed and copied his posture crossing her arms over her chest. "You are asking a lot of questions, but not answering any of mine."

"I just find it fascinating you think as a Fallen, I shouldn't associate with your family." "Don't get me wrong, I love my brothers and father. But you're a Fallen for God's sake." He was flustering her with his invasiveness and it was starting to upset her.

"And being a Fallen" he made quotation marks with his fingers as he said *Fallen*. "That I shouldn't know a Reaper?"

"You've been in Heaven. I would think that you wouldn't want anything to do with us."

"Elysian Fields is different from Heaven," he corrected. "Angels don't get to go to Heaven. Heaven is for the souls of the worthy, not for Angels." He wasn't able to hide the frustration in his own words. "Have you been in Hell?"

Celeste choked and sat forward. "Of course not. A person does not just walk into Hell."

He regarded her for several moments. "As one does not just walk into Heaven."

His words made sense. "You're an Angel," she said more to herself than to him.

He chuckled. "A Fallen Angel," he corrected. "Don't put aspirations on me I do not deserve. And I feel for a reason."

She had to bite her tongue to keep from asking why he had fallen. Because it really wasn't any of her business. "So why cavort with Reapers?"

Marcus shrugged. "They are honest."

Her brothers and father were many things and honest seemed to sum it up well. But why would a Fallen Angel, a being that knew such pure light and love find Reapers to be better company then Angels?

"Do you have any contact with them?" she asked. Using her index finger she pointed upward.

"No."

Very succinct, it was a topic he apparently did not want to discuss. She loved a challenge. "Why?"

"None of your business."

She smiled. "I thought you wanted to be partners. We should share," she said more to irritate him than to get an answer.

"Because I am a Fallen and they consider me an abomination and unworthy of attention," he said with anger. "Now why don't you share why I have never been introduced to you before?"

"No."

"Ah I see when the shoe is on the other foot…" He shrugged again.

Celeste was confused and looked down at her feet. "That makes no sense."

Marcus laughed and she pulled herself up short. The sound was rich and full of life, it wrapped around her making her belly jump.

"It is a saying Celeste." She really liked how he said her name. Celeste forced herself to take several deep breaths but she smelled him and his growing acceptance of her as his partner. His pheromones were relaxed for the first time since she had come to the mortal plane. It was spice and rich and all Marcus. Her mind turned to dust, and her fingers itched to reach forward and caress his jaw, run her finger over his full bottom lip.

She was taking short gasps now and had to clamp her hands around the edge of the chair she sat in. Imprinting the feel of the course fabric against her palm. Forcing herself to relax. But her insides were in turmoil and the small plane they were on was folding in on her.

I can do this. She chanted to herself. "We should have Flashed to Australia. This mode of transport is too slow." She could Flash out now if she wanted to, but with Marcus sitting across from her. And the mere fact this was the first real conversation they had shared she was loath to end it even if she thought she might pass out from the sexual awareness pricking at her insides.

"Why have I never met you?" he asked again this time quietly.

"Gah." She threw her hands in the air in agitation. She needed to get away from him before she did something stupid. Before she blurted out she was an abomination too that she knew how he felt. That they were meant for each other. That she loved him. That she would give her right arm if he would just notice her, see her as a woman, and not a Reaper/Demon hybrid. Instead she bolted out of the chair and made to move past him but he grabbed her hand.

Celeste looked down where his hand held hers and barely controlled the whimper of pleasure his touch caused.

"It is a simple question, Celeste," he prodded.

"No it isn't," she bit back and pulled her hand from his. She stomped to the back of the plane and through the door Marcus had pointed out earlier. A small bed was set up bolted to the wall, but it the last thing she wanted to do was lay down on a bed. Not with Marcus feet away.

Tears stung the backs of her eyes and she kicked the bed. Which left her foot hurting. Celeste leaned against the door and slide to the floor. She was furious at her reaction to Marcus, she knew it was going to be hard but as she stared at her hand his touch still burning her skin. She wondered if being forced to work with Marcus might be more difficult than actually killing Calliope.

****

Marcus watched her walk away and slam the door, he couldn't trust her but he also felt drawn to her.

For the first six hours of the flight he had sat in the same room she was in now going through ever single memory he had of the Infernos but nothing came to him. He had never been introduced to her. But something in him told him he knew who she was. He pushed a hand through his hair trying to figure out what he was going to do with her. Working with someone he could not trust didn't sit well with him.

He leaned his head back and closed his eyes, trying to pull a picture of Jessica up in his mind's eye. He started with her blond hair and then her blue eyes, her pert nose that would wrinkle when she laughed or was thinking really hard.

With the image in his mind he let himself drift to happier times. Jessica in the small house they had, her kneading bread. She would turned to him as he had entered her smile feeling the dark hole that had been consuming him since he had fallen.

As he moved toward her though something changed, her features hardened and her clear sky blue eyes narrowed filling with hate. The look took his breath away.

"You are unworthy," she stormed.

And then the figure changed shrinking down. Violet eyes stared at him rimmed in red, accusing fire stared back at him. "What is it you seek Fallen?"

Marcus shot up from his chair stumbling into the ail he gasped for air and glared at the door that separated him from Celeste. "Who are you?" he asked knowing the answer wasn't going to be as easily had.

Chapter 4

"Why are we checking into the hotel first?" This didn't make any sense to her. They should have gone straight from the airport to the Touched. Checking into a room was a waste of time and she had said as much to Marcus.

"Because, you cannot just go out and grab the Touched, Celeste." She was shocked at the hostility in his voice.

"Have I done something to irritate you?"

Marcus finished at the front desk and turned to her. He looked her up and down. She looked down at her red leather pants and vest she was wearing. She took the key card and stuffed it into her breast pocket. Marcus shook his head. "We need to blend it, Celeste."

"No we do not," she countered.

He took her by the elbow and led her over to a bank of elevators. "The Guardians in the city were alerted the moment I stepped off the plane."

"Then we need to act before they take their Guards and hide them." Celeste started to walk back toward the front door. She wasn't going to stand by while the people they had come to protect disappeared.

Marcus stopped her by grabbing her elbow and shoving her into the elevator. "We will allow the Guardians to do their job. If they can protect their Touched they will be doing it now."

Celeste snorted. "And why would they feel the need to protect them from a Fallen?"

Marcus didn't look at her as he answered. "Because I taint everything I come into contact with."

She was glad he wasn't looking at her when her mouth sagged open in shock. And when she realized her mouth was hanging open she snapped it shut and followed behind Marcus as he made the way out of the elevator and down a hallway lined with doors.

"The rooms are connected inside," he said walking into his room. "Get some rest we'll head out an hour before sunset."

"How long?"

Marcus checked his watch and looked back to her. "Three hours."

"What the hell am I supposed to do for three hours?" she demanded. A vein twitched in Marcus's temple. "Well we just spent what? Like a million hours on a freak'n plane, and now we are just going to sit and wait for sunset?"

"Do you have a better idea?" he demanded crossing his arms over his chest. "Because we have plenty of time to share information or Gods forbid learn to trust each other."

"I have nothing to share," Celeste snapped surprising herself with her venomous answer.

"No I didn't think so."

She was so frustrated. "What do you want from me Fallen?" she demanded.

"I want to know that if the shit hits the fan, that you will have my back Celeste."

"That doesn't even make sense. But if you are talking about working together and protecting each other. You can trust that no matter what happens I will protect you against Calliope." This time it was his turn for his mouth to fall open, and she was glad that she had been watching.

"You will protect me?" he asked incredulously.

Celeste didn't understand his shock. "Of course I will."

"Celeste, you have no idea…" he stuttered.

"Marcus, we are here to work together we need to protect each other."

"What were you doing when your eyes flickered back at the Staten?"

Celeste knew exactly what he was talking about but wasn't ready to share, but she also knew if she didn't share then he would take that as her not being trustworthy. She should just come out and tell him with her Demon side she was able to catalogue body movements. It was part of the survival mechanism of a Demon.

Her hesitation was obviously answer enough. "That's what I thought. I can't trust you Celeste. So how when it comes to a fight how the hell can I depend on you?"

"Because I won't let you down," Celeste insisted.

"And how do I know that?"

"Because I say so."

Marcus shook his head and walked into his room letting the door almost close so only half his body was showing. "Sorry but that doesn't reassure me."

He let the door swing shut, Celeste stood there staring at his door for several minutes. She didn't know why he didn't just trust her. She would do anything to keep him safe, but she didn't know how to make him believe that. Should she knock on his door and do or say something to make him understand?

She took a step toward the door. "They won't understand you." Dante had said to her. She stepped back to her door and went into her room and let the door close behind her. She would just have to prove herself to Marcus.

****

"There isn't anything Other here," Celeste accused looking around the dark streets. They had seen nothing, nor felt anything except pure torture in the thick silence between the two of them. Marcus hadn't said more than a handful of words to her since her comments or lack of comments at the hotel. She thought he was acting like a child, but wasn't about to say that to him after the way he had reacted to the other advice she had given him. It surprised her and she chewed on that thought while she waited for sunset. He was a Fallen, and she pictured him as a calm and serene man. But since they had met, he hadn't lived up to any of her expectations.

"Are you sure your intel is correct?" she accused. Her irritation got the better of her.

Marcus didn't even turn to her. "Sometimes being quiet and watching gives you more information than an informant."

Celeste bit her tongue, refraining from telling him exactly what she thought of that idea. "Fine, we shall do what you want and wait." She launched herself up onto a fourth floor balcony and away from Marcus. She needed to get away from him; his smell was driving her nuts, making her a lot more agitated than usual. They had been together for twenty-four hours and had pissed each other off several times. And her feelings were tossing from irritation to sexual awareness and back to irritation. How was she supposed to work with Marcus? She glared down at him as he blended into the shadows.

Celeste played back the last conversation she had with Victor before they had all come to the mortal plan. "You'll need to build a relationship with him," Victor had explained.

"This from the man who told me to stay away from him?" Celeste had thrown back.

"Things have changed, Celeste. I won't lose you. You will do as I ask," Victor said with feeling.

So here she was with a man that didn't trust, because she had breed distrust with him by refusing to answer his questions. And to top it off they were in a deadly situation. It would be nice to have back up she herself could trust. She racked her brain trying to come up with a way to build a relationship with Marcus.

Easier said than done. She had lived her entire life in the Infernos. Either creatures where terrified of her, or they had no idea who and what she was. She remained in the background. She was a shadow lost in the Infernos. Now she was at a loss as to how to communicate with her new partner, much less how to build a damn rapport with him. She cursed Victor and his stupid ideas.

Crouching down, she blended into the shadows of the metal balcony she stood on and watched the dark street below her. She couldn't see him, but she knew exactly where he was. The smell of a car exhaust and day old trash mixed with the smell of the water off to the east.

They didn't move as darkness swept through the city and Celeste was focused completely on Marcus, so the warning bells of something moving in on her came a little too late.

She froze as the feeling eclipsed her own musings; something tingled at the base of her brain. It shivered down her spine. She breathed out; calming herself she focused on the feeling. Something or somebody was perched on the edge of the building directly above her. She could almost feel the brush of Calliope's black wings as they swayed in the salty sea infused air.

She heard him draw in a breath and then a gush of an exhale as he realized who and what she was. His cold exhale chilled her to the bone. She couldn't control the shiver that worked through her body.

"Sister." The words oozed over her like burnt oil. "Are you sure you fight for the right side?" The words whispered over her right shoulder, but she knew he hadn't moved from his perch. He wanted her to turn to the right. He was testing her.

"And what is right, Calliope?" she asked not even trying to deny who and what she was.

"Ah now that is the question of the day is it not? Father was smart in hiding you from me while in the Infernos. I could have feasted on you." He chuckled and the sound made her stomach roll. She thought she was going to vomit.

"You are too young. Dante has kept you sheltered from this world. A world that should belong to us. A world that would find you an abomination." He dropped silently down in front of her, his wings encasing them both. She was pitched into complete blackness.

Celeste had been trained to fight this kind of evil, but seeing it face to face was something utterly different from what she expected. He was a Reaper, a brother, but his features were nothing like what she knew of as Reaper. His eyes were wide and slanted at the corners. Black hair swept around his bare shoulders. He had a pointed chin and hard cheek bones making his face seem skeletal and inhuman. His collarbone protruded out into his wings. He was shirtless, but wore a nice pair of slacks. Stolen no doubt, but she guessed she couldn't quibble about that. After all, he had killed two of her brothers. Shoplifting was the least of his sins at the moment.

"Do you have any idea how long I lived in that box?" Each word whispered against her making her shudder. "You have no idea what being trapped in a box with that evil and filth can do to a person. I used to be responsible for wiping those atrocities from this plane." He leaned in close. "You will end up in one of those boxes one day, Sister."

Celeste shook her head. "I'm not like you, Calliope."

"Really?" he asked. "You're so different from me? Created by a man obsessed with power? You don't think he won't feed you to a Pandora's box, and all the evil it contains in the end? You're just as much an abomination as I ever was and am."

Celeste looked up into his coal black eyes. How many Others and mortals had looked into that face and seen eternity for the last time?

"This is your opportunity. Kill the Fallen and take me into the Infernos. We will rule there together. They will regret the day they thought us abomination. The day they looked past the fact that THEY created us and cannot turn from that in the end."

Celeste finally sensed Marcus moving in toward them. It was about damn time. Was the Fallen waiting for Calliope to kill her or something? "I won't help you kill my father and brothers."

A cold and calculating smile spread across his face. "Oh, but I would never ask that of you. I will be happy to kill them, watch their blood run through the stones of the Infernos. Where is the Blood Rite Dagger?" He demanded. She shook her head making him snarl. "It is past my reach. The souls will take me there and I will kill your brothers and Dante with my bare hands."

And then in a flurry of wings he was gone, the gust of wind caused by his wings nearly pushed her over the edge of the railing. Strong hands wrapped around her upper arms, pulling her back to safety.

Marcus's beautiful and furious green eyes glared down at her. "Exactly whose side are you playing on?" Celeste didn't fight as his forearm pressed against her throat cutting off her blood and air supply to her brain. It was a matter of seconds before darkness swamped her. The last thing she saw were those beautiful green eyes.

****

Marcus watched as blood vessels burst in Celeste's eyes just before they rolled into the back of her head. The last thing he had intended was to hurt her. Now he was swamped with remorse as she crumpled beneath him. She was so small. He would need to remember that and the fact she was a female and treat her accordingly, regardless of what she said and how she criticized him.

He swept her up into his arms. She hadn't even fought back. Gods, if she had fought back, did or said anything to contradict what he had seen. He wouldn't have totally lost his shit with her. But to just look up at him with those amazing violet eyes almost daring him to finish what he had started.

Dante was going to have a fit over this one. More than a pound of flesh was going to need to be paid. *She was worth it*. Damn. Where had that thought come from?

He held her a little closer remembering the conversation they had had in the plane. She had looked at him then like she had known exactly what he felt. No one had ever looked at him like that. Not even Jessica, he snorted especially not Jessica.

He shook those thoughts away. He had more to worry about then the way she looked at him. He scanned the skies but Calliope had disappeared. Frustration coiled in the pit of his stomach. Why had she done nothing but stare at the Reaper, listen to him?

They had lost the opportunity to take Calliope. And he pulled Celeste closer trying to figure why she tripped up his mind like she did. There was something about her that made him want to touch her. To caress her skin? If he could, he should slam his own head into the stone of the building. He needed to get away from her. She was driving him nuts. Never in his life had he raised a hand to a female and now he had choked one unconscious. For the love of all the gods, what was he becoming?

He vaulted down into the dark alley and took her back to their hotel.

What was he going to do with her? He had been searching for months for Calliope and the minute he hooks up with the Demon, Calliope pops out of the air.

Literally.

Marcus wondered for a moment whose side she was on. But Dante's daughter? He couldn't imagine she would turn against her father and brothers. The Reapers were a lot of things, but loyal to each other was their highest priority.

If this had happened with any of the Tracker brothers, they would have killed her on the spot and walked away with a clear conscience. Marcus couldn't kill like that. He had to have reason and proof. It had to be justified. He looked back down at the woman. She was beautiful. He had let that sway him. That utter look of innocence, not beguiling or cunning, just innocence had starred back at him as he tried to choke the life right out of her. He had the proof he needed, had seen her talking to Calliope. She hadn't even attempted to pull her weapon out.

Marcus pulled his gun out and pointed it at her. She was a Demon. They were the most untrustworthy Others. They killed and maimed, ate raw meat. They survived like scavenger, and she hadn't even tried to stop Calliope, he reminded himself. That was the most damning. But the look in those violet eyes, rimmed with dampened eyelashes as if she had been crying, swayed him.

Swearing, he put his gun away. Just shooting her wouldn't kill her. Besides, she was Dante's daughter. There would have to be more to it than just pulling a trigger. He slammed his hand against the wall. He never felt helpless, never was at a loss. He swung around and glared at her.

"Who's side are you on?" he growled.

The sound drew a moan from the bed. Her eyes opened, not quite focused and were slightly glazed. Dark bruises were starting to show on her throat. Blood vessels had burst in her eyes. When she was finally able to focus, she glared at Marcus.

"What the—" she tried to say, but her voice was scratchy and she reached up to touch her throat. She opened and closed her mouth several times. No words came out. She gave him such a pitiful look he couldn't help but feel a little sorry for her. He went to the phone and ordered a very rare steak. Food would increase her ability to heal.

When he was done, he turned back to her. She was still looking at him like she had never seen anything like him before, like he was the Demon.

"What did you expect? You stood there talking to the enemy for ten minutes."

She shook her head. "Not ten," was all she was able to get out. He couldn't stand to listen to her scratchy voice and went into the bathroom he got her a glass of water.

"Long enough for you to have pulled out that fancy Sword and kill him. But what did you do? You decided to have a little conversation with him? Pass on information on what our plans are?" Marcus was working himself up again.

She only shook her head. "Surprised me." The water hadn't really helped her scratchy voice.

"Gods, STOP talking," he bellowed. Every time she got a word out, it ripped at him for acting before thinking. He had been hanging out with the Trackers for too long.

She launched from the bed as if it were on fire. Her cloak flew off. He got his first real look at her. She wore blood red leather pants that hung low on lean hips, a matching mid-drift leather vest barely covered her full breasts. She had bright red hair pulled into a tight ponytail at the crown of her head. It hung in a thick braid down to just below her knees. A gold chain wound around and around her mid-drift, the chain linking to a stud in her bellybutton.

She was so stunning he just stood there staring at her. When she pulled a gun from a holster under her arm he came to his senses.

"What?" he barked, throwing his hands up.

She had opened the door between their rooms and was now pointing to him with her gun and then to the open door. Marcus sighed. He was doing a brilliant job. First he strangles her, and then ogles her. He should slap himself.

Nodding to her, he walked through the door, but turned to say they would be talking about what had happened later, when she felt better, but the door was already slammed and he heard the lock click into place.

Swearing to himself, he stood by the door until he heard room service come and leave. When he heard the clink of utensils he moved away. If she was eating then he knew that she was going to heal.

Marcus headed for the shower wishing he understood woman just a little bit.

****

"He tried to kill me," Celeste muttered to herself for the hundredth time. At least her voice was back and her throat didn't feel as if she had sucked down lava. She wandered to the mirror and looked at the fading bruises.

She had to admit to herself he hadn't actually tried to kill her, but he had certainly tried to hurt her, and regardless of how fast she may heal, it still hurt like hell. Beyond all that, why had Calliope come to her? Why had he made her the offer he had?

She wasn't about to turn her back on her father and brothers, but what was the Reaper trying to accomplish by getting her to trade sides?

There were so many questions and little time. Celeste stood at the window watching the sunrise. It was an amazing and wonderful thing to watch. Anyone who lived on this plane should never take it for granted. Nothing in the Infernos came close to the beauty she saw whenever she was on the mortal plane and was blessed to watch a sunrise she took advantage of it and gloried in the sunrise. She placed her hand on the cool glass watching the dark colors of night bleed into bright oranges and reds, purples and then blue. It took her breath away every time, bringing with it a calm she hadn't had several moments before. She had a job to do and regardless of what Marcus thought of her, she wasn't working with Calliope. The only way she knew how to convince Marcus of that was to prove it. She added proving she wasn't a traitor to the list she had going for showing Marcus her worthiness. With that in her mind, she headed for the shower, a new day was beginning, and with it a new resolve to make today better than yesterday.

****

"Did you get any sleep?" Marcus accused the moment he set eyes on her. "You look terrible. Don't forget your cloak."

Celeste smiled. "Actually I didn't. I was cowering in the corner of my hotel room in fear of my life from my own partner," she said with as much sarcasm as she could. "And don't you think wearing a cloak around Sydney is going to draw more attention to us then me walking around in normal clothing?"

"I don't know where you got your definition of normal." He looked her up and down, his green eyes finally coming back to hers. He gave her a look like he had been forced to eat something he thought horrible distasteful. "But that is not normal." The last part he barked. Celeste looked down at what she was wearing. Trendy combat boots, with flared distressed jeans, a wide belt, and a white v-neck t-shirt. "Excuse me, but this is the most normal outfit in the world."

"Where are your weapons?" Marcus asked.

Celeste rolled her eyes and lifted her shirt. Marcus jumped back as if a viper was going to jump out of her belly button. She showed him the holster she was wearing. "See? You can't even see it." But all he saw was the silver chain around her midsection. "And I have a knife in each boot. Do I need anything else?"

"The Sword?" he croaked.

"Why don't I stay here in the hotel, and if you need help you can give me a ring. I promise to try to get there in time to save your ass." She crossed her arms over her chest, ignoring the fact they were standing in the hall in front of her hotel room.

He grumbled something to himself and then walked away. Celeste followed. If he was going to be grumpy, she could be just as grumpy.

They were waiting for the elevator when the stairwell door opened up and a figure stumbled through. Celeste stepped back. He was covered in sweat, dirt, and blood and looked terrified.

He looked up, his eyes blood shot. "Fallen?" he reached out to Marcus and then dropped to the floor.

"Is he dead?" Celeste asked looking at the body.

Marcus snorted. "No." He picked the man up and tossed him over his shoulder before he carried him back to Marcus's room. He was coming to when Marcus laid him on the bed.

"Aren't you a little freaked he knew you were a Fallen?" Celeste asked. It didn't seem right that a guy would just stumble out of the stairwell and right into Marcus's lap.

"He's a Guardian, Celeste."

"So? Do you have some type of Guardian beacon or something?"

"Do you have some type of Calliope beacon?" he threw back. She rolled her eyes.

"So how do you know he is a Guardian?" Celeste studied the man trying to discern anything that made him stand out. She didn't smell anything, didn't see anything that would point him to anything other than mortal.

"Because I know, like he knew I was a Fallen. We sense each other. When you see another Demon don't you know they are a Demon?" Marcus asked. Celeste gave him what had to be a strange look because he rolled his eyes. "You don't get out of the Infernos much do you?"

Nothing he could have said to her could have hurt worse. The words like a stab straight into her heart and soul. She turned from him before he could see the pain his words caused.

"Celeste—"

She held up her hand, cutting off anything further he had to say. "Wake your Guardian and let's get this taken care of, Fallen."

****

Marcus had stuck his foot in his mouth, and he wasn't actually sure how he had done it. But he had seen the pain in her violet eyes before she turned away from him. Every woman he came across practically fell at his feet and liked him instantly. And it wasn't just for his looks, but he was a nice guy. But there was something about Celeste that had him on edge and he couldn't seem to say or do the right thing when it came to her. He didn't blame her for hating him. He hated him right then.

There wasn't anything he could do about that now, though. Kneeling next to the bed, he shook the man. He was a nondescript man, and his brown eyes fluttered open slightly glazed, but then rounded to the size of saucers, and he backed himself up the headboard.

Marcus held up his hands. "You're safe. What can I do for you?"

The man looked between Marcus and Celeste. "My guard, something is attacking the Guarded. We split up. Whatever it is can sense me."

"Idiot." Celeste swore. "He can sense you both. Where is your guard?"

The man cringed away from Celeste. "I… I haven't been a Guardian for long. He is one of my first."

"Seriously?" Celeste growled. "This is what the Angels do? Assign a complete innocent and novice to guard a Touched?"

Marcus turned to Celeste. "Shut the hell up."

Her mouth snapped shut, but her violet eyes shot fire at him. She wasn't done. He could tell she had more to say.

"What's your name?" Marcus asked. They didn't know for sure he was the Guardian they were looking for.

"George, sir."

Marcus shook his head. "No need to call me sir. My name is Marcus, and this is Celeste. We are here to help. How many Guarded are there in the city?"

He hesitated. It was strictly forbidden to speak about the special mortals that were Guarded. To speak with them to a Fallen, he would be raked over the coals. But Marcus knew that, and if he had taken the chance to come and find him, then George was already in a great deal of trouble.

"I lost contact with Charles." He checked his watch. "Ten minutes ago. I was headed here. The other Guardians don't think there is anything you can do." He looked from Marcus to Celeste. "You can help, can't you?"

Marcus stood, extending his hand to George. "Where did you last sense him?"

"I told him to hide just outside the city. There is an old estate." George started to ramble and Marcus picked out what was needed.

"You can Shift there. Shift to the last spot you sensed him?" Marcus reassured him.

"Yes, but what about you?" he looked again at Celeste.

"We will be right behind you." Marcus gave Celeste a hard look. "Go now." He patted the man on the shoulder just as George nodded and disappeared.

"We can't use the Portals, but you can Shift, yes?" he asked, advancing on her.

Celeste didn't even take a step back. "We Flash, we do not Shift. There is a difference. And why don't you just Shift there?"

He knew the moment she put the pieces together because light flashed through her eyes. "You don't trust me because you think I'm working with Calliope."

"And because of it, I'm not letting you out of my site for a moment," Marcus said between his teeth.

Celeste narrowed her eyes and glared at Marcus. "Fine. Think about where we are going." She reached forward and placed her palm on his chest. "Oh, and by the way. It hurts."

Marcus sucked in a breath as fire burned through every vein in his body. And then he was on his hands and knees in a grassy plot, throwing up his breakfast and everything else he had in his stomach.

"What the fuck was that?" he growled, right before he emptied his stomach again.

"That was Flashing," Celeste said with a small smile. "I said it might hurt a little, next time try breathing out first."

He forced himself to his feet and grabbed her by the shoulders, shaking her. He just couldn't stop himself.

"Why?" was all he could bring himself to ask.

She smiled, but it was a deadly look that flashed through her eyes. "Because I'm a Demoness, and paybacks are a bitch." She brushed her fingers over the healing bruises on her neck before pulling herself away from him.

Marcus couldn't see straight he was so upset. But he forced himself to take several deep breaths. He looked around for George. The Guardian was curled in a ball at the base of a tree. That wasn't a good sign. Marcus rushed over to him. Blood was coming from his nose and mouth.

"Shit." Marcus gently laid him back in the grass and looked around. "Are we in a fucking graveyard?"

"It would appear so. And I would think that a Fallen would have a more discernible and eloquent vocabulary." Celeste looked around letting her senses spin out to take in her surroundings. It was an old graveyard with tombs and large monoliths. Then she felt it, the tickle at the base of her skull. Calliope was here, and he was doing something horrible. Fear tracked up her spine, and she desperately searched her surroundings.

There deep in the graveyard fresh death thrummed through the air like waves after a rock is thrown into a glassy pound rippling outward. Celeste turned and started to run toward the center of the disturbance. The closer she got, the more the smell of blood swamped her. She slid to a halt at the steps of a tomb. She didn't even hesitate as she bounded down the steps.

But came to a screeching halt when she came to the bottom of the tomb a fire burned in the corner. A man was hung from the opposite wall, his body limp in death. Smoke burned her throat and made her eyes water, the smell of the disemboweled body turning her stomach.

She couldn't see what was holding the body up and wasn't sure she wanted to know. He had been split from chin to groin. His bowels spilled out on the cold stone floor.

Calliope hovered over the body. He reached in and grabbed the still beating heart and with it, the soul. He turned to Celeste, a smile on his lips as a portal shimmered and then opened.

"Shit." She didn't think; she didn't have time. Marcus finally showed up behind her. "Attack him," she yelled over her shoulder. As she rushed Calliope as the portal opened fully, she saw Victor on the other side.

"Close it," she bellowed to her brother.

****

Marcus watched as Celeste leapt into the air, wrapping her body around the soul Calliope was holding up like a prize, and then was sucked into the portal which slammed closed behind her. For several seconds he just stood there, he had never seen anything like what he saw before him, and couldn't even wrap his mind around what Celeste had just done. If she had been a millisecond slower the portal closing would have slammed close killing her.

Calliope screamed in rage, and Marcus pulled himself back to the reality of the situation and jerked out his guns he fired at the Reaper who turned his rage on him. Marcus ducked one wing but was caught in the abdomen by the other. It sent him across the small tomb.

A flash of light from the other side of Calliope, and the Reaper roared again. As Celeste Flashed back.

"I offered you the world, sister," Calliope snarled.

"I'm not really interested in the world, brother," she threw back.

Celeste rushed Calliope as Marcus pushed himself to his feet, trying to find an opening to give her some relief. Black wings swirled and mixed with the red of her hair. They exchanged bone breaking blows. That had Marcus shaking his head, she was tough but Calliope seemed to have strength over her. He proved it when he caught Celeste with a wing and flung her into the air, she bounced off a wall.

Calliope laughed.

"We could have been unstoppable."

Marcus was amazed when Celeste rolled to her feet, staying in a crouched position. Her eyes glittered with the thrill of the fight. She smiled. "I'm already unstoppable." She grabbed a handful of the fire that burned next to her, and flung it at Calliope. Then she vanished and reappeared seconds later with the Black Sword she sliced it through the soft flesh of Calliope's side.

Calliope bellowed in pain and flung out his wings, knocking Celeste out of the way. Marcus rushed him, but it was too late. Calliope took to the air and flew from the tomb, scattering fire and ash everywhere, just as Victor and Christian appeared.

"YOU'RE LATE," Celeste screamed from the corner where she still lay. She pulled herself to her feet, ignoring the fact that she had one or two broken ribs. She spat blood out and advanced on her brothers. "What part of immediately didn't you understand?"

"You look like shit," Christian noted.

Celeste narrowed her eyes and then turned to Marcus. "You know, I've heard that one too many times today."

Christian turned on Marcus. "You told our sister she looked like shit?" he asked with what looked like horror and admiration. "You got balls Fallen. Stupid, but you do have balls."

"Damn, he's a sick bastard," Victor said, looking at the disemboweled body still hanging grotesquely in the depths of the tomb. Not paying attention to a sputtering Celeste and a shocked Marcus.

"Which brings us back to the fact that you were LATE," Celeste yelled garnering everyone attention.

George stumbled into the tomb; saw the body, and then wretched. Everyone moved away from the man.

"Who is that?" Victor asked in disgust.

"He would be the Guardian," Celeste said.

Christian didn't look away from George as he muttered, "He failed."

Marcus had heard enough. "You have all breathed way too much sulfur, because you're all insane."

"We're fighting damned souls. Our humor left a while ago," Christian offered with a shrug.

"I've broken a couple of ribs," Celeste said walking up close to Victor. Her anger obviously taking a back seat to the pain she was now in.

Victor smiled. "Would you like me to fix you, little sister?"

She smiled a real smile at her brother. It took Marcus's breath away. "Yes, please." Victor smiled and wrapped his arms around her. They glowed with fire for a moment, and then he released her. Celeste took a breath and then leaned up on her toes to kiss his cheek.

Marcus was stunned at the show of affection between the two. Christian ignored it as he inspected the body.

"What is that all about?" Marcus demanded.

Celeste glared at him.

"I am able to heal her," Victor offered.

"Yeah, wish he would offer to heal the rest of us. But he keeps that ability just for the girl," Christian said. It was obviously a source of contention between the Reapers.

"Stop bitching. You heal," Celeste snapped.

"Yeah, so do you. But if Victor is around, you heal immediately. You should have to suffer like the rest of us."

Celeste moved over to Christian and put a hand on his chest. "Is someone still pissed over having his ass handed to him?" she asked with mock concern.

"Shut up, Celeste." Christian shrugged her off, Celeste laughed.

Marcus had to admit they acted like a family. And his notion that she may be working with Calliope went out the window. She loved her brothers, and they loved her. Marcus knew from past experience you didn't turn your back on that type of love.

"What am I going to do?" George asked, interrupting everyone.

Marcus helped the man to his feet and led him out of the tomb.

When they reached the fresh air, Marcus took several deep breaths trying to catalog everything that had just happened. Calliope had offered Celeste a partnership, and she had turned it down.

"Charles deserved better than that," George said looking up at Marcus.

Light spread around them, and Marcus sucked in a breath, not having felt the light in over five hundred years. George fell to his knees.

"I failed," he cried.

"Royally failed," Christian said, stepping up behind Marcus.

"This has nothing to do with you, Reaper," the Angel hovering just above the ground said. Her voice was so beautiful it brought tears to Marcus' eyes.

She held a hand out to George. "You must stand before the Arch and explain what has happened."

George nodded and climbed to his feet. Christian stepped forward and stopped the Guardian by placing a hand on his shoulder. George paled, and Marcus could actually see his knees shaking. "He failed. His soul is ours."

George looked like he was going to faint as he looked from Christian to the Angel.

"His soul is not up for debate," the Angel said.

"You're right, it's not. He guarded a Touched. The Touched was brutally murdered, and his soul is permanently damaged. As we speak, the Touched is standing judgment with Dante," Christian explained.

"That is not the way of things," the Angel thundered. Her light pulsed around her like a beacon.

Victor moved forward and shrugged. "Things are changing. Maybe you should come down from your lofty perch and check it out."

The Angel sucked in a disgusted breath. "How dare you speak to me so, Reaper."

Victor shook his head. "You should check the treaty. A Reaper claimed the Touched soul and therefore the Guardian of that Touched now belongs to Dante."

"You have no say here. The Touched already belonged to Dante."

Marcus stepped forward holding up his hands. "If you tell us what other Guardians are watching over the other Touched, we will relinquish George."

Christian snorted. "He has no say in this matter. He is a Fallen."

"And his concern is mired in mortal emotion and not in concern for the Guarded," the Angel accused not even looking in Marcus' direction.

"We are trying to save them from Calliope," Marcus argued. "Doesn't that mean anything to you?"

"Yes. We are aware of the situation, and it does not concern us. George?" She held out her hand.

George tried to move forward but Christian refused to let the man go. "So you understand the Infernos are under attack, and you have chosen to ignore the threat? You and your brethren know that souls are going unclaimed because of the unrest in the Infernos?" His only show of irritation was George sucked in a pained breath, as the hand on his shoulder turned white with the grip he had on him.

"It is not a threat against the Angels. It is a threat that was created in evil, and will be dwelt with by evil." She finally turned and looked at Marcus as she said the last part.

"Why can't you just tell us who is in danger? Save the souls that are deserving and stop another death like that poor soul down there suffered?" Marcus asked. They knew unconditional love, did they not suffer when innocence was brutally murdered? The scars on his back, where his wings had once been throbbed, of course they didn't, and his scars reminded him of that.

"Would it ease your curiosity if I were to tell you that Jessica is not involved yet?" she said with a mocking tone.

Marcus stepped forward. Irritation, pain and embarrassment drove him over the edge. "This has nothing to do with Jessica. Besides, after everything that has happened, I wouldn't believe you. But it has everything to do with the fact if Calliope wins in his quest to take over the Infernos, he will release the souls of the damned into the mortal plane, and your precious Guardians and Touched will be the first to die."

"Pity, it wouldn't be the Fallen," the Angel answered.

"How can you be so cruel?" Celeste asked stepping forward. "Aren't you supposed to be gentle and kind?"

The Angel took one look at Celeste and hissed, backing away from her. "You are an abomination, and will not be acknowledged."

"You're pushing your luck Angel" Victor said coming to his sister's side. His next words spoken to Christian. "Take the Guardian, she has no ground to stand on, and she knows it. If you have a problem take it up with Dante."

The Angel sucked in a breath, bringing her several feet above the ground. It didn't stop as a weeping George was Flashed out of sight with Christian.

"You will regret this," the Angel warned, and then disappeared.

"I need a drink," Celeste said.

Marcus couldn't agree with her more. He pulled a phone from his pocket and called to have the plane readied.

"We are headed to New Orleans," he said to Victor. "How are things going?"

Victor shook his head. "Once you open the doors to the asylum and let the inmates out, they really don't want to go back."

Marcus couldn't blame them. "At least we avoided Calliope from getting into the Infernos today."

"And what about tomorrow?" Celeste asked.

"Tomorrow will be another day and another fight," Marcus said walking away.

"You need to hold yourself together," Victor snapped as Celeste watched Marcuse move away.

"What the hell are you talking about?"

Victor kissed her on the forehead. "Keep your distance with the Fallen. His fate is unwritten and therefore, dangerous."

Celeste threw her hands into the air in agitation. "You told me to build a relationship with him before I left the Infernos."

"Yes, but not that type of relationship," he said.

"What the hell is that supposed to mean?"

"Be careful," was his only response before he Flashed away. Celeste looked around the empty graveyard. The sun was reaching the peak of the day, bathing her in sunshine and light. Victor was right. Keeping a distance between herself and Marcus was the only way she would be able to walk away from this and fulfill her destiny and save her brothers and father. Her heart twisted, but she turned into the light of the sun and took several breaths letting the warmth of the sun spread through her.

This time she took the bed in the back of the jet. She was exhausted and although Victor had healed her, she needed to get some rest. If she was going up against Calliope again she was going to need as much strength as possible. He was far stronger than she had originally thought.

She left Marcus on the phone with a laptop in front of him. She was asleep before her head hit the pillow. Her last thought was of Marcus's past and of the mysterious Jessica. It annoyed her she cared so much. Especially after the stern talking to she had given herself in the graveyard.

Chapter 5

"Wake up." Marcus shook her roughly, and she rolled over glaring at him. He glared right back. "We're going to land soon, and we have some things we need to discuss."

Celeste pulled herself into a sitting position wiping the sleep from her eyes. "Really, I can't imagine what we have to discuss." She blinked innocently up at him.

"You're very good at that," Marcus snapped in anger. Celeste took a deep breath, the smell of Marcus almost making her eyes cross in pleasure. He smelled incredible, like sun warmed skin and the unique smell that was all Marcus and all man. She honestly couldn't think of anything that smelled better.

Celeste mentally shook herself. Lifting an eyebrow waiting for him to continue. Not sure her tongue would work if she tried to speak anyway.

"You have an amazing ability to turn conversations back on a person with sarcasm."

She folded her arms, feeling as if he was just warming up. Her father had done it more times than she could count.

That's when she felt the slide of passion from deep in the pit of her stomach. It flowed into her lower back and started to pulse. She pushed it away and concentrated on Marcus. The time change from the Infernos to this plane was going to be a problem. Time passed quicker here. She had been here three, maybe four days, and the Sex Demon in her was getting restless. She ignored its whine of attention pulsing in her lower back and attempted to concentrate on the lecture Marcus was working on giving.

"If we are going to work together we need to be honest with each other," Marcus started.

She laughed. "As a Reaper and a Demon. I'm sure you can understand I have some issues with trust of any kind outside of my brothers and father."

"But does that include the brother that has gone rouge and killed innocent mortals and Reapers? The same one that is trying, as we speak, to take over the Infernos and unleash them on the mortal world?"

"I will say this one last time, Fallen. I am not working with Calliope. In case you may have missed it, I have a lot to lose if he wins. My home, my family, my very way of life. He also just kicked my ass. That's not really making me eager to join his team." What did he think was going to happen to anyone who stood against the Reaper? The half breeds and mortals would be the first to go. She wasn't an idiot. She had read history from both the Others and from the mortal plane. She had everything to loss here. If he couldn't put that together, she had strongly misinterpreted his intelligence.

"What exactly are your abilities?" Her mouth dropped open when he asked this question. It was like asking Superman who his alter ego was.

She leaned forward placing her hands on the bed. "You tell me yours, and I'll tell you mine." She let some of her Sex Demon pheromone leak out, infusing the room. She hoped it would get him to leave her the hell alone for a moment.

Marcus immediately rose to his feet and left. Well, at least she knew how to clear a room. Unfortunately, he was the one man she wanted to stay, and he really didn't like her.

****

When they landed, the sun was just rising, and she scrambled from the plane so she could catch it. Marcus gave her the strangest look as she pushed past him in her excitement to exit the plane.

As the door opened, she leapt from the plane before the stairs were brought into place. Landing on the balls of her feet, she oriented herself and turned toward the sunrise, smiling when she realized she was in time. She closed her eyes and breathed in the sight and smell of the new day.

"What are you doing? I thought we were under attack," Marcus snarled next to her.

She waved him away. "It's beautiful, and not even your sorry ass attitude can change it."

"What?" he demanded.

Celeste turned to him in utter shock. She reached out and slapped him upside the head like she would do to one of her brothers.

"The sunrise." She pointed. "Now shut up."

Marcus snapped his mouth shut and turned to the sunrise. She ignored him. She had promised herself she wasn't going to let him get to her. She swore she was going to remain completely aloof when it came to him. He was her partner, and when it was done she would go back to the Infernos, and he would go back to whatever it was he did on the mortal plane. When he owed a pound of flesh, she would be there to care for him as she had been for the last two hundred years.

"Can we go now?" Marcus asked once the sun was fully visible.

Celeste turned to him. "Have you become so jaded in this world you cannot enjoy something as simple as a sunrise?"

Her question seemed to surprise him, and he looked back toward the sun, then to her. "I have no idea what you are talking about. I just watched it with you, did I not?"

She couldn't help it. All her promises flew out the proverbial window she reached out and cupped his cheek. "But did you enjoy it? Did you feel the majesty of it?" she whispered as if speaking the words too loudly would break the spell that a new sunrise always spun for her.

He jerked away from her touch as if it burned him. "I have no idea what you are talking about."

Celeste nodded. "I understand."

He narrowed his eyes and walked to a waiting car. She followed, and before climbing into the dark interior, took one last look at the sun and breathed in the clean air. It was enough that she understood.

****

Marcus couldn't understand the woman. One minute she was spitting mad and hitting him. The next she looked so calm, and still she could have been a statue. Her enjoyment of the sunrise baffled him. When had he last taken the time to enjoy the sunrise?

Jessica's face popped into his memory, and he pushed it aside. She was his past. She had moved on, and he had as well. Things were better this way.

"Cameron has been here for two days, but as a Tracker he has to almost be within reach of a Guardian before he knows there is one there," Marcus offered.

"I thought Trackers could track anything?" Celeste asked, not looking at him, but out of the window at everything they passed. She seemed to be memorizing it all as they passed.

"They can, but to get the best results they need to have to have come into contact with something of the entity they are tracking. It must be either by way of a personal effect, or actual contact. They can sense Guardians, but like I said, they have to be very close in order to pick them out," Marcus offered.

"But you are able to sense and know where the Guardians are, correct?" Celeste asked taking her braid she wrapped it around her hand, playing with the silver tipped ends.

"Yes, and the other way around. We have that unique ability so we stay away from each other." And for the last several centuries it had worked, but now Marcus was turning it against them. If he ever believed he would one day be redeemed, it flew out the window. By tracking down Guardians, revealing who they were and not just revealing who they were, but revealing who they were to Reapers. Hell was too good a place for him.

She looked thoughtful, and Marcus watched her, unable to take his eyes off the movements of her hands. As the silky strands were wrapped around her wrist, his palms itched to reach out and touch it, to feel it run through his fingers. Was it as silky as it looked? His entire body reacted, stringing him as tight as a bow, frustrating him in more ways than he could point out at the moment.

Celeste dropped her hair and snapped her fingers in his face. "Hello, Fallen?"

Marcus shook himself. "Excuse me?"

"What are you doing?" Celeste asked, confusion written all over her face.

She was staring at his groin, and he shifted, uncomfortable, and looked down. Not his groin, his hands in his lap. He had snapped the pen he was holding in one hand and crushed the cell phone in the other.

"Damn it." He threw the objects across the vehicle.

Celeste rolled her eyes, her brow creasing as if she was thinking really hard. "So you can sense them? The Guardians? So we send you out to scout them, and then we move in?"

Marcus wished it were that easy. "They don't really trust the Fallen, Celeste. And like in Australia I can't just move on them."

She rolled her eyes, and he realized it was a form of communication with her. He had seen her do it so many times in the last several days he was beginning to at least understand her eye rolling and sarcasm. It was little help, though, because everything else about her was a complete and utter mystery. That particular eye roll meant she had just told him she wasn't an idiot.

"Duh. You sniff them out, and then we'll send the Tracker in. If he can get a lead on them, then we just need to watch and see who the Touched is." She shrugged as if it were really going to be that easy. "I can tell when a mortal is Touched. Or, we could do like we did in Australia and wait for Calliope to find and disembowel the Touched and lose another Guardian. Oh, and of course, the possible chance to stop Calliope from entering the Infernos, but really I'll let you decide." She said picking up her braid she toyed with it again. But her shoulders were tense, and he understood now she was just as uptight about the situation as he was. She just showed it differently.

"Sarcasm much?" Marcus quipped to put her at ease.

She actually smiled at his flippancy, but otherwise kept her mouth shut. She must think she had gotten her point across, but all she had done was irritate the hell out of him.

"The Trackers have a home here. We will be staying there," he snapped.

"Where is it?"

"What?"

"The home? It is close to the city, close to Bourbon Street?" Marcus smiled, his irritation immediately forgotten at her obvious excitement. She couldn't keep it out of her voice. "Celeste, have you never been to New Orleans?" He actually felt the wall fly up between them and had to control the urge to lean away from her.

"No." Her voice was calm, but he saw emotions pass through her violet eyes.

"It's a wonderful place. I think you will enjoy it. I am sure, as we search the city you will be able to see a great deal of it."

She pursued her lips together and turned back to the window. "That would be nice." But he heard the quiver of excitement, the thrill of the possible. It made him wonder what else she had missed out on while being raised in the Infernos with only men to teach her anything.

She was such a contradiction; one minute a spitting mad Demon. The next an excited woman on her first visit to New Orleans. He was definitely going to have to consult Kyra on this issue. Either that, or kill Celeste in a fit of rage because she seemed to touch his every last nerve, and he did the same to her. In fact, this was the longest they had gone without arguing since they met three, no, four days ago. They passed the International Date Line twice, and now he wasn't sure even what day it was.

"How old are you, Celeste?" Marcus scolded himself. He didn't want to know that information. He wanted to maintain a distance from this woman.

"Why?"

Well, he had stuck his foot in his mouth. He might as well continue. "Just that keeping you a secret must have been a great ordeal. I can't imagine it has gone on that long."

She rolled her eyes again, this time saying it was his turn to be the idiot. "Why, because Dante and the Reapers are such a wealth of information? Strike up a lot of conversations with Reapers on your visits?"

"Celeste, I have been in and out of the Infernos for several centuries. I think I would have remembered seeing you."

"Five hundred years," she offered.

Marcus just sat there. That was impossible. He would have noticed her. How could he have missed her? She was a wet dream waiting to happen, and he was damn sure he would remember her. Then he shook his head, where the hell had that thought come from? Not that it wasn't true but damn, he would have liked to think he had remembered meeting her.

"That's not possible."

She leaned forward, her breath whispering against his face. He drew in her smell, and something clicked in the back of his brain. It was gone just as fast. She smelled like clean sheets just pulled from the line. He had never thought that smell was erotic, but with her braid slipping from her lap and landing against his thigh, he went hot all over. Between her smell and that damn hair, all he wanted was to push her back against the seat and kiss her, which shocked the hell out of him. He thought he had grown past those types of physical emotions. Then her words brushed against him like a caress. Whispered so quietly, Marcus had to lean in a little farther in order to hear them.

"That would be, because it was a secret." She barely breathed the last word, and then leaned back, placing her index finger against her full lips and winked at him.

Marcus fell back in his seat and just glared at her, fighting with himself. One side wanted to push her back into the cushions and press himself against her sweet body. The other side of him, the celibate side, wanted to get as far away from her as possible.

However, at the moment, he was trapped in the car with her. She was doing something to him that he couldn't explain, and it was turning him on and pissing him off at the same time.

Finally, she broke the silence. "The black robs, Fallen. They hide a lot."

"Marcus," he said.

"Excuse me?"

"My name is Marcus."

She turned to look out the window dismissing him. "If you say so, Fallen."

He was going to strangle her, that was all there was to it. He was going to wrap his hands around her beautiful throat and strangle her.

Again.

His fingers actually itched to do just that. It was either that, or jump from the moving vehicle, but he didn't particularly want to sustain the injuries that would cause.

"What are you?" he couldn't stop himself from asking.

She turned innocent violet and blue tinged eyes at him. "I'm a Demon and a Reaper. What are you?"

"What kind of question is that?" he barked.

She smiled again. "That is a question only you can answer."

He growled. "Again, this is something that you are very good at."

She laughed. It wasn't one of the irritating laughs that made you want to cover the woman's mouth. It wasn't shrill or high pitched or annoying. It was a throaty sound, and the way she did it made him wonder how often she laughed.

"You could have chosen any path in the world. You could have chosen to do anything you wanted; be invisible to the mortal and Other world by blending in, but you chose to be a Fallen. Wear the mantra and burden of a Fallen." She looked back out the window. "Could have done and been anyone, but you chose Fallen." She turned back and the blue was now missing from her violet eyes. "Always remember that, Fallen. By your choices, therefore you are."

Marcus leaned back and crossed his arms over his chest, unable to argue with what she had said. He had worn the mantra of a Fallen like a cloak that shielded him from the world and human emotion. That she had been able to discern this about him in just a few short days, vexed him.

"And what about you?" he asked.

Celeste shrugged. "I am a product of my mother and father, something that should never have been. I therefore die or disappear in the almanac of time as something that never was."

"And you're okay with that?" Marcus couldn't imagine not leaving his mark on this world. After centuries, he wanted to go out with a bang, wanted to feel more alive than dead, which he hadn't felt for so many years he had lost count.

She gave him a sad smile. "We must all live with the cards we are dealt, Fallen."

He didn't know why, but the fact she wouldn't say his name was starting to frustrate the hell out of him. He was about to say something when she screamed for the driver to stop the car.

They both flew forward as the car pulled to the side and stopped on a dime. Celeste gave Marcus a strange look. "Can you smell that?"

She reached for the door handle, but Marcus stopped her. "What?"

"Death. You can't smell it?" Marcus closed his eyes and focused but he didn't smell anything.

"Celeste, this is a very old city with a strange and varied past. Death is part of New Orleans."

She snorted, and raised an eyebrow. "Not that type of death. Do you think Calliope could have beaten us here?"

Marcus doubted it. He looked pretty bad the last time they had seen the Reaper, and it would have taken him at least a day to heal. Then he would have had to find transportation to New Orleans, unless he was capable of Flashing or flying all the way.

"Can Calliope Flash?"

"Not that I am aware of. Mortals view him as one of them. They have no idea that standing in front of them is a Reaper able to take taking their life without them even knowing it. He wasn't capable of flying all the way from Australia to here, but something is going on here." She pulled her hand free and threw the door open. "And it isn't good."

Marcus climbed from the car, following her, telling the driver they would be right back. "Unless it has something to do with Calliope or Lordus, then I don't give a shit what it is Celeste. Now get back in the car. Cameron is waiting for us."

She turned to him, her violet eyes taking on a slight red glow. "You can be really bossy, you know that?"

Marcus swore. "And you can really irritate me by not listening."

****

Celeste smiled to herself, he was a frustrated man. She could smell it from the Infernos, but it was a choice he had made for himself. Still, this had nothing to do with him. She smelled a Demon. Actually, she smelled a Troup of Demons, and they were feeding. If she wasn't mistaken, they were feeding on mortals, and as far as she knew, it was against the rules for Demons to feed on mortals.

Following the smell, she ignored Marcus's grumbles behind her. They were in an old part of the city, and the alleys were dark, little things scurrying in the shadows. She almost laughed. It was like being home.

Rounding a corner, she stopped dead in her tracks and swore under her breath. Six very large Demons stood at the end of the alley gorging themselves on the remains of a mortal. Piles of bloody clothes, and remains of other mortals were scattered around the dirty dead-end alley. Blood splattered on the brick walls formed a morbid sort of collage of death.

Celeste stepped back before they could see her, and put her hand out to stop Marcus. She turned to him, her finger on her lips again.

"What is it?" he said.

Celeste could feel the blood lust from the Demons and Marcus was doing his damdest to draw attention to them.

"Shut up," Celeste said under her breath. She let him pass her so he could see what was at the other end of the alley.

He jerked his head back. "Get back to the car," he growled in a whisper.

Celeste thought she might have heard him wrong. "Excuse me?"

"I said to get your ass back to the car." Marcus pushed her to emphasize his words.

"And just what do you plan on doing?" she whispered.

Marcus growled again. She grabbed him by the shirt front and shook him, shocking them both.

"You need to stop doing that." She raised her voice slightly. She knew this was neither the time nor the place, but for all the Gods, when he made that sound all she could think of was jumping his bones.

He pried his fingers from her shirt. "What the hell is your problem?"

Celeste needed to kill something. "You are. Stay here." Pushing past him she walked into the alley.

"Morning, boys." She let her sex pheromone radiate out while they all looked up and stared at her. She picked out the one she wanted to keep alive for questioning.

Ignoring Marcus's swearing behind her, she moved forward. "I thought killing mortals was forbidden." She licked her lips giving them the impression she wanted to share the food with them.

The largest of the six sniffed and then took an involuntary step forward. Typically, female Demons were submissive creatures, but female Sex Demons were a totally different ball of wax. They liked the challenge, and would only mate with the strongest male. To get a Sex Demon to mate with you was a crowing point for that male.

The largest of them knew exactly what she was. Celeste wet her lips again and let the blood red of her Demon side bleed into the irises of her eyes. She pushed her neck forward and snapped her teeth together in a show of challenge. Then all hell broke loose as the largest Demon turned to one of his companions and tore his head off. Celeste didn't hesitate, she ran toward the group. She launched herself against the wall. Taking two sideways steps, she pivoted herself, her hair flying out as she whipped the Demon closest to her with the ends of her hair. He screamed, covering the open wounds on his neck. Landing on the balls of her feet, she pulled a short knife from her boot and finished cutting his head off.

The largest male let out a primal growl, thinking she was joining in the killing so they could mate. Celeste turned to the one she had picked out earlier, and threw him clear of the fray. He slid the entire length of the alley, knocking his head against the brick wall. He didn't move. Damn, she hoped she hadn't killed him.

But she didn't have time to stop and think about it because another Demon attacked, wrapping his arms around her from behind. He sniffed her neck. "Sex Demon."

The words brought the other two Demons to a dead halt before the fighting started in earnest. Celeste grabbed the man by the back of the neck, and tossed him over her shoulder. She drove her blade into his chest. It wouldn't kill him, but it would slow him down. His screams of pain were cut short as she slit his head from his shoulders, throwing the head at the last two. It hit the larger of the two in the head, and they stumbled apart.

The smaller guy looked from Celeste to the other Demon, and threw his hands up. "You can have her, dude. I'm gone, like out of this city, gone. You explain it to that bitch why she's down five guys.

He leapt to the top of the building and disappeared. Celeste turned back to the large Demon. He was covered in blood and bits of flesh, which frankly made Celeste's stomach turn regardless of the fact she was half Demon. She liked her meat cooked, and definitely not human. It was the same for the men she slept with. She never slept with Demons. That was just asking to be taken and mated.

He grunted and took a step forward, growling in a very unsexy and dominate way. Marcus had finally joined her and was now standing several feet behind the large man. He looked so pissed she wondered if she wouldn't be better off fighting off the huge Demon.

"Mine," the Demon snarled leaping at Celeste.

"Not even on your luckiest day," Marcus said. Pulling the trigger, he planted a bullet in the back of the Demon's head. It crumpled to the ground.

Celeste stepped forward and severed his head. "And today would definitely not qualify as a lucky day," she finished.

Celeste smiled at Marcus, still crouched over the Demon. "Don't you have a sense of humor, Fallen?"

Marcus stormed up to her and grabbed her braid. He pulled her forward. "What the hell do you have on the ends of your hair?"

"Quills. There braided into the ends, and dipped in silver."

Marcus shook his head and jerked on her braid. She yelped as she stumbled forward. "That's not all their dipped in."

Celeste shrugged. "Demon venom."

She wasn't sure what else to say as he opened and closed his mouth several times. "Get rid of them," he said, reaching for the knife she held. Instead she pressed her knife against his throat.

"Don't touch my hair," she growled. "You have no place or right to cut my hair. And if you do it, I will never forgive you. If the weapons at the tips of my hair are so horrible to you, I will take care of them, but don't you dare touch it to cut it off."

Marcus froze, not sure what it was that had pissed her off so completely. He stepped back, and she lowered the knife, but her defenses were still up.

"You are wearing on your person a weapon that could cause you serious pain." He enunciated each word. "Why in the name of all the Gods would you wear something like that?"

"Because no creature would expect it," she said, more calmly.

"Celeste, it is utterly impossible to expect anything from you. You are a contradiction in combat boots." He moved away from her and to the now semi-conscious Demon taking him by the throat. He lifted him off the ground, pressing him against the stone wall. "What are you doing?"

The only thing he was capable of was shaking his head.

Celeste stepped up, placing a hand on Marcus's forearm. "I know how partial you are to choking people to death, but we need him to be able to speak."

Marcus dropped the man, his frustration getting the better of him. "You…" he started, but he didn't know exactly what he was going to do or say to the woman. She was making him crazy. Maybe Cameron would take her off his hands for a while because he was sure another day in her presence was going to have him leaping off a bridge.

Dropping the man, Celeste bent down. "Hello." He sniffed her so Marcus kicked him. Celeste rolled her eyes. "Not really necessary," she said to him before turning back to the Demon. He was a low level Demon with little to no power. He had a master that ordered him around, and she was going to get that information from him. "What's your name?"

"Why does it matter? You're going to kill me," he muttered, gasping for air.

Celeste gave him a beautiful smile and dragged a finger down the Demon's cheek in a careful caress. "Yes, we will, but the manner in which we do so will depend on how you chose to answer our questions."

"Sarafina", was all he said in response. Celeste was shocked at how quickly he had sold his master out. He would take the punishment of death rather than face the woman again. Luckily, she knew exactly who Sarafina was and what she was capable of, and Celeste had to admit that she was offering him something more palatable.

Celeste stood up and looked at Marcus. "If she is involved, then it's possible that Lordus is close."

They both turned back to the Demon who was staring at Celeste like he wanted to swallow her whole. This only jerked Marcus's anger up several degrees, and he stomped his boot into the other man's groin.

"Seriously?" Celeste shook her head and rolled her eyes. "Where is she?" she asked the Demon.

"House outside city," he gurgled between gasps of pain.

"Address," Marcus barked. The Demon mumbled the location. "Done?" he asked Celeste.

Celeste nodded. "I'll be right back." She reached out and grabbed the Demon by the shirt front and Flashed out. Marcus headed back to the car, by the time he was reaching for the door, Celeste had Flashed back and was standing next to him.

"What did you do to him?" Marcus asked

"I turned him over to Dante. He will claim his soul and either recycle it or place him where he is meant to be." She shrugged.

"It's that easy is it?" Marcus couldn't keep the strain from his voice. "You just turn whomever over to your father and that's that?"

Celeste gave him an incredulous look. "He knew exactly what his punishment was going to be, Fallen. If you ask me, we did him a favor. Sarafina or her brother Evan would have tortured him. This way he will pay for what he has done, which is only right."

She climbed into the car, stopping the conversation as far as she was concerned. But for Marcus, this conversation was far from over.

"Which one of the Trackers is tracking Lordus?" she asked.

"Currently we are all working on your little issue," Marcus said, pulling a new cell from a pocket of the vehicle. "Ryder and Kyra have been trying to track him down, but the bastard seems to stay one step ahead of everyone."

****Celeste leaned back and listened while Marcus spoke on the phone explaining what had happened, noticing he left out her part in the action, which she didn't understand. Was he embarrassed that she fought like a man? Or that she fought at all? Or maybe it was that she won.

When he finally hung up, she had worked herself into a lather. "What the hell is your problem?"

Marcus looked at her as if she had lost her mind. "What the hell is MY problem?" he asked both eyebrows shooting up to his hairline.

"You male chauvinistic, antiquated bastard. What part bothers you most? That I can fight? Or that I enjoy it and do a damn good job at it?" she growled.

"What the hell are you talking about?" he blustered.

"If you don't know, then I sure as hell am not going to explain it to you." She glared at him, waiting for him to understand he had just bypassed her and the part she had played in getting the information. He just glared at her.

"Celeste, you are one of the most complicated, unbelievably, psychotic bitches on any plane of existence. I understand why your father hid you now." He couldn't have said anything that could have possible hurt more.

"I hate you," she said, then Flashed away, back to her room in the Fortress.

She plodded around looking for one of her brothers. She needed to vent, but they were all out fighting. This made her feel even worse because they were all out fighting, and she had just walked away from what her part was to be in the war. She stomped her foot and kicked a pillar, but none of it made her feel any better. Unwanted and unexpected, her lower back released a painful tingle.

"Great, just freaking great," she snarled.

She went to her room and stared out at the fields of red, orange bedrock, the Lake of Souls. After a time it did its job and calmed her. She had a part to play, and she wasn't going to walk away from it.

Concentrating on the mortal plane, she located Marcus and flashed back to him, cursing him up one side and down the other as she did it.

****

Marcus just stared at the spot where Celeste had disappeared for several moments, expecting her to come back. When the car reached the house and she still hadn't re-appeared, he grabbed their things and went inside. She was insane, had been trapped in the Infernos for too long. It didn't matter some part of him was worried about her; that some part of him was upset he had hurt her so horrible. She was a warrior, and he had pushed her to back away and run. He knew it must be humiliating for her. He was a total ass.

Cameron met him at the front door. "Where's the hot Demon?"

"Shut up, Cameron," Marcus barked.

Cameron started to laugh. "It took me four months to get sick of you. You got rid of her in like four days? The guys are going to shit."

Marcus dropped the bags and slugged the Tracker in the face. Cameron's head snapped back, but he didn't stop laughing as blood poured from his nose. "And you hit like a girl." He laughed even harder. "I bet the Demon hits harder than you do."

Marcus saw red. Cameron was probably right. In the several fights they had been in, she hadn't really allowed him to fight. She always took the lead. He had to admit part of his pride was hurt. She ran head first into a fight with no regard for her own safety because she knew she was going to win. He wondered where she had gotten such self-assurance. Then he remembered who her brothers and father were. Celeste had obviously never failed. He wondered what would happen when and if she ever did.

Marcus walked away from Cameron knowing the Tracker, like his brothers, liked nothing more than a good fight. Marcus was tired, irritated beyond belief and frustrated as hell. He wondered if this mission could possible get any worse, or if he could feel any worse about it and the woman he was partnered with.

"So this is all we have?" Marcus asked after he had poured over the Intel the Tracker had uncovered.

Cameron shrugged. "The city is a hotspot of Others and mortals, and they all know something funky is going on. There have been random attacks by Demons and Vampires. The Others are saying there is going to be a war, and the mortals are scared to death. Why the hell wouldn't Dante just give us a name? Why just a location? What game is he playing?"

"That's not how being Touched works. When mortals die, they go to Heaven or one of the levels of the Infernos, or straight to Hell. Or they go into Limbo if they are chosen in Limbo to return and be reincarnated. If the Arch overseeing it wants to track that soul to see if that soul changes its ways, they become Touched. Same with Dante, but sometimes, like in my case and Kyra's, we are singled out, so are the Touched that we are looking for. There are hundreds, if not thousands of Touched, however, only a handful of them are truly special."

"Dante doesn't know who his Touched are because they are reborn, and when that happens, their souls are cleansed. They are new, and the Arch knows who they are and places a Guardian over them in order to keep them from danger. It's one of Dante's greatest irritations that in the process of rebirth, the power of his Touched shifts to the Angels and light," Marcus explained.

"Great history lesson, but it does nothing in the way of finding the Touched or the Guardian, dude. Taste. Touch. Smell. Kinda the Tracker motto," Cameron said. "Besides, what happens to the Guardians and Touched that aren't specially touched by Dante' for a specific reason? If Calliope kills them, what happens?"

"Their soul immediately returns to Limbo. The Guardian is returned to the Angels or to Dante if they have failed so completely that the soul of the Touched is compromised."

"And who decides if the soul is compromised?" Cameron asked.

"If the Touched is killed specifically for its soul, by way of murder or ritual, or in our case, by Calliope in order to gain entrance into the Infernos, the soul is considered compromised," Marcus explained. "Only pure evil would commit that type of crime. The Angels want nothing to do with that or the Guardian they have placed over that soul."

Cameron shook his head. "I'll stick with being a Tracker."

Marcus was tired and pushed himself away from the desk to stretch. "It's been a long couple of days. I believe that we have at least a one or two day's lead on Calliope. I'm taking a shower and going to bed."

"What about the female?"

"She left. I'm not going to go after her. Actually, I can't go after her with the Portals locked. If she wants to be a part of this fight, she will have to make the decision for herself and come back." Marcus wasn't sure how he actually felt, but it was ultimately up to Celeste. He wasn't sure how he felt about her leaving or her coming back.

Cameron nodded. "I'm going to go get laid. Ry and Kyra will be here tomorrow."

Marcus nodded and headed to the room he had taken for himself, glaring at Celeste's bags as he passed them in the hall. The woman would have been the death of him. She was better off in the Infernos fighting alongside her brothers.

So why was he worried about her? Why was he even thinking about her? He wanted to slam his head into the wall.

He took a hot shower, forcing himself to think about anything other than the Demon/Reaper. Climbing from the shower he felt a hell of a lot better, wrapping a towel around his waist, he headed into his room.

The only warning he got was the flash of fire.

Chapter 6

Celeste just stood there. She might have opened her mouth, but couldn't be sure. Marcus stood in the doorway of the bathroom, a towel hanging low on his hips. The Sex Demon in her crowed with glee, and the lust surging through her body acted before her mind could stop it.

She threw herself at him, pressing her lips against his. He was hot and wet and felt so amazing she was surprised her brain didn't just combust right there. Celeste combed her fingers through his wet hair, bringing his head down so she could control the kiss. Sex pheromones surged through her body, making her slightly crazed.

He was so amazing; better than she had imagined he would be, for the last two hundred years. His warmth spread through her like fire. Celeste wrapped one leg around his waist, thrusting him close to her core. She couldn't control the moan from the feel of his erection. This had been the man she had always wanted, and he was in her arms. She never wanted to let him go.

Celeste let her arms drop to the towel she tugged, letting it fall to the floor, and she cupped his butt. Fireworks went off in the pit of her stomach and traveled downward. It was the most wonderful feeling, nothing like anything she had ever felt before. She thought she might burst into flames any second. And for the life of her, she didn't care.

Celeste rubbed herself against Marcus, trying to get closer, only to realize his arms remained at his sides. Pulling away she looked at him. His facial expression was one of pain. Humiliation infused her where passion had been only seconds before. Shame sucked deep into the pit of her stomach.

Celeste let her leg drop down to the floor with a thud. She stepped away from him. His hands were fisted at his side.

"I'm sorry," was all she could mumble through the lump in her throat.

"What was that?" his words were quiet and controlled.

She hesitated, not wanting to give up yet another secret to this cold, hard man. "I shouldn't have done that, I'm so sorry," she apologized again. The Sex Demon in her screaming and her pheromones still out of control, she turned toward the door.

"Celeste," Marcus said her name very quietly. She stopped at the door, but didn't turn around. She couldn't bring herself to look at him, wasn't sure if she was ever going to be able to look him in the eye again. "That can never happen again, do you understand me? I will not return your desires."

"Of course," she said, before walking through the door and leaving him alone

She looked around the house and found her bags and an empty room. She threw herself down on the bed and stared at the ceiling. Her pain was so acute, she didn't want to even move, but it would drive her to do something stupid if she didn't pull herself together. Pushing herself off the bed, she stripped and put on something horribly provocative. Short skirt, leather bustier, high heel boots that went up to her thighs and no tights. She looked in the mirror and grimaced. She looked like a hooker. At the moment, she felt like one, but the part of her that was currently in control wasn't going to allow her anything short of finding a man and getting laid. Either that or go nuts. "Tough choice," she swore to herself.

Throwing her bedroom door open, she was surprised to see Marcus standing there. He took one look at what she was wearing and swore.

"What the hell are you wearing?" He had slipped on a pair of slacks and a turtle neck. It couldn't be more obvious he was trying to cover as much of himself as possible, while she was showing more skin than was necessary. Her palms itched to feel his heated skin, the muscles just beneath the thick sweater, roll and jump at her touch. She sucked in a breath and tried to control her Sex Demon.

"My choice of clothing has nothing to do with you, Fallen. Now if you'll excuse me, I have someplace I need to be." She tried to move past him without touching him, but he wasn't moving. They did a back and forth dance in the hall. He wasn't going to let her leave.

"You are not going out looking like that," he growled, making her knees a little weak.

She couldn't look at him and instead, stared at the flower wallpaper over his right shoulder, praying to the Mother of the Gods to just let her get past him.

"Please Marcus, just get out of my way. This has nothing to do with you, and I would appreciate it if you would just let me pass." Each word was enunciated precisely.

"What are you trying to prove, Celeste? What is going on in that crazy, beautiful head of yours?" He actually sounded interested.

Her eyes moved to his beautiful emerald green ones. She took a couple of short breaths. "I am a Sex Demon. And if you don't get the fuck out of my way, right this minute, I will not be able to control myself."

"The Sex Demons were banned to the Infernos." He didn't so much as move an inch, like saying that would make her less of one.

"Yes, I am aware of that. It was six hundred years ago," she said defensively. "My mother tried to buy her way out by becoming Dante's concubine. All she got from it was me. When Dante turned from her, she was sent to Lust where she remains."

"How often do you need sex?" She moaned with him just saying the word. She turned back into her room and slammed the door in his face. It was either that or jump him. She headed for the window.

She wasn't thinking. Her brain was turning into a mush of lust and need. He threw the door open just as she swung a leg over the window sill. "Oh for the love of all that is holy in this world, can you please just leave me alone?" she snarled.

Marcus stormed into the room. "If I am mistaken, and please let me know if I am, you were the one to Flash into my room half an hour ago and maul me. It wasn't the other way around. So you'll pardon me if I want some god damn answers."

She stopped moving and took a deep breath, holding it in her lungs for as long as she could before releasing it.

"I came back. I came back because there is a war being fought in the Infernos, and the answers are here in the mortal plane. I don't want to lose another brother, nor do I want the souls of the Infernos to be released on this world. I came back—" she bit her tongue because she almost said I came back to you. "I came back because it was the right thing to do. I followed your light path because I didn't know where you had gone. That is why I ended up flashing into your room. It was an accident, one I promise will never happen again." She finished, throwing her other leg over the sill and jumped. It was only two stories, and she landed on her feet like a cat, regardless of the five inch heels she was wearing.

"Damn it, Celeste, come back here and fight this out with me," Marcus bellowed out the window, but she ignored him and walked down the long drive. She had no idea where she was going or how she was going to get there.

When she reached the end of the drive she looked left then right and saw nothing but a tree lined road. When tail lights illuminated the road from behind her, she knew she didn't have a lot of time and decided to throw caution to the wind.

Flashing, she set her mind to a place with music and people. Lots of people.

The hard bass and gyrating bodies hit her like a ton of bricks as she Flashed into the night club. Luckily, with the light show going on, her Flash in didn't seem to alert anyone. Looking around she tried to pick out suitable prey, but every guy she looked at more than once came up short. His hair wasn't dark enough. He had blue eyes. He had green eyes, but blond hair. After an hour, she wasn't sure if she wanted to scream or cry. Four days. Four days with a man she had made into a god, only to find out he was a total jackass, yet every man she saw still didn't compare enough to him.

For two hundred years she had always been able to find a replacement someone that looked enough like him to get her attention. Frustration boiling a little too close to the surface, she Flashed out of that club and into another. It was Goth and S & Minspired with pale woman dressed in all black, men with chain link shirts and spiked collars who wore black lipstick.

Celeste couldn't help it. She laughed. None of these people had any idea, did they? Maybe opening the Infernos was a good idea.

"Not your idea of a Saturday night out?" a gentleman asked, coming to stand next to her. He wasn't like the others. He was dressed in casual jeans and a button down shirt. She turned to him fully and smiled. He was a Vampire with a great deal of power.

"Not really, but what's a girl to do?" she shrugged her shoulders.

"Not Flashing in like a Demon from hell might be a good start." He said it so casually that it left Celeste blinking at him several times.

"Saw that, did you?"

"I don't miss much, but your secret is safe with me. Half the mortals here are hyped up on some type of drug, and the Others don't really care." He motioned to the bartender. "What can I get you to drink, sweetheart?"

"Vodka tonic, extra lime." She told the bartender. Holding out her hand to the Vampire she said, "Celeste."

He looked at her hand for a moment then gently grasped her fingers and brought them to her lips. "It is a pleasure to meet you, Celeste."

Celeste smiled back, letting all her Sex Demon needs flow through her as she replied. "No, the pleasure is all mine."

****

Marcus checked his watch. It was now three a.m. and Celeste had still not returned. Where in the hell had she gone?

"To get laid, you dumb ass, because you froze like someone was holding a gun to your head when she threw herself at you," he muttered back to himself.

He didn't know what happened. One minute he was standing there in the bathroom door, and the next there she was, looking so beautiful in her tight jeans and even tighter t-shirt, which showed off her cleavage in a way that had a man wanting more. Then she had thrown herself at him, touching him and kissing him. His entire body had gone into shock. He hadn't touched a woman like that in over five hundred years. Her hands had been everywhere, and he had acted like a fifteen-year-old virgin; frozen with fear.

She had tasted so good, like champagne and strawberries and that smell she had about her. Gods, he hadn't wanted anyone like this since Jessica. Marcus stopped pacing and lowered himself to the floor resting one hand on his bent knee. If he was being honest with himself, he had never wanted Jessica in the sexual way that he wanted Celeste. That realization stunned him, and he leaned his head back against the wall he stared at the crystal chandelier, wondering what he was doing.

Jessica.

Even thinking the name had hurt for so long he had stopped doing it. He had stopped looking for her in crowds, stopped hoping he would see her again. She had been a simple, yet beautiful farm girl when he met her.

He had fallen for her hard, wasted no time in making her his.

"So selfish," he whispered to himself. He had been selfish back then to claim a mortal woman. How would he explain that he didn't age? How would he keep her alive? Keep her with him forever?

Fate was a fickle and cruel mistress. But being a Fallen Angel, he had thumbed his nose at Fate one too many times in his century and a half, and she punished him by taking Jessica. Then he had begged the Angels to make her a Guardian and Fate taunting him further had done exactly what he asked; made her into a soul bound to earth to serve at the mercy of the Angels in the hopes of becoming one.

She had hated him for what he hadn't told her. Hated him for what she had become. She refused to listen to what he had to say, or hear his offers of help to adjust to her new life.

No, she had turned her back on him, taking the help of Uriel of the Betweens. He hadn't seen her again for another hundred years, but then, by chance, he ran into her on a London street, of all places.

Still beautiful, still young and full of life. Still his Jessica. That is what he had told himself at the time. Then she had said the words that would change his life. "You are a Fallen, not worthy of the life and light of the Gods. I understand now that you squandered the gifts the Angels bestowed upon you. I will not allow that to happen to myself or my charges."

"Jessica," he had pleaded with her, but she had turned from him.

She looked back to say, "You are dead to me, Fallen. Go find a place that won't judge you for your sins and your betrayal of the Gods that loved you. And know that I certainly do not love you any longer."

And then, just like that, she walked away. Marcus wandered the streets of London for weeks after that, trying to find her, trying to explain he hadn't meant for any of that to happen to her. Then he had stopped looking and found himself in front of a church. A house of God, something he hadn't been in for centuries. It was said that if a Fallen entered a blessed church, he would be struck down. Marcus was willing to take that chance.

He entered and waited. For six days nothing happened. People came and went, ignoring the man in the corner. Even the priest, after speaking with him and making sure he wasn't a danger to the people, left him alone.

On the seventh day, he got up went to the altar and vowed to make the world a better place, to feel the warmth and love of the Gods and Angels again, to be worthy of Jessica, his final vow was that of celibacy. If he couldn't be with Jessica, he wanted no other woman. The sins of the flesh would not be his downfall. He would be worthy of Jessica, and when the time came and the judgment was held, he would show her that he was again worthy of love; her love.

But that had been five hundred years ago, and he was beginning to question his promises and vows. He wondered what else he was expected to do. Give up?

He hadn't seen Jessica since, but the Angels, when he came into contact with them, never let the chance go to taunt him. They thrilled in the knowledge that he suffered on a day-to-day basis. He was starting to understand the fruitless battle for the love of a woman and a God that had turned from not only him, but their creations, their own flesh and blood. It made him sick to even think about. What more was he expected to do? He wanted to scream it to the heavens, but knew it was useless. His pleas were heard and disregarded.

And then there was Celeste. Just the thought of her made him hard. He stood and started to pace again. What the hell was he going to do with her? She was a contradiction, but in the last four days he had seen more in her to like and care for than in all the time he had spent with Jessica. There was something about her that tickled at his memory and made him want to gather her into his arms and never let her go.

Keys jangled in the door, and he threw it open. Cameron fell in on him. He caught the Tracker and pushed him back to his feet.

"Dammit, Cameron, what are you up to?" Marcus growled.

Cameron gave him a bleary drunk look. "Nothing dude, just want my bed right now."

Stumbling up the stairs, Marcus looked outside. There was nothing there to see, so he slammed the door and looked at his watch again. Four a.m. How long did it take to get laid? Even Cameron was back for the night.

Then he heard female laughter upstairs… and not just any female. Celeste must have Flashed back into the house. And she was laughing? He took the stairs two at a time when a male voice joined in the laughter.

"Hell no." Marcus stormed down the hallway and kicked the door in. If she had brought her conquest back here she had another thing coming, there was no way he was going to sit by and let her get laid in a room down the hall from his.

A large man leaned over Celeste pulling off one of her boots. The other boot lay on the floor at the end of the bed. Marcus had never experienced jealousy before, but seeing another man touching Celeste in such an intimate way drove green envy and jealousy straight through his body like a finely honed blade.

Roaring, he charged the man, and they both flew over the bed.

Marcus was lucky enough to land on top and pulled back to plant his fist in the other man's face when he recognized him.

"Aiden?"

"Marcus? Damn I knew she smelt familiar." Marcus didn't like the sound of Aiden smelling Celeste so he let a fist fly with a punch directly into Aiden's nose.

Aiden bellowed, and then Marcus was flying across the room and into the wall. He had forgotten how powerful Vampires were.

"What the hell is your problem?" Aiden said standing over him now.

Marcus shook his head. "Dammit man, I wish I knew."

A giggle from the bed had both men looking. "I think you just committed a horrible crime," she said, rolling over on her side she gave them both a fuzzy look.

"And what would that be?" Marcus demanded.

In the loudest whisper he had ever heard she explained. "I think he might be someone important. You shouldn't strike someone important."

She was so drunk Marcus was surprised she was able to finish the sentence. Then her eyes drifted shut, and her head fell onto the mattress.

Finally," Aiden offered. "I didn't think she was ever going to pass out. Who knew Demonessess could hold their liquor like that?"

"And you brought her back?"

Aiden gave him a strange look. "Actually, she told me she was too drunk to have sex with me, but she didn't know how she would feel in the morning. Then grabbed me and Flashed us here. Where she then made a really bawdy joke before thrusting her foot in my face and demanding I remove her boots."

"Flashing hurt like hell?" Marcus asked hoping the Vampire had felt a little pain. Since he didn't seem to have been bothered by Marcus' little hit.

Aiden gave him a sly smile. "You forget, Vampires don't have the same sensory limitations as others. But it was a different experience. Not one I would jump at again, but not painful."

"What are you doing here, Aiden?" Marcus asked still leaning against the wall where he had landed.

Aiden crouched down next to him. "City's been a little different the last month or so, so I thought I would check it out."

"And what have you found out?" Marcus asked.

"The answer depends on whether or not you are still close acquaintance's with those uncivilized Trackers or not." Aiden raised one perfect brow.

"Ryder didn't mean to insult you, Aiden."

"Oh, of course not. I never doubted that he did. However, the fact remains that he needs to apologize."

"Bloody hell, Aiden. That would be like getting the sun not to rise."

Aiden snorted. "Yes, well if you want information from me, not saying I have anything so it may not even be worth the bother of asking, but if you do want information, the Neanderthal must apologize."

"Just tell me this; are you aware of Demons attacking and eating mortals in the city?" Marcus watched the vampire closely. He rarely, if ever, showed his cards unless absolutely necessary.

"Yes, Sarafina is behind it."

Marcus wanted to shout "hurray!" That would be enough to get even Ryder to apologize. Sarafina was one of Lordus's go to gals. She and her brother wreaked havoc anywhere they went.

"Do you know where Lordus is?" Marcus had to ask.

Aiden laughed quietly. "Now isn't that the question of the century?"

Rising to his feet Aiden looked at Celeste and then back at Marcus. "Who is she?"

Marcus shrugged. "Can't say."

Aiden raised an eyebrow. "Even to a trusted confidant?" When Marcus didn't answer, Aiden whistled through his teeth.

"Must be someone important. Please remember who brought her back tonight safe and sound, will you?" Damn it, Marcus had fallen right into that one, and they both knew it.

Pushing himself from the wall, Marcus extended his hand to Aiden. "I appreciate it."

Aiden moved to the window his eyes lingering on Celeste. "It's a pity though. I think we might have had an amazing time in bed together." And then he was gone, the sound of his laughter flittering by in the wind.

Marcus growled and turned to Celeste. Although her boots were off she still had on the tiny scraps of clothes she had left in earlier. Marcus knew the gentlemanly thing to do was to cover her up and put her to bed, but when it came to Celeste his ability to maintain his gentleman attitude flew out the window.

Digging through her bags he pulled out a pair of yoga pants and a t-shirt. He had dressed and seen woman naked hundreds, if not thousands of times, but when he turned back to the bed, he froze. His body reacted to her in a way that was painful in its intensity. Placing the clothes at the foot of the bed he maneuvered her so that she was lying beneath the covers.

A Sex Demon? Who would have thought? And she was in his care. If something bad happened to her, Dante would have his hide, along with all the Reapers, and he just didn't know if he had that much flesh to offer up to the blood thirsty bastards.

Chapter 7

She was tired, overly so and burrowed farther down into the bed. Something wasn't right. She felt as if her body had been placed in a rack. Pulling her knees up to her chest, she moaned. She wanted her mother. Before Lexi had been sent away, she had often crawled into bed with her daughter. They would just lay there holding each other. Lexi would whisper to her that she would always love her.

Dante never did anything like that. His most affectionate touch would be when he stroked her hair. Right now she wanted the comfort her mother would give her by just being close.

She totally blamed Marcus for the pain she was in. If it wasn't for him then she would have been able to find someone last night. She would have gotten the sex she needed and they could go on with their investigation. But no, now she was in so much pain she wasn't going to be able to even find someone to have sex with. It was probably going to kill her. She growled to herself, as her door opened.

"I've been reading up on Sex Demons," Marcus said from somewhere to her left.

"Good for you, now go away." Her throat was dry, and felt like her tongue had been staked out to dry in the Sahara.

"It says here that physical contact with another being will ease the symptoms of the sexual drive of the female Sex Demon." The way he said it sounded like he was reading it from a book. Celeste peaked out and, sure enough, he was holding a dirty old tomb of a book.

"You don't necessarily need sex, just physical contact. That should hold off the symptoms for four to five days to even a month. If the contact is consistent." He said it with a note of pleasure. He actually thought he was offering her a better alternative.

He looked down from the book and smiled. "So we have this issue solved. You need physical contact with another hot blooded individual, and you won't go lust crazed."

"If that is all you have to offer, Fallen, I would appreciate it if you would get the hell out of my room so I can die in peace." He didn't know the first thing about Sex Demons and whatever book he was reading looked older than she was. She would rather beat him with it than have him try to treat her with anything that actually came out of it.

She heard the thump of the book as he put it down. "Yes, but that is the problem. We have a job to complete, and until then I need you at full Celeste princesses' warrior status."

Celeste nearly jumped from the bed when it dipped as Marcus sat down. She peaked out just in time to watch him pull his shirt off.

"Oh god, Marcus, please get out," she begged.

He smiled at her. "You used my name." Then he gathered her into his arms, pressing against her chest and face.

Celeste couldn't help it. She moved as close as she could get to him. He was amazing and filled the places that were empty both inside and out. After several minutes, her tight muscles started to relax, and the tingling in her back reseeded to a dull ache.

"How do you feel?"

The last thing she wanted to admit was that he was right, so she lied. "I hurt like hell," she muttered.

Marcus grunted and pulled her closer turning her over so her back pressed against his chest one arm wrapped around her stomach and the other above her chest. She relaxed her head against his forearm, and he threw a leg over her, moving so they were spooning.

Celeste was in Heaven as the last bits of the unbearable lust eased from her body. She breathed in a relaxed breathe. The last person who had held her had been her mother, and she couldn't help but just enjoy having another person's arms around her.

"Celeste?" Marcus asked his voice rumbling against her back.

"Shut up," she growled, not wanting to talk. She just wanted to enjoy his touch.

He didn't say anything for several long minutes, and Celeste soaked up his warmth, but she knew he was gearing up for something because he grew tense as the minutes ticked by.

"Do you remember how you got home last night?" he finally asked.

Celeste thought back to the night before. She remembered drinking with a great looking guy…and drinking and drinking. But no matter how much she drank, she couldn't make the beautiful man look more like Marcus.

"No."

"No idea how you got home last night?" Celeste had a sick feeling he was fishing for information.

She rolled over slightly so she could look into his green eyes. "No Fallen, I have no idea how I got home last night?"

"How much did you drink?"

Celeste pulled out of his arms and scooted to the other side of the bed feeling the loss of his touch as a physical blow to her stomach. She sucked it up and turned to him.

"First of all, if I don't remember how I got home last night what makes you think I have any idea how much alcohol I ingested? What's with all the questions? Your fishing for something so spit it out already." The warmth and kindness from just moments before were totally gone, and she had the urge to slap him just so he could get to the point.

"I thought you might have found it interesting that Aiden, the King of the Vampires, brought you home. Or more to the point you Flashed the two of you back here."

Celeste had the sudden urge to throw up. Of all the people in the world she had run into the King of the Vampires? What were the odds of that? And how pissed would her father be?

Celeste looked under the covers. Her clothes were a little askew, but thank the gods she was still wearing them. "Well, he was a gentleman, unless he dressed me after."

Marcus snorted. "If you had had sex with the King of the Vampires don't you think you would have remembered it?"

He had a point.

"What's going to happen next time? What if someone working with Lordus or Calliope were to find you? They would have a way into the Infernos. Do you want to put yourself and the Infernos in that type of danger?"

"Okay, Fallen let's get to the point." She waved a hand.

"You are not allowed to go out alone. If something were to happen to you, then your father and brothers would kill me."

Celeste climbed from the bed, irritated. "Oh yes, and all you want is to feel alive, sorry, I forgot."

Marcus launched from the bed and grabbed her by the shoulders painfully. "What did you just say?"

Celeste wanted to slam her head into the wall. She hadn't meant to say that. She didn't have an answer. If she told him that she took care of him while he healed from his punishments, he would hate her for seeing him weak and out of control. If she knew anything from growing up with brothers, men did not like to feel vulnerable.

She put as much sarcasm as she could into her words as she spoke. "Isn't that what all Fallen want? To feel alive? You envy the life and love of mortals. Having been blessed with the love of the true light." She rolled her eyes. "But finding happiness can only be done from within." She stabbed him in his bare chest with her index finger.

Marcus released her... "Why can we not have a single conversation without it turning into an argument?"

At the moment Celeste was wondering the same damn thing, but wasn't about to admit it to him. She must be more like her brothers than she wanted to admit. The very last thing she wanted was for Marcus to see her vulnerable. Anyone else she might be able to get past, but Marcus seeing her helpless, that might just do her in.

"I guess we just rub each other the wrong way, Fallen," she said quietly. "Unless necessary, we should just stay away from each other."

"We are partners, Celeste, and your father and brothers entrusted you with me. I do not take that lightly."

She rolled her eyes at him. "So gallant of you, but I can take care of myself."

She moved to the door and opened it. "If you don't mind, I would like to take a shower and change my clothes. Thank you for helping me this morning."

Marcus walked to the door and hesitated. "If you need help again, Celeste, I don't mind helping you out." But it will mean nothing and be physical without feeling, was left unsaid and burned like acid in her stomach.

It took everything she had to plaster a fake smile on her face and thank him, and not slam the door on him as he moved through it.

He didn't mind helping out? Her temper flared so strong she thought she would set the house on fire. He wouldn't mind helping out? Like she couldn't take care of herself? Just the thought of asking him for the time of day made her want to grind her teeth together.

She stormed into the bathroom and turned the shower on, climbing under the hot spray; she relaxed and let herself cry. She never cried in front of people, never allowed anyone to see her weaknesses. But here, Celeste looked around at the cool marble shower stall, she was alone, completely and utterly alone, and admitting that hurt like hell.

****

"So the bastard will give me some information. Information that may or may not get me what I need, only if I apologize?" Celeste heard Ryder's voice and almost turned back down the hall. But she was too damn hungry to let that ill-tempered Tracker persuade her out of food.

"It could be very valuable to have Aiden on our side, Ryder." Celeste almost burst out laughing at the forced calm in Marcus's voice. She was sure the Fallen wanted to shake Ryder, and to be honest, she would have paid to watch it.

She walked into the kitchen, and the conversation came to an abrupt halt. "Don't let me interrupt. I'm just looking for something to eat."

"There's meat in the fridge," Marcus said turning back to Ryder and Kyra.

Celeste opened up the fridge and sure enough, there was a package of raw steak at least an inch thick. The Demon side of her really wanted to just pick it up and throw it in her mouth like a crazy person. But she was civilized, and she reached past it for the gallon of milk.

"Is there cereal?" she asked turning back to the group.

"You don't want the meat?" Marcus asked, surprised.

"I might like it for lunch, but not for breakfast." Kyra pointed to a cupboard by the stove. Opening it up, she let out a little yelp of pleasure. They had Fruit Loops, her favorite. Grabbing the box she turned and searched for a bowl and spoon. Her inhabitations of the other people in the room temporarily forgotten. Once she had everything she went to the table and sat down. She was now as far away from the group as she could get.

"You should ask Celeste. She became quiet friendly with Aiden last night," Marcus accused. Celeste just rolled her eyes as she spooned some of the tasty flavored cereal into her mouth.

"How do you know, Aiden?" Kyra asked. Celeste couldn't help but notice the Element had a little irritation in her voice.

"Met him at a bar last night. Had no idea who he was, until Marcus told me this morning," she said around a mouth full. "You might want to ask Marcus how the hell he seems to know everyone 'cause that's just freaky."

"How exactly do we get in contact with him?" Ryder practically snarled.

Kyra laughed. "It's not going to kill you."

"Yes it is. Damn blood suckers think they are better than the rest of us, but they are just like as weird and freaky as us Others," Ryder snapped

"I will make some calls and should be able to get ahold of him by nightfall. But meanwhile Celeste, and I need to continue to look for the Touched." Marcus pulled a phone out of his pocket.

Celeste did the same she and pushed the saved number she had been given the night before and wasn't surprised when Aiden picked up on the first ring.

"Good morning my beautiful Demon. I hope you slept well," he purred through the phone.

"Like the dead, but you should know all about that," she said, making Aiden laugh which had her smiling.

"So who should I thank for having the pleasure of speaking with you this morning?" She loved the way he spoke so proper, enunciating each word perfectly.

"Well, first I wanted to say thank you for making sure I made it home safe." Celeste looked up at Marcus who glared at her. He put his phone down. "Second, Ryder is here, and he is way excited to speak with you."

Aiden laughed again. "First of all, it was my pleasure to ensure you made it home unharmed, although I am withholding judgment on your mood of transportation. And second, if Ryder is so very excited to speak with me, I would be happy to take his call."

"You want me to give him the phone?" Ryder started waving his hands around like a crazy person while Kyra nodded.

"Hmm, interesting dilemma," Aiden said and paused for a moment. "Why don't you let him know when he is truly ready to speak with me, you are permitted to give him my number, but until it is his idea, then I shall keep my distance as well as my information?"

"What exactly did he do?" Celeste asked looking at Ryder as she asked the question. He looked like a biker and acted like a Neanderthal half the time, but whenever he looked at Kyra everything about his visage changed and softened. Celeste wasn't really surprised he had upset Aiden.

"Ah, Little Red, that is a story for another time."

"Okay, but I'll get it out of you," Celeste promised.

Aiden laughed again. "I'm sure you will, and we shall both enjoy the games, wins and losses, it takes to procure said information," he said suggestively making Celeste smile.

With that, he hung up, and Celeste put her phone down and shoved another spoonful of cereal in her mouth.

"Well?" Marcus barked.

Celeste looked up. "Ask the Tracker, he heard every single word. And it was regarding him, not you, so he can share or not."

Celeste turned to her breakfast with the intention of ignoring everyone else in the room no matter what.

"You're impossible," Marcus growled.

"Yes, you've said that before."

Marcus stormed from the room, which was fine with Celeste. She meant it when she had said they should stay away from each other. She had built someone up in her mind of the romantic Fallen Angel, and he was nothing like what she'd expected. That's how fantasies worked. And the thing was, he had turned out to be more human than anything else. And she had no one to blame but herself.

"What have you done to Marcus?" Kyra asked as she moved to sit across from Celeste. She brought a bowl and poured herself some cereal.

"What do you mean?" Celeste asked

"I mean, in all the time I have known Marcus he has never stormed out of a room." Kyra spooned some cereal into her mouth and raised an eyebrow in question.

"Really? Hmm, have you ever known him to choke a woman into unconsciousness? Shake a person until their teeth rattled?" Kyra's eyes bulged in surprise.

"Of course not, he is a Fallen Angel. He is kindness personified." Kyra's words actually made Celeste choke on her cereal.

Kyra jumped up and patted her on the back until she could breathe again.

Celeste pushed her bowl away, losing her appetite. "Personification of kindness," she said with sarcasm and complete shock. "Not really the Fallen I know."

Ryder laughed. "I knew it."

Kyra glared at her mate. "Knew what?"

"That Marcus would become a frustrated jackass. Five hundred years without a woman, now he is partnered with you." Celeste didn't miss the disgust in his voice when he mentioned her. "He's bound to just combust at some point." He laughed again.

"I don't understand," Celeste said. Leaning back in her chair she regarded Ryder. "What is wrong with being partnered with me, and why is his pain so funny?"

"You, because you're freak'n beautiful. No offense," Ryder said to Kyra who shrugged.

"I know where you sleep at night so if you see a beautiful woman, she is beautiful. You're the more jealous one in the relationship," she explained.

"And it's damn funny because his frustration was bound to catch up with him one day," Ryder said.

"You think its funny someone you consider a brother is in pain?" Sometimes Celeste just didn't understand men.

Ryder glared at her. "No, what I think is funny is that he is too stupid to figure it out."

"Who is stupid?" Marcus asked coming back into the kitchen.

"You are," Ryder said.

"Yes, well you think everyone is an idiot," Marcus said and looked at Celeste. "Are you ready to go?"

"And just where are we headed to?" Celeste asked.

"I think a slow cruise through the city is in order. I can feel Guardians in the area."

"So the two of us are just going to go out and drive around until you feel a Guardian?" The thought of spending the day trapped in a car with Marcus made her want to crawl up the wall and howl.

"Do you have a better idea?"

Kyra interrupted them. "Marcus, why are you so angry?"

"Because he's a dumbass," Ryder answered.

Kyra glared at her mate. "Since you are in such a wonderful mood, I think I will take Celeste's place and go for a drive with Marcus."

"The hell you will," Ryder snapped.

"See the jealous one? He calls you beautiful I don't blink. But I want to go for a ride with a friend, and the caveman comes out pounding on his chest." She rolled her eyes and turned back to Ryder. "Oh so you're going to call Aiden and apologize?"

"Hell no!"

She smiled, rising from the table, she kissed Ryder on the cheek. "Then I will enjoy a ride with Marcus."

Marcus growled causing shivers to spread up Celeste's spine. "And just what are you going to do today?" he demanded of her.

A countless number of sarcastic answers clawed at the back of Celeste's throat, but she clenched her teeth together and thought for a moment. "I think I am going to the Infernos, to question George. He may have more information than he was prepared or able to give us."

Marcus looked surprised. "That's a good idea. But don't be gone too long. Let's get this taken care of."

Celeste glared at him. "Oh I'm sorry. What's my curfew, Daddy?"

Marcus threw his hands in the air. "That viper's tongue of yours is going to get you into a lot trouble one day."

"And let me guess, you can only hope to be there when it happens?" He looked so frustrated she thought his head might explode.

Marcus leaned down so they were nose to nose. "Just one conversation. Just one, that doesn't involve your viper jaded tongue."

She smiled and leaned forward so her forehead actually leaned against his. "But if my vipers tongue wasn't involved, I wouldn't be able to speak." She licked her lips after she said it. His eyes glued to the action.

He jerked back. "That would be the point."

Celeste just shook her head and Flashed to the Infernos.

****

"Why are you letting her get under your skin?" Ryder asked, as soon as Celeste disappeared. Marcus felt as if he was going to combust from the sexual frustration clawing at him.

"She snaps sarcastically at me every time I open my mouth." Marcus shoved a hand through his hair. He would dearly love to know the answer to that question himself. That way at least he wouldn't feel so helpless or out of sorts when it came to Celeste.

"Look, brother, I'm not the best person to give out advice on the issue, but maybe, just maybe, you are frustrated because she is a beautiful woman, and you're celibate," Ryder quipped. "Sex can be a dangerous powder keg. The situation between the two of you is bound to strike a match and blow up at some point."

Marcus sighed. "I have been celibate for five hundred years and have been around beautiful woman before. Your mate and I have worked together in the past. But Celeste—there is just something about her that rubs me the wrong way."

Ryder shook his head. "Rubs you the wrong or right way? There is a fine line, my brother. You should figure out where it is before you trip and land into something you aren't prepared to defend yourself against."

Marcus again sighed. Ryder was right, and if he was right then there was something really wrong with the world, which only frustrated him more.

He felt terrible admitting it. He typically liked everyone, and that emotion usually went both ways. He had never been with someone who acted as if they truly disliked him. And if he had to admit it, his feelings were just a little hurt on the matter. So he lashed out at her, and each time he did it, he promised he would be nice next time. But she evoked such strong emotions in him he didn't seem to have control sometimes.

"You know she is a Sex Demon?" Marcus asked Ryder, who whistled and shook his head.

"Son of a bitch." Ryder laughed. "That would explain some things."

"That's all you have to say about it?" Marcus asked, incredulous. "They have been banned from this plane because of what they are and what they can do, and you say it explains some things?"

Ryder slapped Marcus on the shoulder. "She fits the bill of a Sex Demon. The only question is how are you going to handle that? After all, she is your partner, and Dante entrusted her into your hands."

"She was having some issues—" Marcus could feel the blood rush to his face, and he wanted to turn and walk away but he had to get this out. "So I did some research on the Sex Demons. They need contact, not necessarily sexual contact, but contact with a hot blooded species. I offered to help her out by holding her."

Kyra snorted once before bursting out in laughter, which, of course, only fueled Marcus's irritation.

"She was in pain, Kyra. What was I supposed to do?" he snapped.

"Maybe you could have slept with her," Ryder threw the words out.

"I don't have sex, or did you miss that part?" Marcus snapped and turned to Kyra. "And why the hell is this so funny?"

Kyra pulled herself together enough to speak. "Marcus, she is a Sex Demon. She is a physical being one of the most physical beings in all of creation, and all you did was offer to hold her?" she held up her hands as he started to interrupt. "Not that it didn't help because it obviously did or she wouldn't have been able to come down this morning. However, from what I know of the Sex Demons they feel things very differently then you or I. You might have put her off for a while, but eventually she is going to need sex. Just like the Trackers must share their pheromone with their chosen, she needs to have sex in order to survive."

"I understand all that."

"Yes, I know you understand it intellectually, but she is a Sex Demon. She needs sex, and holding her will only help for so long. Eventually it will only make it worse," Kyra said.

Marcus thought about it for a minute. "I think I have more studying to do."

"And why can't you just let her have sex with someone else?" Ryder asked.

Marcus felt like someone had pulled the rug out from beneath him. "Because we are partners."

Ryder shrugged. "Marlee and I are partners, and I wouldn't sleep with her for any reason." He actually shivered.

"That, and she has bigger balls than you do," Kyra said, laughing. "But that is a thought, Marcus. Just let her have sex with someone. She seems to have made a connection with Aiden."

The thought of her sleeping with another man made Marcus want to commit homicide. "She is my partner, and we don't have time for her to go out and find a man to have sex with. She is my partner, and I will find a way to work around this."

"Stop studying. Try being nice, even if she snaps at you. Just be yourself." Kyra patted him on the back and reached out for Ryder's hand. "If you won't sleep with her then you have a great deal of studying to do."

"I thought you were going to go with me?" Marcus asked as she pulled Ryder to his feet.

Kyra smiled. "I think that maybe you should spend some time thinking about what we've discussed. Time alone always helps. Enjoy your recon. Besides, Ryder has some questions to answer."

Ryder gave her a confused look. "What?"

"I'm curious how you know so much about female Sex Demons."

Ryder cursed. "You know just as much as I do," he snapped.

Kyra glared at him "But my information came from years of study. Where did yours come from?"

"Dammit, Kyra." He grunted as she pulled him from the room.

Marcus did smile at that point. Finally someone else was getting their ass handed to them. It helped to assuage some of his tension.

Grabbing a set of keys, he headed toward the garage. Kyra was right. Time alone to think was probably the best answer for everyone concerned.

****

Celeste rushed up to Victor. He had a gash in his side and was bleeding from a wound in his head.

"Why didn't you send for me?" she asked

"Never really had the time, little one." He leaned against her and put one arm around her neck as she led him to a bench.

"Is it really that bad?" If she had known how dire the situation had become, she would have come back immediately. "And you damn well know I am one word away."

Victor laughed, and then cringed with pain. "We've got most of the levels contained now. It's basically clean up, but we are shorthanded."

"I will do whatever needs to be done," she promised.

Victor pulled her close and hugged her. "You need to make sure Calliope doesn't make it back into the Infernos. How are things going?"

"I am not enjoying myself," Celeste said honestly. "Not that this was a vacation or anything, but I am my mother's daughter, and the time changing has been difficult to adjust to."

Victor gave her a hard look. "And Dante placed you with the one person in any plane of existence that wouldn't sleep with you."

Celeste laughed. "Is that why he put me with him?"

Victor raised one blond brow. "You tell me."

Celeste sobered. "Are you and the others going to be okay?" She worried about them.

Victor cupped her cheek. "We will be fine and always there for you if needed, but this is a fight only you can fight. The Black Sword would turn any of us into what Calliope was born into."

Celeste lowered herself to the bench next to her brother and leaned on his good side. "I understand all of that, but I don't understand the workings of the mortal plane, and Marcus is making me want to kill him."

Victor shook his head. "Men will do that. And you being a Sex Demon doesn't help. You reek of sex, baby girl."

"But it's not my fault," she wailed and then pulled herself together.

"Of course it's not. But it is different on the mortal plane for you." Victor patted her on the shoulder. "Take it one day at a time, and if the Fallen touches you, his ass will be burned in the pits of Hell."

Celeste wished he had been joking, but she knew he wasn't, and the thought of Marcus being hurt like that made her want to cry.

So she decided to change the subject. "Where is the Guardian you took? It was George, wasn't it? "

"He had the most pussy ass name. How can you be a Guardian if you're named George?" he asked shaking his head. "Anyway, we were short two Reapers, Dante gave him the choice of going back into Limbo, and seeing if the Arch would take him back, but honestly if they had really wanted him, wouldn't they have fought for him? George isn't stupid and placed the question to Dante. Who, of course, answered by offering him a deal: become a Reaper by drinking Dante's blood, which is how it was done in the old days, or Dante could put him to eternal rest?"

Celeste was shocked. "And what did he choose?"

"Reaper, actually." Celeste had to pick her jaw up off the floor in her shock. This just wasn't done. Hadn't been done since the First, and they were fighting Calliope now because of it. How would George react? Would he become evil like Calliope was now? "Would you like to see him?" Victor asked.

"Has the transformation completed? To make him a Reaper would be difficult, and he may not have survived? And aren't you worried he would end up like Calliope?"

Victor laughed. "Calliope was a corrupt soul before he became a Reaper. George wasn't utterly clueless, but nowhere near corrupt. He did have a pure soul. Becoming a Reaper for him would just enhance what he already had in him."

"So he survived the change?" Celeste asked.

"Oh, he survived alright and came out a better man for it. Some people's destiny lies within losing, not winning." He stood, the gash in his side already closing. The head wound had healed as they spoke.

"We gave him a new name though. How could he be a Reaper with a name like George?"

Celeste laughed. "And what did you come up with?" she was almost afraid to know what they had named him.

"Dante chose the name when he came through the transformation," Victor said, opening the door to the great hall. A man standing a head taller than Celeste stood in the middle of the room. He was heaving as if he had just run, and he was completely naked. He turned to Victor and Celeste as they came through the doors. His dark hair hung down into nearly black eyes. He flipped his head back whipping his hair out of his eyes.

"Celeste, Garrett," Victor made the introduction.

"Holy Gods." Celeste couldn't keep her mouth shut. She clamped her hands over her mouth to keep anything else from rushing out.

Garrett tipped his head back and laughed, when he calmed he looked back to Celeste. "I will take that as a compliment."

"Um, you probably should," Celeste offered.

Garrett grabbed a robe and threw it around his shoulders.

"Garrett shall make a good Reaper", Dante said from where he sat on the dais.

Celeste moved forward and kissed her father's cold cheek. She turned back to Garrett still shocked at the change. "Garrett, I have some questions."

Garrett nodded his head. "I am at your disposal, sister." His voice was deep.

She looked back to her father who nodded, giving permission. Celeste hugged Victor. "I don't want to come back and see you beaten like you were again. You probably took several years off my life."

Victor snorted. "I'll try to stay out of trouble." But the smile he gave her said otherwise. Being the head of Violence, he often was injured or hurt and loved what he was and what he did. Celeste kissed his cheek and moved to an alcove, Garrett behind her.

She sat down on a bench, and Garrett sat next to her. "Are you sure this is the path you wish to be on?" She still couldn't believe a Guardian had chosen to become a Reaper instead of an Angel.

It must have been a question he had been asked because he smiled. "I was a Guardian, Celeste, it is not a glamours job nor is it a guarantee I would have ended up as an Angel. How would you like to live an endless life protecting ones that are special and never knowing if you would be chosen to become an Angel? Or live immortally serving the Angels with tasks they deem unworthy for their own?"

"You paint the Angels as a selfish lot," she couldn't help but say after his explanation.

He shrugged his large shoulders. "I was a wandering soul, Celeste. When I was chosen to be a Guardian I believed it was a blessing. But even after the short term of fifteen years, I have come to realize it was not where I was meant to be."

"And what happens fifteen years from now? Will you want something different?" Celeste asked with complete seriousness.

Becoming a Reaper was not something done thoughtlessly. In fact, a new Reaper hadn't been created or born since Celeste. No one outside of the family knew about her. She wondered what the Angels would think about this.

Garrett shrugged again. "It is a road I will have to cross when I come to it. However, deep inside, I feel this is my course. I finally feel like the person I was meant to be." He smiled showing her straight white teeth. "And it feels amazing to know, in your very soul you're where you should be. But you didn't come to hear my story, what are you in need of?"

Celeste wondered if changing him had been a good idea or a desperate attempt to feel a hole in the Reaper world, but it was a question for another day. "I need to know what you remember from the day when your Guard was taken."

Garrett leaned his head back. She could see in his eyes the pain he felt for what had happened. "I should have been stronger. I shouldn't have left him alone. We knew something was going on."

"That's what I want to know about. How did you know?"

"A darkness entered the city. Like a shadow falling over you after lying out in the sun. The Guardians aren't really allowed to be in contact with each other, but we knew about each other. Calliope killed two other Guardians and their wards before he caught up with Charles and I." He shook his head and rested his elbows on his knees before he put his face into his hands.

"I see it every time I close my eyes, what that monster did." Celeste squeezed his shoulder. "His soul was given to Dante, and Dante granted him access to Limbo. He took it."

Garrett smiled. "I am glad he will be renewed, given another chance to live a life that was cut to short this time."

After an hour of questioning him, he didn't have any other information she didn't already know.

"Thank you for your time, Garrett." She rose from her seat, as did Garrett. "I need to get back."

He nodded and walked with her toward the dais. Dante had left and the room was quiet.

"Good luck, sister," Garrett offered.

She nodded. "Thank you." She was just about to Flash out when Garrett grabbed her arm.

"Celeste, I do remember one more thing. The one other Guardian I spoke with prior to the murder said he believed the Angels had forsaken us. I tended to agree with him. I'm not sure if that will help you out or not."

Celeste filed that way. "Thank you again." She Flashed back to the house she was sharing with Marcus and the Trackers. She immediately felt Marcus. He wasn't in the house, but he was close. She checked the time, it was close to ten p.m.

Her stomach growling, she headed to the kitchen. Ryder, Kyra and Cameron sat around the table. They were laughing at something when she entered, but their talking stopped the moment she stepped into the room.

"I'm sorry, I was just looking for something to eat."

Kyra stood. "No, please join us. I made plenty." She motioned to a casserole dish of something. Ryder and Cameron both shook their heads wildly until Kyra turned to look at them.

"Um," Celeste didn't want to hurt the Element's feelings, but the way the men acted she wasn't sure she wanted to say yes. But in the end, how could she say no? "Thank you, that is very kind."

Cameron rolled his eyes, and Ryder gave her a strange look before shaking his head.

"Here sit down, and I'll get it for you." Kyra rushed past her, and Celeste took a seat at the table.

"Hope you're not hungry," Cameron whispered.

"Just chew and don't think," Ryder offered. "She can kick your ass, but she can't cook."

They were all smiles when Kyra returned to the table with a set of dishes she spooned a large helping of the casserole onto Kyra's plate. She smiled so nicely Celeste just couldn't hurt her feelings.

Taking her fork she took a large portion and put it in her mouth and started to chew. Her very first instinct was to spit it out. Her mind screamed for her to spit it out. Spices and something sweet mixed with rice. Gods, she hoped it was rice, and some type of vegetable. But she'd be damned to Hell if she could place it at the moment.

Everyone stared at her as she swallowed and smiled up at Kyra. She had to swallow again, even her stomach tried to spit it out. Planting a smile on her face, Celeste clamped her teeth together and looked up at Kyra.

"Thank you so much. It's different. I like different," she reassured. Not a complete lie.

Kyra heaved a sigh and sat down hitting her husband on the shoulder. "See, I told you I can cook. She doesn't seem to mind it at all." Celeste took another bite to prove Kyra right.

"Really?" Ryder asked looking directly at Celeste. "How does it taste?"

His voice bounced off the walls of the kitchen and into her head like a rubber ball, and she opened her mouth to answer that it was terrible, horrible, the worst thing she had ever eaten. But she slapped her hand around her mouth forcing the words down with the food she was trying to eat.

Kyra immediately hit him so hard he almost fell out of the chair he was sitting in. "That's just not nice, apparently you don't mind sleeping alone."

Ryder winked at Celeste. "My compulsion doesn't work on the Reapers, but you being only half I thought I would give it a try. And as to your threat—" He turned to Kyra. "—we shall see about that."

Celeste tried to eat the dish as quickly as possible without seeming to be rushing through it just to get it over with.

"You are hungry," Kyra said with a smile. "Would you like more?"

Celeste placed her fork on the plate with what was left. She couldn't put another bit in her mouth if her life depended on it. "No, but thank you."

"Are you sure?"

"I've never been surer of anything in my entire life." She hadn't meant to be so serious or honest, but that was just who she was.

"You know what?" Kyra said leaning in close to Celeste. "I had my misgivings about you because you're a Demon and all. I mean I've never met a Demon that was civilized or that I liked, but you? I like you." Kyra nodded as if that settled that.

"Um, thank you?" Celeste wasn't sure what that meant. She was saved by Marcus as he walked into the kitchen from the back door.

"What's going on?"

"We're eating. Would you like a plate?" Kyra asked jumping up to get a plate for him.

"Who cooked?" Marcus asked.

"Oh, I threw something together for the guys. Celeste liked it."

"I ate already," Marcus said without hesitation.

"Really?" Kyra turned on him.

"Yes, I ate while I was out." He didn't even blink.

"Did you find anything?" Celeste interrupted trying to change the subject.

"Not much, but I know where to start tomorrow. You?"

Celeste shook her head. "Nothing new, except that the Guardians think the Angels have forsaken them to the fates of the world."

Marcus's brows drew together. "What the hell does that mean?"

"I don't know but, that is what Garrett said."

"Who is Garrett?"

"George the Guardian?" Marcus nodded. "He joined the Reapers since we were down two and was renamed Garrett."

Ryder snorted and Marcus huffed. "The Angels are going to have a fit when they find out Dante turned one of their Guardians into a Reaper."

"It will cause another war," Ryder agreed.

"But it won't be our concern," Cameron said calmly. "Another war between Heaven and Hell isn't one war you take sides on."

Celeste reached over and hit the Tracker in the forehead with the palm of her hand. "How many times have you been hit in the head? I mean, real brain damage kind of hit?"

Ryder and Marcus both burst out laughing. Cameron just smiled. "You know what, Demon? I like you." He leaned forward and kissed her on the tip of her nose.

Celeste couldn't not smile at the Tracker. He acted so much like her brothers.

"I guess you'll do," Celeste said with a smile on her own face.

"Are you ready to go out?" Marcus asked her. His smile was gone now.

Celeste stood up. "Where are we going? I thought you wanted to wait until tomorrow."

"Nope, still have a couple of things to go over. Let's go," Marcus said moving past her toward the back door.

She followed him out to the car. "You shouldn't lead him on," Marcus snapped at her.

"Excuse me?" Celeste asked, some of her good humor leaving at his sharp words.

"Cameron, you shouldn't lead him on," Marcus said holding the car door open for her.

She was so surprised she just stood there for a moment. "I was not leading him on."

"You're a Sex Demon. You lead on every man," he said.

She was so insulted she couldn't stop the back hand that whipped out sending Marcus several steps back. "Take it back," she growled. Slamming the car door, she advanced on him.

"Damn it, Celeste, you hit like a man,"

"You know what else I do like a man?" she said. "I kick ass like a man."

She swung on him but he moved out of the way, expecting the move, she stepped to the side, catching him in the side of the stomach with her elbow. The air rushed from his lungs. Bending him over, she kneed him in the face, and he flew back, landing on his back.

She pounced, landing on his chest she pressed her forearm over his throat. "You're not the only one that can choke someone."

Furry blazed in his green eyes as he bucked her off, throwing her a good five feet. She rolled to her feet, a trick her brothers had taught her. In a low crouch she watched him closely as he bounded to his feet.

"Are you insane?" he shouted wiping blood from his face.

She heard someone move behind her, but kept her focus on Marcus. "You have no idea what insane is. Maybe one day, if you're a really good boy? I'll show you what real insanity looks like."

Celeste blew to her feet in an explosive move, spinning in the air, she whipped the man behind her with the ends of her hair and then nailed him on the chin with one combat covered boot. He dropped to the ground like a ton of rocks.

"I'm glad I sent Stephan in first," Aiden said, stepping out of the shadows. He took Celeste by the hand and brought it to his lips to kiss her knuckles.

"God dammit all to Hell," Marcus swore. "Is there a man on this plane who isn't wrapped around your finger?"

Aiden laughed. "It would seem you would be that person."

"We have work to do, Aiden. What do you want?" Marcus moved forward so he was standing next to Celeste, trying to control the urge to push her behind him.

"Did Ryder call you?" Celeste asked.

"No, but something has changed in the city. The Others are frightened and leaving." Aiden helped his friend who was regaining consciousness to his feet.

"Um, we might want to have his wounds looked at. The ends of my hair are covered in Demon venom," Celeste said a little ashamed at what she had done.

Aiden smiled. "He will be fine. His bloodline of vampire is immune."

Celeste turned to the blond vampire. The venom should have started to cause him pain, but the wounds were healing as she looked at them. "His bloodline is very pure."

Aiden smiled. "Would I surround myself with anything less? But let us get back to the point. Others are fleeing, and I wondered if it had something to do with what you are doing here, my little Demon," Aiden said turning to Celeste.

Celeste smiled and shrugged her shoulders. "I have that effect, but—" she turned to Marcus who was glaring at her. She was actually becoming used to the look. "That is exactly what Garrett said. The night before the death, they said a darkness had entered the city."

"Calliope is in town," Marcus swore. "And what about you, Aiden? Where do you stand on this?" Marcus asked.

Aiden thought for a moment. "I am inclined to step away, this was not my fight to begin with."

"However?" Celeste asked.

Aiden turned a devastating smile toward her. "The thought of you fighting against such a formidable foe leaves me uncomfortable."

"I'm sure you'll get over it," Marcus said, pushing Celeste back toward the car. "WE don't need your help."

"Wait." Celeste ground her heels in. "We could use all the help we can get. Although if father finds out I'm working with the Vampires he may not like that much."

Aiden laughed. "As long as your father doesn't have the ability to cut my soul from my body, then we shouldn't have a problem."

Celeste looked at Marcus and then back at Aiden. "I wouldn't say he has the ability to cut your soul from your body. Take if forcefully, but there wouldn't be any knives involved."

Aiden, and his friend froze and looked at her. "This is not possible."

"Yeah, well, join the crowd of shocked and unbelieving. She is Dante's daughter." Celeste smiled. The way Marcus said it made it sound as if it were a compliment.

Aiden's next question was to Celeste. "Is he still pissed that Vampires have found a way to avoid the Infernos?"

His friend snorted.

"I would say upset, but he is looking for a way around your ability to move forward without Limbo, and the Infernos, or the help of Angels," Celeste said honestly. She leaned forward. "Would you mind sharing that with me? What exactly happens to the souls of a Vampire when they are—?"

Aiden threw his head back and laughed. "When we are no longer dead or the living dead? Yes, but I would have to kill you afterward."

"You aren't attached to that soul of yours are you?" Celeste said knowing if she was harmed by Aiden Dante would bring all the levels of the Infernos down on the entire race of Vampires.

"Were you headed out, after she kicked your ass?" Aiden asked casually.

"She wasn't—" Marcus swore, but decided it really just wasn't worth it. "Yes."

"We should talk first," Aiden said, looking back at the house. "But I do not believe the Tracker would allow me entrance."

Marcus swore and motioned everyone toward the house. "Tell Ash she can come out of hiding."

Aiden chuckled and made a slight move with his head. A beautiful blonde stepped out of the shadows. She was loaded down in leather and weapons.

She smiled at Stephan and slapped him on the back. "Thanks for taking point tonight. It looked like it hurt like hell."

"Shut up, Ash," Stephan said.

Marcus led them to the kitchen entrance and threw the door open. Cameron, Ryder and Kyra still sat at the table, but they all came to their feet when Celeste and Marcus re-entered.

Celeste turned to Aiden who stood in the doorway, a grim look on his face, he eyed Ryder. Ryder snorted. "Knew you couldn't stay away."

"Contrary to your belief the world does not revolve around you, Tracker I am here for something that eclipses even you."

Ryder sighed heavily and Kyra elbowed him in the stomach with a glare. Ryder closed his eyes and then took a deep breath. When he opened them he moved around Kyra and stepped up to the door, everyone was surprised by what Ryder did next.

"Aiden, King of the Vampires, I apologize for insulting you. Would you please come in and let the hospitality of my home show you we can be allies."

"Damn, I didn't know he knew such eloquent words," Cameron muttered.

Kyra hit him with a napkin.

"I would be honored," Aiden said, stepping over the threshold and taking Ryder by the hand they shook on it.

"I still want to know what happened," Celeste threw out to the group at large.

"Again, my sweet little Demon, a story for another time." Aiden nodded to her as he walked past her.

"Stop calling her those little pet names," Marcus said.

Aiden turned to him. "And just why would I do that? Because you said so? When the lady asks me to stop, I shall. But until that happens, I shall call and do whatever I like with her."

Marcus lunged at the Vampire who didn't even flinch. Ryder stepped in between them. "Geez, man, take it down a notch."

Marcus realized what he was doing and stepped back, he took several deep breaths, then moved into the dining room where they could all sit around the table. He felt like his head was going to explode. Things with Celeste we getting out of control, and he knew he had to do something before he made a complete fool of himself.

Kyra rung her hands. "Um, I feel like I should offer you something."

"My colleagues and I are fine, Element. Please sit."

Kyra pulled up a chair and sat next to Ryder, who wrapped an arm around her and pulled her close.

"So what's your news?" Marcus asked.

"Sarafina left the city early this evening. She didn't take any of her people save her brother. The Demons she had collected are going to go into the city and party," Aiden said the last with a small laugh. "Which means they shall attempt to feast on whatever they get their hands on. They are not a well-controlled race. Present company excluded, of course." Aiden smiled at Celeste who nodded back at him.

"Okay so Demons attacking New Orleans," Cameron said as if he were taking notes. "Next good news?"

"Sarafina left because something more powerful and deadly arrived." A sick feeling grew in the pit of Celeste's stomach.

"And that would be?"

"My spies say it was a large black winged man."

"But if you are in town why would he seek out Sarafina? And not go right for the heart of the Vampires?" Ryder asked.

"If he was feeling out the power in the city, there are several other creatures that would rate higher in the hierarchy than Sarafina," Cameron added.

"That is a fine question and one we don't have the answer to," Aiden supplied. "My only conclusion would be he was either letting her know of his presences, and she bolted or he was sending her a message she should take back to Lordus."

"He couldn't possibly want to join forces with Lordus. That would be insane," Ash said from her position standing to the right of Aiden.

"Either that or Lordus has something that he needs," Aiden said. "I would tend to believe that before anything else. Calliope, from what I understand, is not a creature that works with others. But he has gotten the Demons riled up." Aiden turned to look at Celeste. "I think that has something to do with you."

Celeste shrugged. "I might have pissed him off just a little the last time we had a run in."

Marcus checked his watch. "What time are the Demons heading into the city?"

"Midnight, of course. They are Demons after all, and imagination is not one of their strong points," Aiden said.

"It doesn't make any sense." Kyra finally spoke up. "Why would he come in and make his presence so obvious? Why would he incite Demons to attack mortals? It will only bring the Tribunal down on them. It actually sounds like a trap or a diversionary attempt. He wants something else."

Ryder smiled and kissed his mate. "And that is one of the reason's I love you."

"He knows we won't stand back and let the uncontrolled Demons rampage through the city," Cameron said. "Makes sense. While we are fighting off the Demon hoard, he is going to find the marked and kill them and get back into the Infernos."

"I have enough men in the city to stop the Demons," Aiden said. "But the marked, those will have to be dwelt with by you five, have you identified them?"

"Not really," Celeste said honestly.

"You have been here two days? What exactly have you been doing, site seeing?" Ash asked.

Celeste turned to the woman. Her short white hair was spiked out in several directions. "Okay, you, I don't like and can kiss my Demon ass."

"Sweetheart," Ash said, leaning in so they were nose to nose. "It would take a great deal more than you to stop me."

Celeste pushed herself to her feet. "Sweetheart," she said, using the same amount of sarcasm as Ash had, "you have no idea what the fuck you're dealing with. You might want to step back and let the adults talk."

"Girl fight," Cameron announced just as Ash threw a punch Celeste easily caught just inches from her face. Ash swung with her other fist and Celeste pulled away so it didn't make contact with her face, but just barely.

She was sure Ash didn't even see Celeste's move as a palm connected with her face. Everyone in the room cringed when they heard bones break and Ash flew across the room, caving in part of the wall.

"Geez, Aiden, you're the freaking King of the Vampires, and I've knocked out both of your bodyguards, explain to me how you're going to take out the Demons tonight," Celeste said in disgust.

Aiden stood. "Celeste, I promise you not all Demons fight quite as well as you. As for my bodyguards, as a personal favor, please don't knock them around like rag dolls. They pout for weeks."

"I don't pout," Stephan said.

"Pick her up. We have a job to do," Aiden said to Stephen.

"How do we get into contact with you?" Marcus asked.

Aiden nodded to Celeste and winked at her. "My little Demon has my personal cell number."

Chapter 8

"The city is beautiful from here," Celeste said, trying to break the stony silence that had been forced on her by Marcus who refused to speak to her. He hadn't said a word directly to her since the Vampires left, and they loaded up. They quartered off the city with Cameron, Ryder and Kyra.

She stood on the top of an old church. Crouched on the tallest spiral where she held on with her fingertips. Her body swung out above the church, and the four-story fall to the ground.

"This city has so much character. I think if I were to choose a place to live in the mortal world, I would choose New Orleans."

Marcus snorted.

"Oh, you don't agree?" she asked him, not really expecting an answer, and when none came, she continued. "You might be right, this is beautiful. But someplace open, where I could see the sunrise every single morning." She closed her eyes and leaned her head back. "Bask in the glory of that beautiful miracle every day without any buildings or anything else short of a tree to block my view. Or a high-rise in New York or London above all the mortal bullshit."

"Ivory towers are for fairy tales, Celeste," Marcus muttered.

Celeste turned toward him. She couldn't see him, but she knew exactly where he stood. With his arms crossed over his chest, he stood like one of the gargoyles watching over the city like the Fallen Angel he was. Beautiful, majestic and powerful. She wanted to leap down and grasp him in her arms hold him close, feel his power and strength, pretend he loved her as much as she loved him. She wanted him to know all the times she had cared for him while in the Infernos. She sighed and looked back over the city. They were fairy tales.

"Can't we have just a little fairy tale, with a happy ending? Is that too much to ask?" she said it knowing how wistful her voice sounded. It was something she would never dare say to her brothers or her father. They dealt in death; they didn't do happily ever after. But her mother had told her they existed, and she hoped that her daughter found hers one day.

"Yes," Marcus sighed heavily.

That pretty much summed it up for her, and she pursued her lips together. She had fantasized about this man for two centuries, and the reality was a disappointment, but really, what did she expect? To spend five minutes in his presence, and he would drop to his knees and promise his life and love to her for all of eternity?

A tear slipped from her eye, and she whipped it away. She needed to grow up. Marcus was right. There was no place in their life for a fairy tale ending.

She turned to face the city, blocking out the blinking lights and the beauty for something other than the red, orange and dusty light of the Infernos where time passed in the blink of a mortal eye.

****

Marcus couldn't keep his eyes off her. She crouched at the top of the spiral like an avenging Angel a long coat covered the dark red leather she had changed into. Her long braid hung down behind her blood red in the dark. She was the most deadly female he had ever come across and wasn't afraid to show it. Was unrepentant for the strength she possessed and wasn't afraid to use.

She had shown more gumption and strength in the last five days than he had seen in men over centuries. But there was a part of her that was a little girl desperate for a fairy tale, and her obsession with the sunrise was driving him crazy. He wanted to be there with her when she saw it, wanted to bask in her light when the sun rose because she thought it was the most beautiful thing in the world, and it brought so much joy to her it lightened his soul. Celeste would never give half. She would give all she had or she would die trying.

He shook himself and focused on the city. They were waiting. No fighting had broken out, but they were prepared for anything.

His eyes inevitably drifted back to her. He thought about the slop of her back and the curve of her neck; her smell, gods what he wouldn't do to pull her in and have it all. The smells, the tastes. The feel of her soft skin against his. The sound it would make when he pulled off the leather pants she wore. The gritty sound of the zipper as it slid down giving way to the creamy flesh beneath. He had no doubt in his mind that she would be a vocal lover. How could she be anything but vocal? He could almost feel the soft flesh beneath his hands, the look on her face as he kissed her. The way her voluptuous breasts would fill his hands. The sounds she would make when he made her cry out with the pleasure he would shower her with. She would need no other man ever again.

Damn, where the hell had that thought come from? He couldn't make her his, could he? The thought made his already hard cock jump in anticipation. To be linked forever to this woman. A man could ask for nothing more, and he would count himself a lucky bastard if after everything they had gone through, said to each other in anger over the last couple of days, if she would even consider being with him. But first he needed to traverse the chasm of anger between them.

If he hadn't been so hyper focused on her, he would have missed the slight stiffening of her spine. "What?" he whispered.

She nodded to something in the distance. Marcus moved so he could see what she was motioning to. A large, dark bird flew in the distance over the waters of the Gulf of Mexico, but as it dipped and swayed, Marcus realized that it wasn't any bird. Cold terror seized him, dread coiling in the pit of his stomach.

"Why is he flying so erratically?" he whispered to Celeste.

She shook her head. "I don't know. Could he still be injured from fighting us in Australia?"

"It's possible, but I doubt it." Marcus watched as Calliope dipped and circled and then eerily turned toward them and moved with the speed of the wind.

"Celeste," he urged.

She didn't answer at first. "What is he doing?"

She stood, placing herself in danger of falling the several hundred feet to the ground.

"Celeste, get down. Now," Marcus shouted. "It's a trap; a trap to catch you, not the Touched."

Celeste turned to him. "What are you talking about?" And then everything went very quiet.

He started to climb the spire, scrambling to get to Celeste as screams started to echo up from the city below.

"Celeste, get down." Marcus slipped but continued to climb several of the tiles digging into his palms making him bleed.

"Marcus, stop. I'm coming down." He turned toward Calliope, but it was too late. The Reaper was too close.

"Celeste!" He screamed for her as Calliope swooped down, slamming something against her head. She collapsed, and Calliope grabbed ahold of her around the waist and flew away. Celeste jolted as he grabbed her and screamed for Marcus.

Marcus hung onto the roof and watched, horrified, as Calliope carried her off. It had happened so fast, but the scream Celeste had made would haunt him forever.

****

She felt like hell, and she knew exactly what that felt like. Rolling over, she starred at the cement ceiling above her head and tried to remember exactly where she was.

"Ah sister, so glad to see your beautiful violet eyes." Celeste jerked into a sitting position making her so dizzy she almost emptied her stomach. Calliope sat leaned against the opposite wall. His knees were drawn up, hands resting on them. He looked as if he had all the time in the world.

Celeste back peddled until her back came up against a wall. Putting the distance of the room between them. "What are you doing?"

"I'm trying to go home." His wings contracted, bringing him off the floor as he swung away from her. One long fingernail carved a rounded doorway into the cement wall. "Let me back into the Infernos, Celeste."

"No," Celeste said with conviction glad her voice didn't betray the terror she was feeling.

He moved so fast one blink had them nose to nose. "You don't quite get it, sister. I am not really asking. I allowed the Reapers to throw me from the Infernos; I needed souls. But Dante has learned from past mistakes. I did not know he had the ability to lock the portals. He can't stop you or the others from opening them or Flashing in. You are my key. I don't need a mortal and Demon army, I just need to get back into the Infernos, and the chaos will put me exactly where I should have been all this time. I will rule the Infernos the way there were meant to be ruled."

"You know what? I think the Infernos are being ruled just fine."

He flew back as if she had swung at him. "You would say that, but I think I can change your mind. You might have been able to hide my Dagger from me, but it's just a matter of time before even that is back where it belongs." He was mad, that was the only answer, stark raving mad.

Celeste wasn't prepared when he reached forward and grabbed her ankle. She kicked out and fought against him with everything she had, but he was stronger than she. Celeste screamed for Victor, for Christian. Her pleading only made Calliope laugh. She panicked and clawed at the cement and rock floor. He dragged her through rooms and corridors until her hands bled.

"They can't hear you here." He laughed as she screamed for her brothers. Celeste looked around and saw only cement and darkness. "And no one will look for you, because sweet sister you don't exist in this plane or any plane for that matter. In fact you were a complete surprise to even me. Who would have thought Dante would dip and slum with a Demon whore?" His words cut deeply, and she swung her free leg catching him in the chest he fell back but didn't release her ankle and twisted it at an odd angle as he went down, she heard the bone break before her brain recognized the pain, and she screamed out.

"Fuck you," she cried out.

He clamored up her body, pressing her into the cold floor so that his cheek pressed against her. Wild black eyes starred at her from the corners, and tears rushed down her face. "Tears of blood, how endearing. But not enough to sway me."

He grabbed her by the throat, lifting them both off the floor, he slammed her against the wall making her head swim. By the time he released her, she was chained, her arms holding her body mere inches off the floor. She jerked on her restraints, feeling like one of her shoulders would dislocate any second.

"I will never open the door for you," she finally grasped out. "Yes, you'd rather die first," Calliope said, sounding bored.

Celeste's stomach curled, and bile rose in the back of her throat when Calliope faced her. His dark, fathomless eyes looked through her, making him look as evil as Celeste knew he was. "But you don't die do you?" He laughed and then backhanded her. Her head whipped to the side, and one of her teeth flew out. Damn, he hit harder than any of her brothers, in fact she had never been hit so hard in her life, and her head swam with stars. "Fortunately for me you can't die," he cackled. "It's just a matter of what you can withstand before you do exactly as I ask."

Celeste spit blood out, she was terrified for the first time in her life she was scared, and tears streaked down her face from the pain. "We're going to be here a while, because nothing you do will make me give you access to kill more of my brothers."

"Ahhh but we disagree on that. I thought the same thing when first placed in the box." He leaned in and licked one of the bloody tears that streaked down her face. "But eventually you will break, and I don't need to get into the Infernos today Celeste, not even this century. But I will get there, and you will be the one to open the door for me."

He stepped back. "How long before the lust drives you insane? Makes you do and say things you would never do in your right mind."

"I'm going to kill you," Celeste promised. "I will be the Reaper that sends your soul into the pits of Hell its self, those years spent in that box will look like Heaven when Lucifer is done with you."

Calliope actually threw his head back and laughed. The sound buzzed across her skin, making her feel as if she had been staked out on a fire ant hill. Celeste glared at him knowing she might be eating those words before this was all said and done.

****

"What do you mean you can't feel her?" Marcus stormed at Victor picking him up and slamming him against the wall.

"The moment I lost contact with her I immediately came from the Infernos," Victor snarled. "Explain to me why she is no longer with you?"

Christian and Garrett both grabbed Marcus by the arms but he wasn't about to let the Reaper go. "You sent your sister here to die?" he accused.

"It was never my idea to send her here, allow her to be put in any type of danger. We entrusted her with the only species on this plane we thought could protect her," Victor snarled. "And she was plucked off the top of a church like a sacrificial lamb. While you just stood there. Who is guilty here?"

Marcus threw an elbow into Christian's face and a fist into Victor's.

Garrett slammed a fist into his ribs making him double over. He fell to his knees, but he was far from done. He slammed a fist into the bundle of nerves in Garrett's thigh, and the Reaper hit the floor howling in pain. Lunging to his feet he barreled into Christian planting his shoulder into the Reapers stomach he nailed him into a bookshelf.

Victor swore and pulled him off Christian throwing a punch into Marcus' face that actually picked him off his feet and sent him backwards. When he hit the floor all the air was pushed from his lungs.

"Dammit." Cameron swore from somewhere to his left, and then he was in the fight as well.

Within seconds everyone in the room was fighting including Kyra who was just protecting her mates back because not even a Reaper would strike a woman especially a woman mated to a Tracker.

It was Aiden who actually stopped the fight when he entered and threw a severed head into the fray.

Everyone scrambled back. "Freak'n hell." Cameron kicked the head away.

"What the fuck is that?" Marcus snarled.

Aiden smiled; flanked by Stephan and Ash he placed his hands on his hips. "That would be a Demon, the last one that was attacking in the city. I did my job, and now we will need to get Celeste back."

"And exactly what does the head have to do with it?" Kyra asked, she looked slightly queasy.

"Two points," Aiden started. "First, it stopped the fight. Second it had some interesting information for me before I ripped it from its body."

"And what exactly does that have to do with my sister?" Victor snarled. "And why the hell are you all working with Vampires? That wasn't part of the deal."

"The deal was to retrieve the Touched and kill Calliope. If we call in help from our allies to get it done what does it matter?" Marcus snapped spitting out blood.

"We don't work with Vampires." Christian glared at the trio standing in the doorway.

"Then go back to the Infernos because we do," Ryder threw in.

Victor glowered. "What information do you have?" Marcus asked Aiden.

Aiden glared back. "I am doing this for Celeste, and not for you or your brothers, understand that now. I will not bow to you or your father."

Victor stepped forward so he was nose to nose with Aiden. "Get anywhere near my sister, and I will happily wipe your ass from this world."

"You and what army?" Aiden taunted.

"Just give us your damn information and get out," Victor demanded.

Aiden gave him a deadly smile. "I will not be locked out of the search and rescue. You may not approve of me and mine but Celeste has become a friend, and I will not stand by and let that Reaper spawn hurt her."

Marcus was so shocked he couldn't speak for a moment. Despite the jealousy he felt it was obvious the King of Vampires had bonded with Celeste, and they all wanted the same thing.

"We all want her safe return," Marcus said. "We will work together for that outcome."

"Calliope is a Reaper and knows how to block against Reaper senses. Celeste is half Reaper and half Demon, if you were to get another Demon preferable one related in some way to Celeste that Demon would be able to sense her," Aiden said, obviously willing to work with them to get Celeste back regardless of what Victor and the other Reapers said or did.

Victor started to swear up a storm. "Dammit why didn't I think of that? But the female Sex Demons were banned to the level of Lust centuries ago."

"Her mother," Marcus said. "She said her mother was in Lust."

Victor looked at him like he had lost his mind. "Do you have any idea how many Sex Demons are in Lust?"

Marcus shook his head. "How many could there be?"

Christian snorted. "You have no idea."

"Dante can pull her," Victor announced.

"But will he?" Christian asked.

"Why the hell wouldn't he? It's to get Celeste back." Marcus couldn't even understand why they were discussing this.

Victor turned to Christian. "You and Garrett stay here and start searching. Marcus and I will speak with Dante."

"Why do I need to go? I am staying here to search for her," Marcus stormed.

"Because Dante entrusted her to you." Marcus's back twitched at the thought he had failed and was going to have to pay in a pound of flesh again.

"Ready?" Victor asked.

"You'll take care of things here?" Marcus turned to Ryder and Cameron.

"Of course," Ryder promised.

"We will find her Marcus," Kyra promised.

He nodded and turned back to Victor. "I'm ready." As the Reaper reached forward Marcus remembered what Celeste had told him, and he sucked in a deep breath. As the Flash started, he exhaled.

He landed on his knees again, but this time at the foot of Dante's dais. It hadn't hurt as bad but dammit all to hell it didn't feel good either.

Bare feet appeared in his site as one swung back and slammed into his face. Marcus flew back and landed on his back several feet away.

"Where is my daughter?" Dante stormed advancing on Marcus.

Marcus held up his hands. "We are working on getting her back."

"*Working on* and *doing* are two separate things, Fallen." Dante wasn't a large man but he didn't need to be. He held more strength and power than any creature on this plane or any other for the matter, and Marcus was sure he could rip him limb from limb.

"Dante, the King of the Vampires had information." Dante swung from Marcus at Victor's words.

"Now you're working with the undead?" he bellowed making the rafters above shake and dust floated down.

"Not I, Father. Marcus and the Trackers."

Marcus had to give it to Victor swinging the punishment back toward Marcus.

Dante swung back. "And what untrustworthy information did he have?"

"We need Celeste's mother," Marcus said pushing himself to his feet.

Dante's expression didn't change but a muscle ticked in his temple. "Calliope can protect against Reapers, he can't protect against a blood related Demon. We need her mother."

Dante stood looking at Marcus for several minutes and then turned and walked over to one of the large columns it was made of marble, and Dante slammed his fist into it. Shattering it, pieces fell, and the ceiling started to collapse. Victor swore and scrambled to Marcus grabbing him they Flashed out.

When they reappeared they were in the courtyard at the bottom of the hill that led up to the Fortress.

"Never actually seen him that angry before." Victor and Marcus watched as part of the Fortress above collapsed.

"Is he going to help us?" Marcus asked. Victor shrugged.

"Not good enough," Marcus said and started up the path toward the Fortress.

"Why do you care so much?" Victor asked falling into step with him. "She is our sister, our responsibility."

Marcus stopped and turned to Victor. "I have no idea, but she is my partner, and I will not let Calliope win by taking her. And every second we spend here is an hour there. She can't die Victor."

Victor blanched.

"How much torture do you think she can stand before she breaks?" Marcus asked. "Do you want to see her broken?"

Marcus asked the question only to realize he didn't want to see that, he would give a pound of flesh and then some to not see the bright spirit that was Celeste be extinguished. They fought like hell, but he didn't want that.

"Interesting," Victor said as he started walking back up the incline. "Marcus, did you know she cared for you?"

Marcus was so stunned he didn't move for a moment and then had to run to catch up with Victor. "What are you talking about she hates me."

Victor shook his head. "Not in that sense, every time you gave your pound of flesh she cared for you."

"How long?" Marcus asked.

"Couple of hundred years, she said it was the least she could do. You were a warrior and deserved to be cared for by a warrior," Victor said it offhandedly. "Personally I think she just liked being with a man that wasn't one of her brothers."

Marcus didn't have anything to say to that. He didn't remember much from his times of being whipped. But he knew he was cared for, that someone sat with him until he slept without pain. He had imagined that person as Jessica. And now to know it had been Celeste made him rethink who the woman was and explained why sometimes when he looked at her something in his mind clicked.

"But she hates me," Marcus repeated.

"Yeah well, she didn't like to see you suffer." Victor shrugged. "It was the good in her, I don't have that weakness," he announced proudly.

They both stopped as the mountain rumbled. "Damn he is pissed." Victor looked up and then turned around.

"Where the hell are you going?" Marcus snarled.

"You know what?" Victor said over his shoulder. "I would rather search through the Sex Demons myself than deal with him when he is that mad."

Marcus looked from Victor to the Fortress and then followed Victor.

As they swung through the large gates Dante appeared with a woman clinging to his arm. The woman had short red hair that spiked out in several different directions and looked so much like Celeste that Marcus took a step forward before he realized her eyes were different, they were a dark purple almost black, and her skin had an orange hue to it. Fingernails like talons scrapped across Dante's chest.

"Get me my daughter back or I will have your soul on a spit over the River Sticks." He thrust the woman at Victor. "She is your responsibility," he said as Victor took the woman by the arm, and then he was gone.

She looked at Victor and then at Marcus. "I want neither of you. I want Dante, take me back to him."

"As soon as we find Celeste," Victor lied.

The woman swung on Victor, her eyes brightening, "I can see Celeste? My Angel?"

"Yes," Marcus said this time.

"I don't want to speak with you," she said over her shoulder. "How is she? I've missed her so."

"She has been kidnapped, and we need you to locate her." The woman screeched and clawed at Victor.

Victor tried to push her away. "No, please god's no. Not my Angel," she wailed."

Victor shoved her away as blood started to trickle from the wounds on his chest. "This is going to be a lot of fun," he said to Marcus grabbing him by the shirt front and the woman by the arm.

They were back in the dining room; Kyra was pacing in the corner, and the sun shone down through the window.

"How long have we been gone?" Marcus asked.

"About twelve hours," Kyra said. "They haven't found anything, not even a trace."

"Where is my daughter?" The woman screeched.

Kyra took a step back. "You are Celeste's mother?"

"Yes." She looked around the room in horror. "I feel her but she is in pain, where is she?"

"What's your name?" Kyra asked.

The woman snarled at Kyra. "If you must know, it is Lexi, now get away from me."

Lexi turned and left the room. "Pleasant woman," Kyra said.

"She is insane," Victor explained. "She fell in love with Dante, and Dante didn't not return her affection. It made her mad."

The woman screamed from somewhere in the house, and everyone ran, she stood in the foyer holding her stomach. "She is in pain, why is she in so much pain?"

Lexi clung to Victor. "Get the car."

****

Celeste spit blood out, she was bleeding somewhere internally, and a rib had punctured a lung making it difficult to breathe, and she kept spitting out blood. But she took some joy in the fact Calliope was getting frustrated.

"Bring it on you son of a bitch," she taunted. All she was really hoping for at the moment was that he would knock her out so she could at least take some comfort in oblivion.

Calliope had turned from her but swung back, the tip of one wing slashing just below her collar bone and across her chest, the talon sunk deep scraping across her breast bone, Celeste screamed out in uncontrollable pain.

She was seeing stars at this point and hoped from either blood loss or a hit she would pass out already. Calliope might be getting frustrated but even she was surprised at what she had been able to stay conscious through.

"Don't you want it to stop?" Calliope said calmly. He switched moods so quickly one second he was furious and pummeling at her like she was a punching bag, and the next he was stroking her cheek and whispering he wanted to stop the pain.

"That would be nice," Celeste said between swollen lips and gurgling gasps of air.

"All you have to do is open a portal," he said calmly.

"What part of 'Dante has locked all the portals' don't you understand?" he side kicked her in the stomach, throwing her back against the cement wall behind her. She couldn't breathe, and she was sure this was the point where she would surely pass out but then she sucked in a breath, pain radiating throughout her entire body. "I couldn't open one if I wanted to. Does that make enough sense to you? Or had being locked in the box make your brain so messed simple explanations like it's out of my control our beyond you?" Her head fell forward she was just too tired to even hold it up for the moment.

"Celeste," he said she lifted her head and looked at him. She had decided he slightly resembled Dante, had some of his features the shallow face, and the shape of his eyes and mouth. It hurt her to look at him and see her father in his face.

"I know you can get into the Infernos, I know you Flash in and out. I feel it whenever any of you Flashes. I feel the small flicker it shivers through me letting me know that the Infernos are close. You can take me there; know more mortals need to be harmed. No more souls need to be collected."

Celeste laughed but her voice was dry as paper. "Until you reach the Infernos. Then the souls will feel the levels to bursting."

"Sacrifices will have to be made Celeste, do you want to go down in the notes of history as a casualty of the war or sit on my right side as the Queen of the Infernos and of Hell?" he asked caressing her cheek.

Celeste laughed again. "So now it's the Infernos and Hell? Good luck with that one. You do not cross Lucifer."

It was Calliope's turn to laugh. "I fear nothing." He threw his head back and screamed making the walls shake. He pounded on his chest. "I am one of the first, and the last survivor of the Original Reapers, and we were feared and worshiped."

"I feel sorry for you," Celeste said honestly. Calliope whipped around, a winged tipped talon slicing across the soft part of her underarm. She sucked in a breath. "You could have been all of those things, and could have had all of that if you had just followed some simple rules."

"And exactly what were those?" he asked quietly leaning in he rubbed his cheek against her softness.

Celeste pulled away. "If you had just shut up and listened instead of taking the power you were given by a man greater than you. Because no matter how strong you get Calliope, no matter what delusions you have that tell you you will eclipse the power of the one that created you? You never will, that's the thing about creation. You were created by something bigger, something more powerful, and in the end your self-importance and believing you have overcome your creator that is what will destroy you."

Calliope growled and slammed a fist into her stomach, she bounced against the stone wall behind.

"Don't you ever ask yourself why?" she asked when she had her breath back.

"What?"

"Why he locked you and your brothers away?" she spat more blood out.

"Because he was jealous," Calliope said with lofty regard. "He couldn't stand the way the mortals quaked at the thought of the Reapers, his creations becoming more powerful than the creator."

"Dante is many things Calliope, but jealous of the power of his sons is not one of them."

Calliope made a mulling noise before leaning in and rubbing his cheek against hers again. "You know so little? You the protocol child, a girl, in the army of male offspring. Do you really know what your father is capable of?"

Celeste shook her head. "I know him a great deal better than you, I would think."

"Really?" Calliope leaned back and stabbed her with his black eyes. "I am one of his creations, one of his sons. And he locked me away in a box and threw me away in a cave."

Celeste swallowed past the pain that choked her. "He would never do something like that now. The Reapers now have a strain of light."

Calliope threw his head back and laughed. "Ah yes, the light of love and kindness," he spat. "Lying with Angels, the very thought is sickening. It's a weakness, and you're a stupid child to think otherwise."

She hurt too much, and she just wanted it to be over for a few minutes. "You know what I think, Calliope?"

His eyes narrowed at her question, and he grabbed her by the chin squeezing until she was sure he was going to break her jaw.

"I think you are the one that is jealous. You are the one that covets what Dante has and what he is." She held her head up proudly. "I think you know deep down in your heart that you will never be as powerful as Dante, and that is killing you inside."

As she spoke she felt him tense, felt him start to shake in rage, and by the time she was done he was focused with his black eyes on her. Calliope swung a wing around slicing her throat open. For just a moment she thought for sure it was over. She was beheaded, there was nothing left to say or do. But then the pain radiated in her brain, and the spray of blood covered the walls she realized he hadn't severed her head from her own shoulders but she was surely going to die. Not in a totally dead kind of way, she would eventually heal but for the moment Calliope had won.

Celeste felt her head fall to the side; she tried to turn and look at him. To laugh but when she opened her mouth only blood poured from it, when she tried to move nothing happened.

"Maybe when you heal from your wounds you'll have a better attitude," Calliope said walking through a door she actually hadn't noticed before.

She was suddenly swamped with exhaustion, and she closed her eyes. Blackness coming and going, she wasn't sure for how long, she knew nothing but pain. She thought of her brothers, of Dante, of her mother and wished that she had said goodbye to them. She wished that she had told the jackass Fallen that she had fallen in love with him two hundred years ago, if anything just to see the look of horror in his eyes. If she had been capable of it she would have laughed. She released everything and sagged down, the chains digging into her wrists, and her shoulder popped out of its socket.

Celeste knew she would wake up healed but it would be days. And then it would start all over again, but she also promised herself as blackness swamped her that one day she would get away, and when she did, she would hunt Calliope down, sever his head, and feed him to the lava pits of hell with a smile on her face.

She closed her eyes and smiled, keeping the image of Marcus in her mind's eye she let go of everything.

****

"She's dying," Lexi screamed as they drove through the city. The closer they got the more pain the woman sensed. "Can't this contraption go any faster?"

Marcus had the pedal all the way to the floor had barely avoided several accidents and was completely surprised the police hadn't stopped him yet.

"STOP," Lexi screamed.

Marcus slammed on the breaks, everyone in the car braced themselves. They were in an old part of the city, monolithic buildings raised to the sky. They had been driving through the streets the majority of the night, and now the sun was about to rise, and Marcus would be damned if Celeste was going to miss it.

Everyone exited from the vehicles, Lexi ran toward a building the bricks were crumbling she scrambled over the falling rocks and disappeared into the darkness.

"I wouldn't follow that woman through a fully lit park of children and I'm about to follow her into a dark abandoned building. This world has totally gone to hell," Cameron said pulling out his guns he checked them and was the first to climb in through the rubble.

Victor and then Marcus, Christian and Garrett followed behind.

****

She heard the gun fire, but for a moment thought maybe it was her imagination. Either that or Calliope had decided to shoot her. But she didn't feel any more pain. So it had to be her imagination. Or a memory, just a memory. Celeste tried to hold onto it, even that was too much and blackness swamped up to take her before she was able to make sense of what was happening.

When the door flew open and her mother flew into the room, letting out hysterical screams as gun fire followed her. Lexi was bleeding but it didn't seem to slow her down it still didn't seem real. If she could have she would have smiled, her mother, and not even gun fire would stop her from what she wanted. Except for the gates of Lust, she couldn't get past those, but that was because of Dante.

Celeste tried to say something but her voice still didn't work.

"Don't let him out of the building," Victor screamed amid more gun fire.

Then everything was silent except for her mother, who screeched like a banshee clawing at the restraints that held Celeste to the wall. Celeste wanted to beg her to stop she was doing more damage than good at the moment. Scratching at Celeste's arms as she tried to free her daughter.

Marcus came into the room next and stopped dead. "For the love of all the gods." He rushed forward lifting her head he looked into her eyes.

"Please don't be dead." He kissed her forehead. "Don't die, we still have more fights to have." She would have laughed would have explained she wanted to fight with him as well but between him moving her, and her mother scratching at her she just couldn't take anymore and let the blackness swallow her. Her last thought was hope that this wasn't some kind of dream but they really had come for her she really was being rescued. Calliope wouldn't torture her anymore.

****

When he had entered he thought for sure she was dead her neck was sliced open, and blood poured from the wound. She was broken and bleeding in so many places he didn't even bother to try to count them. He held her head in place, as he reached up and pulled the chains directly from the wall.

Lexi cried screaming for Victor. "Give her to her brother."

Victor took one look at Celeste and started to swear. He offered his arms out.

Marcus didn't want to let her go. "I'll carry her to the car."

"No," Lexi screeched. "He has the power to heal her."

Reluctantly Marcus placed her into Victor's arms who hugged Celeste close whispering into her ear. They shown like a black light making the blood she was covered in shine eerily. And then she gasped for air, only to let out a scream of pain.

Victor stumbled back as she twisted and screamed in pain. Marcus watched in amazement as her broken bones moved back into place, and her neck wound started to stitch itself back together. Christian wrapped his arms around his brother, Garrett and Marcus doing the same. The three men held Victor on his feet while Celeste screamed in horror and pain begging them to make it stop.

"Just a few more minutes." Victor crooned softly. Lexi flapped her arms screaming and pacing around the men.

And then Celeste was silent, Victor handed her back to Marcus as he fell to the ground exhausted.

"Can you Flash us back to the house?" he asked Christian.

"Yes, with Garrett's help." Everyone grabbed onto either Christian or Garrett, and then they were standing in the dining room.

Marcus stumbled almost falling to his feet but he would be damned straight to hell if he was going to allow Celeste to receive any more injuries due to him. He forced himself to walk up the stairs and into her room. Her mother hovering over his shoulder the entire time.

"We need to bath her. Victor wasn't able to heal all her wounds but he corrected the most grievous of them." She ran into the bathroom and started the tub.

Marcus started to pull the remains of her tattered clothing from her body. Victor might have healed her wounds so they didn't kill her but she still had several open wounds one that stretched across her chest, another he suspected had severed the muscles and tendons under one arm. There wasn't a part of her that wasn't bruised. That bastard had her less than twenty four hours, and by the looks of it had used every single minute of that time to torture Celeste.

Lexi came back into the room and clucked over her daughter as she helped Marcus remove the rest of her clothing. "If you will please place her in the tub I will wash her, and then we can move her to the bed."

Marcus steeled himself against the naked woman pressed against his body and did as Lexi instructed.

"Wait." Lexi stopped before he placed her in the water. She took the time to unbraid Celeste's hair.

"Did you know her name means heaven sent?" Lexi asked as she unwound Celeste's long hair. "She was a gift from heaven, Dante didn't believe it. But she could be nothing else but sent from heaven." Tears flowed down the woman's face, the insanity he had seen in her in the last hours completely gone as she worked over her daughter. "She is my Angel."

Lexi cupped Celeste's face. "Okay put her in the tub."

The tub was so large it looked like three people could sit in it comfortable. And the minute she was laid into the bath the water turned pink and then brown with blood. It made him sick.

"I will take care of her from here. If you wouldn't mind waiting outside I'll call you when she is ready." Marcus nodded and headed for the door turning he looked back. Her eyes hadn't opened once since they had found her, and Marcus had never felt as helpless as he did right at that moment.

So he went for a drink, Victor was sitting in the library with only the fire burning. When Marcus reached for the light switch, Victor stopped him.

"Please my head is banging so hard, the light hurts." Marcus acquiesced and came into the room pouring himself a large glass of whiskey. He wasn't a big drinker, had seen and done things he wasn't proud of but what he had seen tonight was something he would never be able to erase from his mind or heart.

"How is she?" Victor asked quietly.

"Lexi is taking care of her, she hasn't woken up yet. Where is everyone?"

"Garrett and Christian have returned to the Infernos to report to Dante. I have no idea where anyone else is." Victor's words were quiet and subdued.

"Why have I never known of your ability to heal?" Marcus asked trying to feel in the silence.

"Why would you have, like I explained in the hole in the ground the monster had my sister. It is a gift I can use only with my siblings." Victor had leaned his head back against the chair his eyes closed.

"And what does it cost you to use this gift?"

Victor opened his eyes, the iris of both were filled with blood. "I feel every wound, Marcus. She may be immortal, but you and I know that is relative. She was closer to death than I would have ever wanted her to be."

"Calliope needs to die," Marcus said throwing back the rest of the whiskey he stood and filled his glass again.

"Yes well many things in the infernos should not be and are, but I would have to agree with you on that matter. I will speak with Dante when I return." Again he leaned his head back and closed his eyes.

"Would you like a room, there are plenty?" Marcus asked, Victor must be exhausted.

He didn't open his eyes as he spoke. "Will a bed erase what I felt my sister go through? Will it make that memory disappear?"

"No," Marcus said quietly wishing he could take some of that pain.

Victor chuckled. "As I thought, then I shall remain here with the fire. I am cold, and it helps."

Marcus nodded and left Victor tossing the glass of whiskey back he headed back to Celeste's room. Kyra was standing outside the door her ear pressed to it.

She jumped when Marcus tapped her on the shoulder. She swung around and hit him in the shoulder. "Are you trying to scare me to death?" she whispered urgently.

"Why don't you just knock?" Marcus asked.

"I want to help. But I'm not sure if she'll allow me to help," she insisted.

"She is being nosey instead of warming my bed," Ryder grumbled as he walked down the hall toward them.

"How is she?"

Marcus looked at his friends, his family and let them see the pain in his eyes. "She almost died, but I think we were in time."

"I put up Druid wards the moment I heard you all return. Calliope won't be able to get past them," Kyra said as she leaned into the listen at the door again.

"OH for the love of the gods," Ryder snapped, he reached forward and opened the door and pushed his wife inside and then shut the door.

"For a warrior class sometimes she is so timid." Ryder shook his head in irritation. "By the way you look like hell. Want to talk about it?"

"You know something brother, I feel like hell," Marcus agreed.

"That bad?"

"I can't even put into words what I saw tonight. Nor would I put that on anyone's conscious."

Ryder nodded. "I understand."

They stood outside the door in silence until Kyra cracked the door open, tears streaking down her face. "Marcus can you please come in and carry her to her bed?"

Marcus immediately pushed past Kyra, and went into the bathroom. Celeste was still naked, and he could see the wounds clearly now she was clean. There wasn't a single spot on her body that hadn't been cut beaten or bruised. Fury irrupted inside of him so strong he shook with the inadequacy he felt toward exacting revenge on Calliope.

"Hold it together," Lexi said quietly.

Marcus wrapped Celeste in a towel her hair had been pulled up on the top of her head in an ornate bun. He knew Celeste would hate and carried her to the bed. The room had filled with Victor, Cameron, Kyra, Ryder and Christian had returned.

Marcus laid her down on the bed and covered her up, He looked at all the occupants of the room they all looked like he felt, helpless and impotent, wanting desperately to fix this. Take away all her pain.

"She lost a great deal of blood, her body will of course heal but she needs to have sex as soon as possible to give her the extra strength she needs to heal completely." Lexi looked around the room.

"Fuck, don't look at me I'm her brother," Victor snapped. Christian nodded his agreement.

"I'm taken," Ryder said grabbing Kyra and pulling her close.

"I'd do it but frankly she scares me," Cameron said.

Marcus shook his head. "Everyone get the hell out of here."

"Marcus," Kyra said, startled.

"Kyra trust me," he urged.

She gave him a hard look before nodding and leaving with Ryder. Cameron with them.

Victor and Christian stood there; Marcus knew they were fighting an internal battle at the moment. Marcus pulled off his shirt.

"OH gods." Victor swore, anger lacing each syllable. "If this wasn't going to help her I would kill you right now."

He stormed from the room; Christian held back and looked at Marcus his head tilted to the side for a moment. He had never been one for conversation, and when he spoke you stopped and listened. "If you hurt my sister in any way be prepared to die." Leaving Marcus in the room with Lexi and Celeste.

"Well?" Lexi snapped.

Marcus took a deep breath. "She is going to be fine Lexi. I will take care of her from here, you must trust me."

She glared but left the room. Marcus finished undressing and climbed into the bed. He wrapped himself around Celeste her body was cold, and he rubbed her arms and legs.

"Thank you," she whispered.

Marcus's eyes snapped up to hers. "For what?"

"Getting everyone out of here, and not letting that boy Cameron have his way with me." She smiled.

"When did you wake?" he asked still rubbing warmth back into her body.

"When you wrapped me in the towel." She reached up to her head and groaned. "My hair will never dry. Can you please help me?"

She tried to lift herself up but Marcus pushed her down. "Let me." He rolled her over and pulled the many pins from her hair letting it fall like a red water fall all over her back and his chest. Wet it clung to him, he caught his breath and tried to move but couldn't. Taking a strand he rubbed it between his fingers and brought it to his nose. It smelled like lavender, and he wanted desperately to bury his face into it.

"Um would you like me to braid it?" He knew she preferred that.

She laughed but he could tell it hurt her to do so. "Can you braid hair, Fallen?"

Marcus climbed from the bed and went into the bathroom for a brush. "I have many talents that you are unaware of."

"Then I am glad you saved me so that I could learn them," she said quietly.

Marcus started at the ends which he noticed no longer had the quills her mother must have removed them. He brushed the red locks slowly moving up her back. And chastised himself, five hundred years without a woman, and this was so erotic for him he wasn't sure he was going to get her hair braided without coming and embarrassing them both.

"Why do you have such long hair?" He asked trying to fill the silence so that he didn't roll her over and have his way with her like her mother wanted.

"Mating," Celeste said, and the one world jolted through Marcus like a bullet. "My long hair indicates to other females and males that I am single. When I blood rite I will cut my hair." She said it with no emotion, and Marcus couldn't figure out why the thought of her cutting her hair upset him so much.

"But it will grow back right?"

"No. Once you cut the hair of a female Sex Demon it stops growing."

"But then after five hundred years it should be dragging behind you like Rapunzel." Marcus commented, unbraided it reached below her knees. It also explained why she had flipped out in the alley when he had threatened to cut it. He had no right to cut her hair, and for some reason that stabbed at him. What were these strange feelings he had for this woman? He hadn't known her for a week, yet he desperately wanted to break centuries old vows if only to just argue with her.

"I cut it once," Celeste said so quietly that he almost missed it.

"What?"

"I thought I had fallen in love. So I cut it to where it is today. But it didn't work out, and my hair of course stopped growing. It's best the way it is though, for fighting," she explained.

Marcus gripped the brush so tight he snapped the handle off. "You were in love once?" he asked the words slicing through him.

"I thought I was yes."

Marcus tossed the handle of the brush onto the floor and finished brushing her hair and braided it. "Better?" he asked placing it over her shoulder so she could hold onto it. Something he had noticed she liked to do when she was thinking. It was like her security blanket, something she turned to when she needed to busy her hands while her mind worked something out.

"Yes, thank you." Her voice had grown very quiet. "You can leave now; I promise I'll be fine."

"Of course you will." Marcus climbed back into the bed and pulled her close, she resisted. "Celeste we both know you need this."

"Marcus?" she breathed his name making him so hard he was sure he could cut glass with his cock.

"Yes."

"Please tell me you are wearing something."

He chuckled. "I may be celibate Celeste, but I am not stupid. I have left my boxers on."

'She breathed a sigh of relief and he wasn't sure if he should be insulted or happy she didn't want to have sex with him.

He curled himself around her instead just enjoying the feel of her, she had warmed considerable. She took his arm and placed it between her two and laid her cheek on them drawing him in even closer. He buried her face in the nape of his neck breathing in her scent, she smelled amazing. He couldn't imagine being anywhere else in the world at the moment. What was it about this woman that made him forget all his vows?

It had been two millennia since he had been in the Elysian Fields but holding Celeste in his arms? Her needing his body and comfort, it was like a piece of heaven for him. It was the selflessness of being an Angel. It shocked and comforted him at the same time.

He had almost drifted off when something splashed against his arm he jerked up, as another drop of blood splashed against his arm to join the first.

"You're hurt." He jumped up and ran into the bathroom for a towel. Celeste had pulled herself into a half sitting position. And took the towel waving him off as he searched for the wound.

"Please Marcus. It's not a wound." She lay back down holding the towel to her face.

"What the hell?" he growled.

"Please stop doing that," she whispered, her words muffled by the towel.

"God dammit Celeste you're bleeding again, what the hell is going on. Do I need to get Victor? And what do you want me to stop doing?" She grabbed his hand.

"Marcus I cry tears of blood." She looked at him as another tear slipped from her eyes and streaked down her cheek leaving a bloody trail.

"Gods sweetheart." He climbed back into the bed and gathered her into his arms. He knew she needed to cry, needed to get her emotional pain out, or it could eat her alive. He felt utterly helpless as she exhausted herself.

"I never cry in front of people," she said which only made her cry harder.

"Cry all you like," he crooned, wrapping his body around her smaller form. She fit him like a glove, was soft where he was hard and vice versa. He molded her against him thrilling in the feel of her pulled up against him so closely.

She cried silently eventually wearing herself out. "He really hurt me, Marcus. Calliope is not right in the head, being in that box did something to him. I need to have those boxes destroyed."

Marcus actually had to agree with her. "Don't cry, we will take care of it," he promised.

She nodded and wrapped her arms around him. "I know how much you must hate this right now but I need you Marcus I need you more then I need to breathe right now."

Her words were husky, and she moaned deep in her throat as she pressed her face into his neck.

He caressed her back pushing her closer when he should have pushed her away. "Celeste I can't." He breathed the words, his body betraying him, and they both knew it because it was pressed against her stomach.

She shook her head. "Then why are you here?"

That was a damn good question. "Because you need me, and I'm your partner."

Celeste hiccupped. "Then leave, I don't want you here if it's an obligation."

Marcus was dumbfounded, he tried to pull away but he couldn't. "I can't leave you Celeste." He couldn't, just the thought of it made him light headed. He was shocked, after five hundred years he had found a female he wanted.

When he didn't release her she moaned. "I need you closer to me then."

Marcus was in acute pain, but maneuvered them so that they were entwined he wasn't sure where he began and she ended. His body screaming and his mind wracked with the vows he had taken.

"Marcus" she moaned his name, and for all the oaths he had taken, for all the promises he had made her next words undid all of it. "You're such a good man. I'm sorry I fight with you so much."

It cracked him, that wall of vows, everything he had worked for was to be recognized just as she had put it. He broke, was putty in her hands. He kissed her, he couldn't help it. It was exactly what he needed to hear, what he longed to hear. He promised himself that he would stop at a kiss. But she moaned and kissed him back with such fervor that he couldn't have pulled away even if he had wanted to. If the gates of hell had opened up and spouted forth the damned, he would have continued to kiss her.

When he did finally pull away he let his lips roam across her face. "I never want to feel like that again Celeste," he demanded in a gentle voice.

She pulled back slightly her eyes dazed with passion. "Feel like what again?"

"When I walked into that room tonight, and saw you…" He couldn't continue instead he kissed her showing her with his body, what he had felt. What he didn't want to feel ever again. He tore his lips from hers. "Promise me. Promise me you will never put yourself in that type of danger again."

"Kiss me again, and I'll promise you anything," she whispered. Marcus smiled and kissed her, only tearing his lips away so they could both gasp for air.

"Marcus," she gasped. "The sun is rising," she said in awe.

Marcus looked over his shoulder the sun was just coming up, he rolled over taking Celeste with him so she was facing the rising sun he cupped a breast losing himself in the feel of her. His vows lost in the beauty of her eyes, and her wonderment of something as simple as the rising of the sun. He kissed her neck his other hand moving down to the apex of her thighs. She didn't hesitate but opened for him. It was something he knew she would do, she never didn't anything halfway. The smell of her passion drove him nuts he gritted his teeth together and resisting the urge to roll her to her back and thrust deep within her.

She pushed back into him making him smile he dipped his head and bit her shoulder tenderly. The thin scar there from the shoulder wound reminding him that he had almost lost her. Uncontrollable range spread through him causing him to pull her a little closer. She was right, they couldn't get close enough.

"So beautiful." He groaned, she gasped as he buried his fingers in her she stretched back her hands reaching over her head she wound her fingers into his hair gripping him close. Marcus whispered nonsense into her ear as he drove her toward her climax her smell and feel of her body feeling a hole inside of him he hadn't realized was there.

"Yes, Marcus." She leaned back thrusting her breasts forward as he continued to make love to her with his fingers. He felt her climax just as the sun cleared the horizon, it was the most beautiful thing he had ever experienced in his entire existence the closest he had ever come back to heaven. He wrapped her in his arms as she shuttered, coming down from her peak.

"What about you?" she whispered her words slightly slurred with sleep.

"Next time." He kissed her shoulder she nodded, and he held her while her breathing evened out in sleep.

He rolled away from the sun bringing her with him. Not wanting to lose an inch of the connection they shared. He was in trouble, and questioning everything he had been doing for the last five hundred years. And it all hinged on the woman curled up against him.

He wondered what had happened to Jessica, if she was happy. He questioned what he had been saving himself for all these years? A woman who had turned her back on him not once, but twice.

It did occur to him though he had taken that oath the same time Celeste had been born. Had the Fates always been pushing him toward this end?

He looked down at the woman in his arms a woman he fought relentlessly with, but in seven days had fallen desperately and incomprehensibly in love with. He sent up a silent prayer that Jessica was where she was supposed to be and that she was happy. He was done living in the past, now the fight was on for the future. The worst part he wasn't sure what the plan was, and if he could win it. The first thing he needed to do was find and kill Calliope.

Celeste had admitted she had been in love once, the very thought drove knives of jealousy through him. He just had to convince her that whomever that other man was Marcus was better either that or find the stupid ass bastard and kill him. If he wasn't smart enough to figure out he was losing out on he was too stupid to share oxygen with the rest of the world.

He fell asleep with a smile on his lips, and the blood of her supposed true love on his mind.

Chapter 9

A quiet knock woke Marcus. He shifted, untangling himself from Celeste and pulled on his pants.

"What's going on?" He looked up. Celeste leaned forward on her elbows, one long leg and butt cheek displayed. He froze, wanting, no needing to climb back in bed with her, but another soft knock stopped him.

He grabbed her bag. "Celeste what do you sleep in?" he searched for anything resembling night ware.

"Marcus." He looked up, her violet eyes sparkling mischievously. "I sleep nude."

"For the love..." He blew out a pent up breath, grabbed his t-shirt, and threw it at her. "Put this on."

She shrugged it over her shoulders, and even though he had seen her in skin tight leather, even naked she looked more adorable and beautiful in his over large t-shirt than he had ever seen her before. Shaking himself, he opened the door.

Kyra stood there with a tray. "It's been eleven hours. I was starting to get worried. I wanted to make you a big breakfast, but then I remembered, okay Ryder reminded me, how much Celeste loved Fruit Loops. Is she able to eat?"

"Fruit Loops?" Celeste asked. Marcus shook his head, but couldn't keep the smile from his face.

"It sounds like she is." Marcus pushed the door open and allowed Kyra inside.

He moved to the other side of the bed as Kyra placed the tray on Celeste's lap.

"You didn't have to do this. I would have come down. I feel much better," Celeste said.

Kyra smiled. "It was my pleasure."

Marcus should have shut the door because within minutes the entire household was standing there, including Lexi. She walked in the room her nose in the air and glared at Marcus.

"I told you to have sex with her. Why didn't you?" Celeste almost spit her Fruit Loops across the room.

"None of your damn business," Marcus said as pleasant as possible.

"How is she supposed to heal completely if she doesn't have sex? She is a Sex Demon for god's sake." She slapped Victor on the chest. "What type of idiot is he?" she demanded. She turned to Christian. "Go out and find a man that will service my daughter."

This time Fruit Loops came flying out of Celeste's mouth, and milk came out her nose. As she choked, Marcus gave her back a slap.

Kyra frantically tried to clean up the mess. Victor started to laugh, and Christian only crossed his arms over his chest not moving.

"What has this world come to?" Lexi demanded of the room in general.

"Celeste, I will be returning to the Infernos with your mother. Would you like a few moments alone with her?" Victor finally said after calming himself.

Marcus could see in Celeste's eyes it was the last thing she wanted, but she agreed. Marcus took the tray, brushing his hand against hers, hoping he infused some of his strength into her. It bothered him that he was leaving her with her mother when she obviously didn't want to be left alone with the woman.

"I'll be right outside."

She nodded.

Marcus followed everyone out of the room. Victor slapped him on the back. "Better man than me. If I had a woman that beautiful in bed with me for twelve hours the very last thing I would have done was sleep. You're not so bad, Fallen."

Marcus shook his head. "Thank you, I think."

"Oh, it's a complement. If you had taken advantage of her, regardless of whether she needed it or not, I would have taken you to the Infernos and feed you to my father on a spit." Victor said it so nonchalantly it gave Marcus the chills. "But now I don't have to. Dealing with that crazy bitch is work enough."

Christian grunted, which Marcus took as agreement.

"What is the plan?" Marcus asked, changing the subject.

"We have the Infernos under control for the moment. So once I return Lexi, I will return here and relieve Celeste. She will return to the Infernos where nothing like this will ever happen again," Victor said.

"The fuck you will," Marcus snarled. Victor raised one eyebrow in question. "The Black Sword is the only thing that will kill Calliope, and she is the only one that can wield it. We will finish what we started."

Lexi threw the door open. Her head held high, tears streaming down her face. "I am ready to go with you, spawn of the devil," she said to Victor, who only rolled his eyes at the woman.

"She's talking to you," he said over his shoulder to Christian. Victor took Lexi by the arm, and they Flashed out.

"Please let Celeste know we will be back soon," Christian said, and then he Flashed out as well.

Marcus shook his head and headed back into Celeste's room. She had rolled over and curled up in the bed. "What's wrong?"

"It just upsets me to see my mother," Celeste admitted, rolling away from Marcus. "I'm tired can I be left alone. Please?"

His first inclination was to do as she asked, but instead he climbed back into the bed with her. "Why does it upset you to see your mother?"

"I don't want to talk about it, Fallen." Marcus bristled at the lack of use of his name.

"So we're back to 'the Fallen' are we?" he asked.

He rolled her over so he could look into her eyes. "Celeste, just say my name. Not because you're in the throes of need or passion. Can you please just say my name because it's my name for god's sake? I am not just a Fallen I am a man, and I have a name."

"I would say you are both, Fallen and Marcus. Now are you happy? Can you please leave me alone?" She was holding back something.

"What did that woman say to you?" he demanded. Lexi had said something that had popped the bubble that had been created between them. Gods, if he could get his hands around her neck he would shake the hell out of her.

Celeste closed her eyes and leaned her head down resting her forward on his chest. "She told me the truth," she whispered.

"But are you going to tell me what truth it is she shared with you?" he asked trying to control his angry.

Celeste shook her head.

"Dammit, Celeste." He pushed away from her and climbed from the bed. "Get some sleep, I'll check on you later."

He stormed from the room, not able to do anything else. She was keeping things from him. There was always something she held back from him. Except for this morning, she hadn't held anything back. When his body reacted, he headed for his room and a cold shower. Furious at himself, furious at Celeste, he didn't want it to be about sex. Regardless of the fact she was a Sex Demon. He wanted Celeste because of her strength, her sense of humor, her ability to find utter and total joy in things that others took for granted every single day. But she had this wall she hid behind, and he'd be damned if he knew a way around it.

****

Celeste cried after Marcus left. He had been so kind to her last night. Giving her everything she could need in order to heal, and he had taken nothing in return.

"If the Angels find out about you, the Tribunal, the Council, they will have you killed. You are an abomination." Her mother had cupped her face and kissed her forehead. "I love you, and that is why I tell you this. Keep that Fallen at a distance. Go back to the Infernos were you are safe. How could you possibly let a Fallen get so close? Of all species, why a Fallen? They were thrown from Heaven and the fields for a reason. He could never possibly love or care for someone like you."

"Yes, Mother," was all she was capable of saying by the time her mother had finished. Throwing ice cold water on the small fire, she let herself build between herself and Marcus. The pain so intense was as if she were back in the cement room with Calliope all over again.

Marcus had come in and had been so gentle with her, not walking away, but pressing her, trying to fix it. She cried harder and slammed her fist against her pillow. It wasn't fair. The Fates were cruel. To give her a taste of the love she craved more than her own life, only to rip it out from beneath her, before she realized she hadn't taken the opportunity to savor it like she should have.

Eventually she cried herself to sleep, hoping she dreamed of Marcus and his quiet whispered words of comfort. She thought of caring and love. Now it burned like ash in the pit of her stomach.

****

Marcus had the night to think about what was going on with Celeste. He'd even spoken to Ryder and Kyra which hadn't been casy for him.

"I don't understand her," Marcus growled.

Ryder laughed out loud. "Brother, no man in the world understands a woman. They are complex creatures that need constant compliments, reassurance and if none of that works, sex."

Kyra had slapped her mate upside the head at his words. "What I want to know is why you care for her. The two of you fight like cats and dogs."

"Not sure if you're aware of it, but you and Ryder fight all the time," Marcus pointed out.

She huffed. "It's different."

Ryder shook his head where Kyra couldn't see him. "Fight it out. Passion is good in any form."

Kyra turned to him and nodded. "I agree. But are you willing to go back on the vow's you have made?"

Ryder leaned forward. "About that vow—"

Marcus had never spoken about it to anyone. Ever. He supposed it was time.

"I did it for a woman."

That started Ryder laughing again. "Sky owes me five hundred dollars."

Kyra rolled her eyes and turned back to Marcus. "What happened?"

"I found a mortal female that I thought I had fallen in love with. She was gentle, kind, and God-fearing. A soul so pure she shown with it." Marcus remembered how beautiful Jessica had been, probably still was. "So I married her. I tried to make a life for the two of us."

Ryder shot forward nearly out of his seat. "You're married?"

Kyra shook her head. "You might want to mention that to Celeste."

"She died," Marcus said, remembering the pain he had felt at her death, the helplessness.

"I railed at the gates of the Elysian Fields, pleaded for her soul, her life." Marcus felt ill talking about it again. "They gave her a reprieve because she was such a good soul. They sent her back as a Guardian."

"So does that mean you're married or not?" Ryder asked in obvious confusion.

"I'll get to that. She hated me, hated me for never telling her what I was. She was disgusted to know I was a Fallen Angel. She feared for her own soul, having slept with someone as tainted as I was." Kyra reached forward and took his hand. "She told me I could never be or do anything good enough to make up for the sins that brought me to this place in my life."

Marcus was surprised at how much it still hurt, but it was an old pain instead of an ache of need for a woman that he would never have, should never have had.

"Jessica hated me for being a Fallen, and for not telling her, and for begging for her soul to be brought back. She paid for my punishment as well, in the service of the Angels."

"That's not true, Marcus," Kyra said with tears in her eyes. "You could not have known what she would have become upon her death, whether or not you had been in her life."

"She begged to have our marriage dissolved, but she was recorded as dead, and therefore her death voided our marriage contract. What else could I do? I walked away from her." Marcus closed his eyes and leaned his head back, remembering how hard it had been.

"I saw her one more time, about a year later," Marcus said, not looking at his friends. "Her judgment had not changed. She told me if I wanted to repent and be seen in her eyes as worthy, then I would do everything in my power to make the world a better place and pray the Angels would take me back. She said it didn't matter to her, because she never would, but I held out hope if I did enough good, then she would see and love me as much as I did her."

"Love comes without restriction, without ultimatums," Ryder said, subdued.

"Yes, something I didn't figure out for some time. But by then I had given my vow, given my blood to make this world a better place. I had no desire to be with anyone else, no one could take Jessica's place in my heart." *Until now.*

"What do you think your reaction would be if you were to run into Jessica tomorrow?" Kyra asked. For just a moment Marcus was filled with joy at the prospect. He looked for her everywhere he went, around every corner. Every blond-haired female got a second glace, even though he knew he had promised he wouldn't look for her.

Ryder shook his head. "You care for Celeste, but I think lust drives you more than love, my friend. You must put Jessica to rest in your brain and heart before you can fully open it to Celeste."

Marcus looked down at his hands. "How do I do that?"

"Oh Marcus, you once asked me what it felt like, remember?" Marcus did remember, he had asked Kyra what if felt like to be in love with Ryder.

"If I remember clearly you said it hurt like hell?" Marcus said looking at Ryder as he said it.

Ryder threw up his hands. "Every bone in my body. Victor broke every damn bone in my body. Otherwise, I would have followed her right into hell itself if needed."

Marcus shook his head and turned back to Kyra. "Explain mortal love to me."

It was a similar question to the one he had asked then. Kyra reached for Ryder's hand and squeezed. "I sometimes wake in the night in a panic that it isn't real, that Ryder won't be there, because the thought of him not being next to me hurts so badly it takes my breath away. It can be so painful you want to die, and at the same time so wonderful if fills you to the point of bursting. Life isn't about what I can do to change the world or what I do on a day to day basis. It's based on the love that fills your heart and the person you share it with." She smiled and Ryder rolled his eyes. "Love consumes you, Marcus, every fiber of your being. This may be hard to hear, but if you loved Jessica as much as you say you did, then you would never have walked away. If she had loved you equally, she would have never walked away. I mean, look at what I put up with being with Ryder," she finally said, mimicking Ryder's eye roll.

"Lust will take you a long way, buddy, but love with stands the true test of time. Be its own entity, a force for the two, not against you," Ryder said with as much sincerity as Marcus had ever seen the Tracker have.

"So now what?" Marcus asked.

"Jessica or Celeste?" Kyra asked raising one eyebrow.

Marcus sighed. "Jessica was part of my past, and you're right if I had loved her as much as I professed I would have fought for her. I gave up, and she walked away." He wondered if Celeste would ever walk away and not look back. Just the thought hurt so badly it almost made him sick. "I have stood so long on my morals and virtue of celibacy for the sake of it. Dropping that mantel leaves me feeling freer than I ever have as a Fallen."

Kyra smiled. "Then Celeste it is, if she can relieve you of that pain. And you still allow her to kick your ass. It has to be love." She stood and kissed him on the cheek. "Just think about it Marcus."

Kyra and Ryder left him there in the kitchen, and he watched the sun set, trying to come up with a plan. When he decided on a course of action, he was sure it was going to cause some rip roaring fights. But Gods willing, in the end, it would show them both they were meant for each other. Marcus had braved the gates of the Elysian Fields for Jessica, but he would break down the barriers of the Infernos and Hell for Celeste.

****

Celeste was having the most wonderful dream. She often dreamed of making love to Marcus, feeling the roll of his muscles over his back, the feel of his body pressed against hers. She grasped at the edges of her dream holding onto it for as long as possible.

"I want to make love to you at sunrise every day for eternity."

Celeste jolted awake, as if someone had thrown a bucket of ice water on her and scrambled away from the man on her bed. Landing flat on her butt with a thump.

"What are you doing here?" she demanded trying to not notice how wonderful he looked his hair mussed, sleep still lingering in his eyes.

"Actually I slept here, Celeste. By the way, you sleep like the dead." He sat up and stretched. "But…but…" she stammered. "You have a room, go sleep there."

"I prefer to sleep here," he said simply. Celeste wanted to hit him. She stood up and did just that, slapping him upside the head.

"Have you lost your mind?" she demanded.

Marcus shook his head. "Not that I am aware of, sweet. But keep hitting me like that my mind might not make it that long."

"Get out," she demanded, but part of her brain was screeching for her to get back into bed with him.

Marcus stretched again and stepped out of the bed, naked, completely and utterly naked, his erection evidence of his desire. Celeste's mouth gaped, and she just stared, unable to look away. Marcus's chuckle brought her out of her daze.

She pointed at his amazing erection. "Put it away," she shrieked.

"You're naked Celeste." She looked down, not even realizing she had been standing there arguing with him just as naked as he was.

"You've lost your mind," she said. Grabbing a blanket, she covered herself. "What happened? Why are you acting like this? What about your vow? What happened to you?" she stammered.

Marcus grabbed a pair of pants and pulled them on, zipping them up but not buttoning them. She looked at him and thought he was the sexiest man in the world. Nothing could compare to how beautiful he was. She had to look the other way or she was going to lung across the bed and lick his abs.

She kept her eyes averted as he spoke. "If you don't want me to see you naked, then you may want to think about wearing something to bed."

Unable to control herself, she turned to him, sarcasm foaming at her mouth. "Or you could stay in your room where you belong. That's why they gave you a room of your own."

Marcus smiled, such a sweet and endearing smile she melted just a little. "But your window faces the east, and I have really taken to watching the sunrise with you."

He smiled and left the room, shutting her door behind him. Celeste just stood there, her mouth opening and closing for several minutes. He had lost his mind, that was all there was to it. Lost it completely. She stomped into the bathroom and got in the shower, convincing herself that it had been a fluke and it wouldn't happen again. She was going to remain aloof, a bitch if she had to be. But she was going to keep him at a distance.

****

"What the hell are you wearing?" Marcus said the moment Celeste walked into the kitchen. She had on low slung jeans, barely hiding her hip bones and sexy ass, with a black wife beater t-shirt that enhanced her large chest and thin waist. She was the epitome of a wet dream for any male between the age of fifteen and a hundred and ten.

"I'm sorry. Do I need to check off my wardrobe choices with you?" she asked with such a snarky attitude it actually made Marcus smile instead of infuriate him.

"Eat your Fruit Loops." He shoved the box at her. "In fact, eat the whole damn box of Fruit Loops." Maybe then she wouldn't be able to fit into those damn jeans that were mere inches from heaven on earth.

Marcus swallowed hard and shifted his position at the kitchen table. She smiled at him and poured more cereal into her bowl.

"Marcus?"

"What?" he barked at Kyra, only to feel like a complete heel for doing it. "I'm sorry Kyra, was there something you needed?"

"Yes, I need you to stop kicking me under the table." Marcus jerked his chair back, not even realizing that he had been crossing and uncrossing his legs trying to find a comfortable position for his raging hard on, without anyone noticing.

"My brothers will be here soon," Celeste said, sitting down next to Kyra.

"I have an idea," she said, shoveling Fruit Loops into her mouth. "But we are going to need several of my brothers to make it work."

"They want to take you back to the Infernos," Marcus told her, wanting to know what her reaction would be.

"Of course they would. They think I will be safer there. I'll change their mind," she said with a shrug.

"Exactly how do you plan on doing that?" Marcus asked. As far as he knew the Reapers did whatever they pleased and damn the rest of the world.

Kyra rolled her eyes. "I don't know her plan, but I do know that she is a woman, so she'll get them to do what she wants."

Marcus shook his head. Had he woken up in the Twilight zone? First Celeste, a Sex Demon, had thrown him out of her room. Now Kyra and Celeste were somehow communicating with some female power Marcus couldn't begin to understand.

Ryder came in, and Marcus stood. "They're speaking in tongues," he said as he passed him on his way out.

"They always do. You should hear her, and Marlee go at it. Can't understand a damn thing," Ryder said to his back as Marcus left the kitchen and headed for his room. He needed to check his inventory. He wasn't sure what Celeste had planned for the day, but he wanted to be prepared for anything.

****

"MARCUS!" Celeste bellowed his name from the bottom of the stairs and giggled. She had never been allowed to do anything like that in the Infernos, and she had to admit it was slightly funny. So she did it again.

Marcus appeared at the top of the stairs. "Are you done screaming like a lunatic?" he asked, his hands on his hips.

"What if I had been calling for help? You took a great deal of time to answer my summons," Celeste said, putting her own hands on her hips.

Marcus came down the steps. Stopping, he kissed her on the nose. "Sweetheart, if you were in trouble you wouldn't have called for me. You would have kicked ass and then laughed when I showed up late for the fight." He took her hand as she smiled, unable to stop the warmth that spread through her at his words. "Where is everyone?"

"Dining room."

He led them into the room, shocked to see the Trackers, Kyra, three Reapers and Aiden with his entourage. "Well, if anything, this will be an interesting meeting."

He pulled out a chair for Celeste and sat down next to her.

"First of all, I would like to thank you all for coming to my rescue a few days ago." Grunts and mumbles answered her welcomes. But she hadn't expected much. They were men and didn't do well with complements of any kind. "Second, I have a plan, something that Calliope said to me while he had me. Stuck in my brain."

"Your brain that got so scrambled you almost died?" Victor snarled. "That brain?"

Celeste smiled at her brother and reached over the table to take his hand. "Yes, Victor, that brain. It's also a brain that is completely healed, thanks to you."

He jerked his hand away, but not before he squeezed her fingers quickly. "What did the bastard have to say?"

"He said he didn't need the Touched, he felt it like a shiver in his spine each time someone Flashed from the Infernos to the mortal plane or back. He said if he was close enough he could smell the sulfur."

"If we are going to capture him and take him to hell, or just straight out kill him with the Black Sword. We will need to confuse him, draw him out make him vulnerable," Celeste said.

Kyra leaned forward. "I like that idea. Having the upper hand will switch this from hide and seek to a full on assault."

Victor grunted. "What's the plan?"

Celeste smiled. If she could get Victor on board her other brothers would follow. "We need to confuse him, Flash throughout the city. Get him running in circles and lead him back here."

"Okay, stop right there," Ryder said, leaning forward. "Falcon really likes this house, and I'm pretty sure he doesn't want it destroyed. We can bang it up a bit, but full on destruction like what Calliope is capable of, not going to happen."

"But that is the best part. Calliope doesn't know we have an Element on our side, and she can protect the house. Calliope is balancing on a very thin line of sanity. We screw with that, and he is putty in our hands," Celeste finished. Leaning back, she crossed her arms over her chest and waited for the information she had just tossed on the table to be looked at and digested.

In her head she started at fifteen and started to count down.

Fifteen

Fourteen

Thirteen

Twelve

Eleven

Ten

Nine

"It's a sound plan," Marcus said, leaning forward. "Cameron, get a map of the city."

Cameron jumped up and left the room. "If we all Flash throughout the city in an exact enough pattern it will look as if we are looking for something and bringing whatever it is back here."

Cameron came back and laid out a map of the city. "If we start on the outskirts here," Marcus pointed to the farthest point from the house. "And grid up, we can Flash through the city. Maybe even come across the damn Touched we came for and draw Calliope out at the same time."

"We have one small problem," Aiden said from his seat at the head of the table.

"Vampires don't Flash."

"Yeah and neither do Trackers or Elements," Cameron added.

Kyra groaned and shook her head. "But an Element with just a little help can create something that will simulate a Flash and that is all we need correct, Celeste?"

Celeste wanted to hug the woman. "Yes, that is all we need."

"Perfect. When do we start?" Ash asked, speaking for the first time. "Let's get this party started so we can get the hell out of here."

"We will begin as soon as I take Celeste back to the Infernos," Victor announced, pushing himself away from the table.

Celeste didn't move. "I'm not going back, Victor."

"She's not going anywhere," Marcus said at the same time.

Victor ignored Marcus and looked at Celeste. "It wasn't a request."

"I am going to finish what I started."

Victor leaned over the table. "He won't capture you and torture you next time. He will kill you, dismember you, and disembowel you like our brothers. I will not have that."

Celeste loved her brother and his show of pain at the mere thought of her being hurt tugged at her heart strings, but she wasn't giving in on this one.

"I love you too, Victor, but who else will wield the Black Sword? If any of the Reapers use it, it could turn them. If a mortal touches it, it could kill them. Some Others can handle it for a short time without causing any real damage. If Marcus used it to kill Calliope, it would turn him into a Dark Angel. I am the only one that can do this," she explained.

"Wait a minute." Marcus slapped the table getting everyone's attention. "If I used the sword, I would be turned into a Dark Angel?" He didn't know of any Dark Angels in all of his existence. In the dark times they had been prolific, but were so dangerous that they had been hunted down by the Angels and killed.

Celeste gave him a shy smile. "Didn't we mention that to you?"

"No, and it would have been nice to know I could have become a slathering blood thirsty Dark Angel before I picked up the sword and used it to kill something evil."

"If it makes you feel better, it would only turn you if you killed something truly evil. As a former Angel you would be the perfect vessel for the evil in the sword." She shrugged.

"But what about a Reaper or Element?" Kyra asked.

"All I can say is that you should not handle it. And if necessary for a very short time. It won't turn any of you into evil if you use it, but it won't feel good either," Celeste explained.

"Get your things, Celeste," Victor snapped.

"She isn't going anywhere," Marcus said.

Celeste put a hand over his. "Victor, I am finishing this."

Victor growled deep in his chest, and turned to Marcus. "If so much as a hair on her head is damaged, I will break you in half."

"Excuse me?" Celeste turned to Marcus who nodded at his brother.

"I can take care of myself." She growled now, Celeste glared at Marcus. "I can take care of myself." She said directly to him this time.

"Of course you can." Marcus spoke to her like he was speaking to a small child.

Celeste couldn't help it. She turned toward him and pushed as hard as she could against his chest. His chair went flying back against the wall with jarring force leaving a dent in the wall.

"You are all really starting to piss me off. This is not a male-dominated world," she vented. "I am old enough to know what I am capable of and do as I please."

"Really?" Victor growled. "Because at the moment, you're acting like a petulant child."

Reapers have tempers, and Demons have tempers, but combined it could be deadly. And as the words flew from Victor's mouth, Christian stood and pulled Garrett back. The rest of the room unaware of what was about to happen.

She did it without any telegraphing. One moment she was standing, and the next, Celeste had launched herself over the table taking Victor down with a close hanger to his throat.

****

Marcus scrambled over the table, only to have Christian stop him.

"Let them fight it out."

"She's a girl," Marcus demanded.

"Yeah, but she doesn't fight like a girl. And we all learned a long time ago to not treat her like anything other than what she is; a Reaper/Demon hybrid." Christian pulled Marcus to the side as Victor rolled free of Celeste, slamming her in the ribs with an elbow as he did so.

"He just healed her," Marcus snapped and shrugged off Christian. Christian laughed and stepped back as Marcus joined the fray.

He was elbowed, kicked and punched in the face before extracting himself. Holding Celeste around the middle, he swung her so she was on the opposite side of Victor. Her body and mouth flayed a mile a minute.

"Enough," Marcus shouted over the two combatants.

Victor started to laugh. "Now you have a Fallen fighting for you? You're getting soft."

Marcus gave Victor an incredulous look. "Have you lost your mind?"

Celeste spat out profanities like she would get a prize if she came up with the most inventive combination. She continued to struggle to get out of Marcus's grasp.

Victor only shrugged wiping blood from his lip with the back of his hand. "Why? Because I have the balls to say what everyone is thinking?"

Marcus had heard enough and turned Celeste back to Victor. Victor showed just a moment of shock before Celeste slammed her fist into face.

Marcus shook his head and turned to Kyra. "What do you need to protect the house?"

Kyra looked from the fight and back to Marcus. "The flashing shouldn't be a problem." She pushed Marcus aside as Victor slammed into the wall beside him. "But to protect the house, I'll need Eric or Fiona's help."

"I will be happy to retrieve Eric," Christian offered.

Kyra smiled and pulled a phone from her pocket. "You won't be able to Flash into the Haven or the lands surrounding it." She held up her finger. "Hey, I need some help." She paused. "No, I am not in trouble, jackass." She paused again. "Whatever. I'm sending a Reaper for you." Pause. "Of course I know he can't Flash into the Haven. That is why you will Shift to the gates."

Christian nodded and was gone. "It shouldn't take long at all. Why? Do you have a hot date or something?"

"Yeah? Oh by the way—" she looked at her phone and then jumped back as Christian Flashed in, Eric in one hand. The Element crashed to the floor and vomited.

"I hear Flashing can be a little uncomfortable," Kyra finished shutting her phone.

"Five damn seconds," Eric growled and looked up, his blue eyes turning dark. "Information I could have used five damn seconds ago."

Marcus turned from them to Aiden. "Can you get a couple more vampires?"

"I have as many as you need at my disposal," Aiden said, still sitting at the table his arms crossed over his chest.

"Four more should be good." Aiden nodded, finally standing.

"We shall meet back at say, nightfall?" Marcus nodded, and Aiden and his sidekicks left.

"We'll have to pair up," Marcus said to Christian.

"What the hell is going on here?" Eric asked, standing. He looked at Ryder, who was sitting at the table. The two Reapers stood near Marcus. Cameron looked as if he were about to fall asleep. Celeste and Victor still fought, yelling at each other as they did so.

Kyra linked her arm with her brothers. "I will explain everything in the kitchen. I'll need the two of you," she said to Garrett and Christian.

Ryder pushed himself to his feet, looking at the couple on the floor. "Are you sure you care this much?" he asked, not taking his eyes off the siblings.

"I'll question it after this mission is over."

Ryder barked out a laugh. "Yeah, cause that's a good thing to do. Just put it on the back burner, hoping it will make sense one day."

Ryder patted him on the shoulder. "I tried that once. It almost killed me. Not physically, but mentally. We may be immortal Marcus, but I regret every moment I could have spent with Kyra and didn't. Eternity will never be long enough for me to love her."

Marcus thought about that for several hours as he got ready for their plan. He wondered why he had never thought that way about Jessica, but the thought of not seeing Celeste again made him physically ill.

He looked over his weapons, strapping everything on. He threw on his overcoat and decided he wanted to see her right then, before their night started, and the gods only knew what would happen at that point.

He knocked on her door, and she grunted, which he wasn't quite sure meant, so he let himself in.

She was just pulling a leather body army suit top over her head. He glimpsed a pair of lovely full breasts and a toned flat stomach and a belly button he would give his right arm to dip his tongue into. Low slung blood red leather pants rode her hips, enhancing her small waist and flared hips, making her look so enticing he couldn't resist even if someone had a gun to his head.

"What the hell?" Celeste barked.

Marcus just started at her for a moment and then closed the distance between them. He picked her up by the waist and pushed her against the wall pressing his lips against hers. Feeling as if he didn't touch and taste her right then, he would die.

She didn't feel like any other woman he had ever touched or tasted before. He dipped his tongue into her mouth to rub it against her wonderful taste of strawberries and champagne. He breathed in the clean scent that clung to her, and knew this was his Heaven. What he had been searching for all this time? Two centuries searching for the feel of this woman. She was what he had been waiting for all this time; not for the Angels to forgive him, not for Jessica to redeem him. But for this small, feisty mean as hell little sex Demon reaper that fought him at every corner.

When he finally pulled back he was panting for air. "Gods you taste good."

Something flickered in her violet eyes before they turned nearly black.

"Let me go, Fallen."

Marcus closed his eyes, pushing past the fact she wasn't calling him by name. Leaning his head down he placed it on the wall just above her shoulder. He held her body up with his own and breathed her in. He let every inch of his body touch hers and just thrilled in the fact that right at the moment he had her.

"Let me go," she asked again, but her voice quavered just a little.

Marcus smiled. "Why?" he whispered, leaning in so he could murmur it in her ear before dipping his tongue into the shell, following the lines with the tip of his tongue. "We are heading into a fight tonight, Celeste. Forgive me if I want a few moments alone with you."

"But you are celibate, and you may give me pleasure, but I need my partner to experience pleasure as well. I'm not about to open myself up for your later rejection."

He leaned back and stared into her violet eyes dark with sexual need. "And what if I told you I would take my pleasure with you?"

"I wouldn't believe you. Five hundred years and after seven days of fighting with me you want to throw it all away?" she accused.

He couldn't blame her. He had done nothing to show or prove to her this was a done deal on his side. But he saw the pain in her eyes; saw the hope there as well.

She hadn't moved, and he wasn't sure if she was even breathing. Right now he didn't want to speak, didn't want to hash out all the verbal bullshit. He just wanted to touch her, give them both something to hold onto before going out and fighting.

He rubbed his hands up and down her thighs, eventually coaxing them up and around his waist. "Did Victor hurt you?" he asked nuzzling her neck.

"Yes," she gritted between her teeth. "Why are you doing this?"

Marcus leaned back. She had her head leaned back and her eyes were closed. "Where did he hurt you, Celeste?" he asked instead of answering her question.

Celeste opened her eyes and looked at him, anger and passion melding together in her eyes. "He broke my nose," she whispered.

Marcus looked down. If Victor had broken it, he must have fixed it because it looked perfect to him. But he leaned forward and placed a kiss on the tip of her nose.

"Where else?"

"Right cheek." Marcus brushed kisses along her cheek bone to her ear sucking on her earlobe.

"And?"

She was breathing heavy her words breathless now. "Cracked a rib."

Marcus smiled, letting her slide to her feet, he kneeled down and pulled the tight body armor top up to just beneath her breasts and covered her ribs with kisses and licks, taking the time to run his tongue along each rib, nip at her six pack abs. He also took the opportunity to dip his tongue into her belly button like he had wanted to just a few moments before. And it was better than he had hoped it would be. So he did it again, before moving to her hip and kissing her there as well.

"Anywhere else?" he asked, spreading his hands across her flat stomach and ribs. He rubbed circles on her flat stomach with his thumbs watching her closely as she sucked in breath. Her head leaned back. He couldn't see her eyes at the moment, but he could smell her passion, feel her body warming to his.

She looked down her hands, threading through his hair. Shivers of pleasure cascaded down his spine, and his hands moved to her hips gripping her tight. He placed kisses along the line of her stomach and hips where her leather pants pressed against her soft skin.

"Bruised thigh?"

His hands moved from her hips to rub along the outside of each thigh, rubbing circles up and down her leg, his thumbs brushing across the apex of her womanhood, making her jump and moan each time. He smiled. She was so responsive, almost as if she couldn't control her reaction to him, that everything he was doing to her was new and exciting. This only turned him on the more. He rubbed his face against one hip bone.

"Celeste?"

"Hmm?" he looked up, and she stared down at him intently, passion glazing her eyes.

"Celeste, baby, I can kiss your thighs better with these pants off. And I would very much like to kiss your thighs better," he moaned, Gods, if he got her pants off he would be lost. His erection jerked painfully with anticipation.

He tugged at the hip-hugging black pants she was wearing, sliding a finger in between the leather and her skin, running it along her until it came to the button. It gave her time to stop him.

He flipped the button open, licking her stomach as he did it, pausing before sliding the zipper down.

"Marcus," she moaned his name.

Knock, knock.

Marcus froze swearing under his breath as Celeste bolting away from him.

"Fuck me," Celeste moaned. She hurried to fix her clothing, knocking Marcus on his ass as she did so.

"I was trying," Marcus muttered, more to himself than to her as she stepped over him and threw her door open.

"What?" she asked so abruptly even Marcus flinched.

"They need you and Marcus downstairs, but I can't find Marcus," Cameron said.

"Oh he's on the floor." Celeste thumbed at Marcus over her shoulder, pushing past Cameron he heard her rush down the hall.

Cameron leaned against the door jam and starred at Marcus for a long moment. "You know something?" he asked.

"What?" Marcus snapped. Looking up at Cameron from his position on the floor.

"With a woman like that…" He turned to where Celeste had disappeared. "I think you're going to end up on your ass a lot." Chuckling, Cameron turned and walked away.

Marcus let his head fall back on the hard wood floor. He starred at the ceiling thinking of anything but the woman he had just had in his arms. The woman he wanted to bury himself in and couldn't. He had waited, thinking he was saving himself for something and now knew it was Celeste. But now that he knew that, he wanted nothing more than to be with her, and felt as if he were going to go insane wanting her so damn much.

"FALLEN?" Celeste bellowed from somewhere on the first floor of the house like a vapid fishwife.

Marcus pulled himself to his feet. He knew getting past her walls wasn't going to be easy, but he hoped getting into her body would be easier, and would pave the way around that damn wall she held onto so tightly.

Chapter 10

Celeste stood at the bottom of the stairs waiting for Marcus, only to have Victor come rushing down the hall. He grabbed her by the arm, dragging her ups the stairs.

"What the hell?" she stumbled, but Victor kept moving dragging her when she stumbled.

They ran head first into Marcus as he left her bedroom.

"What were you doing in there?" Victor growled. Then shook his head. "Never mind. It doesn't matter." He pushed Celeste into the room.

"What is your problem?" Celeste asked finally, pulling her arm from his.

"Aiden showed up with several vampires, as requested. However, one of them travels with a Demon." Victor started opening draws and throwing items of clothing over his shoulder.

"Shit." Celeste's mind started racing. "I could just wear my cloak," she offered.

"He already smells you," Victor snarled, looking over his shoulder. "Damn it, get your hair up."

Kyra rushed into the room. "Ryder said I was needed up here."

Celeste was unbraiding her hair. "We need to braid my hair into three sections and wind them around my head."

Victor finally found what he was looking for. "We need to get a man's scent on you," Victor snarled.

Celeste felt blood rush to her face and looked up at Marcus. "What is going on?" Marcus asked.

Victor threw another item at Celeste. "She is an unclaimed female, and on top of that she is a Sex Demon. It drives other male Demons nuts."

"Tell me he is kidding?" Marcus turned to Celeste.

She shrugged. "It wasn't necessary to explain because there are not that many Demons in the mortal plane. They aren't civilized enough, so I didn't. A small detail like that shouldn't matter."

Marcus let out a stream of curses.

Celeste would have laughed at the look that Marcus had on his face, but she was too busy trying to redo her hair.

"We need to hide her hair and dress her down." Celeste actually felt bad for Victor. He looked like he was about to jump out of his own skin.

"Victor, it's going to be okay." She tried to comfort him as she showed Kyra what she needed help with.

"Full explanation. NOW," Marcus demanded.

This was the last thing she wanted to do, but she was backed into a corner. "Female Demons are subservient to the males. I shouldn't be seen without a male escort, and my brothers don't count because they are Reapers.

"You're a Reaper," Marcus said.

"Yes, but I am also a Sex Demon," Celeste said, sitting down so Kyra could wind her hair around her head in a cornet style.

"By going around unescorted I am offering myself to any male that is powerful enough to take me." This was so embarrassing she wanted to crawl under the bed and hide.

"And with my hair down, it's another sign that I am single."

"This isn't making any sense," Kyra said.

"Female Demons let their hair grow until they are blood righted to a male. Then they cut it."

"But you're five hundred years old," Kyra said. "Your hair should be dragging behind you."

Victor snarled. "She cut it a couple of centuries ago, thought she was in love."

****

Marcus felt rage surge through him so quickly he wanted to kill someone. The last thing he wanted to talk about was the man she thought she had been in love with him. "What do we have to do to keep this damn Demon off of her?"

"She needs to smell like a male, and then we need to cover her up. Her hair has to be pulled up, and she needs to stay close." Victor nodded as Celeste pulled a large t-shirt over her close fitting clothing and then strapped the sword to her back, swinging her cloak around her shoulders. The handle protruded through a special opening at her left shoulder.

"What are we going to do about your scent?" Victor asked.

"You don't have to worry about that," Celeste said, not looking at Marcus.

Marcus smiled. Damn straight he had just licked her stomach, kissed her neck. If his scent wasn't all over her, he was doing something wrong.

Victor looked from Marcus to Celeste and swore. He stepped forward, slamming a fist into Marcus's face. "You bastard."

"Victor," Celeste stepped in between them. "We so don't have time for this. And for a moment just remember you forced him on me the other night so I would heal."

Marcus didn't take that as a compliment, nor did he like the tone in which she had said it. She had wanted him as much as he had wanted her. Why couldn't she have just said that?

Victor opened and closed his mouth several times. "That was different."

"Get over it. I'm a big girl," Celeste muttered. "Now let's go see if we can avoid a riot in the living room."

She left the room, Kyra directly behind her.

Victor stopped Marcus. "You hurt her, and I'll kill you."

"So you've said." And then he took pity on the Reaper. "Her life for mine, I will do nothing to hurt her and everything in my power to protect her."

"Stay close to her. And be ready to fight. I don't care if you don't want her, your scent is on her right now, and if that Demon decides to fight you, you better win." Marcus nodded. He had never in his time as a Fallen worried about his ability to fight.

They followed the girls, and Victor stopped them before they entered the room, letting Kyra go in first.

Marcus turned to Celeste and kissed her, rubbing his hands along her cloak covered arms. He kissed her until they were both breathless. He leaned back and looked down into her lovely violet eyes. "Just making sure."

Celeste shook her head but there was humor in her eyes. "You have to go first."

Marcus smiled. "I might like this."

He turned, and she punched him in his right kidney. He stumbled a step before he straightened up and was able to walk into the room upright.

"We aren't done," he said over his shoulder. She had pulled up her hood so he couldn't see her face.

"We'll see." Her voice drifted from the darkness of her hood.

He stumbled, and flashes of times he had spent in the Infernos assailed him: a slight figure leaning over him with bright kind and loving eyes. That figure had him going back over and over for punishment just to feel that soft touch. It was the only touch he allowed himself. Was that who Victor had been talking about? He smiled. She felt something for him, Otherwise she wouldn't have been his caretaker all these years.

****

Celeste could smell the flood of testosterone in the room as she entered. She kept her head down, but looked around. The Demon stood in the corner next to a vampire with dark brown hair and rugged looks. The Demon was large and his eyes locked on her and his nostrils flared, his eyes taking on a red glow, he rumbled deep in his throat.

His Vampire friend put a hand on his arm. The Demon turned to the vampire. Celeste knew if something was going to happen, it would be now and every muscle in her body tensed for the fight. But then the vampire whispered something to the Demon that seemed to calm him he nodded and turned away from her and back toward the vampire.

Celeste stumbled into Marcus when he stopped she was so shocked. She had never met a Demon with control enough to not even approach her.

Marcus stepped back to steady her. "I think it worked," he whispered and winked at her.

Celeste didn't believe it, but was keeping it to herself. That Demon was either already mated or had control she had never witnessed exhibited by a Demon before.

"Now that we are all here, I will need a blood sample from each of the Reapers," Kyra said, standing next to Eric, her brother.

"Why?" Christian asked, stepping forward he opened his palm and cut his palm.

Kyra gave him an endearing smile, and Celeste knew that Kyra had just earned herself a friend for life. "The protection around the house can't be completed until I add the blood of the Reapers. That way, you can cross it, but Calliope can't, and neither will any other Reaper that isn't in the room here tonight."

Garrett and Victor stepped forward also cutting their palms with a knife they pulled from their cloaks. Celeste stepped up and nudged Marcus. "You must do it," she whispered.

Marcus gave her a strange look. "Give my blood?" he asked.

She wanted to hit him. "No you must be the one to bleed me."

"Dammit," Marcus growled, stepping forward with her, she offered her hand over the bowl like each of her brothers had made and pulled a knife from her sleeve handing it to him.

He held it for a moment. "I'm sorry," he whispered so that only she could hear, then sliced into her palm. She forced herself to not make a sound as her blood dripped into the bowl.

Once that was done Eric, picked up the bowl, Celeste turned to Victor who took her hand and healed her. Marcus felt helpless. He had injured her, and he couldn't even heal her.

"Everyone needs to pair up. As many with a Reaper as possible," Kyra said. She handed out small bags to each person, except the Reapers.

"This concoction will simulate a Reaper Flashing, even the opening of a portal," Kyra explained. "You need to be prepared to get out of the area as quickly as possible. From the contact we have had with Calliope, it is obvious he is sitting on a precarious line between sanity and complete madness. So don't hang around. Trust me when I say that in the small groups you will be in you will not be able to defend against him. He will kill you, regardless of being immortal or not. Does everyone understand?"

When everyone agreed, Victor and Garrett pulled out the map. They worked on showing everyone where they needed to be and each destination. "Six hours. That is all the time we are allowing, and then everyone must be back here."

Everyone nodded and then left. It would take a half hour to get everyone where they needed to be besides the Reapers.

When they were ready, Celeste offered her hand to Marcus. "Ready?" she had pulled her hood down so he could look into her eyes.

He placed his hand in hers. "Yes." He sucked in a breath and blew it out as she Flashed him. They ended up in a dark park where swings hung fluttering in the wind. The darkness oppressive and thick.

"Who did you think you were in love with?" Marcus asked as soon as he had his breath back.

Celeste just looked at him for a moment. "Seriously?"

Instead of answering, she Flashed them again, this time Marcus reappeared and fell to his knees, sucking in cool air. "God Dammit, Celeste."

He swept her legs out from beneath her so she landed on her butt next to him.

"Do you enjoy picking on woman?" she asked.

Marcus growled, and Celeste growled back. "Just stop doing that."

"You know, you ask me that a lot. But never once, have you explained exactly what it is I do that you want me to stop doing." He looked up into the night sky trying to figure this woman out.

"Ready?" she asked, irritation lacing her words. It was the only warning she gave before they Flashed and landed in a cemetery.

"You know this Flashing thing isn't getting any easier. In fact, I feel sick."

"Oh, I'm sorry," Celeste said with little emotion.

Marcus pulled himself to a standing position. "Sometimes I wonder if you even have a heart."

She grabbed him, not warning him at all as they Flashed again, ending up in an alley. He knew where each Flash would lead them and where they would end up. He stumbled out of arm's reach. She wasn't going to pull another Flash out without him knowing it.

"STOP." He was done, and they were going to have it out whether she wanted to or not.

"What do I have to do to get past that damn wall you have built between you and the world?" he demanded.

"I have no idea what you're talking about." She reached for him, but he side stepped her.

"Celeste, talk to me."

"I have nothing to say, Fallen."

Marcus wanted to shake her, but knew that if he did, she would Flash them somewhere, and he wasn't ready for that. His ability to shift was a much more comfortable way to travel. "Who were you in love with?"

"None of your business, Fallen. He wasn't the man I thought he was, and what I thought I felt for him is gone." He could tell it hurt her to just say it, which could only mean she still had feelings for him. Rage surged through him, and he felt as if he was going to internally combust.

"He was an idiot." Marcus couldn't imagine a man walking away from her. She was beautiful strong and took joy in things people took for granted.

"I agree completely. We need to move." She reached out a hand, and he took it.

They Flashed to a business district. Empty buildings stood like avenging Angels in the dark with sad windows that were broken out, and black shadows hid behind them. The mortal world was falling to darkness, and the mortals didn't even know it. He wondered briefly how many would care?

"How did you fall?" Celeste asked, shocking Marcus back to the here and now.

He looked at her. Her violet eyes glowed in the darkness. He could brush her off, refuse to answer, but he didn't. He wasn't going to hide from her. He hoped his honesty would help to draw her out.

"Have you heard of Pompeii?"

She nodded, and laughed. "You fell because of Pompeii?"

He turned away from her; he still felt the pain of those souls. "You may laugh all you like, but it was something that should have been avoided. Men, women and children were killed. Innocence was burned and wiped from the earth that horrible day. I gave everything I was and more in protest." Turning back to her, he let her see his emotion. He had never spoken to anyone about how he had Fallen, not even Jessica. But he wasn't going to hide this from her. "The Elysian Fields are full of love and kindness. Angels should guide and show mercy. That day none was to be had. So I chose to be exiled rather than not give mercy where it was deserved."

Celeste just looked at him not speaking. The humor from a moment before was gone. She held out her hand, and they Flashed into a side street off of Bourbon Street. They could hear the merriment of the city just beyond the shadows were they stood.

"It doesn't matter," Celeste said, looking down the street at the brightly lit bars and tourist attractions. "But I think you did the right thing."

He touched her shoulder, turning her around. He pressed her against the brick wall of the alley. "It does matter very much. Thank you, Celeste." And then he kissed her. It was a gentle kiss, one of gratitude, one of caring and kindness. But he felt the power of his need and lust just under the surface, desperate to be released.

When he pulled back, she smiled at him, taking his breath away. "Gods, Celeste, I wish you would do that more often."

Her smile faltered. "What?"

He rubbed his thumb along her full bottom lip. "Smile at me."

"That's all you want from me? A smile?" she asked, laughing.

Marcus moaned and leaned against her, pressing his proof of his need for her against her belly. "No that is not all I want from you, but it's a good start."

"Ready?" she asked. He nodded, and they Flashed back to the deserted business district.

"Why did you never reveal yourself in the Infernos?"

She looked at him hard. "By the time I was born, Mother was already starting to lose it. Dante had pulled away from her, she got pregnant on purpose. She stole his blood and bonded herself to him. She knew she was losing him, and did everything possible to stop it."

She shrugged but he could tell what she was saying was hard for her. "I am an abomination, something that should have never been. When I was born, Dante took me to the river of souls to get rid of me. But he says I looked up at him with my violet eyes, and he couldn't do it. He fell in love with me, regardless of the fact I should never have been born; that he should have never been capable of love after descending from the heavens."

Those words stabbed at Marcus like nothing ever had before. "You feel like you're an abomination?" he asked.

She nodded with complete honesty. "Of course, it's what I am."

Marcus took her in his arms. "Every soul has meaning and purpose, Celeste. You are the furthest thing from an abomination that I could think of."

"Marcus, you say that as if I should be ashamed or hurt by what I am. I am neither. It is just the way things are. We need to move." He nodded, not letting go of her as they Flashed into an open field.

"You are not an abomination," he whispered into her ear and held her, partly because she was allowing him to and partly because he wanted her to know that he really didn't think she was what she thought. "You're one of the most amazing women I have ever had the pleasure of meeting." He leaned back and looked into her face; her eyes glowed in the darkness. "So you hide from the world because of being told you are an abomination?"

She laughed. "I was kept safe, Marcus. My brothers and father deal with the worst of the world both in mortal and Other. They did what they had to do in order to keep me from being hurt. And I left the Infernos and came to the mortal plane all the time."

Marcus stepped back. "Why?"

"Sex," she said honestly. Marcus let his arms fall to his side, and he fisted and released his hands several times. The thought of her coming here just to seek out sex with nameless and faceless men made him want to kill every single one of them.

He turned away from her and took several steps trying to control his temper. With one word she had pushed him from zero to a hundred on a scale of angry.

"Marcus I need sex. I'm a sex Demon, it's a fact." The way she said it made it so he didn't have an argument against it. Not without sounding like a total fool.

"What happened to this man you fell in love with?" he demanded, angry at a man who could have stopped the nameless sex, but was too stupid to know what he had. If she had fallen for someone she would have been kept safe in the Infernos.

Her face fell. "I explained, Marcus he wasn't the man I thought he was and therefore my feelings for him have changed."

She didn't want to talk about it, he could tell. "But the thought of you with nameless men—"

She put her hand on his mouth stopping his words. "Don't think about it. You didn't know me, didn't know I existed. It is the past."

He grabbed her by the shoulders, feeling as if he needed to place a mark on her, mark her as his so she would never need to have sex with nameless men again while he was here. As far as he was concerned the vow was broken. She was his, and he was going to do whatever he needed to do in order to keep her.

He pressed his lips to hers urgently. She didn't fight him, kissing him back. For the first time they were on the same page.

He finally pulled his lips away, and looked around. "What I wouldn't give for a bed." His hands roamed all over her body.

"Breathe," she warned, Flashing them back to the cemetery. Monoliths and slabs of granite lay out around them.

He leaned back. "Not exactly what I had in mind but—"and kissed her, his hand sliding down to cup her butt. His fingers slipped inside the seam of her legs, and he pulled her up so she wrapped her legs around his waist. He backed her up against a large slab of granite.

"Marcus I need you so bad, I can't think," she growled into his ear as she pulled his shirt from his pants. Celeste ran her hands up his ribs. She could feel his muscles twitch and jump as her fingers ran along him.

"Does it help that I feel the same way?" he moaned in her ear. She melted against him as he said it, giving into him.

Celeste pulled away, pinning him with her violet eyes. "Are you sure?" the question held so many different questions: his vow, his life, what he had fought for and believed in.

He answered her by kissing her and pulling her into his arms.

****

She had never felt so safe and so cared for in all her life. She was with the one man she had dreamt about for over two hundred years. He touched her like he worshiped her. He made her feel like she was the most important thing in the world, and that was a new feeling to her.

Cool hands touched her lower back, and she arched forward, gasping.

He chuckled. "Sorry, it's a chilly night."

"Then why am I burning up?" she asked. She cupped his face and pulled him down to kiss. She never wanted this moment to end.

His hands moved to the front, and she pulled her cloak off, tossing it over her shoulder. Marcus pushed her down so she lay flat on the granite. He pushed her top over her breasts and stood staring at her for a long moment.

"You're so beautiful," he said. Leaning down, he took one nipple into his mouth.

Celeste had to bite her lip in ecstasy. She arched up into his mouth, wanting to be as close as she could to him. She felt like no matter how close they got, it would never be close enough.

"Damn, Celeste." He lapped at her body. His free hand pinched her other nipple, and he switched sides as he rubbed his erection against her. "I need you."

She laughed. "Yes, I can feel that."

He moved so that he could look into her face. "You think this is funny?" he asked with mock indignation.

Celeste rotated her hips in a way that would drive him crazy, and he closed his eyes tight, not breathing.

"Never," she said, pulling him down by his hair so that she could kiss him.

When she finally released him, he buried his face in her neck, moaning. "Sweet Mother of all the Gods."

She pulled back, her smile lighting up the night. "No. Celeste, Sex Demon Reaper."

This time he laughed and kissed her again.

"Marcus." She whispered his name when he pulled his mouth away to move kisses down her throat.

"Hmm?"

"We need to keep moving, we are on a mission, remember?"

He leaned up on his elbows, a sour look on his face. "Celeste, one of these days we are going to finish what we start before it kills me."

She pulled her shirt down and grabbed her cloak, straightening out the long sword. "Haven't heard of a cold shower?" she teased. "Besides, you haven't had a woman in five hundred years. What's another couple of days, weeks, months? Self-satisfaction?" She laughed at the look he gave her. "What?"

"Celeste I haven't, I mean… Gods," he stammered, pulling away.

"What?" had she done something wrong? Said something wrong?

"Celeste, when I took my vow of celibacy?" she nodded. "I haven't been with a woman since then nor have I taken pleasure for myself. Besides wet dreams that I can't stop. And lately those have involved you in so many different ways I can't stand it. I haven't—"

"Marcus are you blushing?" she asked as he tried to turn from her.

"You know what? I don't want to talk about it. Where are we headed next?" he asked. He took her hand refusing to look at her.

"Why did you take that vow?" she asked, squeezing his hand.

He took a deep breath in order to answer, and she Flashed them to a bridge overlooking the river.

"A woman," he answered. "For a woman I thought I loved and couldn't live without, but it's amazing what you can live through." His voice dropped, and he shook his head as if he couldn't believe it himself. "For a woman, Celeste. A woman I could never have."

She noticed he hadn't said a woman he didn't want, but a woman he couldn't have. Celeste felt like someone had thrown a bucket of cold water on her. If he could have this mythical Jessica would he turn away from Celeste? Forget that she existed again? The pain that caused almost doubled her over.

"I'm sorry," she muttered without any real sympathy.

Marcus stared out into the slow moving river and shrugged. "Nothing to apologize for. You had nothing to do with what happened." He turned, smiling down at her, and as he had said earlier, she wished he would smile at her more often as well. "You're here now, and that is all the matters."

Celeste backed up as if he had struck her. "So, I'm your second choice because it didn't work out with the woman you took a vow of celibacy for over five hundred years ago?"

"That is not what I said," Marcus growled, but this time it did nothing for her but piss her off. "You took that wrong."

"Really?" she asked pushing him as hard as she could. He gasped as he started to tumble over the railing of the bridge. At the last moment, she grabbed his ankle and Flashed them back to an alley on Bourbon Street.

"Son of a bitch," Marcus bellowed. Landing on his back, his head cracked against the dirty cement. Celeste actually felt bad.

"Was that really necessary?" he snarled with his eyes closed.

She crossed her arms. "Yes," she said, masking her hurt with sarcasm.

"I swear to all the gods in heaven and hell, I will never ever understand you." He finally pushed himself to his feet. "One second you're moaning to bring down the heavens, and the next screaming like a banshee and pissed as hell. You are impossible to understand."

"Then it's a good thing we won't be around each other for all that long isn't it?" she said, turning from him and walking down the alley.

"Don't get your hopes up, sweetheart. I'm not nearly done with you yet."

She stopped dead in her tracks and turned on him. "Excuse me?"

Marcus approached and enunciated each word carefully. "I'm not done with you." He looked her up and down as if she were a piece of meat. "In fact I haven't even started."

She saw red and swung at him. He caught her wrist, smiling at her. "You'll have to try a little harder," he taunted.

That was one of the last things people did: taunt her. Dropping into a squat, she swung one leg out, sweeping his legs out from beneath him, but he refused to let go of her hand, and he took her down as he fell back.

Celeste cringed as her wrist popped painfully. She flipped over him so she was crouched at his head, and her wrist no longer bent at a different angel then it should have been.

Marcus immediately let her go. "Celeste," he said, urgently. "Your wrist."

She shook her head as he tried to rise. Elbowing him straight in the temple, he dropped to the cement like a ton of rocks, out cold. "I'm not sure if you know this, Fallen, but I play dirty and stopping a fight for sympathy is a sure way to get your ass handed to you," she whispered to his unconscious face. Patting him on the chest, she Flashed them back to the house.

****

Marcus woke as he was thrown to the floor. He stared up at the ceiling. How many times had he been in just this position in the last several days? And he owed each time to that crazed Demon/Reaper who he had fallen in love with. And whom he had broken her wrist that she now cradled to her chest.

"Victor, I need you," she said to the room.

The next instant Victor appeared with Cameron. "What?" Victor asked.

Marcus asked still lying on the floor.

Cameron looked down on him. "See? What did I say? Ass down on the floor again." The Tracker just shook his head.

Marcus pulled himself to his feet. "Don't make me hurt you," he growled to the Tracker. Cameron just shook his head and laughed.

****

"What happened?" Victor asked taking Celeste by the arm and gently placing his hand on her wrist. After several moments, he removed his hand, and Celeste flexed her fingers and rolled her wrist.

She smiled at her brother. "Good as new."

"Would you like to explain to me how this happened?" Victor asked motioning to Celeste's wrist.

"She attempted to kick my ass again," Marcus snapped.

Celeste stepped between Marcus and Victor, facing her brother. "I never attempt as you well know. He is just a sore loser."

Marcus turned her by the shoulders. "We have some unfinished business you and me." He couldn't ever remember being so pissed off in all his immortal life. "So you have exactly two choices. You can follow me out of this room or I will throw you over my shoulder and carry you out."

"The hell you will," Victor said, pushing past his sister, he glared at Marcus.

Marcus wasn't going to back down. "Celeste, the last thing I want to do right now is hurt you. And fighting your brother will upset you. So decide."

He could see she was vacillating. "You have exactly five seconds."

If he hadn't been so pissed he would have laughed because Celeste stomped her foot like a petulant child, then turned and walked toward the door.

"I will be fine, Victor," she said over her shoulder.

Marcus followed, Victor stopping him by the arm. Marcus waved him off. "I know, I know, if I hurt her you'll kill me. I got it already."

Victor snorted. "I was actually going to tell you not to let her hurt you. Because you should be a little worried. She doesn't get this mad that often. Oh, and she totally fights dirty. Be ready for that."

Victor grabbed Cameron and Flashed out.

Celeste was waiting at the bottom of the stairs, her arms crossed over her chest. "First of all, I will not be ordered around by you."

Marcus just shook his head, picked her up and threw her over his shoulder. "And I will not be told what you will and will not do."

She growled as he swatted her on the butt. He walked up the stairs and into his room tossing her on the bed. Celeste scrambled off the other side.

"What do you want?"

"Simply put, sweetheart. I want you." He moved around the end of the bed. "And I'm done playing this cat and mouse game."

"We are nothing to each other," Celeste demanded.

Marcus stopped for a moment. "Celeste, do you really think that? Do you really think after everything we have shared, we mean absolutely nothing to each other?"

She shook her head. "We are partners, but that is all."

"Who was the man you loved?" he wasn't even aware he was going to ask the question until it tumbled out.

"What?" she asked in shock. "This is all because you want to know about a man I thought I loved?"

"Thought enough you cut your hair for him. He must have meant something." Uncontrollable jealousy surged through him.

"Kettle meet pot," Celeste said. "Why don't you tell me about the love of your existence? The love you vowed your body and spirit to five hundred years ago?"

She had a point. He turned and sat down on the bed. What was he doing? What had come over him? Then she moved so she was standing in front of him.

"Can we agree to leave the past in the past?" she asked.

Marcus looked up into those violet eyes. He wasn't sure he could just turn his back on the fact she had been in love before. Something in him demanded he be the only one. But he knew he couldn't ask that of her, not after Jessica.

"Explain something to me," Celeste said, sitting down next to him on the bed. "You took that celibacy vow for a reason. Why doesn't it matter now?"

He looked at her, incredulous. "Have you looked in the mirror lately, Celeste? I would have to be dead not to want you."

As soon as the words were out, he knew he had said the wrong thing. He could physically feel the wall come back up. "So because I have the ability— No, it's not even an ability. It's something I was born with like my red hair, my requirement for sex and the pheromones I excrete inciting men who are around me for any amount of time to arousal. You want me? Something I cannot change, by the way. You're attracted to me because of what I am, not who I am. Frankly, Marcus that sucks."

She tried to leave the bed, but he put a hand on her shoulder holding her down.

"Celeste, if I wanted any good looking woman, I could go out and find one." He turned her face so he could look into her eyes. "I have had plenty of opportunities to break my vow, but never a good reason."

She pulled away from him. "You're not making any sense."

Marcus snorted. He wasn't making any sense, and he knew it. "When I took my vow, at first it was difficult. I had led a lifetime, no several lifetimes, of debauchery. I was a Fallen. I had nothing else to lose, so I gorged myself on what the human body had to offer. Taking the vow was one of the hardest things I had ever done. But after a time, it became a way of life. It became who I was, but I have come to realize I have become the vow. Am I a Fallen or am I am man, just Marcus? All of the above, but a man?"

"Still not making any sense."

Marcus stood and started to pace. "Don't you think that if she had been the one I was meant to be with, then it would have been harder? I would have gone back, never given up? I didn't do any of those things. I took my vow and lived the life of a monk until you. I became that stupid vow. I don't want to be a vow anymore. You were right, Celeste, I want to feel alive. With you in my arms, I feel more alive than I have since I fell." He stopped pacing. "And as to the vow, I haven't kissed a woman since then, touched a woman in the way I've touched you." She didn't move, could barely breathe. "Never wanted to, but you? You drive me mad with need and wanting. Not just the sins of the flesh, I want to see your smile." He rubbed a thumb across her lips. "I want to see the sun rise in your eyes." He leaned forward and kissed each eye.

"I love to fight with you. I go to sleep at night hoping to wake before you just so I can see you open your eyes in the morning. Because you greet each day with such zest and glee."

"I never know where I stand with you, and it frustrates the hell out of me."

"I love how you can take care of yourself, how you give so much more than you take. The way you love your brothers."

"Did I mention I even love fighting with you?"

"Fallen, how many times have you actually won a fight with me? Verbal or otherwise?" she asked, and he noticed that her voice was just slightly breathless. He was getting to her, and he knew it.

He couldn't give up now, he wanted her and damn it, he was going to have her. For now and forever.

He pounced, drawing her back on the bed. He rolled so he took the brunt of the fall even though they were landing on the bed. "Sweetheart, there is always a first time."

She pushed away from him. "You realize that everyone is out there hunting down Calliope, and you want to stay here and have sex?"

Marcus thought about it for a moment. "Actually, you have a point. And yes I would rather stay here and have sex with you. Then go fight a creature who is trying to destroy the world and take you away from me."

With that said, he brought her down for a searing kiss, fussing his lips to hers as if his life depended on it. It was true. A monster was roaming the earthly realm, hell bent on killing the woman in his arms. He'd be damned straight to hell if he was going to miss the opportunity for his piece of heaven while it was here.

He leaned back, pulled his holster off, and pulled his t-shirt over his head.

"Gods you're beautiful," Celeste whispered, running the tips of her fingers down his chest, causing the muscles to jump in reaction. Just that simple touch, and he knew he was putty in her hands. If she asked him to jump straight into the fires of hell, he would do it if she would just touch him one more time.

She leaned up on her elbows and replaced her hands with her lips. Marcus wound her braid around his fingers, the strands bound together felt like a rope of silk.

Just this moment, this one moment in time, he knew he had more feeling and more love than all the moments he had shared with Jessica. And he knew, without a shadow of a doubt, Celeste was the one. He leaned back and tilted her head so he could look into those eyes that held his future, and he wanted to drown in them forever.

"Celeste, this isn't just sex," he said, as he moved to pull her tight body armor off. "This isn't just sex."

****

Celeste was speechless, the practical side of her brain was screaming for her to run. But the part of her that was in love with this man she had imagined him to be, was screaming to stay. She pressed her cheek against his six pack, trying to calm her breathing.

She had to make a choice: take his offer and give up all other men. Because just after the few encounters they had had she knew she wouldn't be able to go back to random men. It would mean being damned to Lust for eternity. Wrapping her arms around him, she listened to his strong heartbeat, enjoyed the warmth of his skin. His hands pressed her closer as he caressed her skin, making her feverish to the point of breaking.

She knew he had no idea what he was asking, but she did. "Not just sex," she agreed and leaned back, taking all of him. His lips searched for hers, kissing every inch of her neck and face with his on his way to her lips.

She grabbed handfuls of his hair, trying to find purchase in a world that had suddenly spun out of control. "Fallen," she whispered, running her tongue along the shell of his ear.

He backed up. "Marcus," he growled, turning her belly to Jell-O. "Say it. Say Marcus.

She smiled. "Fallen."

He growled again, her hips thrust up without her permission. "It's a simple name, Celeste," he said. "Or is it—" he growled low in his throat, and it vibrated over her chest. One of his legs had worked its way between hers, and his thigh rubbed at her as he growled her name.

Celeste threw her head back and moaned as an orgasm racked through her body, making her shake all over. She thought she saw stars, and she bowed her body into his, trying to touch every inch of him as she could in that moment. Finally, she drifted down her hips, still riding his thigh, moving back and forth, causing friction that was almost unbearable.

Marcus smiled and leaned away from her. "So, that is what has you so worked up all the time?"

She blushed and hid her face in the crook of his arm. "I'm a Sex Demon. When you growl, you show dominance, and it drives me a little nuts. The Sex Demon in me wants to be claimed."

Marcus leaned down, licking the shell of her ear and sucked her earlobe into his mouth before growling. "I'm not going to forget that Celeste."

She arched up into him again. "If we don't get naked soon, I'm going to go a little crazy."

"I agree." Marcus leaped off the bed and grabbed her pants at her hips. She barely got them unzipped before he was pulling them and her panties off.

Seconds later, he stood naked in front of her. She stared at his very large, very engorged manhood. "Damn."

He leaned down, pressing against her, chuckling. "I'm going to take that as a compliment."

His hands were everywhere. She just lay there so engrossed in how he was making her feel, she forgot she could participate. This was Marcus, the man she had dreamed of making love to, the man she had imagined was all those empty faces from her past. The Demon in her surged to the surface, and she flipped him over. The civilized part of her brain screamed for her to take it slow and stay in control. But the Sex Demon was in control.

"Celeste?" he asked breathless.

"Gods, Marcus." She couldn't say any more as she rubbed herself against him. "I don't want to hurt you."

He cupped her face, forcing her to look at him. "Isn't that what I am supposed to say?"

She nodded. "But I need you. I want you." She leaned back, positioning herself for his entrance. "And the Sex Demon in me can't wait."

Celeste impaled herself onto him. Her head fell back, and she let out a primal moan as she sank to the hilt.

Marcus grasped the bed spread as she surrounded him, squeezing him to the point of pain, he grasped for purchase. "Celeste?" she looked down at him. Her skin had taken on a red hue, her eyes were black with blood, red swirling within them, and she looked the Demon she was. She growled as she started to rock back and forth, milking his cock with every move she made.

She leaned forward and Marcus wrapped her braid around his wrist as he flipped her over. "My turn to be in control."

Celeste growled and thrust up to meet him, but he held her steady with his hips. One hand wound in her hair, the other held her hip as he slowly inched out of her, the pleasure so intense he knew it wouldn't take long. Even now he felt his sacks tighten. He pushed back in slower.

"Faster," she urged, trying to wrestle free, but he wouldn't have it. He moved like that until she was nearly sobbing with need.

"Say it," he said into her ear, pulling out so just the head of his cock lay against her opening. He rotated his hips, the hand holding her hip moving so he could circle the nub at her center with his thumb.

She screamed, both in rage and passion. He kept up the torture.

"Say it," he moaned this time, pressing just a little farther into her. With a hand in her hair, he moved so he could look her in the face. Violet swirled with the black and red of Demon. Pronouncing exactly what she was, and he loved every inch of it.

Then he plunged so deep he felt the entrance to her womb. He did it several more times, moving one leg over his shoulder, he rocked against her. He moaned her name. "Say it Celeste, and I'll give us both what we want."

She looked at him, fathomless emotion showing deep in her eyes. "Marcus," she moaned his name.

He smiled, leaned down pressing a gentle kissing on the tip of her nose, before sliding out and then giving into their passion he ground into her over and over again, rocking the bed until one leg gave way. But that didn't stop them. He continued to pound into her.

She locked her free leg around him tilting her hips so that he could get deeper. Then she exploded; warm juices soaking his cock and sack she vibrated around him like somehow she had been plugged into an electrical socket and it pushed him over the edge. His body strung tight as a bow. He growled her name as he spent himself into her.

Celeste watched as his orgasm overcame him. His strong muscles tightened making him look the conquering warrior from times past. Her conquering warrior, she thought as she dragged her hand down the center of his chest.

Finally, he collapsed on top of her. Small vibrations and ripples shivered through their bodies. "I've waited five hundred years for you," he whispered pulling her tight against him.

The words were meant as an endearment, but stung like salt in a wound. A wound that had started over two hundred years ago. He hadn't even known she existed until a week ago, but she had loved him for the last two hundred years. No, he hadn't been waiting five hundred years for her. How could you wait for something you didn't know existed? But she knew. Tears stung her eyes, and she pushed away from him before he could see them.

"I need a shower," she said. Getting out of the bed, she headed into the bathroom. The hot water hit her, and she let the tears fall. The water stung like needles against her overly sensitive skin her Sex Demon demanded she go back and get physical attention. Instead she turned the water hotter. The last thing she needed was more Marcus, her heart hurt badly enough.

She couldn't blame him for not knowing who she was, what she had been to him while he healed in those times he had been in the Infernos. If she had revealed herself to him, she knew nothing would have come of it. He would have thought her one of her brothers', or worse yet one of Dante's concubines.

She let her tears fall, and when there weren't any more, she washed and climbed from the shower. Just as the entire house shook with such intensity it knocked her off her feet.

Chapter 11

"What the hell?" Marcus bellowed as he and Celeste came running into the living room. The majority of the teams were there.

"Calliope has taken our bait, and now he wants in," Ryder growled. Kyra was sitting on a chair behind him, her eyes closed. Eric sat on the floor next to her his eyes also closed.

The house shook again, and Kyra screamed out in pain. Eric flinched.

"Kill it now," Ryder shouted at Marcus.

Celeste Flashed back to the room grabbed the Sword and Flashed outside.

Calliope flew above the house and every once in a while he dipped and slammed into the invisible barrier. However, when he saw Celeste, he stopped and dropped to the ground, his toes barely touching the dirt.

"Ah, sister." His voice grated over her like sandpaper. "You've brought the Sword as I asked." He held out his hand as if they had been working together the entire time.

Someone from behind her swore. "I knew we couldn't trust the Demon."

Celeste ignored whoever said it and walked forward. "If you want the Sword, I would be happy to bury it in your chest."

"Please, step outside your Druid safe haven. I would love the chance to taste you again." She shivered with fear, but refused to allow him to see it.

Victor stepped forward and whispered urgently, "Did he taste your blood when he had you?"

Celeste thought back. "Yes," she said, wanting to kick herself. This had been a big game to Calliope. He could have come for her anytime he had wanted. "Victor, I forgot."

"He's Tracing you," Victor snarled. "Kill him now before he gets too you. No one can protect you now."

They both took several steps toward the barrier, when Calliope stepped back. "Do you really think I would make it that easy? I'm not nearly done with you yet."

His body shivered, and then his black eyes rolled into the back of his head. Celeste had seen it enough to know what he was doing. Reapers held souls within them, and Gods only knew what Calliope had within him.

"Everyone get away from him," she yelled, as she headed toward the house.

Victor was right behind her as they turned and ran for the house. Calliope's laughter taunting them.

"What the fuck?" one of the vampires said. "I'm not running from the flying piece of shit. Isn't he the one we came to kill?"

Celeste turned, trying to grab his arm, but he was already moving, and Victor had ahold of her hand. Marcus was on the other side. They stood at the threshold of the house as Calliope continued to regurgitate until something black and inky seeped from between his lips, then his nose and ears and finally, his eyes. It congealed into the form of a man. And then a horrible looking woman with hair black as pitch, exploded out of Calliope.

Calliope swung up into the air, hovering over the invisible barrier. "Have fun. Until we met again, I'll be back for you, sister."

****

"Mother of all the gods, is that what I think it is?" Ryder asked from the doorway.

The blackness stepped across the wards and enveloped the vampire that stood there and the other two just as quickly.

The female stepped across the wards as well and lifted her head into the night air and sniffed.

She turned the most malevolent look at the four remaining individuals. "I smell innocent Air Element." Her head tilted to the side. "And she owes me a soul."

The inkiness lurched forward, just as Aiden and four of his men, including the Demon, surrounded it. Holding it back, Aiden turned to them. "We have this."

"Get in the house," Marcus demanded. Throwing Celeste back, she landed on her butt, watching as the woman phased into shadow and flew toward the house.

"KYRA!" Ryder bellowed. It was so loud, the house literally shook.

They raced into the living room. Eric had Kyra in a corner and was throwing balls of fire at the unphased woman. Celeste couldn't believe that Kyra hid behind her brother. She had never imagined the Element would hide from anything.

It snapped sharp teeth at Eric. "Her soul belongs to me." It shrieked the sound, making Celeste want to cover her ears.

"What is it?" she asked

"A very demented banshee," Ryder said. Pulling his gun out, he fired it at the banshee several times, but it phased out, only driving it back, but not stopping it.

The banshee turned and looked at Ryder. Her eyes and face changed until she looked just like Kyra. Celeste shook her head. "We could have been beautiful together, you and I," she screeched in Kyra's voice.

"Really?" Ryder asked moving forward. He was inches from her when she completely materialized black gauze hanging off her emaciated body, her true form showing through.

"All I asked for was one night." This time her voice was quiet.

"But your price was too much," Ryder said. Kyra had moved behind her.

"And my body to go with it." The banshee swung around just as Kyra pulled the trigger. It went straight into the other woman's forehead, picking her up off her feet and throwing her back. Ryder barely stepped out of the way.

She twitched on the floor. Celeste rushed over to Kyra. "Is she truly evil?" she asked Kyra. "Does she belong in a box?" Celeste asked.

Kyra shook her head, looking over Celeste's shoulder. She knew the banshee was recovering. Nothing on this earth would be able to kill her. They could trap her body and soul, but only one thing could destroy her.

"Does she deserve retribution, another chance?"

Kyra shook her head, as the banshee started to screech. Celeste pressed the Black Sword into the Elements hands. "You are pure goodness and this is pure evil. Handling it could be painful, but her death belongs to you. This sword will wipe her from the face of existence. Are you willing to take the chance? To wipe her soul from the world?"

Kyra nodded and took the sword. She wavered for a moment as the darkness in the sword recognized what she was and revolted.

"Hurry," Celeste urged, pushing her forward.

Squaring her shoulders, Kyra stepped around her mate, brandishing the sword.

The banshee still lay on the floor, but the wound in her head was starting to close, and Kyra stood over her body until her eyes focused on the woman above her.

"Sophie, you don't deserve to go to hell. You deserve nothingness, and while you languor in that latitude of emptiness, remember who sent you there." Then Kyra plunged the sword down straight into the heart of the banshee.

Kyra released the sword and fell. Ryder caught her before she hit the floor. Celeste moved forward and pulled the sword from the heart of the banshee and watched as she turned to dust. In moments even the dust had disappeared.

"Now let's take care of the thing outside," Celeste said, moving toward the door.

It was easier said than done, but they didn't lose anyone else before Celeste was able to step in and plunge the sword into the center of the being. It dissipated quickly, leaving them all in the dark staring at nothing.

"That was extremely anticlimactic," Aiden said, one eyebrow raised. He wasn't even breathing hard.

Celeste smiled, she couldn't help it. "But you enjoyed my ass kicking moves anyway."

"Yes, but that still leaves my bed empty for the day," he said, leaning down into her space. "Unless—"

Celeste shook her head imperceptibly and whispered, "As you well know, I have someone to share my bed."

Aiden clutched at his chest. "Say it isn't so, my little Demon."

"She isn't your little Demon," Marcus snapped.

Celeste shivered. He wanted to fight for her, which only made her want to take him upstairs and have her way with him.

Celeste winked at Aiden and shrugged. "I have your number if it doesn't work out," she whispered so only he could hear.

"What did you just say?" Marcus asked coming to stand next to her.

Aiden patted Marcus on the shoulder. "She says she is fine with the partner she currently has." With that, he turned to Ryder and held out his hand. "I have enjoyed the opportunity to fight alongside of you."

Ryder nodded and took the King's hand.

"Lordus is in hiding, even from me. Spies within my circle are alerting him of my movements in trying to locate him. He has created several creatures and beings that need to be destroyed," Aiden said, with all seriousness. "My spies are saying he has created something that will be impossible to destroy. Something that will change us all forever," Aiden explained.

"He won't get away with it," the vampire with the Demon sidekick announced.

"If you continue to hunt him, our paths will cross again," Aiden said solemnly to Ryder. "He is staying one step ahead of me and mine." He motioned with his head to the four that stood behind him.

"A sharing of information among the Other's who would rather avoid an apocalyptic type of catastrophe would be a good idea," Ryder said, holding out his hand again.

"I agree completely." Aiden smiled. "We shall be in touch."

"How do I contact you?" Ryder asked.

Aiden laughed softly. "Celeste has my number on speed dial." With that he and his men left, none of them said anything more as they sifted into the blackness of the night and were gone.

"Give me your phone," Marcus demanded.

Celeste made a point of searching herself. "I seem to have misplaced it," she said with absolute innocence.

"We have a bigger problem," Victor said, getting everyone's attention. "Calliope pulled two souls from the ones he has reaped. Gods only know how many more he has. He can also Trace Celeste."

"What does that mean, Trace her?" Kyra asked.

"He tasted her blood when he tortured her," Victor shook his head in disgust. Celeste saw Marcus flinch as if he had been the one to be tortured. "Now he can sense where she is. Tracing her like a Tracker might, except it's linked to her very soul. He can feel her wherever she is, follow her wherever she goes. She has become a liability, and if father finds out about it, he will have all our heads."

"She is a walking time bomb." Ryder shook his head.

"I have now become the main focus, with his ability to Trace me. If I go back to the Infernos, he would be able to follow me there if he were close enough to me when I Flashed. However, if I stay here in the mortal plan, I am more vulnerable. He can attack any time he wants," Celeste finished.

"So we return to the Staten," Ryder said, making up his mind for the rest of the group.

"No," Celeste said. "I will not put you all in danger. We need to split up. He can't Trace you, only me. I will go in the opposite direction. Hopefully, he will follow me. We still need to find the Touched."

"Oh that," Victor said, a little sheepishly. "Dante informed me when things went sour here, the Touched left and went to Boston and I am needed back in the Infernos." Celeste turned to him, her emotion written all over her face. "I know you must do what you must," she said, hugging him. "Please tell Dante I am safe for now."

Victor nodded. "I will try to not be gone long," he promised and then turned to Ryder and Kyra. "It took a great deal of power to do what Calliope did this evening. You have at least a twenty-four hour head start on him. I wouldn't let one second of that time be wasted."

And then he turned to Marcus. "Walk with me." It wasn't a request. So Marcus fell into step with Victor as they moved away from the house.

Finally Victor turned to Marcus. "She is my only sister. The one sibling I am closest to above all the rest."

Marcus nodded, knowing baring himself like he was doing was difficult for the Ruler of Violence. "I trust you Marcus to be fair. I trust you to protect her not only from Calliope but from herself. Please do not let me down."

Marcus was stunned at Victor's words. He had been expecting to be threatened. "I trust you not to break her in anyway. Because I truly believe causing her pain at this point would cause you pain." Marcus nodded. "She doesn't know what she feels. Be at peace with her and maybe she will let you in."

Victor turned and then looked back over his shoulder. "But I wouldn't count on it, Fallen" and then, laughing, he Flashed out.

Marcus turned back to the house. It was quiet now and the sky just beyond the line of trees turning a lighter shade of blue. Celeste stood in the doorway. Silhouetted from the light of the house, he could see only her shape, but he knew he would be able to pick her out of a crowd of a million silhouettes. He hadn't lied to her that night when he told her he had been waiting five hundred years for her. Now he just had to make her understand that.

He walked back to the house. "Ryder and Kyra are leaving within the hour. They should make it back to the Staten by nightfall."

Marcus nodded and wrapped an arm around her shoulders. He shut the door behind them and headed up the stairs. "Will you be going with them?" she asked.

"I can't even believe you would ask that question," he said.

"That's what Ryder said."

He led her into her room. "Why my room? Your bed is bigger," she said as he tugged at the shirt he was wearing.

Marcus smiled at her. "Because your room faces east, and you once said you never wanted to miss a sunrise. I will not deprive you of that."

Celeste stepped out of his reach. "We should be making plans on leaving, Marcus, not having sex."

Marcus crossed his arms over his bare chest and she had to take a deep breath to keep herself from throwing herself at him. "I will, in this instance, give you the choice, Celeste. And only because you have used my name several times this evening." She glared at him, and he growled back.

"Which would you rather do? Make unnecessary plans, because we know you are in danger, and the only other person Calliope could use to get into the Infernos is in Boston so that is where we are headed. Or spend the day making love?"

"If we leave immediately, we will get a head start on him, Marcus. Tactically this makes absolutely no sense," Celeste said honestly.

"You're completely right," Marcus said, reaching for the shirt he had just discarded.

"But Ryder is taking the plane. We will have to take a commercial airline. How long will that take to arrange?" Marcus smiled at her question and pulled his phone out of his pocket and dialed the number of someone he knew that worked at the airlines. It helped to have people in every occupation.

Ricky picked up on the first ring, and Marcus explained what they needed. Putting his hand over the receiver he looked at Celeste. "There are two flights leaving today, one in an hour which we would never make, or one at 4:30 this afternoon getting into Boston around ten?"

Marcus couldn't control his smile as Celeste looked from him to the bed and back. "I guess 4:30," she said, her voice having gone just a little husky. Marcus went back to Ricky, but his attention was totally on Celeste as she started to undress by pulling her t-shirt slowly over her head.

Marcus took an uncontrolled step toward her, but she backed up, her thumb sliding into the waistband of her leather pants she slipped them down her hips.

"MARCUS?" Ricky bellowed into the phone, and Marcus had to turn away from her.

"What?"

"You're set man. Terminal 9, and I heard you lie to the woman. I could have your plane ready for you anytime," Ricky said laughing.

"Shut up Ricky, and I'll see you then." Marcus shut his phone off and tossed it into the corner. He turned back to Celeste as she shimmed out of her pants.

"I've fought blood thirsty Wer's," he said, moving around the bed toward her. She crawled quickly across, her round ass mocking him as it moved away from him. "Vicious vampires, hell-bent on draining me dry."

She climbed off the other side of the bed and grabbed her braid. She started to undo her hair. He had never thought hair was erotic, but Celeste had the most erotic and beautiful hair he had ever seen. It was the color of a sunset, and he wanted to wrap them in it.

"You were saying?" she asked, shaking it free. Her breasts bounced in the soft lace that covered them. Her skin took on a slight reddish pink shade.

"Hordes of Demons. What does it mean when your skin changes color?" he asked unbuckling his pants.

"Depends on the color I turn." She ran her fingers through her hair, drawing it around her shoulder she reached behind her and unhooked the bra she was wearing. It fell to the floor.

"Red?" he breathed unable to take his eyes off her.

"Red?" she asked sarcastically. "Is the color of passion, but you were saying something else, Fallen."

The use of Fallen brought him back to the present. Shaking his head, he looked up at the ceiling. "All those creatures I've fought, I never feared for my life, never worried for my safety. But you?" He looked down. She had kneeled on the bed and was slowly crawling toward him and for the first time in his life, he wasn't sure if he should run or attack. This is what she had driven him to. Complete and utter disillusionment of himself.

"You scare the hell out of me."

She laughed, and the sound bounced around him like an embrace. He looked down as her pink tongue came out and rimmed his belly button before moving up his stomach she stopped to kiss each muscle, suckle on each nipple. His legs actually shook. "You're going to kill me, Celeste."

She looked up again; red bleeding into the violet of her eyes. "Marcus?" she asked leaning back until she lay flat on her back. Her hair fanned out around her, she was completely naked and the most beautiful creature he had ever seen. He had missed her removing her underwear, and he was still wearing his pants.

"Hm?" was all he was capable of. She was the most beautiful woman he had ever seen with proud, firm breasts, nipples hard pointed toward heaven. Arms wide, she waited.

"Heaven is for the boring. Hell?" she asked arching one scorching beautiful eyebrow. "Is where all the fun is."

She let her legs fall open, and he was lost. He fell on her like a starving man at a feast. He kissed every inch he could touch as her skin turned rosy red wherever he touched her. The blood in her veins streaked just below the surface of her skin, black as night.

He looked up, eyes black, pupils violet.

"Do I frighten you?" she asked, knowing in her current form she looked anything but human and more Demon than any man would care to tangle with. An Angel would run screaming from any kind of Demon, and here he was falling all over one, knowing that he would never walk away from her.

Marcus licked her stomach, watching her skin turn bright red as he dragged his tongue down toward her body.

"Actually, I was thinking that you are the most beautiful creature ever created." And then his mouth was busy, and all his words left him as her scent and taste filled places in him he didn't know had been empty.

Celeste lay physically unable to move as he worked magic on the center of her body. Sucking in breaths, she searched for the control she knew she had to keep from giving him everything he wanted, everything she wanted him to have. She spiraled out of control, letting her climax drive her into the bright light of the glorious morning that bloomed over Marcus's shoulder.

When he looked up, he had an entirely too cocky look on his face. "Your climax is amazing," he growled, and her hips bucked up without her control, which only made his smile widen. He bent down, thrusting his tongue deep within her, circling her opening until she screamed through her second release.

"Someone is over dressed," she finally growled. Marcus fully understood why his growls made her crazy with passion. Hers were doing the same to him.

Standing, he started to pull them off only to have her crawl over to him and take over, sliding her hands down the inside of his pant legs so her hands glided along his bare legs. She pushed them down, and he stepped out of them.

She wanted him so badly she was a little afraid she was going to hurt him. The sex Demon in her was in control. She ran a hand up his chest and one down the inside of his thigh as her mouth closed around the head of his large cock. Knowing she was bordering on the point of pain, she eased and then drew him in as far as he would go, as she fisted the soft hair of his chest. Her other hand came up to cup the tight sacks as the base. She moved on him, drawing him out until he was begging for more, only to pull away at the last minute and run her tongue along the length of him all the while rolling the balls in the palm of her hand. Her other hand rubbed his chest and abdomen.

"Gods, Celeste," he breathed, barely able to get the words out. "I can't stand much more."

Celeste turned to the clock on the bedside she smiled. "But it's only eight in the morning, Fallen. We have hours yet," she said, pulling him deep into her mouth she swallowed around him, squeezing the tip at the back of her throat.

"Mother of all the Gods," Marcus swore. Pulling himself from her, he stumbled backwards, grasping the base of his erection. He took several breaths. He snarled at her and stumbled to the bed. He threw her back, spreading her legs, he planted her thighs on his hips and drove into her. Her entire body bowed up until just her shoulders touched the mattress. He pounded into her like a man possessed. He watched as the colors of her skin shifted from pink to blood red, only making him drive into her harder. Pressure built in him to the point of pain.

She opened her eyes and looked at him, no longer a Reaper, but in full blown Sex Demon. She sat up, using muscle control he didn't think was humanly possible and wrapped herself around him.

She rotated her hips as she grasped each ass cheek with her hands pulling him close. She sank her teeth into the muscle where his neck and shoulder connected, and the pain bled into pleasure. He swung her around and pressed her against the wall, driving into her until she screamed out her passion.

Her climax clinching him, pulling him deeper and milking him, he couldn't control his own orgasm. His head fell back, and he growled with the release that was forced from him as she milked his cock.

"I lied," he finally said when they had fallen back onto the bed. He pulled her close, wrapping the blankets around them.

Celeste immediately lifted her head, fear shining in her eyes. He cupped her face.

"I thought you were what I had been looking for the past five hundred years. But it goes much farther back than that." He leaned down and kissed her gently. "I think even in the Elysian Field I searched for you, Celeste. You are the reason I fell, the only reason I have existed. For this moment, this time with you."

His words were both sincere and burned like fire in the pit of her stomach. He was baring himself, and she had to hold back, knowing they didn't have a future together. She swallowed past the tears and climbed on top of him.

"Then you have a lot of time to make up for," she whispered over his skin, biting his shoulder so she could hide the emotion in her eyes. She slid him into her, holding this time for the two of them.

****

Marcus helped her out of the car. She smiled and moved toward the jet. He had bared his heart to her earlier, and she had thrown up a wall. It was a wall he had enjoyed. Several times, in fact. But it didn't change the fact she was still holding something back from him. It ate at him like a fire in the pit of his stomach.

She turned and glared at him "I thought we were taking a commercial flight because Ryder took the plane?"

He couldn't help but smile at her "Just a little white lie."

Marcus couldn't stop from leaning down and kissing her nose. "Don't be mad."

The look she gave him let him know she was definitely going to be mad. "Marcus, this is bigger than the two of us and sex." She glared.

"The hell it is," he argued. "Sometimes taking a step back is more important than barreling forward with all guns drawn, Celeste."

"Or after five hundred years without sex, you are letting your cock make the decisions."

Marcus grabbed her by the shoulder. "Tell me you didn't enjoy the day? Tell me you didn't forget about Calliope even if for just a couple of hours? Tell me the multiple orgasms you had weren't worth putting it off."

Her only response was to glare at him and stomp off toward the jet.

They didn't speak during the flight. Celeste had curled up in a chair the moment she got on the plane. Her sword leaned up against her, she had fallen asleep immediately.

He sat across from her watching her sleep, wondering what he was going to do. How was he going to break down that damn wall she hid behind?

With Jessica it had been an open book. He always knew where he stood with her. She told him exactly how she felt, feelings be damned.

Celeste, on the other hand, kept everything so close he was afraid if he tried to break through her walls, it would break her. He had seen one woman broken this year. The look on Kyra's face after leaving the Infernos had broken his heart he never wanted to the kind of pain that had been deep in her eyes.

She still had it, and Marcus knew Ryder saw it as well. When no one else was looking, darkness would pass through her, making her shiver. The thought of Celeste experiencing anything like that made him want to commit murder. He wondered what she feared, and why she refused to let him in.

"Yo, we're almost there. You wanna wake the beauty?" Ricky asked leaning out of the cockpit.

Marcus nodded and leaned forward he placed a hand on Celeste's shoulder.

"Baby, it's time to wake up." He shook her lightly.

One moment she was still as the dead, and the next she was crouched on the seat with the Sword plunged deep into Marcus's shoulder.

"Mother fucker!" Marcus fell back, darkness bleeding into him from the Black Sword. Something bleed deep into his soul. And just as quickly as she had stabbed him, Celeste pulled the Sword free and straddled him. She pressed against the wound, bloody tears filling her eyes and streaming down her face.

"You frightened me," she whispered. Tearing his t-shirt, she wadded it up and pressed it against his shoulder.

Marcus looked from his shoulder and back to her. "Ya think?" he took a couple of breaths. "Get off," he urged. Celeste scrambled off him so he could sit up.

"It went straight through," she said, looking at him. "That's good, right?" She pressed her hand against his chest, touching something within him. "Your soul is untouched. Your good right?" she asked again.

"You know what would be good? If I could wake you without being stabbed in the shoulder," Marcus snarled his anger from his words earlier, his affection being unreturned, and his inability to get through to her, only to have her stab him.

"I'm sorry, Marcus," she said, leaning back on her heels.

"Yep, sorry. Great, makes it all better, Celeste. Thanks." He pulled himself to his feet and moved to the back of the plane where the attendants were sitting and talking. They immediately jumped up when they saw him.

****

Celeste followed him, only to see the two pretty attendants doting over him like he was going to drop dead any second.

"How could this happen?" the blond one asked pouting her big full lips and batting her simple brown eyes.

"Too close to the end of a sword, sweetheart. Make sure you don't make that mistake," Marcus said with no emotion.

The other stewardess giggled. "Not the kind that would slice you open like this. What type of barbarian carries a sword like that? An accident was bound to happen," she mewled, pressing gauze to his shoulder.

Celeste had seen enough. She was a barbarian. No, not a barbarian; a god damned Demon. From a line of Demonessess that had been banned to Lust because they were a scourge to the mortal and immortal population. She sat down and pulled her legs up. Wrapping her arms around her legs, she looked around. How had she gotten here? What had pushed her to want to save the world from Calliope? She had nothing to prove. She should be sequestered in the Infernos right now, letting the real warriors fight it out. But nooo, she wanted to be part of the action, was sick of hiding from the worlds. She desperately wanted to be heard and seen, not just as a Sex Demon, but as a person with a soul. Regardless of the fact she shared the blood of a Reaper and Sex Demon, she was a person with a soul.

Marcus stomped up and took the seat across from her. "Buckle up, we're landing."

"I'm sorry," she said again, but he only waved her off. She pulled her seat belt on and swallowed passed the lump in her throat. She forced herself to look out the window at the lights of the city blinking in the darkness of the night. This is where she belonged; in the darkness of the night and they all knew it. Otherwise, she wouldn't have stabbed the man she loved or spent the day making love to him instead of planning an attack that would rid the world of Calliope.

Celeste felt her stomach tighten into a ball. She had been told her entire life she was an abomination. But for the first time in five hundred years she actually felt like one. The plane bounced to a stop and as soon as the doors opened she scrambled out, wanting to get just a little distance between herself and Marcus. Where she could think straight. She really should have known better.

There was no warning, just the gently brush of black wings against her throat and the quietly whispered, "Sister."

Chapter 12

"Stay on the plane," she screamed as she rolled away, catching her elbow on the stairs. She thanked the gods she had been the first one off the plane. Because the stairs she had been standing on blew into a million different pieces.

Another wing flew out, as the black feathers whipped across her face, and Calliope knocked her from her feet. It felt as if someone had splashed acid in her face, and she screamed out in pain.

"Victor," she called as Calliope took flight. Celeste rolled under the plane as she came out on the other side she searched the darkness above her. She was hoping to draw his attention away from the mortals and Marcus.

He came out of nowhere, dipping down from the dark sky and knocked her off her feet, just as three Flashes surrounded her.

Victor picked her up. "Are you okay?"

"Yes, just scratches." She searched the night sky. Christian and Garrett did the same. Then they heard Marcus's bellow, and the screams of the women on the plane.

"Destroy everything," Victor said to Christian.

"Wait, Marcus is in the plane." Celeste took off toward the door, but Victor stopped her.

"Do you really think he is going to survive?" The screams of the dying echoed from the inside of the plane.

She yanked her arm free of Victor's and headed up the steps anyway before she slipped and fell. When she made it to her feet, she didn't even recognize the inside of the plane. Blood was splattered against every surface.

A head of one of the stewardesses rolled down between the seats, causing bile to rise in Celeste's throat. And then the plane shock, and Marcus came flying through the air. She stepped into the path of his body, taking the brunt of the impact, she rolled with him.

He looked at her, his eyes bleary with pain. "Get out," he gurgled, blood spilling from his mouth. Calliope stomped down toward them, and she pushed Marcus out of the plane and grabbed the sword, swinging it without thinking. She clipped Calliope on the shoulder.

He shrieked and backed away. "Why?" he accused, actual hurt filling his eyes.

Celeste eyes bulge. "Look around you. That is why," she shouted. Swinging the sword again, she advanced on the Reaper.

"But they were mere mortals, nothing. And the Fallen? He is two steps away from a Reaper himself," Calliope argued. "You touched him with the sword." He laughed.

Celeste stabbed at him, burring part of the sword in his leg. "These are souls," she shrieked. "They must be allowed to make the choice in life."

Calliope laughed at this statement, and Celeste stopped backing him up, still holding the sword up. "They did make the choice, sister. They just chose the wrong side." He touched his chest. "And now they belong to me."

With that he turned and burst through the back of the small plane. As soon as he was out of sight, she ran from the plane.

Marcus lay on the asphalt face down. "Is he—" she choked on the words.

Victor snorted. "No, but I knocked him out and erased his memory of the events."

"Why?" That didn't make any sense to her. Marcus was on their side.

Victor nodded for her to follow him, which she did, and found claw marks and scratches embedded into the back of the plane. "Calliope caught a ride."

"He's getting closer to me," Celeste said.

"Yes, and I don't think Marcus is going to appreciate that much. Plus, Christian, Garrett and I are going to stay until we can corner him. Marcus needs to be unaware of this." Victor looked down at the Fallen.

"Christian, take care of anyone in the tower. Garrett, blow the plane, and make it look like it had an accident landing." Celeste felt terrible, she was causing more problems than she was solving.

"Victor, this is getting more and more complicated." She wasn't sure if it was possible to achieve their goal anymore. "I was taught to fight. But to lose so many of those I cared for."

Victor pulled her into his arms. "Now is not the time to question. We are in the eleventh hour. And we know he won't fight more than one or two of us at a time."

She pulled away from Victor and she knew her heart was in her eyes. "Have faith, little one."

She nodded. "Celeste," he said her name more seriously now. "Marcus looks as if he has been in a plane crash and he will heal quickly." She looked over at him lying unconscious and then back to Victor.

She rolled her eyes. "Do I have to actually be in the damn thing when Christian blows it?"

Victor smiled. "No, but close. Garrett will have your flank. I don't think Calliope has a read on him yet. Christian and I will be close, and of course Marcus because he's done such a damn fine job up to this point."

Celeste rolled her eyes again and hit her brother. "He is doing the best job he can considering the circumstances."

It was Victor's turn to roll his eyes. "If you say so."

"Ready," Garrett called from somewhere in the dark.

Christian stepped up and smiled, which was something rare. "Do we get to blow her up now?"

"This isn't funny," Celeste snarled at her brother.

"Neither was the beating you gave me a month or so ago. So pardon me if I stand back and watch," he said with Christian-style sarcasm. He moved into the shadows and disappeared.

"He needs help," Celeste said, walking forward with Victor.

"Don't we all." Victor sighed. "This should be close enough."

She hugged him. She would survive, she was almost positive.

"I am one word away, and we will be close," Victor whispered, and then he melted into the shadows as well.

She took several deep breaths. This was going to hurt, damn it. The light was the first thing she saw; a flash so brilliant it burn into her eyes, and then the concussion of the blow hit her, picking her up, debris flying by cutting and imbedding into her skin.

She was out before she hit the ground.

****

Everything hurt. Marcus rolled over, sucking in air, and he tried to figure out where the hell he was.

The last thing he remembered was telling Celeste to put her seat belt on.

Celeste!

He pushed himself to all fours and looked around. The plane lay burning and in pieces. Celeste was several yards from him. He crawled over to her.

"Sweetheart." He touched her face gently. "Celeste." He patted her face.

She moaned and then sat up abruptly and called out in pain. "Gods that hurt." Then she fell back down. Rolling into a ball, she held her stomach.

"What the hell happened?" Marcus asked

"Calliope," Celeste moaned. "I saw him out the window as we were landing. He rammed the plane."

Marcus staggered to his feet. He heard sirens in the distance and knew they needed to get out of there but, Ricky and his daughters were on the plane, and he had to make sure they had made it out.

Ignoring his injuries, he tried to get close to the crash but saw no other bodies. Pain swelled in him, Ricky was a good guy' and Marcus had pulled him from the gutters of drunkenness when his wife had died of breast cancer twelve years ago.

Now Marcus had killed him and his daughters in one fell swoop. He felt horrible, but knew his mourning would have to wait. Turning back to Celeste, Marcus found her still on the ground.

"Celeste, the police are coming. We need to get out of here." She waved him off.

"Don't care, let me die here." Marcus rolled his eyes and turned her over, then gasped when he saw the large piece of shrapnel from the plane imbedded just above her right breast.

"Dammit Celeste, why didn't you say something?" he barked.

"Hurts," she gurgled, spitting out blood.

He picked her up, cradling her in his arms. He headed toward the hanger where he kept a SUV. The way she was acting made him think that part of the metal had pierced her lung. He wasn't about to pull it out, but he knew someone that would be able to.

He laid her on the backseat. "I'm going to take you to a friend."

She grabbed his hand. "I live in the Infernos," she muttered. "And I've been hurt here more than there in the last five hundred years. I want to go home," she said quietly. He almost missed it, but the words cut into him like a knife.

He climbed behind the wheel. He only had scratches and a bump on the head. She was impaled, and just wanted to go home. But he didn't know if he would ever be able to let her go. He wasn't going to tell her that. He needed to get her to trust him completely first.

It took an inordinate amount of time to get to Evelyn's, and Celeste had passed out half way through the trip. He pulled up to the security box and pressed the button.

A very British and proper voice replied. "May I be of service?"

"I need Evelyn, is she in residence?" Marcus asked trying to be calm.

"She is, however at this late hour I fear I am unable to disturb her."

Marcus wasn't in the mood to play this game. "You have exactly five minutes to tell Evelyn that Marcus is here and needs help. At the end of those five minutes if these gates haven't opened, I will break them down and come up there and beat the holy shit out of you."

There was no answer so Marcus looked down at his watch, exactly four minutes and forty-three seconds left.

"Marcus," Evelyn came over the speaker as the gate buzzed and started to open. "What do I need?"

"Plane crash, one wounded." And then he floored it, driving down the lane as fast as he could.

Evelyn was waiting with the door open. She was a beautiful, dark-haired gypsy he had known for several hundred years. This century she had decided to become a doctor and worked days saving lives at the local ER. But at night she saved the lives and worked on the Other population.

She waved him to stay in the vehicle and climbed in the back seat. "Drive around back. I've had a little clinic built there with everything that I need," she said as she bent over Celeste.

When he pulled up to the entrance a gentleman stood there with the door open and a gurney. "It's a good thing you didn't pull it out, it's punctured her lung."

She motioned for the man to pull Celeste from the car, but Marcus pushed him out of the way and gently picked Celeste up before he laid her down. She moaned. "I want Victor."

Marcus actually looked around. Every time she had asked for Victor before, he had appeared. But nothing Flashed and they wheeled her into the clinic.

"Wait here." Evelyn motioned to a small waiting area.

"No," Marcus said. Evelyn gave him a hard look and shook her head before she led them into a room that would rival any ER. Just as Celeste woke up, with strength he wouldn't have imagined, she vaulted off the gurney and into the corner as far from everyone as possible. Blood was starting to trickle down her brow, and he realized that she also had a head wound.

"What the hell is going on?" She wobbled on her feet, catching herself against the wall.

"Celeste, the plane crashed. You're," Marcus said calmly. He held up his hands and took a step toward her.

Celeste looked at him and then down at the piece of metal protruding from her chest. She gasped and yanked it out as both Marcus and Evelyn screamed no.

Her wound made a sickening sucking sound, and she tried to take a breath, but it only made the sucking noise worse. With what she was sure was the last of her breath she muttered, Celeste said, "Victor, god damn it."

Victor caught her as she fell to the floor. Marcus snarled at the Reaper. "You couldn't have shown up half an hour ago?"

"I was busy," he snarled back, holding Celeste close. Marcus saw them both take deep breaths. Victor shuttered.

Celeste didn't open her eyes when she spoke. "I love you." She put her arms around her brother, and Marcus knew she was out again as her body went limp.

Victor glared at Marcus. "How many times are you going to get my sister killed?"

"She isn't dead, you dumb ass." Marcus snapped.

Victor nodded. "Okay, let me put it this way, how many times are you going to put her life in such danger so if I don't show up she will die? Is that better?" he bellowed.

Marcus got right into Victor's face, leaning over Celeste to do it. "You and your brothers and father put her in danger. Let's not forget that part."

"But it was you and your friends that let Calliope out in the first place. She would be safe and sound in the Infernos right now if it wasn't for that," Victor bellowed, his eyes bleeding to black. "She is the most beautiful, kind and strong creature in any plane and she has spilt more blood in the last week on this plane than in her entire life in the Infernos." The words cut at Marcus because they mirrored what she had said to him at the airport just an hour before they hurt all the more.

Victor gently placed Celeste back on the gurney and turned back to Marcus. "One job, Fallen. One simple fucking job: protect her until she finishes her mission. Is it possible to do that without killing her?"

His words hurt, but Marcus wasn't about to admit it. "Get out," Marcus growled. "You healed her, now get out."

Victor shook his head and Flashed out.

"What the hell is going on?" Evelyn asked from behind him.

Marcus sighed he was tired and his injuries from the plane crash hurt like hell. He couldn't remember the last time he had felt so torn up, both on the inside and out. His mind reeled for a moment and then pinpointed it. The day he had fallen was the last time he had felt like this mentally and physically.

Shaking his head, he turned and froze, so shocked he wasn't even sure he was breathing.

"Marcus," Jessica breathed. She seemed just as shocked as he did. So many things ran through his mind he couldn't pinpoint any one thought.

Evelyn saved him. "Marcus please explain to me why you brought a Reaper into my home?" she asked, angrier than he had ever seen her before. "I do NOT treat Reapers."

Celeste snorted from where she lay. "Bitch, nobody asked you to."

"Celeste," Marcus warned. He turned, Celeste was pulling herself to a sitting position. She was pale and covered in blood, but otherwise looked like she was going to survive and Marcus sighed with relief. At lease he didn't need to worry about her any longer. "I brought you here to be cared for, and the least you could do is be polite."

One shapely eyebrow shot up to her hairline, and she sighed like she was just too tired to argue. Leaning around him, she addressed Evelyn. "Sorry, thanks for trying."

As apologies went, it totally sucked, but considering it was coming from Celeste, it was the best she was capable of.

He turned back to Evelyn. "I do not accept your apology," she said and turned to Marcus. "I hope this will not affect our relationship, Marcus, because it is one I value, but get her off my property."

"You haven't changed at all have you?" Jessica asked, looking unsurprised.

Marcus looked at her trying to see the woman he had loved so much so long ago and saw nothing. What he saw now was lacking in what he wanted, what he needed, no spark no light. Not anything like Celeste. He turned as Celeste eased herself off the gurney. She held onto his arm. "Thanks."

To Jessica she said, "You know Fallen, idiots and fools the lot of them. Why else would they have Fallen?"

She was joking, he saw it in her eyes, but when he turned to Jessica he realized Jessica believed every word.

"You disgust me," Jessica spat out.

"Who are you?" Celeste asked obviously ready to come to Marcus' defense.

"His…" She motioned to Marcus with such repulsion it was palatable. "…wife."

Chapter 13

"Shut the fuck up," Celeste shouted from beside him. Marcus turned to Celeste, ready to explain, but she was swinging a fist at his temple at the moment and her furious eyes were the last thing he saw before he was knocked out.

Again.

"I'm leaving," Celeste said to the women, before Marcus's body had even hit the floor. "How exactly did he bring me here?"

"There's an SUV out front," Evelyn said, obviously more than ready to see the back of her.

Celeste took several steps and then stopped. This had to be Jessica, the one person Marcus wanted above all others. She looked at her blond hair curled around an angelic face, but her eyes shown with anger and revulsion.

"You're Jessica aren't you?" she wasn't going to pass this opportunity up for anything in the world. So, he had been married to her? The lying bastard.

The woman sniffed and flipped her perfect blond hair over her shoulder. "So he's told you about me?" she asked with a little too much arrogance in her voice, as if she knew she had been torturing Marcus for the last five hundred years and found pleasure in it. Celeste had the strongest urge to punch her in her perfect nose.

"A little," Celeste said, emotionless, as she bent down and started searching Marcus for the keys. She sighed and stood. If she knew him, he probably left them in the damn ignition. "The marriage thing was a bit of a surprise."

"I couldn't tell." Jessica's voice was waspish, which put Celeste on the defensive; that was a bad thing for everyone. She felt her skin heat and knew she was turning a shade of orange. If they hadn't known she was a Demon before they were getting their proof now.

She ignored the surprised looks of the woman at her physical change. "Since you haven't seen him in what?" Celeste tapped her finger against her chin as if in thought. "Oh, that's right, five hundred years. I'll let your sarcastic bitchy attitude pass. But for your information, you have no idea who this man is, so why don't you take all your notions and ideas about him and shove them up your tight condescending ass. That is, if you can remove whatever it is you already have up there."

She pushed past the two women and headed for the door. The first thing she was going to do was find Garrett and kick his ass. A little less explosive wouldn't have been too much to ask for regardless of the fact she was immortal. Being impaled by bits of plane still hurt like hell. Christian could expect her wrath as well because he was probably somewhere still laughing his butt off at her expense.

At least Victor had showed up to heal her, but he was getting really close to being on her list as well. What the hell had he been waiting for?

"And what do you know about my feelings for Marcus?" Jessica barked, raising Celeste's hackles even higher.

Celeste told her feet to move forward, told herself this woman didn't matter to her. But her body had something else in mind altogether, and she turned and moved so fast Jessica gasped as Celeste pressed her nose into the other woman's face.

"Five hundred years, he has loved you. Five hundred years he has fought evil and the sins of the world just so he could be worthy of you," Celeste growled, trying to not let the tears threatening spill down her cheeks. She felt her small quills stab through the skin of her palms, which meant, at the moment she was a whole lot more Demon than Reaper. The quills could kill a mortal, and the Demon venom in them could cause an Other sever pain for days. She fisted her hands, stabbing herself instead of slapping the stupid out of the Guardian in front of her. She was immune to her own venom.

"All for what?" Celeste spat, forcing herself to step back. "For you to turn your back on him once again. You make me sick."

For the love of all the gods, she just wanted to go home. She turned back to the door. She wanted to get away from this mortal plane of pain and love and a man that made her feel things she had never shouldn't feel.

"You are not a full Reaper," Evelyn said, following her.

"Nope." Celeste didn't even turn around, but kept walking.

"What's your other half?"

"That would be—" she paused for effect, but still didn't stop walking. "None of your damn business considering you despise the Reaper side of me. I could care less of your other interests in me."

A black SUV stood in front of the Clinic, and she threw open the door. Yep, keys in the ignition. She climbed behind the wheel and took a deep breath. She had been taught to drive seventy years ago, but had never really needed to drive anywhere. This was going to be interesting. Plus, she had absolutely no idea where she was going. She needed Marcus, and that frustrated her so much she couldn't hold back the scream of rage, she shook the steering wheel as she did it.

"I'm going to kill him when this is done. Cut him into bits and feed him to Cerberus one piece at a time," she stormed. Climbing from behind the seat, she slammed the door. It made a strange crunching noise she ignored as she pushed through the women.

"Are the two of you attached at the hip or something?" she asked as she pushed past them.

"Of course not. I volunteer here nights to help out Evelyn," Jessica snapped.

Celeste decided it was time to ignore the sainted Jessica because just hearing her voice made her want to kill her, or, at the very least, crack her stupid skull for hurting Marcus like she had.

Marcus was pulling himself to his feet when she made it back into the exam room. He growled at her and grabbed her by the throat pushing her up against the wall.

"Marcus?" Evelyn screeched, stepping forward she put her hands on his forearm.

Celeste glared at him. "This is awful familiar," she said, and he dropped her.

"Are you done?" Celeste asked, not even blinking. Her eyes glowed violet.

"That would depend on whether or not you plan on listening to me or just knocking the hell out of me," he snapped.

She actually laughed, but there was no humor in the sound. "I think I'll go with the latter. It's more fun for us both." Celeste narrowed her eyes. "Besides, you know what, Fallen? You have absolutely nothing to say I want to hear right now, so pick your sorry ass up off the floor and let's get this shit over with."

"Why?" Marcus practically screamed and threw his hands in the air. "Why now?" he asked the ceiling.

Celeste looked up at the ceiling before turning a quizzical eye back to Marcus. "How hard did I hit you?"

He glared, pointing a finger at her. "You need to be quiet for five minutes or you'll be the one on the floor."

Celeste crossed her arms over her chest and laughed. "Bring it on Fallen. Bigger men then you have tried and failed."

Marcus closed his eyes, and Celeste was betting he was counting trying to regain control of his temper. When he opened them he turned from her to look at Jessica.

"Tell her the truth," he snapped.

"And what truth would that be?" Jessica asked with such nastiness it made Celeste gnash her teeth together.

"That we are no longer married." Marcus's voice was so menacing it would have left even Celeste slightly scared. It should have scared Celeste, but it did nothing but turn her on which only pissed her off.

The beautiful blonde leaned around Marcus glaring at Celeste. "Our farce of a marriage was considered voided after he betrayed me and sentenced me to a life of servitude to the Angels instead of leaving me at peace in death."

So that is what had happened. He cared enough about her to ask for her to become a Guardian, and she was ungrateful for that? Loved her enough to never want to be parted from her?

"Was she this stupid when you were married to her?" Celeste asked Marcus.

Marcus snorted, Jessica sucked in a breath. "You cross bred bitch."

Well that was just going too far. Pushing Marcus out of the way she stepped forward and was warmed when Victor and Christian appeared on either side of her.

"Listen up, Jessica," Celeste started as the woman finally took a step back. "That man behind me loved you so much he didn't want to be parted from you and begged the very Angels that had turned their backs on him for your soul and made you what you are today. You should be kissing his feet. And I'd rather be a cross bred bitch any given day than an ungrateful stick up the ass bitch."

"You have no idea what you're even talking about," she snapped. "He is a Fallen." She said it with such contempt and disgust that it startled Celeste.

"So?" she barked.

"They expelled him from the Elysian Fields because he was unworthy," she said, standing tall, her shoulders back, as if she had just imparted the most important information in the world.

Celeste was done talking with her. She turned and smiled to her brothers who gave her identical looks and then they Flashed out. She looked at Marcus, his green eyes filled with pain, and she hoped it wasn't because he realized that Jessica was never going to love him back, the way he loved her.

"Your vow was for that?" she thumbed over her shoulder. "I'm ready to go, you unworthy Fallen piece of shit."

Marcus snorted. "Well then, let's get going, you half bred bitch."

He motioned for her to go ahead of him and she started back toward the car. "You know, I kind of like that "Half Breed Bitch." I might get a t-shirt with that on it. What do you think?"

"I'll pay for it." Marcus laughed.

Celeste turned to him, narrowing her eyes. "I'll hold you to that Fallen."

"Gods, its Marcus." He leaned down so his nose touched hers. "Marcus."

"Of course it is," she whispered back and then turned and headed toward the front door. Evelyn caught up with them there.

"I apologize for the way I treated you. It was a surprise to have Marcus bring you here. That doesn't explain my actions, but I am sorry."

People didn't often apologize to Celeste. So when it happened, she always took a moment to asses why they were apologizing and what it would mean in the future for them both before accepting or rejecting it. It was the father in her. Nothing for nothing.

"Thank you," Celeste said for Marcus's sake. He obviously had a relationship with this woman and as much as that rattled her cage, she wasn't about to ruin that for him.

"Evelyn, you know the Guardians in Boston?" Evelyn nodded at Marcus's statement. "They are in danger."

"What are you talking about?" Jessica snapped.

"Can't she just go away?" Celeste asked to nobody in general.

"What type of danger?" Evelyn asked.

"A Reaper, one of the first, has escaped. It is searching for a way to get back into the Infernos. There is a Touched here in the city. I don't know who it is, but their Guardian would know. Whoever it is needs to get their guard out of the city as soon as possible."

Celeste had been watching Jessica as Marcus explained what they were doing here, imagining ways to maim and kill her. But when Marcus mentioned a Touched, the woman perked up.

"Fuck me sideways," Celeste muttered.

Marcus turned to her. "Excuse me?"

She didn't answer him and pushed past him to Jessica. "Who is your charge Jessica?"

"None of your damn business, you bitch!" Celeste held up her hand, stopping her.

"Yes, we have established exactly what you think of me, but that isn't the question. Who is your charge?" Celeste practically bellowed the words. "Because if she is the Touched, she is in a great deal of trouble. Did you just return from New Orleans?"

Celeste had a sinking feeling in the pit of her stomach and turned to Marcus. "If Calliope can trace me, and he is close, he will know now."

"What have you done?" Jessica snapped and then disappeared.

"Thank the Gods she is gone," Celeste said with honesty.

"I know who her charge is," Evelyn said quietly.

Marcus and Celeste both turned to the woman. "Marcus, if I give you the information, promise me it is because she is in mortal danger."

"Evelyn, I swear to you I wouldn't do any of this if it wasn't life or death." Evelyn looked from him to Celeste and then back.

She sighed and headed down the hall with Marcus and Celeste following. They followed her into an office, and Evelyn unlocked a hidden safe and pulled out some files.

She wrote something down on a piece of paper and handed it to Marcus. "If anyone finds out I have passed this information on to you, I will be murdered."

"I swear I will protect you," Marcus said with a hand on his chest. Evelyn smiled, and Marcus leaned down and kissed her on the cheek. "Thank you, Evelyn."

Celeste made a face behind him. He kissed the woman. Right in front of her, and she didn't know exactly who she wanted to kill at the moment Marcus or Evelyn? But her heart was leaning toward Marcus, the big bastard.

They walked side by side as they left the building. Evelyn stopped him at the entrance. "I'll be right there," Marcus said to Celeste's back. Celeste lifted a hand and he had to be glad she hadn't given him the one finger salute. With how angry she currently was, he could have gotten much worse.

"Marcus, are you sure you know what you are doing?" Evelyn asked, concern creasing fine lines in her beautiful face.

Marcus looked at Evelyn and then back at the SUV. Celeste had climbed into the back seat and was muttering to herself, probably damning him to hell and back.

"Believe it or not, I do know exactly what I am doing." This felt right, and he didn't know how to explain that to Evelyn, but when he looked at her, she had to see the emotion on his face.

"Isn't having your heart broken once enough?" she asked, tears slipping from her dark brown eyes.

He laughed humorlessly. "I think this time it will kill me, considering what I feel for that half bred bitch eclipses what I had for Jessica tenfold."

Evelyn shook her head. "I will kill her with my bare hands if she hurts you."

Evelyn rarely ever showed anger, and Marcus was touched she cared so much. "Believe me Evelyn, as much as we argue and fight, she is my one and only."

He leaned down and kissed her again before heading for the SUV.

****

Celeste watched as Marcus and the beautiful Evelyn exchanged several words, and then he leaned down and kissed her again. Lightning green jealously streaked down her spine making her lower back stab with such intense pain it took her breath away. She grasped the door handle trying to not scream out in pain.

Marcus climbed behind the wheel, completely unaware of the danger he was currently in. Everything in her wanted to claim him, mark him as hers.

"Victor." She moaned the name, and he instantly showed up in the back seat.

"What?" Marcus turned to Celeste and to Victor.

Celeste felt Victor's eyes on her for a long moment. "Just drive away, Fallen."

Marcus started the vehicle and pulled out into the drive. "Celeste?"

Celeste glared at him before leaning toward Victor. "I don't understand why it hurts so much here. I need to go back to the Infernos," she muttered.

"Not going to happen," Marcus said from the front seat. This had Celeste reaching for him in her need. Victor wrapped his arms around her, holding her, he rubbed her back. She had never hurt Victor, but she growled at him now.

"Mine," she whispered so only her brother could hear.

"Damn it, Celeste. What have you done?" he asked. Celeste looked up into what were usually black eyes, but shown a bright blue at the moment.

She felt tears slip down her face. "I'm sorry. I didn't do it on purpose. I couldn't help myself."

Celeste was almost dislodged from her place on Victor's lap as Marcus slammed on the breaks, and the large vehicle screeched to a halt.

Marcus climbed out and threw open the back door. Celeste looked up and smiled, but she wasn't sure if it reached her eyes.

Concern and anger was written all over his face. She knew, somewhere deep inside of him, he cared for her.

"What's wrong with her?" he demanded of Victor. "And why the hell aren't you healing her?"

Victor growled. "Because what is going on is not something I can heal for her. You did this to her, you will need to fix it. And may all the gods, Angels and anything else of light be on your side when Dante finds out."

Celeste clung to her brother, but he Flashed out leaving her sitting alone in the back seat.

"Why Celeste?"

"Why what, Marcus?" she asked between clenched teeth.

"Why when anything happens, do you call for Victor?"

"Are you hurt because I call for my brother rather than for you?" she asked, so shocked she couldn't keep her mouth from falling slack.

Marcus racked a hand through his hair. "Yes, dammit, and I don't appreciate you throwing it in my face. Now just explain it to me."

"He can heal me Marcus, do you have that ability?" she said, shoving herself as far away from him as possible. The base of her back ached so badly she thought she was going to be sick.

"No by all the gods, I don't have that ability," he said, climbing into the vehicle. Celeste pulled her legs up, and she wrapped her arms around her legs, curling into a ball, making herself as small as possible. If he touched her, she was done for, and she prayed to whatever Gods were feeling merciful he wouldn't touch her.

"Celeste, what's wrong?" he asked, his words so gentle she cried harder.

"Marcus, if you care at all, you'll get behind the wheel of the SUV and drive. Ignore me," she begged, not sure who she hated more as each word came out. He reached out for her, and she flinched away. "Just drive, Marcus. I want to go home, and in order to do that we have to finish this mission."

This time it was Marcus that flinched. "Was it because of Jessica?"

Celeste laughed. "Of course not. That insignificant piece doesn't really deserve my time," she said honestly. One day she was going to ask Marcus why he had cared for her for so long. But that would have to be after her lust died down just a little and she could think clearly.

"Celeste, why is your skin turning a slight shade of red?" Celeste laid her head down on her knees.

"You know why," she whispered, wishing the world would stop so she could jump off.

"Celeste, what has you so—" she looked up as he hesitated. Confusion was written all over his face. She would have laughed if he hadn't reached over and brushed a tear from her face."

God Marcus, why?" she asked just before she lunged across the seat and slammed into him, driving him back against the seat. She pressed her mouth so hard against his she tasted blood, which only turned her on more.

She rubbed against him, feeling his hesitation with her. Celeste felt like she was raping him, but couldn't seem to stop herself. Her fingernails elongated into talons, and she ripped his t-shirt to shreds as she searched for hot skin.

When she did find it, she pressed her hands flat against his warm chest soaking up his heat. "So warm," she growled, taking her lips from his and running them down his neck.

"Celeste?"

She leaned back, and saw the surprise in his face. She had changed, she knew she had. "No talking. I need sex right now. I need you right now. If you want to heal me, make it better, I need you to have sex with me right now."

"What the hell happened?" he asked, but he was unbuckling his pants as he asked the question.

Celeste tried to keep the words from tumbling out of her mouth, but she couldn't. "Twice," she growled and licked the column of his throat and moved to his bottom lip. She bit him, drawing blood with her elongated canines. When his warm hands slid into the back of her pants and cupped her ass, she threw her head back and moaned, letting the orgasm from just his touch roll through her.

When it was done, she looked back and him. "Mine," she growled, so low and menacing, it scared her a little. And then she was scrambling out of her own clothes.

Once she had her pants off, she positioned herself, straddling him. She looked down into his face, cupping it with her hands, and she stared into his beautiful green eyes, knowing she would never turn from him of her own choice. Celeste kissed him as gently as she could and slid onto him, home deep inside of her.

****

Marcus was never going to be able to figure her out. Tears fell, unbidden, down her cheeks as she rocked on him, her tight passage squeezing him to just this side of pain. She muttered words, mostly 'mine,' which he couldn't argue with, but it seemed to upset her.

He pushed her forward as he reached for the lever that would fold the driver seat forward. Finally in control and on top, he slowed their movements, feeling as if that little bit of control wasn't costing him dearly.

"Explain," he growled, pulling out so just his head lay within her hot, wet passage. He leaned down and bit one turgid nipple.

She tried to jackknife and pull him into her, but he was in control and rolled his hips away losing contact completely. Celeste growled and bellowed in rage.

Marcus leaned up and looked down at her. Her skin was a dark red and her fingernails as well as her canines had elongated. Her eyes had changed and bleed red and black. She was a totally different creature, but with her fire red hair, he couldn't help but think in either form she was the most beautiful thing he had ever had the pleasure of having contact with.

"Explain," he said again.

"You kissed that bitch twice," she growled, not trying to role away from him.

"Kissed what bitch? What—" And then he remembered that he had kissed Evelyn on the cheek twice as they were leaving.

He smiled, he couldn't help it. "Are you jealous, Celeste?" he asked rolling his hips forward so that he pressed and circled the button at the apex of her legs, making her scream in pleasure.

"I hate you," she growled, scratching at him as she desperately tried to regain control.

Marcus leaned forward and pressed slightly into her. "Celeste, are you jealous?" rotating his hips, he slid farther in.

When she didn't answer him, he started to withdraw, but she screamed and sank her claws into his buttock. "Yes, are you happy now, Fallen?"

She looked anything but happy, but he couldn't have been more pleased. If she was jealous, that meant she felt more for him then she wanted to admit. Sinking deep into her, he ripped her t-shirt down the center from the hole that was made by the plane shrapnel and pulled the bra away he sucked a nipple into his mouth thrilling in the wonderful taste of her. She arched up to meet every one of his thrusts her hot wet canal sucking him deeper with each thrust.

Of all the women he had been with, all the time he had been without a woman, looking down at his beautiful Demon, he knew each second had been worth it. He felt her shudder and let out a low growl of a scream as she bit her bottom lip, drawing blood, he bent down and licked the trickle of blood away. The second it touched his tongue something tingled through his body, but he was too mindless to figure out what that was and then he was thrusting into her over and over again, each time getting closer to her feeling her contract around him, milking him.

When he finally came, he gave into it, throwing his head back and growling her name.

When he finally came to his senses, he rolled off her. "Sorry," he mumbled.

Celeste said something under her breath he didn't catch, but before he could question it, she was speaking. "You have nothing to be sorry for. I was the one who attacked you."

She scrambled to collect what was left of her clothing. "Celeste, I wasn't apologizing for having the best sex of my existence. I was apologizing for crushing you, after I came."

Celeste just stared at him for a moment as if he had changed and was speaking a different language. "Aren't you repulsed at what happened?"

Marcus felt his mouth sag open. "What are you talking about?"

"Nothing." Celeste shook her head and then crawled over the seats giving him an amazing view of her ass. Making him want her all over again.

She turned in surprise as she rifled through a duffel bag. "What are you doing?" she snapped.

Marcus smiled, He really liked it when he caught her off guard, she was such a snappy thing. "Hmm" he said leaning forward in the cramped space. He didn't touch her, but he noticed the goose bumps rise on her arms and legs.

"Celeste, I want you. I want you more than I want my next breath." And then he tongued her earlobe, making her shake.

"Marcus," she breathed.

"Hmmm?" He wasn't really in the mood for conversation. His hands pushed her back against the duffel. She turned and scrambled away from him, putting the luggage between them. But all he saw was the angry scaly red welts that covered her lower back. Shame, and irritation shot through him.

"What the hell happened to your back?" All thoughts of having sex with her flew out the window. He reached for her, but she avoided his hands.

"It's nothing," she said, still avoiding him. She grabbed for the bag and swung around, hitting him in the head. He tumbled into the luggage.

"Bloody hell," he growled. When he untangled himself, she pulled a t-shirt out and put it on. "Celeste," he said her name very slowly, trying to gain control of his temper. "What is wrong with you back?" She shrugged her shoulders as an answer. "Woman, one of these days I am going to shake the holy shit out of you." He knew her well enough when she dug her heals in, she wasn't going to tell him a thing about her back until she was damn good and ready.

He climbed over the seats and pulled his clothes back on. She threw one of his t-shirts in his lap as she passed him and climbed into the front seat. She sat down and pulled her seatbelt on as if they were going for a Sunday drive.

Marcus pulled on the t-shirt and climbed out of the SUV. He stomped around it several times, knowing that if he got in he was going to kill her.

On his third pass, she rolled her window down. "Did you forget where the driver's seat was?" she asked.

Marcus was so not in the mood for her smart mouth and ignored her as he continued to count and walk around the car. What was he going to do with her? One minute she was screaming his name in passion, and that he belonged to her, and the next she was acting like they were on a first date, and an uncomfortable first date at that.

More secrets. She was wrapped in them. They surrounded her, and she had built her life on them, and he was beginning to realize he may not be able to get through to who she really was, touch the heart he desperately wanted for himself.

He had no idea how long he had been pacing when Christian appeared. "We have a problem," he said.

"What?" Marcus growled. Of course they had a problem. This whole mission was one big problem.

Celeste climbed out of the car, and Marcus stepped away from her. He needed to be away from her and her smell for a moment and the mere fact that she was so close was slowly driving him nuts.

"Jessica's Touched?" he asked, looking at both of them.

"Yes?" Celeste answered.

"She isn't just Touched. She's a Descendent."

Marcus threw his hands in the air. "Of course she is," he snarled and turned he slammed his fist into the brick wall of the building they were parked in front of. It crumbled in that spot to dust.

"So like, a real Descended?" Celeste asked.

Christian must have said or done something to confirm her question, but Marcus didn't see it with his back turned to them. Celeste's next comment let him know her fist question had been answered.

"We need the Elements."

Marcus agreed and pulled his phone from his pocket. Ryder picked up on the first ring. "Damn, man, do you have any idea what time it is? And if you wake up Kyra, I'll kill you."

"We need the Elements," Marcus stated, deciding to ignore Ryder and his threats.

"Yeah?" Ryder asked, the one word dripped in sarcasm. "Then give them a call and leave me and my woman alone."

"Ryder," Marcus heard Kyra snap from somewhere close. And then she was on the phone. "What is the problem?"

Marcus explained the situation. "If Celeste gets within a mile of her, Calliope will be able to sense her. And Jessica will be able to sense everything else Other coming at her."

Kyra laughed softly. "Everything but an Element, that is."

Marcus could have kissed her. "Exactly."

"Well then, I think I am going to need Fiona's help on this one. Give me twenty minutes and have a couple of the Reapers met us at the gates."

"Thank you, Kyra," Marcus said with genuine empathy.

"Explain to me why every woman you met falls at your feet?" Celeste snarled.

"Seriously?" Marcus asked. "You're worried about other woman falling at my feet, when there is a crazed Reaper stalking the night of Boston, and you are worried about Kyra?"

Celeste had folded her arms over her chest as he shouted at her. "Just making an observation. You know what, Fallen? I really don't have any idea how the hell you stayed celibate for five hundred years, what with every woman on this plane wanting to get ahold of your large cock."

"Gods," Christian muttered, looking up into the night sky. "I don't want to be a part of this conversation."

Celeste turned on him, and the look in her eyes had even Marcus stepping back. "You slimy overrated, high intensity blow it up son of a bitch laughing your ass off in the grass somewhere." She slammed her fist into Christian's face, who stumbled back. She followed that up with a punch directly in his stomach. As he doubled over, she gave him a knee to the face that sent the Reaper several feet away.

Marcus grabbed Celeste before she could attack her brother further. "Have you lost your mind?" he shook her slightly before letting her go. He moved to Christian and offered him a hand. The Reaper took it, and Marcus pulled him to his feet.

"Has a bit of a temper," Christian groused as he spat blood from his mouth.

"Really?" Marcus asked with sarcasm. "I couldn't really tell."

"I swear, I'm going to kill you both," Celeste said as she climbed back into the SUV and slammed the door.

What crawled up her—" Christian stopped when Marcus rose an eyebrow at him.

Something is wrong with her," Marcus admitted. "She has soars on her back that she won't talk to me about."

Marcus was surprised when Christian's mouth dropped open in shock. "Man, don't touch my sister," he said, shaking his head, and then swore. "Aww. If you've seen her back that means—" he shook his head. "I wanna vomit man."

"Explain to me what is wrong with her back?"

Christian shook his head. "It's where the change starts. Hurts her like hell, but when she needs sex that's where the change starts."

Marcus couldn't process the information for a moment. "So you're saying when her back looks like that, she needs sex?"

Christian nodded. "It happens faster here on this plane. That is why she lives in the Infernos and rarely comes here, only for sex, because of the change, at times she can't control her urges as much here as she can in the Infernos."

"And Tracing. Explain that to me," Marcus demanded.

"Man, you're full of questions," he sighed. "Tracing is the ability to locate someone on any plane of existence. It's done with a transfer of blood, and something unique to Reapers. If I were to take your blood, I would be able to locate you anywhere in the world, on any plane. I could link myself to you in a way that would make it so if you shifted to a different location, and I was close enough, I would be able to catch a ride. Being Traceable is the last call. Once a Reaper has a Trace on you, its game over. You can't hide. All the Reapers are Traced to each other, one word, and we can be there for each other."

Something clicked, and for a moment Marcus saw red. Celeste could Trace him. It was why she had been able to Flash out of the car and then back to him in the house in New Orleans. It was why she could find him anywhere. He smiled. She had to care a little if she had taken his blood. But how long had that been possible and when had he shared his blood with her?

Marcus had a hundred questions, but Kyra appeared with Fiona, Victor and Garrett.

Marcus swore. "Where is Ryder?"

Kyra smiled. "He couldn't come with us, not enough Reapers."

"You do realize he is going to try to kill me now, don't you?" he snarled at Kyra.

Kyra only smiled back. "Yes, of course I realize that, but this is far more important than the fact that Ryder doesn't like me to be out of his sight for more than ten minutes at a time. He will be fine." She patted Marcus on the arm.

Marcus swore to himself. "Keeps getting better."

Kyra laughed at the look Marcus gave her. "I will calm him down."

Fiona stepped forward and smiled, and Marcus leaned down and kissed the older women's cheek, then heard a bellow of rage from the car. He just hoped that Celeste stayed in the car for the moment.

"What have you found out?" Marcus asked.

"We placed wards around her apartment that will repel Reapers," Kyra explained. "Jessica isn't very nice, by the way. She was really pissed, but Fiona convinced her to work with us as long as her ward never finds out what is going on."

"I gave her a charm that the ward can wear when she is outside of her home, and the wards we placed there will make her invisible to Reapers. But it will only last six days."

"So now we have a time constraint," Marcus said.

"Yes, but we also have a plan," Kyra offered.

"What plan?" Marcus asked.

"We need to lure Calliope out into the open so Celeste can fight him with the Sword and kill him," Fiona said. "Jessica has offered to work with us, but it means her ward will be spared. She doesn't want her ward to know anything about what is going on. She doesn't know who she is."

Marcus raked a hand through his hair. "How is that even possible?"

Fiona shrugged her shoulders. "We do not need the answer to continue nor is it any of our business."

Marcus was going to shake Jessica until her molars rattled. She was making things difficult because he was a part of the mission.

"When do we need to put this plan into action?" he practically growled.

"Tomorrow," Fiona said, looking down at her watch. "Four hours."

Marcus nodded, and they made plans for everyone to meet up. And then he was left standing on the sidewalk alone glowering at the SUV and the very pissed Reaper who sat within it.

Marcus started to put some things together with the way that Celeste acted. She had always been the one to care for him when he was punished in the Infernos. Why she hid things from him, and didn't allow him to get to close he didn't know.

A smile spread across his lips, she loved him. Gods how stupid he had been. The woman in the dark robes he had imagined as Jessica, had fantasized over, had been Celeste. Somewhere deep inside he had known it when he laid eyes on her that first night. But he had been so crazed with lust he hadn't been able to put all the pieces together. She was a fighter and wanted nothing less from her partner. On the other hand, she was a woman and a Sex Demon demanding things he hadn't understood until then.

Well, he knew what to do now, by the gods. He was going to get her to confess her feelings and open up to him before they headed out on this death mission. He wasn't going to go down without a fight, but neither was he going into a fight without knowing exactly how she felt about him either.

****

Celeste watched Marcus out of the corner of her eye. He hadn't said anything since climbing behind the wheel of the car, but had a smirk on his face which made her feel as if she was about to be bested at a game before she was given the full set of rules. That only pissed her off.

When they pulled up a ramp, and Marcus got out to throw open a large elevator door that would fit the SUV, she half expected him to push the button and be gone, but nothing like that happened. He casually walked back to the SUV, opened the door, winked at her and climbed behind the wheel.

The elevator took them and the SUV, now turned off, up to the thirteenth floor.

"Home sweet home," Marcus said as the elevator stopped, and he climbed out of the vehicle. "This is my exclusive elevator, doubles as my garage. I'm starving. Would you like something to eat?"

Celeste nodded, but didn't immediately follow him as he shut his door and headed off into the recesses of his condo. She took a look around. It was all slick, black surfaces with silver highlights. She would have thought a Fallen's home would be filled with everything light.

Climbing from the vehicle, she moved into the main part of the condo. Medieval weapons of all kinds adorned the walls from floor to ceiling. She was stunned as she looked over the massive array of deadly weapons. Even from where she stood she could tell they were honed to deadly sharpness and she didn't doubt he could pull any one of them down and regardless of its age kill with it.

She felt Marcus behind her. "Have you carried each one of these into battle?" Somehow, she knew the answer before he nodded confirming her question.

"How many are there?" she asked in awe, turning to him.

He smiled a gentle smile that melted her heart. "Too many to count, but enough to spread across a two story building wall."

She chuckled. "I can see how one could lose count."

Marcus stepped up into her space making her suck in a deep breath. He leaned forward, and she froze, unable to move as his breath brushed across her cheek. "I didn't say I didn't know exactly the number of weapons on the wall. Just that there were too many for someone to count, it would be a useless endeavor."

Celeste leaned back. "Then how many are there?"

Marcus kissed her gently on the lips. "Six." He kissed her again. "Hundred." Kiss. "Eighty." Kiss. "Four." The last kiss he lingered for several moments, and Celeste felt like her legs had been locked in place, and someone had glued her feet to the floor. Wasn't she mad at him? His hands had worked around and were massaging her lower back turning her into putty and easing the pain there. He rubbed the exact spot that ached so horribly with need and sexual frustration.

She was saved when some kind of bell went off in the other room. Marcus sighed and leaned back. "You, my dear, have just been literally saved by the bell."

Celeste watched him walk away and couldn't stop herself from following him. Her back ached and she just needed him to touch her there some more. She didn't care how mad she was at him at the moment.

His kitchen was done out in all silver metal and nickel. Matching the inner man, she thought.

"How do you explain your collection to other woman?" she couldn't help but ask.

Marcus placed something in the oven and turned to her. "Not a problem I've never brought anyone here before."

Celeste was shocked. "Not anyone? Not one of the Trackers? Not a friend? Nobody?"

Marcus nodded. "My inner sanctuary." He motioned to the room around him.

Celeste was touched he would trust her enough to bring her here. "Thank you."

Marcus moved over to her. "For what?" he asked, leaning in he breathed deeply.

Celeste shivered unable to control her reaction to him. "For bringing me here, it shows trust. And I'm not really sure if I am deserving of it," she said honestly. "We fight a great deal, and I didn't know if that would translate over into trust of any kind," she said honestly. She knew she could trust him, knew if she put her life in his hands he would do everything possible to make sure she came out of the situation without a scratch on her. How she knew that she couldn't explain, but it was something about him. But she didn't know if that trust was returned until that moment.

Celeste felt a wall she had constructed hundreds of years ago start to crumble just a little, and her flight or fight sensations kicked in. She took several deep breaths. This is Marcus, she reminded herself. He would never hurt her. So, she planted her feet and refused to move away from him as he moved to stand in front of her.

Marcus gave her a surprised look. "Celeste…" He used the tone of voice someone might use if talking with a small child. "I trust you, and I'm pretty sure I'm falling in love with you." He watched her closely as he said the words, not wanting to scare her away, but he also wanted to make sure she truly understood how he felt about her.

She shook her head and turned away from him. "Marcus, you shouldn't fall in love with me."

"And why is that?" he asked her.

"Because my destiny is written and it doesn't involve you," she said with emotion in her voice. "Can't we just have sex and that be enough?" she asked, turning back to him.

He could see the emotion and turmoil in her eyes, and knew getting her to admit she wanted him for sex was a big point for him and, for tonight, that was enough. He reached over and flipped off the oven. The lasagna he had thrown in there would have to wait.

Turning back to Celeste he smiled. "Yes, Celeste we can just have sex." He swept her up into his arms. She wrapped her arms around his neck and rested her head on this shoulder. "But I'm telling you right now," he whispered into her hair, drawing in the scent that was uniquely her. "It's not going to change how I feel. I'm not sure how I'm going to do it, but I'm going to get you to open up and fall in love with me."

****

Celeste stared up at the intricate pattern on the ceiling of Marcus's bedroom. The sun was just beginning to rise, and they had spent the rest of the night making love, and she had never experienced the emotions she had the night before. She knew it was because of what Marcus had said earlier, but the problem was she already loved him. Had loved him for so long she almost couldn't remember a time when she hadn't loved him.

She heard him muttering to himself in the shower and smiled. He did that a lot, she had noticed. When he thought nobody was listening or paying attention, he muttered to himself, working out issues in a logical way.

Celeste felt a tear streak down her face, and she quickly wiped it away. Maybe she should tell him she wasn't expected to survive this mission, that of all the Reapers she had drawn the short end of the stick. Being half Demon and half Reaper made her the perfect vessel to carry the Black Sword. But by using it to kill something as powerful and evil as Calliope, it would most likely kill her. When the decision had been made, she'd taken the opportunity because she couldn't bring herself to live the way she had been for the last two hundred years. Plus, it would give her a reason to exist if even for a short time. She hadn't known at the time that she could possibly love Marcus more than she had in the Infernos, or care about the people of this plane of existence. No, she had taken the mission fully understanding it would be her one and only. Her father had been proud of her. Victor had railed at their father, promising he was going to do everything possible to get her through it.

The thought of living in eternity without Marcus hurt so badly that she curled into a ball and wrapped her arms around her legs trying to hold in a scream that clawed at the back of her throat. But she would sacrifice that and keep what little was left of the wall between herself and Marcus in order to complete what needed to be done.

Squaring her shoulders, she dressed. As soon as she knew what the plan was she would tell him everything: that she had loved him for two centuries and although he had been in excruciating pain and often called out for Jessica, she still loved him, and wherever she ended up when her body lay dead she would take her love for him in her soul with her there and keep it forever.

Her phone rang, startling her out of her thoughts. "Where the hell are you?" Victor barked into the phone before she even had the chance to say hello.

"Nice to hear from you too, brother," she said with as much sarcasm as she could muster.

"I cannot sense you. I have not been able to sense you for the last three hours," Victor growled. "And every time I called I got your god damn voice mail. So where the hell are you?"

Celeste looked around. "Hold on." She rolled from the bed and walked out into the living room.

"What do you have now?" she asked her brother.

"Okay I sense you now." Victor's voice held some relief.

"Flash to me," he demanded.

"You know something, Victor," she said into the phone as she Flashed following her senses to reach out to her brother. She appeared in front of him on a street corner. "Sometimes you can be an over protecting ass." She finished putting her phone back into her pocket.

"Seriously?" Victor asked his voice turning mean. "Your off fucking that damn Fallen, and I'm supposed to sit back and just ignore it. Father would have an aneurism if he knew what was going on."

Celeste threw her hands in the air, and then glared at her brother. "I am the lamb to the slaughter, Victor. Is it so bad that I want to pluck some happiness from this god forsaken world before I am killed?"

"What the hell?" Marcus growled from behind her.

Chapter 14

Celeste felt like the world had stopped for just a moment, and she wanted desperately to disappear and be anywhere but there. She turned slowly, his eyes were black instead of green, and he looked as if someone had plunged a knife into his back.

"What are you talking about?" he demanded.

Celeste opened and closed her mouth several times before Victor opened his damn mouth.

"If she is able to kill Calliope, which I think is totally possible, it will probably kill her."

Several things happened at once. She sensed something from Marcus that she had never thought possible; pure, unadulterated fury. It was a fury that could kill. She also felt shame for having not told him the truth, for letting him believe they may have a future together. It was why she had held onto her walls so tightly.

"Marcus, I was going to tell you."

Marcus didn't even look at her. "You, your brothers, and Father are willing to feed her to that Reaper?"

Celeste stepped up to Marcus. "They can't hold the Sword, Marcus," she said by way of an explanation.

It was the wrong thing to say because Marcus turned to her, his usual bright green eyes were dull and dark. "That's it then?"

"It might not kill me. I may be able to contain the evil that is held within Calliope. The sword may not turn on me."

"That might have been the stupidest thing I have ever heard you say," Marcus growled.

"Marcus, this was not your decision," Celeste said, standing up for herself. She had loved a man who didn't know she existed, and once this was all said and done he would most likely move on. That was what men did. They had no future together, so fighting in the name of her brothers and the Infernos, even if it meant dying, was better than living an existence of hoping that one day Marcus would notice her.

"Wait." Celeste hit Marcus on the shoulder to get his attention. "How exactly did you find me?"

"No, what I want to know, is how the hell he hid you from me?" Victor snarled. "Because that shouldn't be possible."

"How did you find me?" Celeste asked.

Marcus gave her an odd look. "When I came out of the bathroom and noticed that you were gone I just thought of you and Shifted."

"Holy Mother of Hell and beyond," Victor swore, throwing his hands up. "Now he can Trace you?" Victor accused.

Celeste turned to her brother. "I did not share blood with him," she practically screamed.

"I tasted your blood when you bit your lip," Marcus said. "So does that mean I can Trace you anywhere?"

Celeste wanted to crawl in a hole. "This is not a good thing. He isn't a Reaper he shouldn't be able to Trace anything!"

"Speak for yourself," Marcus grumbled.

"Father is going to have both our heads on a spit," Victor said.

"Let's rewind if we could," Marcuse said with obvious false calm. "You are sending your sister to die with a mad Reaper. Can we discuss that stupid ass decision?"

"Not out on the street, you freak." Victor shook his head and Flashed.

"Is your apartment warded?" Celeste asked.

"Of course it is."

"Okay then let's go back there." Celeste flashed, but came up against the cool steel of a metal door. Victor was standing next to here.

"He is starting to really irritate me."

"I have everything under control," Celeste lied.

"I don't believe you."

Marcus threw open his door.

"Why didn't you tell me the place was so well guarded?" Celeste asked immediately. "This could be a great use to us."

He gave her a hard look before answering. "Because this is my private residence, and I don't share it with just anyone."

In fact, he didn't share it with a single person since he had bought it over one hundred years ago. He remodeled as the times changed, but he never let another Other or mortal for that matter come here.

Celeste cocked her head to the side and looked at him thoughtfully for a moment. "Does it bother you to know you have been in residence in the same city as your sainted Jessica?"

Marcus wanted to shake the woman. "No." They were going to have it out regarding Jessica, but now wasn't the time or place.

"So how does the Tracing thing work?" he asked Victor.

"You share a small blood bond with her. If she calls for you will be able to hear her. Or vice versa, you can sense her and therefore Flash, or in your case Shift, to wherever she is. But until ten minutes ago it was something only Reapers had the ability to do. It must be some kind of link the two of you share? I don't understand it." Victor snapped.

"So Calliope has this ability with her as well?" Marcus demanded. "So he could pop in anywhere she is if it is not guarded and just have done with her?" That thought had him breaking out in cold sweat. She could be taken from him so quickly.

"Not if she is being guarded. Hence the fact that you have a guarded residence being a big deal," Victor muttered. "It would explain why Calliope went crazy last night. But neither of you knew that because you were snuggled in, in a guarded residence doing what exactly?"

"What happened?" Celeste asked.

"None of your damn business," Marcus answered the question.

Victor moved quickly so he was nose to nose with Marcus. "Anything that has to do with Celeste has to do with me. And if you think for one second that this…" He flung his hands out to encompass the room at large. "…love nest is going to change anything, then you are a complete idiot."

"Excuse me, but I happen to disagree with you. I have just as much right to seeing to her safety as you do so you can go straight to hell." Marcus wasn't going to back down from the Reaper. He was taking a stand that might very well get him punished to more than just a pound of flesh.

"Stay away from my sister," Victor said before slamming a fist into Marcus's face.

Marcus's head snapped back, but he didn't stumble and instead lifted his head and looked at Victor. "You may think because I come to the Infernos and take your judgment and punishment as weakness but you would be wrong. I care for Celeste, therefore I will not be hitting you back. But never raise your hand against me again or you will regret it."

Victor threw his head back and laughed. When he had regained his control he looked back at Marcus. "And exactly what do you think you can do against me Fallen?"

Celeste stepped in between the two men and slammed them in the chest with the palm of her hands. Marcus flew back and hit the wall behind him. He heard Victor swearing himself as he struck the opposite wall.

"Can't we just all get along?" Celeste asked her words dripping in sarcasm.

Marcus pulled himself together. "Tell your brother to back off."

"Tell the Fallen he is no longer needed. The plan is set into action, and we don't need him any longer," Victor snapped.

"The hell you say," Marcus growled. "I go where she goes." He motioned to Celeste.

Victor didn't even look at Marcus. "He is part of the reason Calliope has escaped. His job here is finished."

"He completes the mission with us," Celeste said in his defense. She was defending Marcus which he took to mean she had to have feelings for him.

"Well then, now that's settled, what is the plan?" Marcus asked.

Victor growled. "It is not settled, I won't work with him."

"Why?" Celeste demanded. "Because I'm fucking him?"

"Damn it, Celeste," Victor said, turning a startling shade of pink.

Marcus couldn't help but laugh. "Are you blushing?" he asked the Reaper.

Victor narrowed his eyes, and glared at Marcus. "You don't have any sisters, so I am going to let that bullshit pass. But the last thing I need to know about is her sex life."

"What is the plan?" Celeste demanded.

"Jessica and her charge are going to be bait," Victor said casually.

"I will not allow Jessica to be bait," Marcus demanded, turning from Celeste, he faced her brother.

Celeste didn't think it was possible to hurt as much as she did at that moment. She wasn't sure exactly who she was more upset at; Marcus or herself for believing she could love him enough for him to forget about Jessica.

However, his quickness to defend Jessica spoke volumes. What had she been doing? Thinking she could possibly take the place of that raving bitch?

"What is the plan exactly?" Celeste asked, refusing to look at Marcus. She felt as if her heart was breaking, and she knew if she looked at him right then she was going to lose control and kill him.

"The Druids are working on a glamour that will put you with the Touched. When Calliope shows up, you will kill him."

"Sounds easy enough. I, of course, will be playing the part of the Touched. However, who will be playing the part of me?" Victor nodded at her conclusion. The Touched would be a much easier target then Celeste.

Victor turned green. "I will be playing you."

Celeste looked at her brother and started to laugh. "Well then, at least I'll get a laugh out of the stupid mission."

"I don't find anything funny about the situation," Marcus snarled. "I want to play the part of Celeste."

Victor stared at Celeste and when she closed her eyes and turned away from Marcus, Victor attacked. "You are no longer needed. This mission will be completed after sunset, and your mission to Dante will be complete. You will stand up for judgment on the lives that Calliope has taken."

Celeste sucked in a breath as she continued to listen to her brother tell Marcus exactly what was going to happen. She knew, no matter what, she would be there in the end to comfort him while he healed from the punishment that was going to come, her heart breaking a little more.

"Can we go now?" Celeste asked Victor, not looking at him or Marcus.

"Yes, since Marcus's apartment is hidden from and spelled for hiding we can actually Flash back to the infernos until it is time." She felt Victor step up behind her and place a hand on her shoulder.

"Not if I have anything to say about it. She isn't going anywhere," Marcus snarled.

Celeste closed her eyes, going in for the kill and dying a little as she did it. She turned to Marcus. "We have no future together. You are a Fallen, and I am a Reaper/Sex Demon hybrid that may not survive the end of this mission." Marcus stepped forward, and she knew he had a rebuttal ready she held up her hand. "I could never be with a Fallen," she said with as much scorn as she could knowing it would stick at the one part of him Jessica still held on to. "I appreciate the sex so I wouldn't lose control, but that was all it was." She looked him dead in the eyes as she said it, knowing her black eyes stared back with no emotion because she had trained herself to be able to say this one thing for two hundred years. She just never thought she would really have to say it to him, and her heart shattered into pieces as the words came out.

Marcus's usual green eyes turned darker, and shadows burned deep in their depths. He stepped back, then turned and walked out of the room.

When the door closed quietly behind him, Celeste stumbled, but Victor was there to steady her and Flashed them into her bedroom in the Infernos.

"You actually love him, don't you?" Victor asked as she stumbled to her bed.

She nodded. "Stupid me."

Victor didn't say anything more, but left Celeste letting her know when it was time for them to put their plan into action. As soon as he was gone, Celeste Flashed into Lust. Bodies writhed and moaned in discontented passion. Screams of pain and unfulfilled desires pierced her ears, and she fell to her knees letting the hot, blood-red rock dig into and slash at her skin. She screamed with the pain of the others, the pain she totally understood now.

* * * *

"Are you sure this is okay, Marcus?" Kyra asked when Marcus opened the door to his condo.

"Yes," he said, letting her and Ryder in, followed by Garrett and Christian. It didn't matter now. She had rejected him. He felt the years of depravation weigh on him so heavily it was hard for him to move his feet. When this was done, he would request the gauntlet into hell. It would either kill him or he would burn in hell for all of eternity, but either way he was done with this world, and the hell he had been forced upon him.

Ryder gave him one look and shook his head. "I came here wanting to kill you, but it looks as if you would appreciate it."

Marcus just looked at a man who had become his brother in the last six months; a man he could count on for anything. "I would rather you kill me."

"Yes, I can tell," Ryder said, slapping him in the back.

Kyra stood back and looked at him a sad smile on her face. "Jessica's a bitch on wheels," she said.

Marcus snorted. "I realize that."

"So are you going to go and get her?"

She hadn't said her name, but they both knew who she was talking about. "She doesn't want me, Kyra. And if I've learned anything, it's that I will not wallow where I am neither wanted nor needed."

Ryder barked out a laugh. "Said the spider to the fly. Don't be an idiot." He slammed a fist into Marcus's shoulder, making him stumble back. "You love her. Go and get her. If she denies you, fuck her until she changes her mind."

"Ryder," Kyra stammered in shock.

Ryder gave Kyra a knowing glance before turning back to Marcus. "Worked for me." He shrugged and turned and walked into the living room, leaving Kyra with her mouth hanging open.

"I will not beg to be loved," Marcus said.

Kyra turned back to him, her eyes turning sad. "I don't blame you, but I do know that she was the one that took care of you for the last two hundred years. And if that doesn't speak volumes of love, then I don't know what does."

She had a point, but Marcus shrugged it off. Celeste had made her choice this morning. He just didn't understand how he could possibly be standing there having a conversation when he felt as if he had a gapping whole in his chest. She hadn't just walked away from him she had gone somewhere he couldn't find her, and it felt like death sucked at each of his steps.

"Let's just get this over with shall we?" he offered, motioning her into the living room.

"So, if I tried to use the sword," Ryder was asking, "and I killed Calliope, I would risk taking a piece of his black soul into mine?"

"Yes," Christian said.

"What about Kyra?" Ryder asked, knowing that she had handled the sword once already.

Christian smiled. "Kyra is an Element, and part of the Light regardless of the fact the Element of Light has been lost. That repelled the darkness of Sofia's soul, and the sword retained it. If she held it for an extended period of time it would eventually consume her."

"So why can Celeste handle it and not you?" Marcus couldn't control of the flinch that racked him as Ryder said her name.

"She is part Demon, part Reaper. As a full blooded Reaper I would have no control over the blackness consuming me. As Kyra is a member of the Light, I am member of the Dark. Celeste on the other hand is neither, nor does she have a choice in the matter, expect for the moment she kills Calliope. At that exact moment she can choose to be dark or light. If she is weak, the sword will make the choice for her."

"What about me?" Marcus asked. "What if I were to take the sword and kill Calliope with it?"

Christian gave him a hard look. "You are the opposite of Celeste. You have been rejected by the Light, but the Dark has not staked a claim either."

"So what does that mean?" Marcus demanded.

Christian bristled. "I believe the Sword would thrive on the pureness of your soul and turn you into a Dark Angel."

Kyra sucked in a breath. "Well, that decides that then. Marcus isn't allowed to take the Sword."

"Exactly."

"Why had none of this been written in the 'Alms of Time'?" Marcus asked. This was information that should have been written down, should be known by everyone.

Christian shrugged as if it didn't really matter. "Lost in time, brother."

Marcus felt fury surge through him like a tsunami. "Lost in time? That's your fucking answer?" he advanced on the man. "You son of a bitch, this is information that should be known."

Christian crossed his arms over his chest not backing up even one step. "And who besides you feels this way? Who could have predicted that Dante wouldn't destroy the sword after the wars between the gods? What about Celeste? She is an innocent in this, but no one could have predicted her either. You think we Reapers are hiding or keeping information, but we are making decisions that you can't make."

Marcus grabbed the Reaper by the throat. "And now you are sending your only sister in to die."

Christian didn't flinch as Marcus squeezed and then in frustration, threw the other man from him. Christian gained his feet and for a brief second, Marcus saw the pain he felt at the idea of losing Celeste, but he refused to let it penetrate too deeply. She had rejected him.

"It wasn't my choice or the choice of my brothers. This was Dante and Celeste's decision. Do you actually think I want to see her hurt? She may be closest to Victor, but she is still my sister."

****

"What the hell is he doing here?" Celeste barked when Marcus climbed from the driver's side of the vehicle that had just shown up on the side of the street.

Victor shrugged. "Ignore him."

Easier said than done, Celeste wanted to scream. She loved him so much it took everything she had to not look over at him and beg his forgiveness for what she had said.

Closing her eyes, she took a deep breath and drew in strength from the cool clean air around her. Better than the thick hot air of Lust where Victor had found her when it was time to return.

"Plans changed slightly," Victor announced to the group. "Celeste is going to be herself for this mission."

"Why does the plan always seem to change at the last minute?" Ryder growled from somewhere to her left.

"I am the only one that can hold the Sword," Celeste said, strapping the weapon to her back and pulling on her shroud. It was cut in the back so the hilt of the sword stuck through.

Jessica suddenly appeared, sneering at the group at large. "I don't want my charge involved in anyway. If you don't kill this thing, and she becomes endangered, the Tribunal will hear about it."

"You're a fucking bitch you know that?" Garrett muttered.

Jessica turned to the Reaper. "And you're a fucking idiot if you think this rag tag team is going to kill one of the original Reapers. He will get into the Infernos and do away with you all," she said as if she was washing her hands of the entire situation.

"And then you'll die, because the first entities Calliope will take out will be the Touched," Victor said, shaking his head. "You take so much time to be disagreeable you fail to see what is right in front of your face."

Jessica's mouth slammed shut, which put a smile on Celeste's face.

"You find this funny?" Jessica asked hissing the words through her teeth.

"I find the fact you hate so much what you are you fail to see the good you do and what can be done with that. You obviously take this world and the generosity of the love that made you what you are, for granted," Celeste said with more passion that she really intended, but damn the woman was irritating.

"You have no idea what you have or had." She finally looked over her shoulder at Marcus who stood as still as a statue his arms crossed over his chest. The setting sun, made his eyes black.

"Okay so, you'll be playing the part of the Touched then?" Victor asked.

Jessica sneered. "Of course."

Celeste had the craziest notion to let Calliope have her so she could appreciate what she had, but knew it probably wouldn't make a difference. Five hundred years of hating oneself; a good beating would do nothing for.

Kyra stepped forward. "Do you have something of your charge with you?"

"I'm wearing the clothes she had on today," Jessica offered.

"Now that would be something I would have liked to see. It's barely dark," Christian said with a smile turning the edges of his lips up.

"If you must know," Jessica began. "I had to drug her. She isn't to know anything of what is going to happen tonight," Jessica snapped.

Celeste couldn't resist. "Is it impossible for you to be nice? We are all here trying to help."

Jessica swung around to Celeste. "You brought the evil here from what I understand, so no, I can't be nice."

"Okay then." She dies first if everything goes south, Celeste thought "Let's get this over with."

Kyra stepped forward and handed Celeste a charm. Then she faced Jessica and took her hands, also placing a charm in the center of her palm. "Do not let this go under any circumstances. If Calliope is to get his hands on this, then he will be able to get to your charge." Kyra then whispered something over Jessica's head.

When Jessica looked up she had an impression of someone else over her, like a picture that had been overexposed with another photo.

"The line we set up is at the end of the street. You will be in a car. It will look as if Celeste is trying to escape with the Touched. Calliope has to understand that we know he can trace Celeste,"

Victor explained. "When Calliope attacks, we will all be there to stop it"

Celeste led the way to the car, climbing behind the wheel. She was shocked when Marcus stopped her. She hadn't even felt him move forward.

"Be careful," he whispered so only she could hear, and then he was gone. Her heart thumped painfully. After everything she had said and done he still worried about her.

She climbed behind the wheel glad she was just going to have to drive down the street and around the corner because she wasn't sure if she had much more in her. Victor had reassured her it was like riding a bike. Unfortunately, she had never learned to ride a bike either so that advice had meant nothing to her.

"You do know how to drive, don't you?" Jessica snapped, climbing into the passenger seat.

"Nope, never sat behind the wheel of a car in my life," Celeste volleyed back just to irritate her. Jessica didn't have to know how close it was to the truth.

"Well, that's just great," she snapped.

Celeste smiled because irritating Jessica was just plain fun. "I certainly hope you know how to fight because things could get really bad, really fast."

Jessica snorted. "Of course I am prepared to fight. I'm not useless."

"Nope, just a bitch on wheels," Celeste offered.

"You have no idea, what I am," Jessica said quietly. For the first time her words held no malice. "I did not ask for this life."

"How many of us did?" Celeste was not going to feel bad for her. "I certainly didn't ask to be what I am. Do you think your charge asked for her fate?"

"Leave my charge out of this."

Celeste started the car and pulled out into the street. "Do you have any idea how much I would give to have a man love me enough to beg for my life from the same people that banned him to what they consider hell?"

She watched Jessica out of the corner of her eye. The Guardian's flinch was almost imperceptible. Good. She needed to understand what she had, and what she had lost. Celeste almost felt sorry for her. To hate what you are for so long would be wearing on both your heart and soul.

"I don't hate what I am," she admitted. "I do good things and my charge is safe because of me. But that doesn't change the fact that Marcus lied to me."

"But have you ever asked yourself why he lied to you?" Celeste couldn't help but ask. "Look at how you reacted. Do you blame him? He loved you and didn't want to hurt you"

The words burned in her throat like acid as they came out.

"What do you know of love?" Jessica snapped.

"And warm and fuzzy just look a left turn onto bitch and heartless," Celeste muttered more to herself than to the very unhappy Guardian sitting next to her.

****

"Tell me she knows how to drive," Marcus growled to Victor as Celeste pulled the car out into the street.

Victor looked at him his eyes black. "Define drive."

"Mother of all the gods," Marcus snarled and headed toward his SUV. He was going to stay close. If anything went wrong, he would at least be there.

Victor pulled him to a stop. "We can't leave the safe zone. Calliope will sense us."

"You are sending her out to die," Marcus said more to himself then to Victor.

"Do not underestimate her, Marcus. She fights better than most men I know Other or mortal." Victor slapped him on the shoulder. "And she has a heart that is just as breakable as the rest of us."

The last part made Marcus stumble. "She rejected me."

"She also doesn't think she is going to survive the night, Marcus." Victor stepped in front of him, his black eyes glowing in the dark eerily. "See this from her stand point. Two hundred years she has pined for you, only to have you, and then know it was all just temporary. If she left you thinking it didn't mean anything, then one day you would get over it. But if she left you knowing how much she cared, then what wouldn't you do?"

Marcus just stared at the Reaper for a moment. He was prepared to die for her, to spend the rest of eternity in Hell because she had rejected him. But if he had known she carried, what would he do to keep her safe? He looked down the street as the car pulled up to the stop light, when they passed through they would be out of the safe zone. Calliope would feel the Touched, feel the power of Jessica and know they were fleeing.

"She isn't going to die, and when this is over, she is mine," Marcus snarled and looked around he focused on the highest building he launched himself into the air and landed soundlessly on the roof he crouched down so that he could watch the car.

Victor, Garrett, and Christian joined him.

"Where are the Elements?" he asked looking down at the street.

"They are safe," Christian said, moving along the edge of the building the four of them moving as shadows. They watched the car pass through the intersection.

Marcus looked up into the moonless night, nothing moved in the expanse of the night sky. It felt as if even the air was standing still waiting for something.

"What happens if he doesn't show up and they move out of our site?" Marcus asked.

"Honestly?" Victor asked. "We didn't anticipate that equation. He wants into the infernos, and this is his chance, why wouldn't he take it?"

"Because he is not an idiot," Marcus snarled and leapt to the next building.

Victor stayed at his side. "If you go any farther you will be out of the safe zone. You could ruin the entire plan, and it won't be one we will be able to do again, he has one chance."

"I won't sit back and watch her die," Marcus said, making the leap to the next building.

He could hear Victor snarling. "You are an idiot."

"Yeah, I've been told that before. I think by you," Marcus whispered back, his eyes never leaving the car.

Calliope came out of nowhere. One moment Marcus was crouched in the shadows, and the next thing he knew Garrett was flying through the air and over the edge of the building.

"Shit," Victor growled. He pulled a scythe from within the shroud he wore and swung it at the Reaper as he swooped down to attack again.

Christian pulled a sawed off shotgun from the inside of his own shroud. Cocking it, he fired it directly into Calliope.

"Do you think me a fool?" Calliope screamed falling back with the blast of the shotgun.

"We could hope." Victor's words were quiet as he stepped in shining the scythe as he went black blood splattered against the brick and tar of the roof.

"They will be mine." Calliope laughed he took flight. "I could care less of the Touched, but a Guardian and a Reaper? I will feed on their blood and make them scream for mercy." Calliope looked down at Marcus. "Just like last time."

Marcus didn't hesitate; he Shifted into the back seat of the car. "Step on it," he shouted.

Celeste didn't even turn to look at him, but slammed her foot down on the gas, and they flew forward.

"We need to get him someplace where we can all fight him." Marcus wracked his brain. "There's an abandoned industrial park about four miles ahead."

Marcus turned and looked back. The Reapers were holding Calliope back, but he knew it would be only a matter of time before they wouldn't be able to hold him any longer.

Celeste followed Marcus's directions. The moment they moved into the shadows of the first building, something huge slammed against the side of the car. The car flipped, spinning in the air it slid on its roof to a stop, glass shattering and metal bending.

"Out, get out of the car," Marcus shouted.

He had hit his head, and blood was trickling down his forehead into his eyes, but he watched as Celeste kicked out the safety glass of the windshield, and he pushed her through the opening. Jessica had at some point Shifted out of the car.

"Bitch," he snarled, following Celeste.

Celeste looked around her breathing heavy. "Bitch left, didn't she?"

Marcus nodded, and Celeste kicked cement. "Chicken shit bitch. When this is done she and I are going to have a serious argument."

Marcus would actually like to see that, but at the moment he was more worried about getting through the next few minutes. Garrett and Christian appeared as a black wing swung at them, throwing Marcus and the two Reapers against the building.

When his vision cleared, he saw Victor standing at Celeste's side. He wielded the scythe like it was an extension of his arm, as did Celeste with the sword.

He was so amazed he was immobilized. Her shroud had dropped away and her beautiful red hair swung around her, slashing with the sword at Calliope. She crouched and swung, using every bit of her body in the fight, not just the sword. Barely stepping out of Calliope's reach or the swing of his deadly taloned wings.

Victor swung the scythe at the Reaper several times, barely missing Celeste. But it only took a moment of watching them to understand they played off of each other picking up where the other left off. Feeling in each other's holes, when Celeste moved right, leaving an opening on her left Victor swung in to protect it.

However, Calliope fought tirelessly. Screaming, blood splattered the walls of the empty buildings around them. He ragged against them.

Marcus scrambled to his feet and pulled out guns he had holstered and fired into the Reaper. Calliope didn't even flinch.

Jessica reappeared, holding a large colander she threw the contents on the Reaper. He screamed and backed away, but not before he caught Jessica with one of his wings he flung her back into the shadows.

"Jessica," Marcus shouted her name, as she flew into the shadows. But he didn't have time to worry about her, Celeste, and the other Reapers were still in danger.

"What the hell was that?" Garrett asked.

"Holy water I would assume," Christian offered, pulling a ball and chain from the inside of his shroud he shrugged the garment off. "Time for that bastard to die."

The three men pushed forward, joining Victor and Celeste as they fought off the Reaper. "Attack his wings so he can't escape," Victor shouted.

Marcus emptied his guns into the Reapers shoulders and base of his wings. Flinching just a little, as he remembered how badly it hurt to lose ones wings. Celeste backed up to Marcus.

"I have a blade in each boot." Marcus bent down and grabbed a blade from each of Celeste's boots. He stood and started slashing at the Reaper whenever he could get into reach.

Calliope howled in pain and attempted to take flight but he wasn't going anywhere.

Celeste moved forward. "Time to die," she said, lifting the Black Sword.

Everything happened so fast, Marcus wasn't sure for a moment if it was real or not. One second Calliope was laying on the asphalt, his blood pouring from him. Celeste was holding the Black Sword over her head ready for the killing blow.

Then one working wing came forward piercing Celeste deep in the chest, it picked her up off her feet, the Black Sword clattered to the ground as she was lifted her hands going to the wing as he shook her.

Marcus screamed in pain and fury. With a shrug Calliope flung her aside. She flew through the air like a rag doll. Garrett and Christian caught her. Victor let out a horrifying bellow of rage as he attacked Calliope, who lay laughing, his blood coating the cement. Marcus knew Victor couldn't wield the sword against him. Knew that the only person that could wield the sword was laying with a gaping wound in her chest.

Marcus stumbled over to her. He grabbed her face in his hands as Garrett and Christian returned to the fight.

"I love you, Celeste. Tell me you feel the same way. I just need to hear the words." He felt tears searing down his face, he hadn't cried since the day he had fallen from the heavens. "I need to know what I am about to do is not in vain."

Celeste opened and closed her mouth her eyes rounding in shock and pain.

"Say it," he barked. Her violet eyes stared up into his. "For the Mother of all the Gods say it," he begged, as the light started to fade from her beautiful eyes.

When her mouth opened blood trickled out, and he knew she was fading and he felt as if the world as he knew it was coming to an end. He had no choice, leaning down he kissed her bloodied lips. "I love you enough for the both of us regardless of what you think or tell yourself."

And then he gently laid her down. If she was going to die, then he was going to go out fighting himself. She reached for him, and he kissed her fingertips, but then turned back, sweeping the Black Sword up he joined the fight.

Darkness tingled up his arm, it was pure power and darkness, and he couldn't help but be thrilled by it, while part of him knew it was wrong. But he was going to avenge the pain Celeste was in, avenge her and everything else Calliope had hurt.

Taking a running step, he blew past the Reapers and landed on top of Calliope the sword burring itself deep in the Reaper's chest. His black eyes shown with surprise. Marcus had never felt as powerful as he did at that moment, and he tilted his head back, bellowing into the black heavens.

"My darkness now belongs to you," Calliope gurgled, his hand reaching up he touched Marcus in the middle of the chest and laughed, splattering blood all over Marcus.

Chapter 15

Marcus laughed, whipping the blood from his face. "Bring it on, bastard."

Evil rolled up his arm where he clutched the sword and penetrated into his soul. He took it all, thrilling in the power, in the pain. It lanced through Marcus as if he had been struck by a bolt of lightning. He rolled away from the Reaper, pulling the Black Sword free as he went he felt as if it were attached to him. He watched out of the corner of his eyes as Calliope twitched and then dissolved into black goo.

Dark shadows, voices like Banshee's screeching, oozed from the ground around him sucking up what was left of Calliope and then seeping back into the ground. And then the pain lanced through him again. He screamed again. His body twitched, and then he seized completely.

"Get the damn sword away from him," he heard Victor scream, but couldn't be sure as his screams, and the pain increased. His back burned, and he rolled to his stomach, but it didn't help. He could feel his back split open. Bones and cartilage rearranging itself.

Images of horrible atrocities, of darkness so black it was ink etching itself into his brain. As it swallowed him consuming any part of light within as it spread. He fought against it, holding onto the light, onto the love he had for Celeste. He opened his eyes, and she floated above him, glowing with light. He reached for her, but the blackness swallowed her before he could reach her, and he screamed in rage and pain for the loss. He had never felt a pain so intense, not even his fall from the heavens hurt like this. He lunged out as someone touched him, slicing through whoever it was. He screamed as souls that had been trapped in Calliope fought for release.

He vomited, releasing the souls, his body racked and heaved as they clamored for freedom. He heaved over and over again as the pain in his back steadily grew. Bones cracked, as he rolled onto his hands on knees. He threw his head back and screamed to the heavens.

Inky blackness sucking at him he fought against it, knowing that if he gave into it he wouldn't ever see the light again.

****

"This wasn't the plan," Dante bellowed. Flashing in, he stood over Marcus as he wailed and screamed, souls oozing from him. "Collect the souls, Christian. Victor see to your sister."

Victor rushed over to Celeste where she leaned against the building. Everything in her hurt, but she pushed herself away from the wall and with the help of her brother, he brought her over to Marcus.

"What is happening to him?" she groaned, blood spraying onto him. She realized she was still bleeding.

"He is changing." Dante narrowed his eyes at Marcus and shook his head. "I should kill him now."

"NO!" Celeste fell down next to Marcus and even though he fought her, she wrapped her arms around his neck. "I beg of you, Father, please do not destroy him. He will come through this."

"And you know this how?" Dante asked.

"Because he is a good man, a soul of light," she cried, her bloody tears mixing with the blood Marcus was spilling. She felt the edges of her conscious blur. "I beg you, Father." It was the last thing she remembered saying as blackness swamped her.

"He should be destroyed," Dante said again.

Victor picked Celeste up, cradling her in his arms. "Hasn't she suffered enough, Father?"

"You question me?" Dante demanded, his voice booming through the dark night.

Victor didn't back down. "Yes. She is everything that is good in any world and you would destroy the one thing she wants above everything else."

Dante swore. He turned to Christian who had collected the last of the souls that had erupted from Marcus. Garrett held his arm where Marcus stabbed him as he had tried to take the sword from him.

"Clean everything up." Christian nodded, and Dante reached forward. He placed one hand on Marcus's shoulder and Flashed them into the catacombs of his Fortress.

Solid granite surrounded them. Marcus moaned in pain. Dante swore softly. "You have this one chance, Fallen." He leaned down to whisper into Marcus' ear. "Fight for what you want, be what you were meant to be. Light or Dark, the choice is yours."

With that, Dante slammed out of the cell. He would put his sons on a constant watch, but the moment Marcus showed signs of giving into the darkness, Dante would destroy him regardless of how Celeste felt about him.

****

Marcus shielded his eyes from the bright light that shown down on him.

"When did a little light hurt you?" Celeste laughed from beside him.

Marcus turned to her, trying to gather her into his arms, but she moved too quickly for him.

"You'll have to try harder than that, Fallen." Her laughter brushed against his bruised and broken skin like a salve.

He reached for her again, pain lancing through his body. She danced just out of his reach. "Hold still," he begged.

Her laughter only increased, turning into something horrible; screeching that drove him to his knees, he covered his ears and closed his eyes, begging her to stop.

Silence encompassed him, and he opened his eyes, but a blackness so thick he couldn't see his own hand in front of his face, surrounded him.

"Celeste?" he bellowed the words like knifes in his brain.

"She is gone," the darkness screeched. "Lost to you forever."

Marcus bellowed in rage. She couldn't be gone. He had killed Calliope for her, ingested pure evil to save her. What wouldn't he do to spend one more minute in her arms?

He railed against the darkness against the very idea that Celeste was no longer with him. The reality of it drove him to his knees.

"I need her," he cried. She was his light, his world. But the darkness laughed back at him. He struck out at it with his bare hands, daring it to contradict him. Celeste was out there, and the blackness was hiding her from him.

****

"Maybe we should bring her down here," Garrett offered, peeking through the bars of the door.

For two days Marcus had raged with fever and pain as his body morphed into what it was now. Sleek muscles, toned and taut prepared for a fight. Black silk wings fluttered and whipped against the confines of the cell.

Now he raged against the darkness, the blackness that would eat his soul and demand that he consume everything in his wake. It had been several millennia since any plane of existence had housed a Dark Angel and Victor wondered if they were going to be able to contain him.

They had tried to tie him down, but he broke through all restraints. And every time one of the Reapers entered his cell he had to be carried out.

At the moment he was screaming for Celeste as if his very life depended on it. Victor was at a loss as to what to do. There was no way he was about to bring Celeste down here to witness the love of her life lose the battle between good and evil. Nor was he willing to give up on Marcus. His sister loved him. It was something Victor just didn't understand.

"She is safe, Marcus," he reassured.

Wings contracted and folded around Marcus. "Then bring her to me." His voice was graveled and deep.

"When you are more under control," Victor promised.

Without notice, Marcus slammed himself against the solid door, his face glowing in the darkness. "Bring her to me now."

"So not going to happen," Victor replied.

Marcus fell to his knees, his head falling back, he bellowed to bring down the very walls that surrounded him.

Victor didn't know what he was supposed to do, and it was a new and confusing situation for him. He couldn't bring Celeste down here. After three days she had regained consciousness and was healing. Dante was about at his limit, he wanted Marcus dead.

"I'm going in."

Garrett shook his head. "It's up to you, but I wouldn't recommend it."

Victor pushed past Garrett and swung the solid rock door open he stepped in.

Marcus immediately stopped raging. The silence after was so profound it made the hair on Victor's arm stand on end.

Slowly Marcus's head swiveled so that black on green eyes stared at him over one shoulder. "Tell me she is alive. Tell me she is going to be okay?"

Victor crossed his arms over his chest and regarded Marcus. "Why did you do it? Why did you sacrifice everything you have and are for a female?"

"She is not just any female," Marcus snarled. Then growled something that sounded awfully like 'Mine."

****

His moment of clarity was waning as the inky black voice in the back of his mind screamed for release. "She is dead, they are not telling you so that they can use you like they used me, and then threw me away." The dark voice in his head voiced his worst fear.

"Tell me she lives," Marcus demanded.

"She lives," Victor said.

"Lies, all lies." The blackness crooned now sympathetically.

Marcus pushed at the darkness wanting to believe Victor, wanting to believe Celeste was still alive. But he had seen her injuries, and he couldn't imagine even an immortal living through something like that.

"Bring her to me then."

"I can't do that, Marcus."

Marcus lurched to his feet, unused to this new body he staggered, but was still faster than Victor had him pressed against the wall one winged talon buried in the Reapers shoulder.

"I will not be used by you." Marcus voiced his worries.

He could see the pain in Victor's eyes but he didn't flinch. "We don't want to use you Marcus, we want to ensure that you will not hurt her."

Dark rage consumed him. "Never" he growled unable to speak a full sentence. "Hurt her." The darkness so powerful it drove him back to his knees.

He looked up into Victor's face. "Hurts, the darkness," he stammered. "So much pain."

Victor knelt so that he was eye to eye with Marcus. "I believe you love her, but you must fight against the darkness in order to keep her." Then he stood and walked out, leaving Marcus to fight this internal battle alone.

****

Celeste sat up straight in bed, light-headedness swamping her. She threw her covers back and stumbled from the bed, falling flat on her face as she did so.

"Bloody hell," Dante growled, Celeste looked up at her father. He bent down and picked her up. She might have imagined it, but she thought he held her close for just a moment extra before placing her back into the bed.

"That's one way to wake up," he said, gently brushing a lock of her red hair behind her ear.

"Where is he?" her voice was so scratchy it hurt to speak and started her coughing.

Dante handed her an old earth worn cup. She sipped the cool water. It soothed her sore throat, and left her able to speak again. "What did you do to him?"

"I?" Dante asked with such sarcasm it was biting. "I did nothing to him."

Celeste couldn't control the tears that rushed to her eyes. "What happened to him?"

Dante sighed. "There hasn't been a Dark Angel in several millennia. They were destroyed for a reason, Celeste."

She allowed the tears to fall. "He was a good man."

Dante did something he had never done before; he climbed on the bed and gathered his daughter into his arms. "Celeste, a Dark Angel would be hunted down and killed by the Tribunal. They would never allow a being such as that to survive."

"Sounds familiar," she said around her tears.

Dante sighed again, and lifted her chin with his index finger. "Yes, it does, and because of that I spared him. He is in the cells in the catacombs. He is fighting the darkness and light within him."

Celeste cried harder. "But he is alive?"

"Yes, but if the darkness wins, he won't be for long. I will destroy him myself Celeste. You understand that don't you?" She nodded turning her face into her father's shoulder. "Rest, he is going nowhere at the moment. He is consumed with madness from the change."

Celeste sucked in a breath. "Is he in a great deal of pain?"

She knew her father wouldn't lie to her, and he nodded. "He is fighting against being consumed by darkness."

"I need to go to him." She pulled herself away from her father. And slowly moved to her feet. "How long have I been out?"

"Several days, get something to eat, and then Victor and I will take you down." He nodded obviously knowing he wouldn't be able to talk her out of going to him.

She conceded knowing when she could win, and when she couldn't. Celeste went and got into the shower, and when she was done she came out to find her room abuzz with women, pulling clothes out and food was waiting for her.

She ate and allowed the servants to braid her long hair. By the time she was done, she was so worried she rushed through everything and grabbed her cloak as she threw her door open. And then looked down at the cloak she had worn for five hundred years and threw it on the floor and stepped through the door.

Victor and her father waited for her. When Victor saw what she did he smiled. "About damn time."

Celeste just looked at him for a moment. "I thought I had to hide from who I was," she said to her brother and father.

"Only you found it necessary to hide," Victor said.

Her father only shrugged. "I only ever wanted you to be proud of who and what you are. Until you were done hiding and prepared to stand proud of who you and what you are the cloak was necessary. Apparently that time is over."

Celeste felt tears fill her eyes again, she had hidden for five hundred years because she was ashamed of who she was, not that her father was ashamed of her. The very idea was stunning to her.

She swallowed the tears and let her brother and father lead her to the catacombs.

Water dripped from the damp cold walls of the catacombs of the Fortress. Moans of pain, and chains rattled behind arctic stone doors. She knew of several creatures that were kept down in the catacombs, and her blood ran a little cold for it.

She knew when they were close because she saw Garrett at the end of passageway. His arms crossed over his chest he waited.

She heard Marcus moan and scream. "Christian is in there trying to calm him down."

Celeste pushed past Garrett. "Let me in."

"No." Garrett shook his head.

"Why?" Celeste snapped

"Because he is getting worse. I won't send you in there to be mutilated by that monster."

Celeste snorted. "Christian is in there right now, and I kick his ass on a regular basis. So get the hell out of my way Garrett or I'll kick yours."

Garrett looked at her with surprise and then back to Victor and Dante then stepped aside. She pushed past him and pressed herself against the thick rock of the cell. With her brothers and father at her side she walked into what she had to describe as hell.

The cell didn't quite contain the wingspan, and Celeste ducked out of the way as a wing flew over her head the talons on the end carving deep wounds into the granite.

"Marcus." Celeste said his name with awe and shock. He stood naked facing Christian his back to her. But the moment she said his name he froze. Heaving for breath, his skin was pale against the black wings that folded in lying slack against his back and then folded again. She watched in amazement as they folded up and sealed themselves within his back making the muscles of his back and sides bulge. But one last bone breaking shiver his back smoothed out and flat muscle replaced and covered his wings.

She took a step forward and said his name again.

"Get out of here," Christian snarled from his position in the corner where Marcus had him pinned.

Without warning Christian was lifted and tossed in the direction of the door. Celeste scrambled out of the way as her brother flew past her swearing as he went.

She took the opportunity to move forward toward Marcus, she knew her brothers and father wouldn't allow her anywhere near him if he was out of control and she wasn't going to leave. She was right when Victor lunged at her grabbing her by the arm he jerked her back. She squeaked in shock as she was brought to an abrupt halt.

Marcus bellowed and turned, his green eyes were gone replaced by blackness Celeste was stunned at the changes in him. He was taller, more muscular and at the moment pissed as hell and beyond. But he was alive and she was going to do whatever it took to keep him that way. He had confessed his love to her before he had taken up the sword, and she knew that man was in there somewhere. She just needed to get to him so she could say the words back to him.

"Let her go," he growled.

"No chance in hell." Victor placed her behind him. "You're not in control Marcus."

Celeste tried to push past her brother. "He won't hurt me."

Victor was physically moved, Celeste was amazed at the speed at which Marcus moved. One second Victor was holding her back, and the next he was gone and she was picked up and placed in a corner with Marcus's back to her.

Her father and brothers went nuts, the four of them attacking Marcus. Celeste screamed and bounded forward she placed herself between Marcus and her brothers only to be pushed aside several times. Tears streaked down her face, she didn't want anyone to be hurt.

Finally she threw herself around Marcus, wrapping her arms around his neck. She didn't care if he was a Dark Angle, a Fallen or a mortal she loved him.

"Stop," she whispered into his ear. "I'm right here, I'm not going anywhere."

"I thought I had lost you," he whispered.

"Never."

"God dammit," Victor bellowed. "She's totally lost her mind."

"I love you Marcus," she whispered back. "I should have said it earlier. But I didn't think I would make it through this, but I've loved you for so long." She couldn't help the tears as they ran down her face.

"I will never forgive myself for what you became in order to save us all." She closed her eyes and leaned her head down so it rested on his shoulder. "Thank you."

"Get them out of here now," Marcus said very quietly.

Celeste moved so she could look over his shoulder but not actually let him go. "He is going to be fine."

"The hell he is. The man's been crazed for days," Garrett growled.

"They wouldn't let me see you. I didn't know if you were dead or alive," he growled. "This new body, this new thing I am, I can't control it yet. I was terrified you had died..." He dropped off. She leaned back to look into his face, and she saw the anguish there the pain he must have been feeling to have lost control of who and what he was.

Celeste wrapped her arms more tightly around him, feeling the wings below the surface of his skin on his back. "I'm here now, and I'm never going anywhere ever again."

"Celeste, step away from him," Dante demanded.

Marcus growled and pressed her closer into the stone and himself. She wasn't going anywhere even if she wanted to.

"He thought I was dead," Celeste said, noting that Marcus twitched again.

"Never say it." His voice hadn't changed, and only she heard his words.

"Why didn't any of you tell him that I was healing?" They could have saved themselves a lot of trouble she thought.

"Actually we did, but because we wouldn't bring you down here he thundered around the cell like a mad man." Marcus chuckled low the sound barely registering except for the rumble of his chest against hers.

"You're idiots," she snapped.

"Leave," Marcus growled.

"This is a bad idea," Victor snapped and stormed out of the cell.

"One drop of blood Dark one, and I'll have your head on a pike outside my walls," Dante said as he turned and left, Garrett and Christian following him.

****

Marcus looked down into her violet eyes, he didn't remember a lot of the last several days. Pain, and anguish he remembered them trying to explain she was alive but she couldn't come down until he calmed down. But he hadn't believed them. But here she was, and she was breathing and warm and the most beautiful thing he had ever seen or felt in his entire existence.

His wings sprung from his back, pain tore through him as they ripped through his back. This was something he was going to have to get used to. They wrapped around Celeste pushing her back against the wall the talons embedding in the wall he had her trapped.

He fought against the urge to devour her to take everything she had to offer the darkness and the light. To suck her soul from her so they would never be parted again. But the light in him revolted at the idea. He took a deep breath sucking in her scent all the way into his very soul it calmed him.

"I don't want to hurt you," he growled.

She looked up at him her eyes shining in the dark cell. "I don't think you could hurt me even if you wanted to," she said cupping his face with her hands.

"I'm a monster now."

"You're beautiful."

He growled. "How can you say that, I'm…" He searched for the words but nothing came to him. He felt so different, he didn't know if he was alive or dead, if he was dark or light. Shades of gray swamped him as he tried to figure it out, hate and mortification at what he had become. But he would do it all over again, wouldn't think twice about picking up the Sword and killing Calliope for just one more minute with Celeste.

"I'm a monster," he repeated.

"An abomination?" she asked throwing words back at him that he knew she had heard her entire life.

"Yes."

She laughed, and the sound filled him with peace and joy for the first time in days. And for the first time since he had picked up the Sword he felt purchase in this new and unknown world. "Then I believe we are perfect for each other don't you?"

He shook himself and stepped back forcing his wings back into his back he shuddered in pain. "You need to leave, Celeste."

"Where would I go?"

"Anywhere but near me. All I want to do is devour you." His voice shook.

"And that is a bad thing?" She smiled at him, in that way that only a Sex Demon can master. Holding so much passion it burned him at the edges. Making him want to fall to his knees and beg for more.

He swung on her taking her by surprise she stepped back as he pressed himself against her. "Yes, because I don't know if I can control the darkness, and if I were to hurt you in any way it would kill me."

"Marcus." She stepped forward and kissed him on the chin. It was a simple light touch but he felt it all the way down into his toes. "You would never hurt me."

"Ten minutes ago you were raging because you didn't know if I were alive or dead. And I was worried you would be consumed by darkness. Neither of those things are true," she said quietly. "You are a Dark Angel because of the evil Calliope held. But your soul is light, it was always light and not falling from the heavens or holding the Black Sword and killing Calliope will change that you are a good person." She smiled making his heart a little lighter.

"You are an Angel again," she said in awe.

He couldn't control himself any longer. She looked at him with such trust, and love. He leaned down and pressed his lips against hers. "Say the words Celeste," He moaned. Pulling away he ran kisses across her faced to her ear. "Say them," he begged needing to hear them more than he needed his next breath.

She leaned forward, and he lifted her, she wrapped her legs around his waist and tilted her head down toward his ear soft hair tickled his cheek and neck. "I love you Marcus, I have loved you for two hundred years. And nothing in this world will ever change that. I love you."

Marcus leaned back so awed by finally hearing the words he was momentarily speechless. "I'm sorry," was the first thing that slipped out.

She quirked an eyebrow at him in question. "No…" he started. "I'm sorry that I didn't realize who you were before now."

"What does that mean?" she asked placing kisses on the column of his neck he concentrated on the words he needed to say before anything else happened.

"I purposely defied Dante, the pain he inflicted meant nothing because I was cared for by a creature that I believed to be an Angel of mercy and kindness." He leaned back so he could look at her. "I pretended you were Jessica in my mind."

Her arms and legs immediately fell from him, and he groaned with the loss.

"Cold shower," she muttered pushing past him.

"I fell in love with that creature that cared for me each time I was punished, and held myself above the sins of the flesh for the creature who cared enough to give more than she received. And I will never forgive myself for not recognizing you when you finally showed yourself to me. I love you Celeste with everything that I am both dark and light." He turned grabbing her arm before she could get farther away from him. "And I will never ever let you go again."

He kissed her then with all the passion he felt for her, all the love he held for her. Centuries of need and wanting encompassed in the melding of their lips. He thrust his tongue between her lips, and she moaned deep in the back of her throat causing him such pain and pleasure at the same time he wasn't sure if he was coming or going.

"Marcus?" she leaned back. His eyes had turned back to the green she knew. "I have something to confess."

He let her slide down, terrified at what she was going to tell him. "My hair?"

"Yes?"

"I originally cut my hair for you. It was always you," she confessed. "I will love you forever," she whispered

"Ah, sweetheart that just won't be long enough." And then he was kissing her again the darkness in him receding back as the light took control savoring each breath and touch. He picked her up and carried her to the bed, shredding the clothes she had on as they went.

"I liked that shirt," she muttered between kisses.

Marcus smiled down at her. "You shouldn't wear anything you don't want torn from you from now on," he suggested, part of him deadly serious. "If I get to rough tell me," he growled.

"Bring it on." She laughed, filling his soul with love. "I'm a Sex Demon, remember?"

He growled so low and deep she felt it all the way to her soul. "My Sex Demon."

Celeste smiled up at him, his eyes were turning a dark shade of green which she knew was from the Dark Angel in him but her Demon side caused her eyes to bleed to red, so she knew they were a perfect pair.

He raised her arms over her head and leaned down to take one of her nipples into his mouth. Her body responded on its own bowing up into his greedy mouth. She gasped and begged for more.

He leaned back pressing the head of his erection into her opening. His wings expanded, a talon came forward slowly. He looked at her, and she knew what he wanted and felt like her world was being completed. She loved him, and they would be together forever.

She opened her hands palms up, the talon slashed through the palm of each of her hands. She hissed in pain, and then he did the same to each of his palms.

He leaned down and kissed her still hovering at her opening making her want to scream in frustration. "By the bonds of blood," Marcus growled breathlessly.

"I give my soul for yours."

She repeated the words, and then they clasped hands fingers entwining. She felt the connection spread through her body, both dark and light it started in her hands and moved throughout her body like warm honey. Celeste moaned in pain and pleasure as their souls blended together.

"Bonded forever," he whispered placing a kiss just below her ear and running his tongue down her neck.

She smiled, and thrust up pulling him deep into her. This time they both moaned, and then he was moving inside of her, and she couldn't think for the pleasure that their joined bodies and souls felt. Just on the outside of her own feelings she sensed something else. The urge for more, the urge to devour, constant dark fighting light only to be eclipsed by passion. She sucked in a breath her eyes flying to Marcus's.

"Can you sense it?" she asked breathlessly.

In answer he projected back to her exactly what she had been feeling, and it heightened the intensity.

"Oh gods," she screamed as her orgasm saturated through her every muscle and nerve ending.

"That was not something I was expecting," she growled, as she felt his climax take him he arched into her thrusting deep, and she felt it from his stand point as well as her own. She gasped trying to find purchase in a world that had turned inside out her body soared to heights unknown as another orgasm racked her body making her scream out.

He collapsed on top of her, and she immediately turned him over. She smiled down at him. "Don't let me hurt you," she whispered the words he had just said to her as she leaned over him biting his shoulder she sank down on him.

This time it was Marcus that let out a loud shout of passion as she rode him milking him for all he was worth. Marcus grasped her hips holding her tightly, he had almost lost her. He had almost lost himself.

"I'm right here. Feel me," she moaned, letting all her walls down she opened to him completely.

Emotion flooded him giving him everything he had ever wanted from her. He took it all in he looked up into her red violet eyes filled with passion and love, and he let it all go. All that mattered was Celeste and the passion and love they shared.

Celeste moved over him, gliding him in and out of her. "I'll never get close enough," she moaned.

Marcus opened his mind to her, and she gasped with pleasure. In the next instant she did the same, the bond growing stronger with every second they spent together. They felt each other, knew the passion they shared was mutual and intense.

When she came, she saw stars before collapsing on his broad chest. He stroked her back letting her come down from her orgasm before flipping her over and driving into her.

"I love you," she shouted just as he came. And he felt it deep down in his very soul, he returned the feeling. The look in her eyes showing him she completely understood.

Chapter 16

"What do you mean his punishment is a gauntlet?" Celeste couldn't believe her ears.

"Not just a gauntlet, but after that is done then he must be able to pick you out." Victor smiled.

"I don't give a shit that you are bonded but for two hundred years he didn't recognize you for who you were."

Celeste slapped her brother on the forehead with the palm of her hand. "You dumb ass, where blood bonded. He would be able to pick me out from anywhere on this plane or any other for that matter. Is that what you have been doing for the last week? Planning on ways to torture him?"

"As a matter of fact," Garrett said sheepishly.

Celeste rolled her eyes, she wasn't going to hit all her brothers but she really wanted to. "Just remember, blood bonded. Anything he feels I feel as well, are you sure you want to put him through a gauntlet?"

Christian threw his head back and laughed. "Has a point."

"I still want to kick his ass," Victor snarled.

"Is this what you do for fun?" Marcus asked from beside her.

They had spent a day in the cell and then had moved to her room where they had stayed for the last week. She had told him about her entire life, shared things with him she had never shared with anyone else. She had apologized for Ricky and his daughters telling him the truth. He hadn't liked it much but he understood.

And in return he had told her about his life, the adventures he had had. He had explained Jessica, which she hadn't liked but again she understood. They made love, and bonded to the point where she wasn't sure where he started, and she finished. It scared her a little to be so close to another individual. But when she had those feelings she would feel him withdraw from her mind giving her the oneness she needed. And it only made her love him all the more.

But now they had been summoned by her father, and they couldn't ignore that. Otherwise she would have stayed in her room forever just enjoying each other, physically and mentally.

"Enough," Dante demanded from the dais.

"You will not go through the gauntlet," he said standing. "You will not be punished. You will be given my daughter's heart, and if for any reason you hurt her I will send you to hell myself," he said this grabbing Marcus by the shoulders; Celeste felt the searing cold burn into Marcus.

"You just Touched him," Celeste snapped. "I have the most dysfunctional family."

"He was already Touched, Celeste," Dante said moving back to his seat.

"Yes, but when he became a Dark Angel your mark was erased. Plus you forget that I was here the first time he became Touched, and he did so willingly. Now you take what he offered and throw it in his face?" She argued.

"Yes, but now it is back, and he shall serve you well or die." Dante turned and sat back down in his chair as if that was that. "Oh, and by the way, I removed the mark on the Element. You completed your task."

"Thank you Dante," Marcus replied.

"Well now what?" Victor growled. "None of us get to kick his ass?"

Marcus shook his head and smiled at Celeste he kissed her gently on the nose. "Bring it on Victor, I'm not afraid of you, I'm bonded to a Demon/Reaper you have nothing that could come close to that."

Without warning Victor stepped forward and slammed his fist into Marcus's face. Celeste felt a wall fly up between her and Marcus so she wouldn't feel the pain. "That might come close," Victor snapped laughing.

"VICTOR STOP" Celeste tried to step in between them.

Victor turned to her. "He asked for it." Marcus slammed a knee into Victor's kidney causing the Reaper to crumple to the floor screaming in pain.

"He's right, sweetheart. Just sit back and enjoy the show." He leaned down and kissed her again. "Have I told you how much I love you today?"

"Yes, but I never get tired of hearing it."

Victor kicked Marcus's right leg out from beneath him, and he went down hard on his left leg. He smiled. "I love you, Celeste."

And then he turned and concentrated on the fight with Victor, soon Christian joined when it was obvious that Marcus was winning.

"Well that just isn't fair." Celeste shook her head.

But Marcus's laughter drowned out her protests.

"You have chosen well daughter," Dante said from next to her. "But you will both need to watch each other's back, the Tribunal must surely know about you and him being changed into a Dark Angel." Dante sighed. "I believe the changes in the mortal plane are far from over. But for what it's worth you have me and your brothers on your side."

At the moment Celeste was too happy to care about anything else and threw her arms around her father kissing his cold cheek. "We shall all meet them head on proud of whom and what we are."

Dante nodded. "What more could a father ask for?"

Celeste smiled. "Now if you don't mind I think I'll help my bonded mate kick my brother's asses."